- Whose parents were irradiated by a mysterious meteorite, thus rearranging their genes to produce a superhero?

- Who had an ape for a mother?

- Who dropped his loincloth in the jungle one day, thus revealing one more of his many endowments?

IT'S TARZAN—
A UNIQUE HUMAN BEING IN THE ANNALS OF HISTORY AND LITERATURE.

Born John Clayton, dubbed Tarzan by his fellow apes, later known as Lord Greystoke, Tarzan's fascinating career spans continents and decades. Philip José Farmer draws upon voluminous research and meticulous reading of all of Edgar Rice Burroughs's tales to piece together the life of this fantastic man:

- The ill-fated voyage that led to his birth on the isolated African coast.
- His adventures in the fabulous golden city of Opar.
- His lifelong love for Jane (38-19-36).
- A carefully documented genealogy tracing Tarzan's family tree through Sherlock Holmes, Doc Savage, and the Scarlet Pimpernel.

NOW IT CAN BE TOLD!
THE AMAZING TRUE SAGA,
THE FULL AND ACCURATE STORY
OF AMERICA'S MOST
BELOVED SUPERHERO.

While they were stagg...
paper being pushed under...

D0877923

PHILIP JOSÉ FARMER

TARZAN ALIVE

PLAYBOY
PAPERBACKS

*This is for the man who is the real "Lord Grey-
stoke" and for the man who brought him to the
attention of the world, albeit in a fictional disguise.*

Published simultaneously in the United States and Canada by
Playboy Paperbacks, New York, New York. Printed in the United
States of America. Library of Congress Catalog Card Number:
81-80084. Reprinted by arrangement with Doubleday & Company,
Inc.

Books are available at quantity discounts for promotional and industrial use. For further information, write to Premium Sales, Playboy Paperbacks, 1633 Broadway, New York, New York 10019.

ISBN: 0-872-16876-X

First Playboy Paperbacks printing August 1981.

I am as free as Nature first made man,
Ere the base laws of servitude began,
When wild in woods the noble savage ran.

—John Dryden

A hero ventures forth from the world of common day into a region of supernatural wonder: fabulous forces are there encountered and a decisive victory is won: the hero comes back from this mysterious adventure with the power to bestow boons on his fellow men.

—Joseph Campbell

There is always something new out of Africa.

—Pliny the Elder

The worlds of Edgar Rice Burroughs are never-never lands, dream worlds where virtue and courage win honor and beauty, where evil can be identified and confronted, and despite all odds defeated. . . . This sense of timelessness raises Tarzan above the clutches of time.

—Richard Lupoff

THE WOLD NEWTON FAMILY, 1795-1901

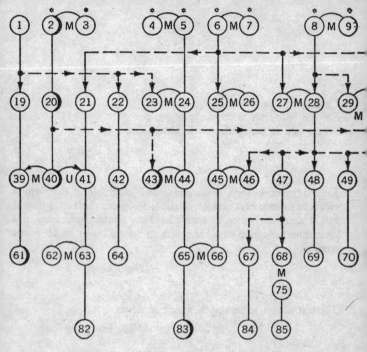

Legend

Duke of Greystoke

Siblings

(1) = 1st M
(2) = 2nd M

M = Married

U = Unmarried

✿ = Exposed to Radiation

1 Karoly
2 3rd
3 Alicia Rutherford
4 Elizabeth Bennet
5 Fitzwilliam Darcy
6 The Scarlet Pimpernel
7 Alice Clarke Raffles
8 11th Baron Tennington
9 Elizabeth Cavendish
10 Violet Clarke
11 Dr. S. Holmes
12 Hugh Drummond
13 Georgia Dewhurst
14 Honoré Delagardie
15 Philippa Drummond
16 Louis Lupin
17 Albert Lecoq
18 Lord Byron
19 John Jansenius
20 4th
21 Mavice Blakeney
22 Julius Higgins
23 Agatha Jansenius

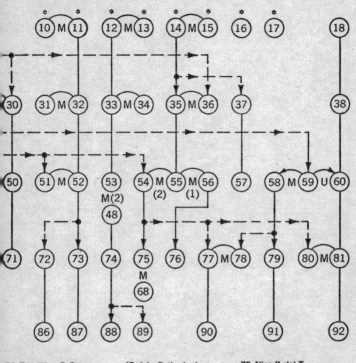

24 Fitzwilliam B. Darcy
25 Percy Armand Blakeney
26 Alexandra Grosvenor
27 Serena Blakeney
28 12th Baron Tennington
29 Scott Rutherford
30 Suzanne Blakeney
31 —————— Vernet
32 Mycroft Holmes
33 John Drummond
34 Oread Butler
35 Paul H. Delagardie
36 Marguerite Blakeney
37 Charles Dupin
38 Ada Augusta
39 Edith Jansenius
40 6th
41 Patricia Clarke Wildman
42 Ellen Higgins
43 5th
44 Athena Darcy
45 Marguerite Blakeney
46 13th Baron Tennington

47 John Rutherford
48 Venetia Rutherford
49 George T————
50 Egidnia Rutherford
51 Violet Rutherford
52 Siger Holmes
53 William Drummond
54 Lucasta Rutherford
55 Francis Delagardie
56 Enid Austin
57 C. Auguste Dupin
58 14th Duke Pomver
59 Joane Clayton
60 12th Baron Wentworth
61 7th
62 Arronaxe Larsen
63 James Clarke Wildman, Sr.
64 Leopold Bloom
65 John Clayton
66 Alice Rutherford
67 Melissa Rutherford
68 Professor Challenger
69 Ludwig Horace Holly

70 Nina (Lola) T————
71 A. J. Raffles
72 Sigrina Holmes
73 Sherlock Holmes
74 Roger Drummond
75 Enid Delagardie
76 P. Austin Delagardie
77 H. Lucasta Delagardie
78 15th Duke Pomver
79 1st Earl Whimsey
80 Rhoda Delagardie
81 Lord John Roxton
82 Doc Savage
83 8th—Tarzan
84 Monk Mayfair
85 Enid Challenger
86 Denis Nayland Smith
87 Nero Wolfe
88 Bulldog Drummond
89 John (Korak) Drummond
90 Lord Peter Wimsey
91 Barbara Collis-Whimsey
92 Richard Wentworth

ACKNOWLEDGMENTS

It is impossible to acknowledge everybody who has contributed, in one way or another, to the making of this book. I wish to thank especially John Harwood and Dr. H. W. Starr for their scholarly articles and their many critical and illuminating letters to me. I thank Dale L. Walker, a scholar in the Jack London field, for his enlightening comments. Sir Alvin Germeshausen of Hollywood was most kind in lending me certain reference books which would have been difficult and, in some cases, impossible for me to obtain. Sam and Florence Russell used their valuable time while in England to dig up much information on the barons of Greystoke in Cumberland and to garner weather data from the May 1888, London *Times*. Henry Eichner gave me some valuable Atlantean data. Vernell Coriell was extremely generous with his time and the loan of his rare materials in helping me with my research. Others whose articles have helped me clear up obscure points, or validated my own independent conclusions (or invalidated them), are Allan Howard, Frank Brueckel, the foremost scientific apologist of the Burroughs world, and John Roy. Peter Ogden, Camille E. Cazedessus, Jr., and Phil Currie should also be thanked for having put so much time and money into their publications, with a consequent enrichening of Burroughsian scholarship. Richard Lupoff and Sam Moskowitz have made valuable contributions to the field, and, therefore, to this book. I owe Larry Ashmead and Diane Cleaver, editors of Doubleday, much for accepting the idea of this book and for giving me free rein to pursue the true Tarzan. Thanks are also very much due to Robert M. Hodes, vice-president of Edgar Rice Burroughs, Inc., for giving me permission to write this biography, and for his many helpful hints, and his enthusiasm.

I thank Doubleday and Company and the estate of A. Conan Doyle for permission to use the quotations from *The Complete Sher-*

lock Holmes, A. Conan Doyle, Garden City edition, 1938; Dover Publications, Inc., for permission to quote from Suzanne K. Langer's Translator's Preface in *Language and Myth*, Ernst Cassirer, Dover Publications, Inc., New York, 1946; to Princeton University Press for permission to quote from *The Hero with a Thousand Faces*, Joseph Campbell, Bollingen Series XVII, copyright © 1949 by Bollingen Foundation, published by Princeton University Press, Princeton, New Jersey. Other acknowledgments are made in the text or bibliography; I express my gratitude to those who kindly permitted me to use the quotations and references.

The two to whom I owe the most, of course, are Edgar Rice Burroughs and the subject of this biography. I am forever grateful to Mr. Burroughs for having written his classical semifiction (which flourishes and will flourish despite so-called literary critics). I am inexpressibly grateful to "Lord Greystoke" himself for granting me an interview and for showing me, however briefly, his father's diary.

I can't reveal my final methods in locating him; suffice it that I did. He answered my letters with an overseas phone call, and he did so only because he wanted to make sure that I would not reveal his true identity. I would never have done so without his permission, nor will I, but he must have felt that I deserved something for my silence. Most people would not think that fifteen minutes of questions and answers would be enough repayment for an expensive flight to Africa. But these nine hundred seconds were far more than I had expected.

Unfortunately, I spent about five minutes of the interview, though not all at one time, in just looking at him. He was the most beautiful, but at the same time undeniably masculine, man that I've ever seen. This was so despite the scars on his forehead and neck of which Burroughs speaks and many more on his face and hands that Burroughs does not mention. I was silenced by the exceedingly charismatic force which he radiated even when he was quiet. Perhaps tigerish would be a better term. Something burns brightly inside him.

I got the feeling that I was in the presence of an immortal, though I knew that he could bleed and die even as I. That he was eighty years old then but looked only about thirty-five seems unbelievable now that I am no longer in his presence. Of course, he did not produce any proof that he was born in 1888, and I didn't ask him for it. I did not have any proof that he was really "Lord Greystoke"; it is possible, I suppose, that I was the victim of a hoax. All I can say is that anyone who met him would not believe that he was anything other than what he claimed.

I was not permitted to take any photographs, and many of my questions were answered with only a word or two or an enigmatic smile. But I do have the final authority for a number of statements I make in this biography. The rest is reconstruction applied with logic and common sense and what I call the analogical approach.

—Libreville, September 1

FOREWORD

This is a biography of a living person.

It should, therefore, be placed by librarians and booksellers on the "B" shelves. It should be subtitled in the catalog cards as *The Life of Lord Greystoke, from 1888 through 1946.*

Some might object that, since the book is also a quest for the identity of the real Tarzan, it could be put into the category of "mystery." Others might object that, since it is based on a semi-fictional series written by a novelist, it should be classified as "fiction." However, this book makes a serious attempt to fill in the gaps left by Burroughs and to explain the seeming discrepancies in his works on "Lord Greystoke." It tries to cull the fictional, the impossible and the improbable from the works by Burroughs. The residue, I trust, presents a fairly accurate picture of the life and times of the very real Englishman who spent his youth among a group of rare hominids who are probably now extinct. Hominids are subhumans, not great apes, and it was a band of language-using pithecanthropoids who adopted the human infant called Tarzan. Burroughs, who based his early novels of Tarzan on incomplete and sometimes inaccurate data, described the "mangani" as great apes and was thereafter stuck with that term. Not that he minded. He was writing novels, and the facts did not always have to be adhered to. Indeed, as I will be demonstrating more than once, he sometimes went out of his way to make sure that the reader thought that his Tarzan books were entirely fictional.

I propose to show that Tarzan is not at all the persona we've seen in so many bad movies about him. I propose to show that he is not quite the persona that Burroughs wrote about, though his character, or temperament, is essentially the same. Burroughs did, however, exaggerate some things for romantic purposes. Thus, the physical prowess of Tarzan, while undoubtedly superior to that of any other living human being, and his ability to travel through the trees are not up to the feats described by Burroughs. Not quite. And it is doubtful that the real Tarzan ever found more than two lost cities or that they or the inhabitants were exactly as described by Burroughs.

This is not a debunking book, however. I propose to show that Tarzan is, in many ways, the last expression of the mythical Golden Age, that his life emulated, unconsciously, of course, the lives of many of the heroes and demigods of classical and primitive mythologies and legends.

Burroughs, it must be said, did for Tarzan what A. Conan Doyle did for his character, Brigadier Étienne Gerard. Doyle did not exaggerate or falsify too much in his tales of Gerard, as has been proved. There was a real marshal of France named Étienne Gerard, one of Napoleon's commanders at Waterloo (see the Encyclopaedia Britannica). But Doyle did not base the fictional Gerard on the marshal. He used only his name.

The real Gerard was the Baron de Marbot, Jean Baptiste Antoine Marcelin, 1782–1854 (see the Encyclopaedia Britannica). His fascinating wilder-than-fiction adventures may be read in his *Memoirs of His Life and Campaigns*, published in 1891 in French and in 1902 in English. More available to American readers is the 1935 abridged edition edited by J. W. Thomason, Jr., *Adventures of General Marbot*.

Those who have read Doyle's Gerard stories and the Marbot autobiography know that Doyle did not exaggerate Marbot's character in the least. Nor did Doyle cross the boundaries between fact and fiction very often. Those adventures of Gerard not found in Marbot could have happened to Marbot easily enough, and he would have acted exactly as Gerard did, though more intelligently. Marbot was not only brighter, he earned a baron's title and married and had children, whereas Gerard never got married and was, supposedly, childless, and ended on a small pension in his old age.

Burroughs' "Lord Greystoke" and the real Englishman are as close in character as Doyle's Gerard and the real Frenchman. But the fictional Tarzan had adventures that veered more from reality than Gerard's did. I propose to show what probably did happen to Tarzan. The adventures as described by Burroughs are given in a very shortened form and in my own words. They are rearranged to fit the proper chronological sequence. The background for the stories, neglected by Burroughs, who was primarily a storyteller, will be filled in to the best of my ability. And the reader will finish the book believing, I hope, that there is indeed a flesh-and-blood man behind the fictional mask of the ape-man.

I warn the reader that I do not intend to reveal his true identity. I will come as close as I can. If the reader cares to spend as much time as I did, four years, in tracing lineages through the several thousand pages of tiny closely set print of Burke's Peerage and correlating his finds with historical phenomena and the Tarzan books by Burroughs and various works by Doyle and many other writers of fiction or fact, then he, too, may track down the real Tarzan. And then he will find that the real Tarzan is reported as being dead. I say *reported* because the man himself has faked his death and taken a new name. The tracker-down will not be as lucky as myself, who got permission from the genuine "Lord Greystoke" to write this biography.

"Lord Greystoke" and Gerard are not the only fictional characters based on, or are very close to being, real-life persons. Recent evidence indicates that there was a "Scarlet Pimpernel," though he did not call himself that and his adventures and ability to disguise himself were not quite as flamboyant as those of Orczy's character. Nor did he become a baronet until after his exploits. He was, however, as I show in Addendum 2, the ancestor of our "Lord Greystoke," the real Tarzan.

Lord John Roxton, the great hunter and Southamericanomaniac of Doyle's *The Lost World*, had a real-life counterpart very much like him. He was also a nobleman's son, though his father was not a duke. Doyle's Professor Challenger was, we know, a Rutherford, though he was not the Professor Rutherford who taught Doyle at Edinburgh University. He was a relative of that Rutherford, and he did go on an expedition to South America. I'm sorry to report that he found no Maple White Land and did not bring back a live pterodactyl, or even a dead one, to London.

Bulldog Drummond, as McNeile admitted, was based on a real man. McNeile's novels are very much romanticized as far as events go, but the character of Captain Hugh Drummond, D.S.O., M.C., is essentially true.

There was also a real-life Sherlock Holmes, three, in fact, and a Doc Savage, a Lord Peter Wimsey, and a Raffles. Sadly, there doesn't seem to have been anyone on whom Sax Rohmer based his Denis Nayland Smith (unless it was the fictional Holmes) or that greatest of villains, Fu Manchu. These are fictional, as is Holmes' sister, whom I postulate in Addendum 2. Addendum 2 is half-fiction, half-true, and the family relationships depicted therein are sometimes, as I admit, made up to fill a requisite slot. But Addendum 2 is mostly literary fun. I hope the reader enjoys it as much as I did.

Addendum 1 is from *The Baker Street Journal* and is Professor Starr having fun. It is also, he has told me, a satire on a certain type of Ph.D. and the kind of "research" done by this type. But, entirely by accident, Professor Starr struck near the truth. The character of Sidney Trefusis in G. B. Shaw's novel, *An Unsocial Socialist*, is based on a real man, a peer of England. He was as eccentric and as radically minded as Trefusis and as the fifth duke of Holdernesse postulated in Starr's essay. I have located him in Burke's Peerage and elsewhere; he was indeed the grandfather of Burroughs' "Lord Greystoke."

He may have been a cabdriver. He held many jobs under many names, as the real-life nobleman whom Shaw calls Trefusis did. One of his names was John Clayton, and he may actually have been questioned by the real-life Holmes. I suspect that he was and that Doyle knew this. Whether or not it was during the case which Doyle calls *The Hound of the Baskervilles*, I do not know. There is no way of proving this. But he was a cabdriver, and Doyle did know of him, and he did live in Marylebone Borough. And the address given is close to his real address.

Whether or not the real Tarzan inherited the title from the eccentric Socialist "Lord Greystoke," or is just a baronet, a sort of hereditary knight, I cannot reveal.

The present "Lord Greystoke" is quite adamant about the limits to be observed in this book. Thus, his lineage and, indeed, half of the events and persons herein are not presented with the real names and places and dates attached. Half are. The other half are analogs or parallels. What I give herein is the truth but the truth looked at obliquely or in a distorting mirror.

That is why the librarians and booksellers should place this work in the "B" section. That is why the reader should realize that he is reading something unique, the first analogical, or parallel, biography.

Each chapter number is accompanied by Roman and Arabic

numerals in parentheses. These are for the convenience of the scholar. Those who do not care about such things may ignore the parenthetical numbers. For those who do care, (I–1), for instance indicates the first chapter in the first of the twenty-four authorized volumes of the biography by Edgar Rice Burroughs. The biography at hand, *Tarzan Alive*, reports the events of Tarzan's life in strict chronological sequence. Mr. Burroughs did not always so report. Thus, he did not go into detail about the ape-man's youth until the sixth book of the biography, *Jungle Tales of Tarzan*. Chapter 6 (Part of I–11; VI) indicates that the sixth chapter of this book concerns part of chapter 11 of Book I, *Tarzan of the Apes*, and all of Book VI, *Jungle Tales of Tarzan*. It was necessary to insert the events of Book VI in Book I for reasons which will be explained.

The following table gives the Tarzan volumes, by Roman numeral, in the order in which they were published.

TARZAN VOLUMES

CONTENTS

1888: *The World*

1898: *The World*

1908: *The World*

CONTENTS

1888: THE WORLD

The population of the world was 1,483,000,000, as compared with more than double that in 1970.

The partition of Africa by the European powers was not yet complete. Africa was, in every sense, the Dark Continent.

Grover Cleveland was President of the U.S.

Victoria was queen of England; Lord Salisbury, her Conservative prime minister.

The automobile was still in its experimental stage. Karl Benz had operated his first automobile only three years before.

It would be fifteen years before the Wright brothers would make the first successful flights in a heavier-than-air craft.

Heinrich Hertz generated radio waves with a spark gap transmitter and detected them with apparatus a few feet away.

Jack the Ripper was prowling London's East End.

Bismarck made his great Reichstag speech, mostly about the Russians, ending with, "We Germans fear God and nothing else in the world."

Count Samuel Teleki, a Hungarian scientist, discovered Lakes Rudolf and Stefanie in East Africa.

Mark Twain was writing the major part of *A Connecticut Yankee in King Arthur's Court.*

The Samoans revolted against their German overlords.

The recording adding machine was invented by Burroughs; transparent photographic film, by Eastman; calcium carbide was by Willson.

Georg Brandes (Georg Morris Cohen) lectured on Nietzsche at the University of Copenhagen, thus bringing Nietzsche to public notice.

Tarzan, a superman unlike the one of which Nietzsche dreamed, was born on the west coast of Equatorial Africa.

Chapter One

(I–1)

Out to Sea

Joyous we too launch out on trackless seas,
Fearless for unknown shores . . .

—Walt Whitman

Without wine, we would never have known the story of the most
famous adventurer since Odysseus or of the strongest man since
Samson.

Edgar Rice Burroughs, an American writer, had dinner with a
retired official of the British Colonial Office. The official had more
than a few drinks, but Burroughs was moderate that winter evening
of 1911. He clearly remembered the Englishman's story the next
day.

The host's pride was hurt by Burroughs' skepticism. He obtained
old records from the files of the Colonial Office and also a diary
of a long-dead man to "prove" his exceedingly strange story.

Half-convinced, the American dug into all the records to which
he could get access. Inspired by what he read, he wrote a biography
which is, in the main, faithful to the facts. However, there were
gaps which he had to fill in with guesses. Some of these hit near
the mark and some missed the target completely. The book was
first published as *Tarzan of the Apes* in the October, 1912, issue
of *The All-Story Magazine*. Burroughs left out much which he did
not think necessary to include because the biography was presented
as pure fiction. It is the purpose of this "private life" to fill in
the gaps and to correct or explain certain puzzling features and
seeming discrepancies.

Burroughs would have been thirteen years old in 1888 (after

September 1). He wrote *Tarzan of the Apes* between December 1, 1911, and May 14, 1912, when he was thirty-five years old. Since he had never been to England, he would have had to get his facts and surmises about the "Greystoke case" from a man who had just returned from England to Chicago. No human being outside of a few isolated blacks knew that Tarzan existed until February, 1909. The civilized world could not have known about Tarzan until about July, 1909. Between then and December, 1911, probably late in 1910, Burroughs talked to the man who had pried the Tarzan story out of the retired official. For greater verisimilitude and speed of narration, Burroughs pretended to be the very man from whom he got the information.

The story begins in 1888, but first we must examine the background of "a certain young English nobleman, whom we shall call John Clayton, Lord Greystoke." Burroughs used the "Greystoke" to include several different titles, since John Clayton would not have borne the same title as his father, who was still living. Clayton would not have been a nobleman. The children of peers still living are considered to be commoners. But the eldest son of an earl, marquis, or duke is usually known socially by the name of his father's next peerage. If Clayton's father's title was Duke Greyminster, for example, Clayton could have called himself Lord Saltire, because his father was also Marquess Saltire. Burroughs concealed the real titles of the family under the catchall of "Greystoke" because he respected the privacy of this ancient family, which was especially sensitive to publicity. A. Conan Doyle, Dr. Watson's literary agent, or perhaps Watson himself, did the same for this very family, if Professor H. W. Starr's theory is correct. Doyle (or Watson) concealed the name of the family as Holdernesse in *The Adventure of the Priory School*. Doyle (or Watson) forgot to correct Holmes' slip in referring to the "Duke of Greyminster" in *The Adventure of the Blanched Soldier*. "Greyminster" was also a pseudonym but it was much closer to the real title of the duke, perhaps too close. It was the "Greyminster" that gave me the clue I needed to track down the real identity of the man known as Tarzan.

The original manuscript of *Tarzan of the Apes* gave Clayton's title as "Bloomstoke." Burroughs, who delighted in codes, could not, however, resist a stronger hint about the real identity of Clayton, so he changed the initial syllable of the title back to "Grey."

Addendum 2 describes in detail Burroughs' method of coding, and, in addition, Doyle's and Watson's. But it is necessary to read Addendum 1 first. This is an article, *A Case of Identity*, by H. W. Starr, which originally appeared in the *Baker Street Journal*. The researches of Mr. Starr into the true identity of the "Greystokes" are admirable and highly ingenious, though his conclusions have been modified and expanded by me in Addendum 2.

Mr. Starr makes a strong case that John Clayton, a cabdriver in *The Hound of the Baskervilles*, was actually the eccentric fifth duke of Greyminster and Tarzan's grandfather. Mr. Starr concludes that the sixth duke of *The Adventure of the Priory School* was the younger brother of the John Clayton who disappeared on the *Fuwalda*. A study of the dates and other facts convinced me that the sixth duke was, instead, the younger brother of the fifth duke. He was the uncle, not the brother, of the John Clayton who became Tarzan's father. Addendum 2 details the argument and also gives the genealogy and the relatives of the "Greystoke" family since 1795.

In 1888, John Clayton, Lord Greystoke, was selected to make a secret investigation of conditions in a British west coast African territory. Most readers of *Tarzan of the Apes* have assumed that the "friendly European power" was Belgium. They are thinking of King Leopold's alleged exploitation of the natives of the Congo Free State. But the nearest British West African territory (not a colony) was the Niger River (Oil Rivers) area. It would be very unlikely that Belgians would be recruiting native soldiers almost eight hundred miles away for operations along the Congo and Aruwimi rivers. Moreover, 1888 was a few years too early for the kind of exploitation of which Leopold's private company was accused. Burroughs knew this but deliberately threw his readers off the track here, as he did at a number of other places, to help obscure the identity and the mission of "Lord Greystoke."

Clayton was given a position in the Royal Niger Company, which had succeeded the National African Company in 1886. This chartered commercial organization was given complete control of the Nigerian area north of the Niger Coast (Oil Rivers) Protectorate.

Ostensibly, John Clayton had resigned his recently acquired position in the British Colonial Office to take up his new job as a civilian administrator-explorer. His area of investigation was to be, at first, just west of the Kamerun, a territory claimed by the Germans only five days before the British tried to seize it in 1884. It was the Germans who were up to something on the Niger-Kamerun border, and Clayton was to find out what they were doing. In addition, he would be making surveys of the topography and the mineral resources. After reporting on the Germans, he was to proceed north and ascertain what the French were doing there in their push to claim more African lands.

Clayton was twenty-four years old, six feet two inches tall, and weighed 195 pounds. If the Olympics had existed then, he could have been as famous an athlete as Jim Thorpe was to be. His face was handsome but very masculine. He had the straight nose, square chin, and short upper lip that his famous son would inherit. His eyes were as dark grey as the winter skies of his native Yorkshire. His hair was almost as black as the hair of the natives he had commanded during his service in the Indian Army.

John Clayton had served as a captain in the Pioneers of the Corps of Madras Sappers and Miners (the Queen's Own). His colonel, Sebastian Moran, took him along on the extended hunting trip in East India of which Moran wrote in *Three Months in the Jungle* (1884). He is the John Clayton whose near-fatal mauling by a tiger is described in Chapter 12. Clayton anticipated his famous son's proclivities by killing the great cat with a hunting knife. But he was so badly hurt that he was invalided home. While recuperating, he decided to resign from the military and make the Colonial Office his career.

Clayton came from an ancient and distinguished lineage. Though Greystoke was not, in actuality, among the titles he would inherit someday, he was descended from the de Greystocks of Greystoke Manor, Cumberland, through several different lines. His family was related to the Howards, d'Arcys, Percies, Nevilles, Cavendishes, Drummonds, and a number of other noble families. He was also descended from the Plantagenets, the Tudors, and the Stuarts.

Clayton was a graduate of Chatham, the royal military engineering college. His experience in the Indian Army, and his powerful connections, could have taken him high up in the military. But, tired of army life, he preferred the Colonial Office, which was swiftly expanding with the growth of Britain's overseas empire. Almost at once, he was given the mission to the Niger.

He was both thrilled and dismayed. He had been married in late

February to the Honorable Alice Rutherford, daughter of Baron Tennington. She was eighteen years old, a beauty with dark hair and large grey eyes almost the same shade as those of her husband. The Rutherfords were an ancient and distinguished family of the Scottish border. "Rutherford" derives from an Old English place name, *hrythera ford* (horned cattle of the ford). The arms of Alice's family bore a wild bull's head and a wild man's head between the horns. This was appropriate, since her son would be as strong and as fierce as a wild bull. Yet he would be singularly controlled by his human intelligence.

The marriage, which was also a double wedding, was one of the great social events of 1888. Clayton's uncle, William Cecil, had decided, at the age of fifty-two, to marry. His bride, the wealthy widow of a peer, had resumed her maiden name for reasons known best to herself. Edith was the daughter of the wealthy and recently knighted financier, Sir John Jansenius. (Watson gives him a different name.) William Cecil, brother to the fifth duke, was a very distinguished statesman and politician. In recognition of his services, Queen Victoria had granted him the titles of Marquess of Exminster and Viscount Passmore. At this time, he was intent on getting his older brother certified insane so that young John Clayton could legally take over the administration of the family estate.

The wedding promised to be not only a happy one but a brilliant one. It was attended by prominent relatives: the dukes of Norfolk, of Westminster, and of Pomver; the earls of Lovelace, of Carlisle, of Perth, and of Burlesdon; the barons of Tennington, Dunsany, Byron, Inchiquin, and Ruthven; and, the most distinguished, the Prince of Wales. Young Clayton's best friend, his tall red-haired cousin, Rudolph, himself soon to make a fateful voyage, was present.

The most outstanding guest was an uninvited cabdriver. He was the younger groom's eccentric father and the older groom's older brother. The fifth duke, John Clayton I, had disgraced his family by becoming a fanatical Socialist, hobnobbing with Karl Marx, Annie Besant, and George Bernard Shaw. (Shaw told the fifth duke's story in his novel, *An Unsocial Socialist*, though he changed names and dates and omitted some things to keep from being sued or perhaps even caned. See Addendum 2 for the full story.) John Clayton I had moved to London to become a common workingman, and he refused to touch any of the great fortune he

derived from his estates. He was as fierce an individualist and as
unconventional as his grandson would be.

John Clayton I, looking quite unducal in his cabdriver's uniform,
went through the crowd passing out socialist pamphlets, even offer-
ing one to Victoria's son. The fifth duke had just gotten out of jail
for the second time. The first time, he had been put on trial for
seditious libel and sentenced to imprisonment, but his sentence
was quashed when his counsel found a flaw in the indictment.
He would be arrested again when he hit Karl Marx in the nose
during their final argument.

Both grooms were mortified, and his son took him aside and
argued violently with him. The two never saw each other again.
This final estrangement so angered John Clayton II that he thought
of his father as dead. This was why, on May 22, he wrote in his
diary that his baby son was "the second John Clayton" when he
should have written "the third."

The young John Clayton could not endure the thought of leaving
his bride behind when he went to Africa. But he could not even
wish that she go with him into that region appropriately named
"the white man's grave." Especially, he could not ask her because
she was pregnant.

Alice Rutherford did not plead, storm, or wheedle. She insisted,
firmly but quietly, that she was going. Clayton finally agreed but
only on condition that she return to England at once if she got
sick or found conditions intolerable.

On a bright May morning in 1888, the Claytons sailed from
Dover for Freetown, the capital city of the British crown colony
of Sierra Leone. The exact departure date and the name of the ship
are unknown. Clayton did not start the diary which would end up
in the files of the Colonial Office until several days before his
arrival at Freetown. Apparently, the earlier diary was either lost or
mailed back to England from Freetown.

(The port authorities of Dover state in a letter to me that the
sailing date and the name of the ship are not available. They do
not say why, so I can only guess that the records were destroyed
by bombs during World War II or the "Greystoke" family has
made certain that they are not "available.")

(Whitaker's Almanack says of May, 1888, "The weather was
mostly fine, and there was much sunshine." However, to the English,
any day, no matter how gloomy, is "fine" if it's not raining. A

reading of daily weather reports of the *Times* [London] and other journals indicates that May 11 or May 23 were the most likely to be bright all morning in Dover.)

A month later, the couple arrived in the hot, steaming, stinking, and muddy town. Lady Alice, knowing that this place was considered to be the most civilized area of west Africa, was sickened. Not wishing her husband to sense her true reaction, she smiled and laughed and exclaimed over this and that exotic item.

John Clayton recorded in his diary that Captain Sir Richard Francis Burton, the famous explorer and linguist, and a distant cousin, had visited Freetown in 1862. Burton, Clayton wrote, had liked Freetown even less than his wife Alice liked it. Evidently, she had not fooled him. He noted also that Sierra Leone was probably the terminus of the famous voyage of Hanno the Carthaginian. There were no gorillas in west Africa in 1888, but Hanno may have encountered some in 500 B.C.

A few days later, they boarded a small ship, the barkentine *Fuwalda.* Clayton had chartered this coastwise trader-freighter to take them to a small village on a tributary of the Niger River. (This site was to be called Obomotu, and, even later, Port Harcourt.) From there, the Claytons would travel up the river and then cut across the country to the Niger-Kamerun border.

They were never seen again.

Two months later, while British naval vessels were searching for the *Fuwalda*, its wreckage was discovered on the shores of St. Helena, the island where Napoleon died in exile in 1821.

(This same year, 1821, the famous explorer of Africa, Richard Francis Burton, and the famous explorer of the dark continent of the psyche, Fyodor Dostoyevsky, were born. It was also the year in which Siger Holmes, Sherlock's father, was born, if W. S. Baring-Gould is right. It is worthwhile noting that Siger Holmes, like John Clayton, was invalided home from military service in India. The "friend" whom Baring-Gould mentions as being involved with Siger in the accident that crippled him was his relative, Richard Francis Burton. Burton was an officer of the 18th Regiment of Bombay Native Infantry, stationed at Bandor Gharra, Sind, south of Karachi. Siger, a cavalry lieutenant, was visiting him.)

After leaving Freetown, the barkentine began its zigzag path toward its destination. It was pushed along by the eastward-going Guinea current, but the southeast trade winds forced the vessel to beat about. It was making about eight knots an hour in a hard wind, which was remarkably swift, considering that the *Fuwalda* was not run in a very efficient manner. Its crew was composed of misfits and criminals of many nations and all races, excluding the Australian aborigine. Its officers were not much better than the crew.

The morning of the second day out from Freetown, the Claytons witnessed a shocking incident, the first of many. They had just finished talking to Captain Billings, a big, broad-shouldered, round-paunched, red-eyed man who always needed a shave. He turned away from them and fell over the back of a little old sailor on his hands and knees scrubbing the deck (because Clayton had complained about its filthiness). The captain sprawled on his face, knocking over the bucket full of dirty water and soaking him.

Alice gave a little shriek. John smiled. He did not mind seeing the loud-mouthed, ill-smelling brute mortified. But he lost his smile when Billings, cursing, leaped up and struck the old sailor to the deck.

The other sailor, Black Michael, was as big as the captain and looked even meaner. His black mustachios stuck out like the horns of a bull, which he resembled in figure and ferocity. Bellowing, he struck the captain to his knees with a single blow of his fist.

The captain's face changed from red to white. Still on his knees, he pulled his revolver from his pants pocket and fired at the giant.

But Clayton struck down the captain's arm so that the bullet, a .44-10, hit the side of the sailor's calf instead. It gouged out a chunk of flesh, and blood ran down his leg, but the bullet had not seriously wounded him.

Clayton roared, "What kind of a beast are you? You don't kill a man for that!"

Furiously, he denounced the officers for their brutalities and declared that he wanted no more such incidents. Otherwise, the British authorities would hear about the *Fuwalda*.

The captain, shaking and white, walked off. Black Michael, supporting the little sailor, limped off, but not before he had growled, "Thanks, Mr. Clayton."

(Dale Walker has suggested, and John Harwood has developed, the connection between Black Michael and Watson's Black Peter Michael Cary of *The Adventure of Black Peter*. I believe that Black Michael was indeed the same man and that he had other reasons than humanity for sparing the Claytons. I also believe that the fifth duke was murdered by Black Michael and that one of the men we know as Sherlock Holmes investigated the case. This will be explained in Chapter 10. Refer also to Addendum 4.)

From then on, the officers avoided the Claytons as much as possible. This did not displease the Claytons, since they had nothing in common with the sullen and dirty brutes. But, though isolated, they could feel the ominous air which settled down like a great spider web over the ship.

The fourth day out, Clayton came up from the companionway just in time to see an unconscious sailor being carried off. The first mate was holding a bloody belaying pin.

The fifth day, when Clayton saw a British warship bearing down on them, he thought about transferring to it. But what excuse could he give to the captain of the warship? He had seen some brutality, and that was all. Nobody had threatened the Claytons. He would be thought a coward, and his mission would be aborted or delayed.

Before the upper works of the ship had disappeared over the horizon, he regretted his decision, which he now knew came from false pride. The old sailor whom Billings had knocked down had warned Clayton that he and his wife should stay below if they heard any shooting.

Clayton told Alice about this. She insisted, despite his reluctance to help the captain, that he must warn him at once.

"It's a lie!" Billings shouted, banging his fist on his desk in the tiny cabin. "And I'm getting tired of you sticking your blue-blooded needle nose into my business!"

There was much more, but Clayton waited until the purple-faced captain was out of breath. Then he drawled, "You're a bit of an ass, don't you know?" and walked out. Returning to Alice, he told her they must go to their cabin at once and check on their revolvers. They found their quarters ransacked but only the guns and bullets missing.

"What are we to do, John?" she said. "Possibly our best chance for salvation lies in maintaining a neutral position."

"Right you are, Alice. We'll keep in the middle of the road."

They were to find that the self-declared neutral may be as much a victim as the defeated belligerent.

While they were straightening up the cabin, they saw a piece of paper being pushed under the door. Clayton strode to the door, but

Chapter Two

(I-2)

The Savage Home

. . . ready to perish in this wilderness. . . .

—William Bradford

The morning of the sixth day out from Freetown, a rifle barked as
Clayton stepped out onto the deck for his prebreakfast walk. He
half-turned to dive back into the companionway as more shots
followed. But he decided it would be wiser to act as if he were not
involved. He watched as the crew, after a brief fight, massacred all
the officers.

Clayton puffed on his pipe as if he were watching a cricket match.
Inwardly, he trembled with fear for his wife. The blood lust of the
sailors was still up, and blood lust quite often led to another kind of
lust. He turned to go down to her, not sure whether he should go
later to Black Michael for protection or kill her at once with his
hunting knife, the only weapon he had to save her from what the
Victorians called "a fate worse than death."

He almost dropped his pipe. She was standing just back of him
and looking around the corner of the companionway.

"How long have you been here, Alice?"

"Since the beginning!" she cried. Her face was pale and twisted.
"How awful! Oh, John, how awful! What can we hope for at the
hands of such as these?"

"Breakfast, I hope," he said, having decided instantly to brave it
out.

They walked toward the men, her arm in his, both seemingly
unperturbed. They saw the bodies of the eight dead men and of
the severely wounded, officers and crew alike, go overboard. A sailor,

bleeding from a chest wound and half his face shot off, screamed as he went into the sea, almost into the mouth of one of the sharks that had been following the ship for its garbage. Alice checked her stride and squeezed her husband's arm, but he whispered, "Steady! Don't act scared!"

A sailor lifted his bloody ax and, crying, "Here's two more for the fishes!" charged them. Before he had gone more than a few feet, he fell on his face, a bullet in his back from Black Michael's gun.

Black Michael roared out, "These here're me friends, and they're to be left alone! I'm captain of this here ship now, and what I says goes!"

To the Claytons he said, "Just keep to yerselves, and nobody'll harm ye."

The Claytons were very happy to obey. They stayed in their cabin, talking about what could happen and what they could do, and sometimes they were silent while they just held each other. Now and then they heard noises which indicated much drinking and brawling and, twice, revolver shots. On the eleventh day out of Freetown, the fifth day after the mutiny, they heard the lookout shout "Land ho!"

An hour later, Black Michael entered.

"I don't know if it's an island or the mainland itself," he said. "If it's livable, ashore you go, bag and baggage. Ye'll be all right there a few months, and by that time we'll have made an inhabitable coast some place, some place civilized, and we'll scatter."

(The *Fuwalda* was off the mainland, the shore of the French Congo. The vessel was halfway between Iguéla and Setté Cama, approximately at 2 degrees south latitude, on the middle point of the coast of the *Parc national du Petit Loango* of the present-day Gabon Republic. This location is far from the 10 degrees south latitude which William Cecil Clayton was to calculate in 1909. It does not agree with Burroughs' statement that the Porter party was fifteen hundred miles north of Cape Town. This location would be on the coast of Portuguese Angola in or near the present-day Quicama National Park. This would place the Greystoke cabin and the Porter party more than three hundred miles south of the Congo River. Gorillas lived near where the Greystokes were stranded, but there were, and are, no gorillas south of the Congo River. Internal evidence from the Tarzan books indicates that the coast of Gabon was the correct location, even if we did not know that from other sources. Burroughs' statement that the *Fuwalda* only sailed eleven days before the Claytons were stranded is also purposely misleading.

Black Michael said, "Then I'll see that yer government is notified where ye be, and they'll send a man o'war to fetch ye off. 'Twould be a hard matter landing ye at a civilized port wi'out a lot o' questions asked, and none o' us here has any convincing answers up our sleeves."

(This use of "*yer* government," not "*the* government" or "*our* government," means that Black Michael was not a British subject. He would have been a citizen of the U.S.A. or, possibly, an Irish expatriate, or both.)

Clayton protested, but Black Michael became angry. He said, "If it was left up to me men, yer throats'd be cut, after suitable use o' yer ladyship, if ye know what I mean. Don't argue wi' me. I've had enough o' that wi' me own men."

At three o'clock that afternoon, the *Fuwalda* came about off a beautiful wooded shore by what seemed to be a landlocked harbor. The rolling surf was as white as the teeth of a shark. Within the lagoon and on the beach were thousands of ducks, pelicans, ibises, cranes, marabouts, and sea gulls. To the north of the sandy beaches was the mouth of a little river and then the edge of a mangrove swamp with the white-and-black fish eagles on the tops of the cotton-wood trees. Inland were low ridges and gentle hills which reared within a few miles to form a series of plateaus.

The vegetation of the plateaus was that of the closed-canopy rain forest of equatorial west Africa. The tall broad-leaved evergreen trees were so thickly intertwined with lianas and other growths that the jungle edge looked like a living cascade of plants on a high cliff. Between the shore and the rain forest were several miles of quite different jungle, thick with bushes but with the skies frequently seen between trees.

The sailors, silent as if touched by the vast and gloomy spirit of the forest, manned a boat. They rowed through the violent surf, the boat rising and falling like a wooden horse on a merry-go-round gone mad. In an hour, the sailors returned to report deep water in the passage and inside the lagoon. Before sunset, the barkentine was at anchor on a surface as smooth as that of a goldfish bowl.

The big white gulls wheeled about the ship in clouds and screamed. From the beaches came the squawk and quack of the ducks and the screams of the other birds. The forest, seen at a closer range, looked even more vast, impenetrable, and dusky, despite the blazing colors of the semitropical verdure.

("Semitropical verdure" was another example of Burroughs' efforts to mislead the reader about the true location of the birthplace of Tarzan.)

Clayton pointed out to Alice that the river ensured them fresh water, the sea would yield plenty of fish, and the jungle would, of course, hold plenty of game.

Then the sun dropped like a piece of red flesh into the mouth of night, and the predators took over in the wilderness. Alice shrank against her husband as a roar, which seemed to her to be a lion's, bounded across the waters. A moment later, the distant scream of a panther rose like the wail of a dying woman.

(When Burroughs refers to the African "panther," he does not mean the puma, cougar, or mountain lion as this big cat (*Felis concolor*) is variously called. Leopards (*Panthera pardus*) were sometimes called *panthers* and even *tigers* in different parts of Africa by whites. There is evidence that Burroughs' knowledge of African wildlife was limited when he first learned of the existence of Tarzan. Later, he made it more extensive and precise, but he was still not above substituting a lion for a leopard when he felt that the story would be more dramatic. However, leopards are the true king of the beasts, according to Jean-Pierre Hallet in his *Animal Kitabu*, Random House, 1967. "Pound for pound, he is the strongest animal on earth, seemingly assembled out of steel muscles and tendons . . . he is, by reason of his intelligence and great adaptability, the most successful and widely distributed of all big cats, ruling regions that lions have never been able to invade and surviving where lions have long been extinct."

(I believe that all the "lions" mentioned in *Tarzan of the Apes*, up to the time Tarzan left his natal territory, were leopards. Lions do not inhabit Gabon, and zebras and rhinoceroses are not jungle animals. The reader should not be perturbed by this. Burroughs was mainly interested in writing a colorful story.)

Early in the morning, boatload after boatload of the Claytons' possessions and their supplies were ferried to the shore. Black Michael accompanied the Claytons ashore to make certain that his men did not try to murder them at the last moment.

As the boats rowed away, John and Alice Clayton stood by their high pile of boxes, chests, barrels, and sailcloths and watched with utter hopelessness.

When the *Fuwalda* had disappeared behind a hill on the promontory to the south, Alice sobbed as if she would never stop. He let her cry because he thought it would be good for her to weep out the repressed terror and grief. At last, she quit weeping and said, "Oh, John, the horror of it! What are we to do?"

His reply was short, simple, and Victorian. Work would be their salvation. They would use work as an armor until the government found them.

After loading his rifles, Clayton began to build a temporary shelter. By late afternoon, he had constructed a small hut about ten feet up on a platform between four trees. Just before dusk, he completed a ladder. He filled a large canteen from the river for the night, at the same time observing two otters catching large frogs and noting several large crocodiles. Then he climbed into the hut and sat down on the blankets beside Alice. They talked for a while, he trying to reassure her, while they looked through the opening between two sailcloths used as combination curtains and walls. So far, there had been no mosquitoes, for which they should thank God, as Clayton said several times. Perhaps the exposure of this area to the strong trade winds swept the mosquitoes off the beach. Or perhaps there was not enough still water in the swamp to provide a breeding place for them.

Suddenly, Alice gripped her husband's arm.

"John! Look! What is it, a man?"

Clayton saw the silhouette of a great figure standing in the shadows of the ridge. A chill ran over him. It looked like a misshapen man, or a demon, hammered out of the raw ore of blackest night.

It stood there for a moment and then retreated, walking upright, into the jungle dusk.

Alice, trembling, asked him again what it could be. He replied that he did not know. It could have been just a shadow cast by the rising moon.

"No," she said. "If it wasn't a man, it was some huge grotesque mockery of man! Oh, I am so afraid!"

He kissed her and whispered all the encouragement he could think of, but it was not much. After a while, he lowered the sail-cloths and tied them down and they tried to get to sleep. But no sooner had they closed their eyes than they heard a leopard scream beneath the hut. The rest of the night, he sat up with his rifle ready.

Chapter Three

(I–3)

Life and Death

Death borders upon our birth, and
our cradle stands in the grave.

—Joseph Hall

A hare's bite may kill a leopard.

—Mpongwe saying

At dawn the bleary-eyed Claytons ate their meager breakfast of
salt pork and biscuits and drank their coffee. He began work at
once on a permanent one-room log house a hundred yards from
the beach. It took him until the first week in August to complete it.
The rainy season would not start for another two months, but here
there was not much difference between the dry and the rainy
season. There would be somewhat more precipitation, and the winds
would not be so strong.

The A-shaped roof was thatched with a layer of branches over
which were placed woven long-grasses and palm fronds. This was
also coated with clay. The single window was barred with a grate
made of interwoven branches one inch thick. The door was solidly
built of layers of planks from packing cases. He took two days
of hard work to shape two massive hardwood hinges, and then he
constructed a lock. By the end of September, they were well
settled with furniture he had built himself, including a cradle.
And he planned on extending the house when he got time.

Burroughs, always one to eliminate details that did not contribute
to the mainstream of the story, did not mention that Clayton also

built a storeroom-annex to the cabin. The small cabin in which
the Claytons lived could not possibly have held the huge store of
goods and tools needed for the planned stay of five to seven years.
There were many pairs of Balmoral lace boots, linen slippers,
leggings for protection against thorns and insect bites, Panama hats,
a hundred pounds of the hardest Marseilles soap, 75 ounce-bottles
of quinine and 30 quarts of laudanum, 10 gallons of castor oil,
50 pounds of Epsom salts, 150 pounds of arsenic to preserve animal
skins, and many other drugs. All were packed in japanned tin
boxes. There were also boxes of beads, mirrors, cloth, and gin for
trading gifts and tribute. There were more boxes of scientific
instruments: watches, sextants, telescopes, binoculars, sun dials, aner-
oids, compasses, drawing instruments, thermometers, nautical al-
manacs, and many other devices. There were 100 pounds of wax
candles, 10 gallons of alcohol for lamps, boxes of matches, and
flints and steels. There were 10 boxes of photographic apparatus
with developing chemicals. There were rifles and pistols, including
an air rifle and a double-barrel .600-caliber rifle for elephants. There
were tents and folding chairs and a portable library for John and
his wife. And there were boxes of children's clothing and of
children's books.

So solidly built was the house, it gave them a sense of security
even when the big cats prowled around the door at night. But the
occasional glimpses of the shadowy manlike figures, like that which
they had seen their first night ashore, did trouble them. Clayton's
opinion was that they were gorillas. He showed Alice drawings of
them in a book by the American explorer, Paul Du Chaillu,
published in 1872.

The illustrations somewhat resembled the creatures. But Alice
was more interested in the sketch-map of that part of Africa
which Du Chaillu had visited. She pointed to the drawing on the
title page and said, "You think we're somewhere there, on the
coast between Cape Lopez and the Congo River. Why don't we
just walk along the shore until we come to a settlement?"

"Because we would be out in the open day and night. Because
we would be subject to attacks by leopards and gorillas and leeches
and poisonous snakes and insects. Because there are cannibals in
this area. We would have to carry many provisions, ammunition,
medicines, sleeping equipment, and so forth. You can't carry much,
not in your condition, or even walk very far with a load on your

back. You're about seven months along, in no shape to do anything but rest, really. No, forget about trying to reach civilization or even a friendly native village. We can do nothing but wait until we are rescued. Black Michael promised to notify the authorities of our position, and I'm sure that he will do so. Here, at least, there are no men—no cannibals—and we have sturdy walls to protect us from the beasts. We will stay here."

A few days later, as Clayton was working in the afternoon on an addition to the cabin, he saw monkeys racing through the trees in terror. The cause of their alarm came swiftly and boldly through the jungle as if it had decided to quit spying on them and to attack. It walked semierectly, occasionally placing the backs of its fists on the ground. It was a huge anthropoid ape intent on its goal: the killing of the human male. It growled deeply but gave a low bark now and then, its four great yellow-brown sharp-pointed canines gleaming wetly. It was huge, standing when erect about six feet three inches high and weighing about 350 pounds. Long black hair covered it except on its face and chest, which were black-skinned. Its forehead was low and slanting, and its black eyes were set under a bulge of bone. The jaws jutted forward, and the lips were thin and black.

(Burroughs gives the above description of the *mangani*. Clayton merely wrote that it rushed at them.)

Clayton, having grown careless lately, had left his firearms in the cabin.

Alice had been sitting by the door while she knitted another dress for the baby to come. He shouted at her to run inside, and she started to obey him, then looked back. The brute was between the cabin and her husband, who was starting to swing at it with his ax.

He shouted at her to lock the door, but she ran on inside and grabbed the only rifle in the cabin, a Lee-Matson. She ran out just in time to see the ax ripped out of her husband's grip and sent spinning toward the bush. Then the great ape was dragging her husband toward his huge canine teeth.

Alice pointed the rifle and pulled the trigger. The recoil knocked her down, but she was up at once and then frantically trying to work the bolt and eject the cartridge. John had tried to get her to learn how to operate a rifle, but she had always been afraid of firearms and had refused to learn. And now the nightmare creature had dropped her husband and was advancing on her. It stood upright on its two legs, its arms held out toward her.

She screamed and at the same time struggled with the mechanism of the rifle. Then it was on her and she had fallen beneath its crushing bulk.

John Clayton leaped up from the ground and ran to the bodies. The ape lay on top of the woman; both were motionless; a bloody hole in its back showed where Alice's bullet had gone. John rolled the heavy corpse off and cried out when he saw the blood all over her dress. But an examination showed him that the blood was the ape's.

Gently he carried her into the cabin and there tried to bring her back to consciousness. Despite his efforts, she did not wake for an hour. Yet she had not a mark on her except for the bruise given by the rifle's recoil.

When she opened her eyes, her first words revealed that her mind was affected. She thought she was in their London town house on Carlton House Terrace. She was sure that she had just had a particularly frightening dream during which she had been attacked by horrible beasts.

That night, while a leopard screamed near their door, a son was born.

Clayton did not record the exact minute of birth. He did indicate it as Thursday, November 22, 1888, shortly after midnight of November 21. The future "Lord Greystoke" was thus ushered into the world under the zodiacal sign of Sagittarius, the Archer. But his birth date was so close to the sign of Scorpio that he was on the "cusp," the line (as imaginary as the equator) where one sign ends and the next sign begins. If we did not have Clayton's record, we would still be able to deduce the infant's birth as being on or near November 22. He shared so many of the basic characteristics of Scorpio, the passionate, and Sagittarius, the hunter.

Sagittarius, the centaur with the bow, could not be a better symbol of the half-animal, half-man who was to be so deadly an archer and killer. He also had a lively, if sometimes cruel, sense of humor (Mark Twain was a Sagittarian). This was to be evidenced by his trickster pranks among animals and men alike. He was also frank, impulsive, restless, had much intellectual curiosity, and loved the outdoors and animals. Sagittarius is the sign associated with long journeys, and Tarzan was to out-Ulysses Ulysses in his wanderings. (Also, Thursday's child has far to go.) This sign is intimately coupled with the tendons of the muscular system, very appropriately for the strongest man in the world. Sagittarians usually have much better than average health, and their recuperative powers are amazing. Sagittarians, somehow, are always at the right place at the right time, and the penchant of coincidence to occur in Tarzan's neighborhood has been noted by many.

A Scorpio is no halfway person; he has extreme likes and dislikes. He is liable to want the world to agree with him, rather than to adapt to the world. He is a fierce competitor. He attracts persons and *situations* (thus Tarzan has a double magnetism for coincidence exceeding the probabilities of chance). He can be aroused to great anger but also to intense sensitivity and kindness.

Scorpio rules the sexual-reproductive organs. Scorpio men exude sexual power, and the readers of the biography by Burroughs have noted the many attempts of women to seduce Tarzan. A Scorpio is also ingenious, creative, a true friend, and a dangerous enemy. He is very deep and mysterious, no matter how unreserved he seems to be.

The young Greystoke was to be all of the above.

Clayton performed the delivery, his only assistance the medical books he had brought along and his determination that the baby would live. He had laudanum and morphine to lessen her pain, but he was afraid to give her much because of weakening her pelvic and stomach muscles and also affecting the baby. Fortunately, the infant came swiftly. Alice did not begin screaming until fifteen minutes before the baby was out, and after that he dosed her with laudanum. He cut the umbilical cord and did all that was necessary and some things that were not. In 1888, the use of soap and water and carbolic acid during birth was well known, though not always practiced. The discoveries of the Frenchman Pasteur, the Englishman Lord Lister, and the Hungarian Semmelweis had reduced fatalities during childbirth, and Lord Greystoke used their knowledge that night in the little cabin on the coast of west Africa. It was a grim, painful, anguished, bloody, and lonely night, but it was successful—as far as the baby was concerned.

Alice never recovered from the double shock of the attack and the birth. Though she was physically healthy, she usually lived in a dream England. Clayton did not attempt to break her delusion. She was happy and could not have been a better mother.

A year passed. The baby did not sicken, as he had feared it would in this climate. Young John Clayton, the future "Lord Greystoke," was a beautiful baby with large grey eyes. He had exceptionally large bones and great strength for an infant. A half an hour after he was born, he was lifting his head and looking around. (Some unusually muscular and vigorous babies can do this. I saw my own granddaughter, Kimberley Dana, lift her head up and stare around, unfocusedly, of course, a half hour after birth.)

In his leisure, Clayton read to his wife or wrote in his diary in the French language. He kept the diary wrapped up in oilcloth inside a japanned tin box.

A year to the day after the birth of the baby, early in the morning of November 22, 1889, Alice Rutherford Clayton died in her sleep. She had not complained of being sick. Perhaps her heart just gave out or her mind wandered so deeply into her dream England that she could not return to her body. It is more likely that she accidentally overdosed herself with laudanum. Clayton's diary records that she quite often took laudanum when she could not sleep. If he knew the cause of her death, he did not note it.

While she lay under a sailcloth on her bed, he made the last entry in the diary. It is a measure of his hopelessness and grief that he forgot to write in French. His final words were: *My little son is crying for nourishment—O Alice, Alice, what shall I do?*

Then his pen dropped from his hand, and his head dropped forward in despair. After a while, he rose, replaced the diary in the tin box, locked it, put it away, and then returned to the table and to his grief.

For a long time, the only noise to rupture the silence of the noonday jungle was the pitiful wailing of the hungry baby.

Chapter Four

(I–4 through I–5)

The Apes

The ape, vilest of beasts, how like to us!

—Quintus Ennius

How tender 'tis to love the babe that milks me . . .

—W. Shakespeare

Clayton described in his diary the "anthropoid ape" killed by Alice. But he was not a trained zoologist or anthropologist. He did not notice how similar the leg and hip structures of the anthropoid were to his. But we know from a later account, indirectly from Clayton's son, that the so-called "great apes" or mangani were far more hominoid than gorilloid. They had speech, and this made them human, whatever their outward features. Their brain development, if not size, was necessarily greater than a gorilla's.

And there were other differences. They may have been a giant variety of Australopithecus robustus (formerly Paranthropus), a hominid supposed to be extinct, but possibly surviving in the remote jungles even to this day. They may have been the *agogwe* of native African legend, noted by Bernard Heuvelmans in his *On the Track of Unknown Animals*.

Burroughs followed Claytons' description of them as "gorilla-like apes" because he had no information, at that time, to the contrary. Later, having gotten a more accurate description, he could not contradict his earlier version. Thus, the error was fossilized in the first two Tarzan volumes. Using poetic license, he permitted the first descriptions of the "great ape" to stand in the later books. But he slipped now and then, as will be noted.

It may be that the "great apes" are a smaller African variety of the Himalayan *yeti* or the giant hairy man, the *sasquatch*, of the Indian legends of the northwest American states. The *Jungle Tales of Tarzan* (The Battle for Teeka, VI-10) mentions ". . . these great manlike apes which the natives of the Gobi speak of in whispers. . . ." Note the *manlike*. Note, also, in the same chapter, that the "great apes" walk considerable distances entirely erect. ". . . unlike the chimpanzee and the gorilla, they walk without the aid of their hands quite as readily as with." Their pelvises and legs are not those of apes.

Note, also, that in the entire twenty-four books about Tarzan, there are only two passing references to chimpanzees. Cheetah is an invention of the people who made the generally bad and misleading movies about Tarzan. Still, it seems strange that Tarzan had so little to do with this likable and inquisitive folk.

Burroughs tells us how Kerchak, the king of the "great apes," was seized by a fit of madness. After killing several apes, he chased Kala, a young female adult, through the trees until her baby lost its hold on her and fell to its death.

Kerchak's maniacal fit passed as swiftly and as unexpectedly as it had come. This endemic madness of the male mangani often seemed to have no cause. Probably, the rages which possessed the old males were caused by a sex-linked recessive gene. This was a nonsurvival trait that had tended to reduce the population of the genus, which had been very low for thousands of years. This instability may have helped them lose out in the race for the kingship of Earth in the dawn of sentience. The gorilla, their closest relative after man, had also lost the race. Both of the hairy genera faced extinction and perhaps knew it in a dim or unconscious fashion. But the huge vegetarian gorillas, though not nearly as intelligent as the mangani, and not numerous, still outnumbered the mangani by a hundred to one. It is doubtful that there were over two hundred of the Folk left in equatorial Africa in 1889.

Kerchak's tribe included almost a third of the entire genus. Its number varied from sixty to seventy, consisting of six to eight families, each comprising an adult male, his mates, and their children. The tribe formed a well-organized group with a definite pecking order, unvocalized rules of conduct, and patterns of behavior as complex as those of many human tribes.

The anthropoids called themselves by a word which means "the Folk" or "the Real Folk." Mangani, however, is not in the great apes' vocabulary. At the time that Burroughs wrote the first Tarzan stories, which he disguised as novels, he had no access to Tarzan himself or to any source of information about the mangani language. Burroughs made up the vocabulary, much of it based on a sort of code.

In fact, "Tarzan" is a word Burroughs made up. When he was writing the first Tarzan novel, he had no access to any documents. All he knew was what his informant had heard from the British official and had seen in the files. Only once was there any mention in the documents of Tarzan's mangani name. This was as a Lieutenant Paul d'Arnot of the French navy understood it, and his comment was that his transcription was a very rough approximation. D'Arnot stated that only a trained linguist could categorize the sounds correctly, and he might have to invent some new symbols for some of them. D'Arnot wrote Tarzan's name as Zantar, noting that sometimes the "Z" sounded to him like a "z" and sometimes like a "d" and sometimes like a soft "g." And there weren't any "a's" in the word; he had put them in to make it possible to pronounce the word.

Actually, according to what d'Arnot had heard from Tarzan, the only vowels were the neutral sound of "e" in "the" and a glottal stop. A glottal stop is the sound produced by the opening, closure, or opening and closure of the vocal cords. Generally, it's classified as a consonant. Tarzan says it's a vowel in mangani. Its presence or absence doesn't mean anything in standard English. Scots English uses it in some words to replace the "t." For instance, some Scots pronounce bottle as bo'l (the "'" here symbolizing the glottal stop). In many languages, its presence or absence makes a difference in the meaning of the word.

When Burroughs was writing the first novel, he used d'Arnot's transcription. But he did not like it, and since he had no need to stick to the facts, he changed it to Tarzan. From an esthetic point of view, the change was for the better. From the biographical point of view, it deviated even more from the truth. Since no one except Tarzan himself knows what the truth of this particular matter is, the change hurts no one.

It's likely that Burroughs derived mangani from Du Chaillu. Du Chaillu writes in several of his books about the Adjiena tribe and their word for "white man." This was ntangani. Also, a native named Rikimongani appears in Du Chaillu's *The Country of the Dwarfs*. These two words may have influenced Burroughs in his invention of mangani. He often made new words for his novels by changing existing words. He then used mangani as the base, and from this created *tarmangani*, meaning "white man" or "white men," and *gomangani*, meaning "black man" or "black men."

Many Tarzan books later, Burroughs gives the baboon the name of tongani. Did he derive this from ntangani? If so, was he hinting that ntangani and tongani shared certain qualities?

Kala was ten years old, the mate of a male called Tublat, meaning "Broken Nose." The child she had just lost was her first. This may explain why she insisted on clutching the little corpse to her instead of abandoning it. She crouched under a bush, moaning, tears running down her cheeks and into the black fur under her chin. The tribe had resumed its activities as if nothing had happened. The bodies of the murdered male and female had been dragged off into the undergrowth where they would probably be eaten by leopards. (This custom had given the local big cats a taste for mangani flesh, which further reduced the population.) The young played about in the trees or bushes, chasing each other, playing tag, king-of-the-mountain, wrestling, pinching, mock-biting, throwing rotten fruit. Some adults rested while others turned over fallen branches and dirt clods in search of tasty insects, worms, and reptiles. Others prowled the trees nearby for fruit, nuts, small birds, and eggs, or anything that could be caught and eaten. Meat eating was much more highly developed among the mangani than in any of their hairy cousins.

After an hour, Kerchak called them to follow him to the sea. For a long time, he had been thinking about the mysterious *wala*, or nest, built by the strange creature which he called tarmangani (white mangani). More than anything, he wanted to kill the big tarmangani and get hold of the death-dealing stick.

He led the band down the steep slope from the tableland to the level seacoast and then up to the cabin. He saw no sign of the man, and the front door was open. Slowly, Kerchak crept toward the cabin. Behind him were the two next biggest males. Close behind them was Kala, still carrying the dead infant. None of the tribe gave way to their impulse to growl. The death-dealing stick had taught them caution.

Kala was ahead of the usual order of precedence because of her curiosity about the tarmangani baby. She should have been far back behind the adult males and the older females, but she had pushed herself ahead without the usual rebukes and bites from those who ranked her. For once, they were willing to let a lesser being precede them. If she was crazy enough to venture so recklessly into the sinister den, let her do so.

But Kala, as soon as she had smelled the dead female, knew what was causing the tarmangani baby to cry. It was as if the molecules of decay from the corpse triggered off a sequence of thoughts ending in life. Life for her as a mother and for the little tarmangani as her baby.

The tarmangani was sitting at a table, his head between his arms. He raised his head just as Kerchak silently entered. (We know all these details because Kala told the young Tarzan about it many years later.) Crying out, the man jumped up, but he was too late. His revolvers and rifle were hanging on the far wall. A moment later, his neck bitten through, he dangled in the bloody hands of Kerchak. Then he fell as Kerchak released him to investigate the corpse of the female and the baby.

But Kala ran by him, dropped the dead infant in the cradle (in a pack-rat exchange), picked up the screaming baby, and raced out of the cabin before the startled Kerchak could get hold of her.

High on a great mahogany, surrounded by a tangle of lianas, loudly colorful blooms, and buzzing insects, Kala held the shrieking infant closely but tenderly. Then she placed her swollen and aching black nipple in the baby's mouth. It quit crying and began sucking noisily, and both were at peace.

She looked down at the little head on which the black hairs were just beginning to grow. Once, he opened his big grey eyes to look up past the blue-black mound of the breast into her big liquid-brown eyes. In a few minutes, she was beginning to love this strange little creature with its white hairless skin and the puzzling thing around its middle. (The Claytons had wrapped up little John only at night, departing because of the heat from the conventional Victorian swaddling of infants. Later, Kala would pull the diaper off and discard it.)

A few moments later, there was an explosion, and those who

had managed to squeeze themselves into the cabin stampeded out
of it. Kerchak had accidentally triggered the death-dealing stick.
And when he came out through the door after the others, he still
held the rifle. Its front sight caught on the edge of the door and
pulled it shut behind him. The lock clicked shut, and no amount of
experimenting by the anthropoids later on would enable them to
unlock it.

The story of that terrifying experience in the cabin was to be
a main topic of conversation in the tribe for a long time.

Kerchak, once he had recovered the firmness of his nerves, called
for Kala to come along with them. They were to return to the
feeding ground. Kala obeyed, but she would allow no one to come
near or to touch the baby until she was assured they meant no
harm. Remembering how her child had fallen, she always traveled
with one arm about him. No baby of hers would ever again fall
to its death.

She kept her promise to herself, but the little Tarzan (Whiteskin)
was the only baby she was ever again to hold.

Up to the moment of his adoption by Kala, the infant was a
human being in extraordinary, although not unique, circumstances.
When he was snatched from the cradle by a sentient nonhuman,
he entered the mythic world of the changeling. Though he existed
as an entity in the real world, though he was flesh and blood, he was
on the road to the superman and demigod. He was to be the hero
of golden myth. He became one with Romulus and Remus, Oedipus,
Hercules, Telephus, and the many other heroes of fairy tale, folklore, legend, and myth. The door to the universe of mundane
mankind swung shut behind him. Now he was the feral man,
the babe suckled by the half-beast. He would be the last hero in a
world where the belief in heroes was dying out.

Of all this the one-year-old knew nothing. He soon lost the few
English words he had learned. He replaced them with the nonhuman speech of the mangani. The memory of his parents faded
as swiftly as if they were transparent ghosts in this green world.
Kala became his only love.

Little Tarzan was born on the coast of an area where Eu-
ropeans often died quickly, and the black natives, though more
resistant, often died, too. Indeed, the Gabonese saying was that a
man did not consider himself sick until he had four diseases at the
same time: malaria, filaria, intestinal worms, and tuberculosis. Nor

was this exaggerated. Even as late as 1968, 68 per cent of the natives had malaria.

Infant mortality was extremely high. However, that first year of his life, Tarzan did not come into contact with other humans bearing diseases. Isolation sometimes has its benefits. Though a mangrove swamp was near, its bed was tilted seaward and its waters were in motion. Thus mosquitoes had little chance to breed. The wind at this point had discouraged insects from flying too near the cabin. Moreover, the elder John Clayton had brought along every available medicine, and his service in India had taught him much about the prevention and treatment of diseases of the tropics.

The next nineteen years of Tarzan's life were to be spent largely in the interior of the closed-canopy rain forest. This type of jungle is, according to Ivan T. Sanderson in his *Book of Great Jungles*, the healthiest place on earth except for the bacteria-free air of the north and south polar areas.

It was seldom too hot or too cold there. Water was plentiful, though it was sometimes necessary to know just where to look for it. Food was usually available. Shelter was never out of reach. Even the bugs were less abundant than in the bush jungle. Clothes were not needed. And if a man was cut or wounded, he would find the antibiotic properties of the soil so strong that the wounds would heal almost while being watched.

The equatorial closed-canopy jungle was not the green tangled hell of which most people think when they think at all of the jungle. The dense impenetrability they see in the movies is the bush jungle. It is true that the rain forest of the highlands of Gabon looks impossible for travel to a man who stands on its outer edge. But once through the tangle, the man would be inside a region which Hudson fittingly called the "green mansions." The lighting is as green as if the traveler is underwater. Now and then, sunlight pierces the multilevel overhead world of branch, liana, creeper, and leaf which gives the designation of "closed canopy." There is comparatively little underbrush. The soil is seldom the many-feet-thick mulch of rotting vegetation which people visualize. It is mostly only a few inches of acid soil easily washed away if exposed to a heavy downpour or a flood. Often the jungle floor *is* bare. Sometimes, it's a carpet of creeper stems. Sometimes, it's a covering of many kinds of varicolored and juicy fruits dropped from one or more of the terraces above. Great

trunks loom in the greenish light like pillars of temples in sunken
Atlantis. Lianas hang down in loops from the tangled ceilings.

Tarzan's life in these green mansions was generally happy.
Kerchak's tribe roamed a territory which extended along the coast
for twenty-five miles and inland for fifty miles. Even when the
tribe ventured out into the bush or into the mangrove swamps,
the little Tarzan never got sick. He never got malaria or dengue
or any of the diseases that killed so many humans, black or white,
in western Equatorial Africa. Nor did he ever have a toothache.
He was blessed in his ancestors, who, though of British stock, had
extraordinarily good dental genes.

(I contend that certain of the "Greystokes" were genetic mutations. The mutations explain a peculiar superiority of intellect and
physique, a tendency toward certain lines of activity, a resistance
to diseases, and a number of other seemingly superman qualities.
The possible origin of this mutation is described in Addendum 2.)

Tarzan was not entirely weaned for five years. But Kala also gave
him fruits, roots, worms, insects, rodents, eggs, and occasional
pieces of bird or monkey meat. These were often prechewed by
Kala. The mangani had massive teeth well fitted for grinding down
and tearing apart roots with a high silicon content. Tarzan avoided
damage to his more fragile teeth by eating them prechewed.

Kala loved Tarzan, but she was distressed because he was so
retarded. His contemporaries passed him in size, agility, learning
ability, and independence as if they were hares and he the tortoise.
The other females commented on this to Kala, though they kept
their remarks about his hideous hairlessness, flat face, and pale
washed-out eyes to themselves. Whatever her private misgivings, she
was ferocious in her public defenses of him. She loved him, and she
felt—with no evidence she could give—that he would improve and
some day surpass his little friends.

One day it struck her that the infant's parents had been quite
physically capable and undeniably the mental superiors of the mangani. Thereafter, she pointed this out to the critics, and even hinted
that, when Tarzan grew up, he would be using the same kind of
death-dealing sticks that his parents had. If the others would shut
up now about Tarzan's failings, they might avoid his resentment
when he grew up.

The story about how Tarzan was adopted was told many times
for some years after the event. But Tarzan did not hear it for a

long time. His contemporaries never knew it, and the older great apes tended to forget it. Kala kept silent until the day that Tarzan discovered the cabin on the seashore. And then she omitted many details, including the all-important fact that he was a changeling. It is possible that she had forgotten this fact. She loved him so much she did think of him as having been born of her body.

During the early years, Tublat wanted to leave Tarzan sleeping someplace where a leopard or bush pig would kill him. Tublat did not like it that Kala would not mate with him while she was nursing the strange hairless creature. As if he had been an ancient Greek, he wanted to expose the defective child.

Kala refused to listen. Tublat waited for the chance to find Tarzan undefended. But he never got it. And Tarzan, when he was a juvenile, repaid Tublat's hatred with a thousand practical jokes, some of them very humiliating and painful.

At ten, Tarzan was as strong as most men of thirty and far more agile than any Olympic athlete. His mangani contemporaries were almost full-grown by then and too heavy to follow him swiftly through the upper terraces of the closed-canopy jungle. His mind leaped ahead of theirs. He was forever making up new games. He invented riddling stories, and he asked a hundred questions every day, none of which Kerchak's people could answer. He had even coined new words, putting together, or slightly changing, existing items of mangani vocabulary. And he had invented something new to the mangani: the pun. Some of the tribe were bright enough to appreciate the less subtle plays on words, and they would grin or give a soft hooting laughter. But that was as far as they could follow him.

Some admired his cleverness. Others, especially the victims of his wit and his practical jokes, resented him. And they waited for a chance to kill him.

1898: THE WORLD
(From the 1899 *World Almanac*)

The total world population was 1,440,650,000.

McKinley was President of the United States.

Victoria was still queen of England; the marquess of Salisbury, prime minister.

Gladstone, former prime minister, and Bismarck, creator of the German Empire, died.

In the United States, diarrheal fever killed 74,711; measles, 9,256; diphtheria and "cramp," 41,677; malaria, 18,594.

Mental worry, said Dr. Herbert Snow, was the chief exciting cause of cancer.

The U.S. battleship *Maine* was blown up in Havana Harbor, Cuba, and two months later the Spanish-American War began.

Bread riots in Italy caused much loss of life.

Colonel Henry of the French Army committed suicide after confessing he forged a letter to secure the conviction of Captain Dreyfus.

Fashoda, on the White Nile, was occupied by the French.

Kitchener, commanding British and Egyptian armies, beat the Dervishes at Omdurman and occupied Khartoum.

A top-class mail-order buggy could be purchased for $21.95.

Dr. Alfred Sanden's Electric Belt Company, 826 Broadway, New York, N.Y., advertising in the *World Almanac*, offered its belt as a self-treatment for men suffering the results of youthful indiscretions or later excesses. The belt could cure drains, impotency, lame back, nervousness, varicocele, etc. The belt gave strength because "Electricity is strength." Dr. Sanden claimed to have over six thousand testimonials of absolute cures.

There were 131,618 known lepers in India.

Radium was discovered by the Curies and G. Bemont.

J. B. Dunlop introduced the pneumatic rubber tire.

Chapter Five

(I–6, I–7)

The Difference

Reason is not man's primitive
endowment, but his achievement.*

—S. K. Langer

It was at the edge of ten that he became sharply aware of the difference in physical appearance between him and the mangani. He had been ashamed of his hairlessness for a long time, and he hated to be called a tarmangani. But not until he went to drink one day from a lake in the bush jungle did he realize how ugly his face was. He was accompanied by a male child of one of Kala's younger sisters and so got a chance to compare his face with his playmate's in the mirrorlike waters.

He became so intent on his distressing comparison that he did not hear Sabor, the lioness, creeping up on them. A moment later, he was getting his first, and possibly last, lesson in how to swim. When the lioness, roaring, had sprung on them, she had forced him to dive into the lake. He came up almost at once, and, in an effort to keep his head above water, discovered how to dog-paddle. His companion was dead, and the lioness was eyeing Tarzan. Tarzan knew that the big cats could swim, and he paddled away, meanwhile giving the distress cry of the mangani. The tribe came and chased the killer away. Thereafter, Tarzan swam frequently whenever he got the chance. The mangani thought this strange but did not complain. They were happy because it helped reduce

* From Suzanne K. Langer's Translator's Preface to *Language and Myth* by Ernst Cassirer, Dover Publications, Inc., New York, 1946. Reprinted through permission of the publisher.

his odor, so offensive to them. Like most rain-forest creatures, they had fewer sweat glands than the dwellers of the open spaces. They were also more vegetarian than Tarzan and so did not have his essential carnivore's stink.

Shortly thereafter, Tarzan again visited the cabin by the seashore. This time he found out how to unlock the door, and he entered the world of man.

(He had never entered the storehouse. It had been hit by lightning, had exploded, and had burned between his two visits.)

In the cabin he found a hunting knife of the best Sheffield steel and a child's illustrated alphabet. These were the keys to unlock the treasure of his human heritage.

> A is for Archer
> Who shoots with a bow.
>
> B is for Boy,
> His first name is Joe.

At this time, he did not correlate the pictures with the words below. Indeed, he not only did not recognize the letters as printed symbols for words, he did not recognize the illustrations as such. He had never seen a drawing before, so he viewed them only as meaningless patterns of color. But, after a half hour of looking at them, something silently clicked in his mind. The patterns swam out of chaos to become configurations, some of which he recognized. This was his first step in his long self-education in reading and writing. It would be an extraordinary, even heroic feat. Admittedly, only a genius could have done it. But Tarzan, as is demonstrated in Addendum 2, belonged to a clan which produced geniuses, both mental and physical.

Looking through the book, he recognized Manu, the monkey, and Numa, the lion, and his old enemy, Histah, the snake. Even the reptile's picture raised a specter of cold on the back of his neck.

The letters of the alphabet he classified as a strange sort of bug.

Finally, at dusk, no longer able to see the books, he left the cabin, carefully closing the door behind him. But he took his new toy, the knife, with him.

It was well he did. Outside the cabin, a giant male gorilla attacked him. Ordinarily, Bolgani was a shy creature and the best of neighbors. But this one was probably an old rogue, mentally sick from a tumor of the brain.

This statement is based on what Kala told Tarzan. The gorilla's skull was broken open with a rock during the Dum-Dum, the wild victory dance of the males, so the brains could be eaten. Part of it was definitely cancerous. Mack Reynolds, in an amusing, if irreverent, pastiche titled "Relic" (*Magazine of Fantasy and Science Fiction*, March, 1966), claims that it was not a gorilla but a baboon. But Trader Horn, speaking of the Gabonese attitude to gorillas, says that "the natives'll always tell you he's mad. Something slipped in his brain that's similar to the mistakes in the brain of a madman. Nature's got a hankering after experiments."

George B. Schaller, who wrote *Year of the Gorilla* and is the greatest authority on that animal, would not agree with this observation. Professor Schaller's studies were of the Uganda-Congo mountain gorilla, however, not of the west coast lowland gorilla. Of the latter creature, little is known, according to Schaller.

The gorilla attacked, and Tarzan would have been quickly killed if it had not been for his knife. Within a few seconds, he learned how to cut and stab with it. The gorilla died, but not before he broke three of the boy's ribs, bit half through one arm, and tore a chunk of flesh out of his neck close to the jugular vein.

If Tarzan had not been nursed so tenderly and intensely by Kala, he would have died.

And if he had not had the knife, he would have died. This was the first time, but not the last, that he would be saved by a product of human technology. Though he was to despise and loathe much of civilization when he encountered it, he owed his life to it.

Tarzan recovered and went back to an active life. But his life was never the same. He soon discovered the linkage between the pictures and the strange little bugs. In five years, he knew the various combinations of letters standing for each figure in the little primer and in several of the big picture books. For a long time, he had only a vague idea of the meaning and use of *a, the, and however, thusly,* and many other grammatical devices. But, at twelve, he found pencils in the cabin and so learned how to reproduce pictures and the letters with them. Later, he began to place the letters in new combinations.

He had not the slightest idea of the correct pronunciation of

the letters of the alphabet and he may never have been sure of
the purpose of the punctuation marks. Indeed, he did not know
that the letters were supposed to be pronounced. But he arbitrarily
gave to each letter a syllable from mangani speech. His pronunciation of the English God was a wonderful example of his method.
He was not sure what or who God was. God could be the Moon
or some entity which sent the wind and the lightning. The great
apes had a very rudimentary form of religion, a vague animism
which attributed evil powers to certain objects—trees, rocks, and
bodies of water—and to certain animals—snakes, leopards, and
poisonous insects. That was the limit of their attitudes toward the
supernatural.

But God had to be masculine. In the mangani speech, there
were only two genders: masculine and feminine. The prefix of
masculine nouns (and of masculine verbs, adverbs, and adjectives)
was bu. Since it was obvious that capital letters, being big bugs,
were more important than lower-case letters, the little bugs, they
were of the masculine gender. The female prefix was mu, so all
lower-case letters were prefixed with mu.

To g he gave the syllabic value of "la." O was pronounced as
"tu"; d, as "mo." Thus, God, when spoken aloud, was "bu-la-mu-tu-
mu-mo": "bu," the masculine prefix; "la" for g; "mu," the feminine
prefix; "tu" for o; "mu," the feminine prefix; "mo" for d. "Bu-la-mu-
tu-mu-mo." A literal translation into English would be: "he-g-she-
o-she-d."

Tarzan did not know how to transliterate his mangani name, of
course. And for a long time he did not come across the words
white or skin. Thus, when he wrote his own name, he wrote he-boy,
basing this on a picture of a little white boy in a primer. He
pronounced this "bu-mu-de-mu-tu-mu-ro." (We are not told what
phonic values he gave the punctuation marks.)

Later, he wrote his name as White Skin, a direct translation of
his mangani name.

Since he did not come across script until years later he knew
only how to print.

Ever since he was ten, Tarzan had been using ropes made from
grass. This was his independent invention, and its principal use was
to bedevil. He tried unsuccessfully to rope the larger animals: the
big cats and the orange-colored bush pigs. More successfully, he
dropped the noose around the necks and legs of monkeys and

civet cats and servals and porcupines and anteaters. And he was always choking or tripping a playmate with his rope. But the main recipient of the strangling or tumbling noose was Tublat, Kala's ex-mate. Tublat's natural tendency to irritation and rage was stimulated a dozen times a day by the ropes launched from above or from behind a tree. Many times, he gave chase, but Tarzan was too swift and agile.

When Tarzan was thirteen years old (November, 1901), he had to face up to Tublat. During the Dum-Dum, Tublat went mad. Even the biggest of the males fled. Tublat cornered Kala, and Tarzan came to her rescue with his knife. Slaying Tublat in a quick but savage fight, he, in a sense, recreated the Oedipal situation. This act was his *bar mitzvah*, his rite of passage. He had saved his mother, killed the foster father who had wanted to murder him, and established himself as a dangerous contender for the kingship.

"I am Tarzan!" he cried. "I am a great killer! Let all respect Tarzan of the mangani and Kala, his mother! There are none of you as mighty as Tarzan! Let his enemies beware!"

This was an indirect challenge to Kerchak. But seven years would pass before he and the hairy old Goliath would battle to the death.

Chapter Six

(I–8 through I–10)

Loss and Revenge

Grief weeps alone.

—L. Knowles

Men must reap the things they sow,
Force from force must ever flow . . .

—Shelley

The best manner of avenging ourselves is by
not resembling him who has injured us.

—Jane Porter

Shortly after he had killed Tublat, Tarzan began his lifelong friendship with Tantor. Tantor was all elephants and also particular elephants. The Tantor that Tarzan knew first was a forest elephant, somewhat smaller than the grey titan of the savannas. His ivory was darker and less valuable than the beast of the open spaces, and his herds were not so large. But Tantor was Tantor, and the thirteen-year-old boy "talked" to Tantor wherever he met him. He established affection and trust, and, somehow, the "word" spread across the continent from one Tantor to the next. Even when Tarzan met an elephant he had never seen, he was recognized and accepted. And he often rode on Tantor's back or would even sleep on it. Who would dare attack him there?

If any think that Tarzan could not speak to the beasts or understand their dumb replies, or be understood by them, if any think this is fantasy, let him read *The Language Barrier: Beasts and Men*.

This work, by Elizabeth Mann Borgese, daughter of Thomas Mann, may not convince everybody. But it should cause them to reconsider their prejudices. She presents strong evidence that animals and men can communicate on a much higher level than generally believed. However, it may be that only especially sensitive men are able to tap this ever-flowing stream around humans and beasts. Tarzan, born in the wild and raised by beasts, had this power to a high degree.

Mrs. Borgese speaks of white-snake eaters, a term derived from an old fable. Once upon a time, the fable says, a man became the most wise and powerful ruler on earth. His secret of success was that he had eaten a piece of a white snake. This gave him the power to talk to animals and to get them to do his bidding. The white snake flesh enabled him to return to the pristine stage of mankind, the primal time, when men spoke with beasts and birds. Men have lost that power now, the fable says. But Tarzan was born to it. He had no artificial barriers, no adults without faith around him, to ruin the inborn gift. He was one with Nature. Not just close to Nature. He was *with* Her, part *of* Her.

Tarzan, though flesh and blood, woundable and killable, of certifiable and datable human ancestry, belongs to the heroes of old. He is like Melampus of Greek legend, who understood the language of the birds because a snake had licked his ears. Siegfried, or Sigurd, of the ancient Germanic legends, tasted the blood of the dragon he had slain, and he knew what the birds were saying. No claim, however, is made that Tarzan could speak with the birds. In fact, his biography has singularly few references to birds. Ska the vulture is most frequently mentioned, and he is no friend of Tarzan. The only other birds described are parrots, and these played villains.

Tarzan does not speak to birds for the simple reason that birds don't have language. Tarzan is legendary, but he also exists, and he is bound by the limitations of real existence. Thus, his communications are only with the higher, the greater brained, animals. And the higher the intelligence, the more the communication approaches the speech of man. The mangani were sentient, of course, and their language had strange, somewhat nonhuman sounds, due to the conformations of their oral cavities. But their language had a grammar. The gorillas, baboons, and other species of monkeys have no genuine linguistic ability, unlike the hominid mangani. It is true that Burroughs often interprets a dialog between Tarzan and the simians as if it were being conducted in proper English. But he makes it clear in more than one place that he is transmuting a simple system of signals into complex symbols for the reader's benefit.

Whatever the form of sound and syntax, Tarzan loved Tantor and talked to him, petted him, and gave him love. And Tantor was to save his friend more than once.

"All else of the jungle were his enemies, except his own tribe, among whom he had many friends."

In 1906, when eighteen years old, Tarzan had extended his knowledge of language in another direction than that of the beasts. He could read and understand much in the books in the cabin. By then he could print words and even sentences he made up. Burroughs does not tell us what simple stories he created in his head and printed on paper. We may presume, however, that a boy who could teach himself to be literate without having heard a word of English could imagine stories.

They must have been strange and, perhaps, as unintelligible as some avant-garde or Joycean works of art to the average reader of the West. Those who would find them in the cabin three years later wondered about them. They saw the work sheets of Tarzan, the papers crowded with his efforts to print letters, to form phrases, and his copying of many pages from the varied, though small, library. These progressed steadily from unreadable scrawlings to precise lettering combined to form quite intelligible, if not elegant, sentences.

Perhaps Tarzan erased his earlier work to save paper, which was in short supply because the storehouse had burned down. He may even have worn off most of the sheets with his palimpsests.

His father's small but select library included the 1887 edition of The Encyclopaedia Britannica, several illustrated dictionaries, a massive King James Bible, books on Africa by Stanley, Baker, Burton, Livingston, Du Chaillu, and Winwood Reade. The latter had made a visit to equatorial western Africa in 1863 to find the gorilla. He was also the author of The Martyrdom of Man, which Sherlock Holmes recommended to Watson. But it is a depressing book, and Alice Rutherford had not cared to have her husband read to her from it. She had preferred their well-worn copy of Dickens' Pickwick Papers, because she could laugh at that. And she loved to have John read to her from the huge, profusely illustrated *Le Morte d'Arthur* by Malory.

Alice also enjoyed Dickens' *Child's History of England*, which John had brought along for his son. His son read it, of course, just as he read everything he found except the French diary of his father. How well he understood is another matter. Without having been raised in the West, without the slightest "feel" of the human world, he would have had great difficulty. And he would have transposed the scenes of history and of legend into terms he knew. His struggles with the Arthurian legends were aided by the glossary of medieval terms in the back of the book. The many illustrations helped him somewhat. Where pictures were lacking, he was to see things clothed in the images of what he saw around him. Thus, the ogres and dragons he read about may have looked more like gorillas and crocodiles than anything else.

Tarzan was often puzzled by what he read and the pictures he saw. Much was repulsive or made him uneasy. Nevertheless, he longed for the day when he would find his first human being. As he got older, he had less and less empathy and interests with the mangani. He wished desperately for the day when he would see another human being, a MAN. Or a WOMAN.

Like many, he got his wish. And, like many, he would half-regret the fulfillment.

One day Tarzan sat in the cabin reading, for the hundredth time, the massive 1886 edition of Burke's *Peerage*. This book had almost twenty-five hundred pages of very small closely set print and many illustrations of family coat-of-arms. It dealt, in the main, with the lineage of royalty, nobility, baronets, and knights. John Clayton had brought it along for his own edification and his child's. He had hoped to show the young boy the arms of the dukes of Grey-stoke, the barons of Grebson and of Tennington, and the other noble families borne on the family shield. He would explain the stories behind the brief and condensed accounts of the *Peerage*, and he would blazon the family arms for young John as his mother had blazoned for him. And he would read extracts from the Grey-stoke lineage, accounts of the great deeds of his forefathers. He would save the accounts of the less glorious, even shameful, deeds of some of the ancestors for a more advanced age. No family was without blots on the escutcheon.

Tarzan had had to tackle this huge book without paternal help.

And on this day he happened to be reading the pages devoted to his family, though he had no idea that it was his, of course. (See Addendum 3 for the lineage as it was to be printed in Burke thirty-six years later.)

While he was struggling to understand fully what he was reading, the first of the longed-for humans entered Tarzan's jungle. They were cannibals, and they were fleeing from their enemy and looking for a new home.

This is all we can know for certain. Burroughs says they were the people of Mbonga. They had been oppressed by the rubber and ivory collectors of Leopold II of Belgium. They had killed and eaten their white masters and their black soldiers, and they had run off before the avengers arrived.

We can discount the four days Burroughs says it took them to travel from the old village to the site of their new one. If they were escaping from the nearest place in the Belgian Congo, they would have taken several months or more to get near to Kerchak's territory on the lower middle coast of Gabon.

Actually, no one knows where the tribe came from, why they came, or even what their tribal name was. It is doubtful that more than four or five of the names Burroughs gave the blacks were genuinely theirs. Tarzan, who was to be a master linguist, never learned this tribe's speech. He may, however, have identified some by name while spying on them. Burroughs made up the story that they were running from the Belgians. And he made up the names of their people, just as he had made up the mangani words in the early books. A storyteller, he needed handles for his people.

Burroughs had read Du Chaillu's books of his explorations in Gabon. One contains an appendix on the languages of Equatorial Africa. One Mpongwe verb is *Mi bonga*, meaning "I take." A slight alteration makes this into the Bantu-sounding Mbonga. And Mbonga certainly "took" things. One of these was the most precious thing of all to Tarzan, for which Mbonga and his people were to pay a terrible price. They were also to cut off all possibility of peaceful intercourse with Tarzan.

After three or four months, the new village, built by the side of a small river, was settled. Crops—cassava, plantain, and yams—had been planted. Meat was badly needed, but the hunters feared to venture far out into the closed-canopy rain forest. Pygmies lived in this dark place with its spooky muted sounds, but the tall blacks dreaded it. And the extraordinarily large and brave leopards of this area had dragged off some women and children and even killed and eaten two men. They had also snatched away the few dogs that had survived the march, dogs being especially choice items on the menu of leopards.

This was to be fortunate for Tarzan, since dogs would have made his nocturnal incursions into the village impossible.

One day, Kulonga, son of Mbonga, set out alone to hunt. Kulonga was a very brave young man, and his courage was reinforced by his hunger for meat. Failing to kill anything, he slept on a tree that night, and he slept relatively well. But he did awaken now and then at a strange sound, and he had to make sure that it was not made by a ghost or a monster. In the morning, he continued his fateful search. About twenty miles to the west of the village, he stumbled across Kerchak's tribe. If he had missed them and continued straight on, he would soon have come to the sea. And, perhaps, he might have run across Tarzan in his cabin. It was well for Tarzan that he did not. Kulonga hated white men and would have shot him with his poisoned arrows. Even if Tarzan had been black, he would have been shot. To Kulonga, all men outside the tribe were simply meat. (Cannibalism was widespread at that time. The Oshebas and the Okellys to the north, for instance, when not at war, sold each other their dead for eating.)

Tarzan, sitting in his cabin, heard faintly the uproar from Kerchak's tribe. He hastened to the mangani, thinking that a leopard had attacked one of them or an enemy mangani had abducted a female.

But they were screaming and yelling because Kulonga had slain Kala with a poison arrow.

Tarzan's grief and anger screamed out through the forest. He roared the bull-ape's challenge and slapped his chest. Then he collapsed, sobbing loudly and weeping, upon her body. He shook and cried as if he were trying to pump up every drop of mourning his body could possibly contain. He was draining out the terrible pain of his mother's death. There was nothing repressed or frozen about his grief; he was uninhibited and healthy.

The huge ugly creature that was his mother, the only being who truly loved him and whom he truly loved, was dead. He mourned her deeply but briefly, though he would never forget her.

There was no neurotic guilt tainting his passion or crippling him. He did not turn his anger inward. He wanted to kill the thing that had murdered his mother.

And so, after a while, the tears decreasing, he rose from the body. He asked the tribe who had done this. The apes were somewhat confusing in their replies, because many had never seen a MAN before, except for Tarzan, and those who remembered Tarzan's parents had only a dim picture of them.

But Tarzan knew at once, because of his picture books, that the hairless black ape with the feathers on its head was a MAN. A MAN who had fled eastward.

And so Tarzan set out on his trail. In time, he overtook him. From the trees, he watched the MAN kill Horta, the orange bush pig, with an arrow on which was smeared a red tarry substance. Du Chaillu says this poison was used by the Fan tribe, which concealed its origin and preparation.

Watching Kulonga, Tarzan became very excited and curious, though he did not forget his vengeance. He saw in him not so much the Negro as the Archer of his children's alphabet book. And, seeing Kulonga make a fire with flint and steel to cook the boar, Tarzan almost fell out of the tree. He had never seen fire except when Ara, the lightning, ignited some great old dead tree, still supported by the tangle of the canopy after its roots had died. Even so, these times had been few, since the rain forest was seldom dry.

Tarzan stole Kulonga's bow and arrows while he slept. In the trees, he followed the panicked man's flight on the ground. Just before Kulonga reached the fields outside the village, Tarzan dropped the noose of his grass rope around the youth's neck. He pulled the struggling killer of his beloved mother up and then rammed his father's hunting knife into the heart.

While the body dangled from the end of the rope, Tarzan appropriated Kulonga's knife and put the copper anklet on his own leg and the feathered headdress on his own head.

Then he lifted his knife to cut off a piece of Kulonga's arm. He was hungry.

He hesitated.

Burroughs says that Tarzan did not eat the black because of "a hereditary instinct," an inborn repulsion against cannibalism. As far as science knows, this instinct does not exist. Tarzan's own ancestors, if one went back far enough, were cannibals. It is more likely that his decision not to eat Kulonga was culturally based.

The mangani did not eat members of their own tribe. And, in this moment of hesitation, Tarzan remembered that he, a MAN, should not eat another of the tribe of MAN.

Moreover, the books he had read must have stopped his knife. The novels and the works of Malory and Homer showed that only ogres, cyclops, and other monsters ate men. Or, if men ate men, they were despised. Surely, Tarzan had read of CANNIBALS, and he may even have known what ANTHROPOPHAGIST meant.

Perhaps, if Tarzan had known that Kulonga was a cannibal, he might have overcome his hesitation. But he did not know that. And when he was to find out, he would by then have no more eaten of Mbonga's people than he would of the despised Dango the hyena.

In this instant, Tarzan took the first step toward the psychic evolution from ape to human. He did not consciously know that he had entered the brotherhood of man. But something deep within him knew it.

He watched the natives all that morning from his tree perch. He saw their terror on discovering Kulonga's body. While the tribe gathered about it, he dropped into the village and stole arrows. He also played the first of many of his grim practical jokes on Mbonga's people. He piled furniture in the center of a hut, put an inverted cooking pot on that, a human skull from a warrior's collection on that, and Kulonga's headdress on the skull. Then he kicked over a pot of boiling poison, leaped up, grabbed the branch of a tree hanging over the palisade, and disappeared like a forest demon.

Why was the branch of this tree uncut? It was such an obvious avenue for man-eating leopards. The only explanation is that it was one of the numerous "sacred" trees of the natives and hence could not be injured or killed. The black savages of the French Congo were like their white brothers of the cities. Logic and religion were two beasts meeting at a crossing in the jungle paths of their minds. Logic always gave way to religion. And why not? Religion is the older logic, the dark science of the unconscious, striving for a light beyond light.

Chapter Seven

(Part of I-11; VI-1 through VI-4)

Growing Up

The red sweet wine of youth . . .
                              —R. Brooke

All true civilization consists in our attaining that
deepest simplicity which is the highest wisdom.
                              —A. Schweitzer

Tarzan returned to his tribe to boast of his adventures and to
practice with his stolen bow and arrows. Before a month passed,
he was a good shot, though not the superb bowman he would
become. Burroughs does not say so, but we can presume that,
during this time, he went back more than once to observe the
humans. Intensely curious, he would not have been able to resist
learning all he could about them, even if they were the murderers
of his mother. Among those closely studied would be the hunters.
He would carefully watch their methods of using their bows,
and he would have copied them. Intelligent as he was, he probably
improved on their technique as time went by.

Some critics have objected that Tarzan could never have become
a champion marksman. Their arguments are based on McLuhan's
statements that illiterate savages lack perspective and hence cannot
be good bowmen or gunshots. But the McLuhanites forget, or
never knew, that Tarzan was a fluent reader (within certain inevitable limitations) before he encountered Mbonga's people. They
also forget (as does McLuhan) that the magnificent longbowmen
of medieval England could not read or write.

Despite the time spent watching the humans, and his archery practice and necessary food-hunting, Tarzan continued to visit the cabin. He found a metal box with a key in the lock. Inside was a photograph of a smooth-shaven young man, a gold locket studded with diamonds and attached to a gold necklace, some letters, and his father's diary. Therafter, he wore the locket suspended around his neck, though he had no idea then that it could be opened and that cameos of his parents were within. He could not decipher the handwriting of the letters or read the diary, which was in French. -

That same day, while spying on the blacks, he saw them drag in a black prisoner. Watching them torture, kill, and eat him, he knew what his fate would have been if he had tried to approach them with friendly intentions. And he was deeply disgusted and repelled by their cruelty. The mangani did not torture their enemies. If they captured one, they killed him outright. (This makes them sound more like apes than hominids.)

Tarzan, of course, knew nothing beyond what he had read of the vast continent beyond the confines of his small tribal territory. He did not know that cannibalism was still widespread over central and western Africa and that it was being conducted in white-held countries whenever the white man had his back turned. Of course, there were many tribes that did not practice cannibalism and looked down on those that did. These Burroughs approves of, but others, such as Trader Horn, claim that the cannibals were among the highest type of blacks. Doubtless, the truth is that cannibalism has little to do with other aspects of morality. Anthropologists claim that most cannibalism is ritual, but the early travelers in Africa, Du Chaillu, Burton, and others, describe a situation where cannibalism was obviously practiced because of shortage of meat. There was little of the religious about many African cannibals, though some may have eaten men solely for religious reasons.

While the villagers were getting ready to cook the dead man, Tarzan sneaked into the village. He stole arrows, kicked over another cooking pot, and took a skull with him. Later, he threw the skull from a tree and hit a man on the head, panicking Mbonga's people. This was his second trickster deed and far from the last. These grim jokes convinced the blacks that an evil spirit of the forest needed propitiating. Thereafter, they left food out for him, food which he ate, and the eating of which convinced them that a Munango-Keewati truly existed.

(I have been unable to find this word in any dictionary of African languages or any traveler's account. Still, it may be a genuine vocabulary item. Tarzan learned this word and wrote it down after he knew how to speak English. Its existence implies that Mbonga's people were not speaking any known Bantu or, in fact, any known language. They may have been the last users of this language, in which case their tongue is irretrievably lost, as we shall see.)

At this point, we must consider a discrepancy in the Tarzan biography. Burroughs says, in *Tarzan of the Apes*, Volume I, that Tarzan killed a lioness and a deer with the poisoned arrows on his leisurely way home after killing Kulonga. Then he boasted of it to the apes and was attacked by the jealous Kerchak. But Volume VI, *Jungle Tales of Tarzan*, describes the many months of his life between the killing of Kala and his final conflict with Kerchak. A chronologist must ignore this collapse of time in chapter 11 of Volume I. Burroughs, writing the first volume, and not wishing to make it too long, skipped the years after Kala died and before the fight with Kerchak.

Volume VI relates Tarzan's first love (after Kala, of course). At least, Burroughs says that the young female great ape, Teeka, was Tarzan's first love. But, if he was eighteen then, he must have had a delayed adolescence. Other evidence confirms this. At eighteen, Tarzan was six feet tall. Two years later, he is six feet three inches tall. His growth was slow but sure; like a great tree, he took his time because it takes time to become the greatest.

Thus, at eighteen, he was going through the pain of his first sexual love. He was also tricking and terrorizing Mbonga's people, pondering on the nature of Creation and the Creator, and searching for identity as a human and for a formulation of his philosophy.

Tarzan, even though not fully grown, was a bronze god, an Apollo, as Burroughs says. His black hair was cut with a sharp clamshell into bangs across the forehead and chopped off behind to shoulder-length. He never wore the headband that became a trademark of the movie Tarzans, starting with Elmo Lincoln. In fact, Tarzan's haircut made him look more like Prince Valiant than anyone else. He wore no clothes; the only things on his body were the locket, the copper anklet, a rawhide belt and sheath for his knife. Thus, he would have been the envy, and the terror, of

his mangani fellows if they were no more sexually endowed than
their gorilla cousins. The erect penis of the adult gorilla is only
two inches long, according to Swiss zoo-director Ernst Lang. If,
however, as I believe, the mangani were actually far more hominid
than Burroughs depicted them, they would have had no cause to
regard Tarzan as a genital monster.

Readers might object to Tarzan's nudity on the grounds that
Volume VI states that he left his leopard-skin loincloth behind
one day when it was hot. But this is an editorial insertion.

Another proof of his slow growing-up is that he did not have to
shave until he was about twenty. At eighteen, his face was still
innocent of hairs.

Burroughs calls him bronzed, and this tells us that he did not
spend all his time inside the closed-canopy forest or inside the
cabin. The rain forest is a twilit place, like a huge green cathedral,
and forest dwellers do not get much sunshine. Thus, Tarzan must
have been on the seashore and in the bush jungle much more than
Burroughs indicates.

Tarzan was an Apollo, not a Hercules, though he had herculean
strength. His gorillalike power would come from the *quality* of his
muscles rather than from their massiveness. It is quality also that
gives the small chimpanzee the strength of two large men. This
is another reason for considering Tarzan a mutant. It is true that
the active arboreal life he led would have developed his strength
beyond that of other humans. But the factor of quality, of mutated
muscle, has to be considered.

So we find the naked young demigod lolling on a tree branch
and admiring the (to him) beautiful young female, Teeka. At
the same time, he was disparaging his own hairlessness, his smooth
brows, his tiny teeth, the washed-out color of his eyes. But Tarzan,
never a self-pitier, soon approached Teeka. He found a nasty rival
in mighty Taug, who also desired Teeka. They began to fight, and
Taug was bleeding from Tarzan's knife, when Sheeta the leopard
tried to carry Teeka off. The two came to her rescue, and Teeka
seemed to favor Tarzan then. He was elated. He would have this
beauty for his mate, and she would bear his young.

Strangely enough, reproduction might have been possible. Burroughs later describes the hybrids of human and mangani. This
means, of course, that the great apes were really much less simian
than Burroughs describes them, as I have noted. Gorillas and

chimpanzees have forty-eight chromosomes, and humans have forty-six. The apes can't have offspring by humans. (However, the primatologist, G. H. Bourne, says there is no physiological reason why they can't.) Thus, the mangani must really have been a type of Java ape-man, Australopithecus robustus, or some other ancestor or near-cousin of man. They would look brutal and probably could never pass for human even if shaved and put into a business suit or skirt. But they are not gorilloids. However, throughout this biography, the great apes will be as Burroughs described them.

Whatever Teeka looked like, she was loved by Tarzan. He was very much hurt when he returned from the hunt and found Teeka and Taug engrossed in each other. And he began to notice how only like paired with like, the leopard with the leopardess, Manu the monkey with the she of his own species, and the young black females of Mbonga's people with the young black males.

He realized that Teeka really wasn't for him. She was a substitute for the dead Kala, his mother. And Tarzan, sadly but firmly, concluded that he was a MAN, the only one of his kind in this part of the world, and he would go through life alone.

Yet he knew from his books that his own kind, white people, did exist somewhere beyond the limits of tribal territory. Why didn't he go looking for them? He was certainly not afraid of the outside world; Tarzan had never been afraid and never would be. And the only person who could have kept him there was dead.

However, Tarzan was still restrained from leaving by the old territorial sense. He had no instinct of the "territorial imperative," of course, and it is doubtful that the mangani did either. The time would come when the tribe would pick up and go across the continent, apparently without much distress at leaving their own area. But they had a sense of property in the same way that one nation regards certain land as its own. Tarzan shared this sense. He fought strange mangani trespassing on his territory, and he avoided trespassing on alien land. Still, the time would come when he would grow out of this feeling and would regard all of central Africa as his.

There is also the indisputable shyness of Tarzan. He was not afraid of human beings, but he did distrust them. As Burroughs says, he had the shyness of a wild animal. This came from the dreadful things he had read that humans did to one another and from his observations of Mbonga's people. So he just was not ready yet to venture forth. And it was good that he was not. He had not yet grown up.

The short and bitter affair with Teeka occurred in February, 1907. A month later, Tarzan was captured by Mbonga's people, who made the mistake of not killing the forest demon on the spot. (Many were to make this fatal mistake in the future.) Tarzan summoned Tantor, the elephant, to his rescue and thus confirmed the natives' belief that he was a demon.

Tarzan's knife was left behind in the village. Burroughs does not mention his returning to get the knife, but he must have done so. In the next adventure, he has it back.

In November, 1907, Teeka became a mother. We know the date because the gestation period of the mangani can be presumed to be the same as a human's, that is, about 275 days. In any event, we could not be too far off. A gorilla's is 265 days and the chimpanzee's is 242 days.

Tarzan wanted to hold the baby *balu* (child), which was called Gazan (Redskin), but Teeka refused. Taug interfered, and once again Tarzan and Taug fought. Tarzan hung Taug upside down at the end of a grass rope from a branch. After a series of dangerous incidents, Tarzan helped save the balu from a leopard. Teeka entrusted Tarzan with her child, and Taug became Tarzan's best friend.

Chapter 4 of Volume VI (*Jungle Tales*) describes Tarzan's problems in learning how to write. This has been detailed earlier in the biography at hand. But Tarzan was also filled with questions about the nature of the universe and of God, Supreme Deity, Creator, mentioned frequently in the books in the cabin. Tarzan wondered who He was, since he had seen no picture of Him. (This means that his parents brought along no large illustrated children's Bible tales for him. Or else they were in the storehouse when it burned down.)

The mangani could not answer Tarzan's questions, which were not even precisely phrased, since he wasn't sure what he was asking about. Some thought that the power which made the lightning, thunder, and rain came from Goro, the Moon. Tarzan climbed up the highest tree and challenged Goro to combat. And he found, as many have, that celestial phenomena are quite indifferent to all forms of life, even the intelligent.

An old male suggested that he ask the gomangani, the blacks, and quit annoying him with his stupid questions. Tarzan set out to discover if the gomangani indeed "had intercourse with God." He saw Rabba Kega, the witch doctor, dancing in his ritual costume. Tarzan thought that the masks and other dress were living parts of this creature, who might indeed be God, he looked so strange. Always forthright, and perhaps carried away in his zeal as a theological student, he dropped in on the witch doctor—literally. He found that under the mask of divinity was only a divine, that is, a man.

But the most revealing event in this adventure was that he passed up a chance to kill Mbonga. For the first time, pity and compassion touched him. Mbonga was just a scared old man, and Tarzan realized this. He spared him, and so marked another step upward from the ape, one more toward being a MAN.

The reader of the *Jungle Tales* will enjoy the details of the young ape-man's conclusions about the nature of God. They are so Tarzanic. But, the youth wonders, could God have made the snake?

Tarzan hated and loathed snakes. Burroughs attributes this feeling to heredity, but we know that human beings aren't inherently afraid of snakes. Gorillas and chimpanzees, however, do seem to have an instinctive dread of Old Belly-Crawler. Perhaps the mangani's fear was instinctual, too. Or perhaps not. In any event, Tarzan's loathing was culturally derived. He was conditioned from an early age by seeing the reaction of his tribe to Histah, the poisonous viper and the crushing python. The mangani would go into a screaming frenzy, but their hysteria was derived from a rational fear. Tarzan, we may be sure, reacted unhysterically, even though the sight of Histah made the back of his neck turn cold.

1908: THE WORLD
(From the 1909 *World Almanac*)

Total world population was 1,522,700,000.

Edward VII was king of England; H. Asquith, prime minister.

W. H. Taft was elected to succeed Theodore Roosevelt as President of the U.S.

Perry was in the middle of his expedition to reach the North Pole.

Liquid helium was first made, and tungsten was proved to be well adapted for filaments in incandescent lamps.

The French Army defeated fifteen thousand Moors on the Algerian border.

A two-cent postage rate for mail between the U.S. and Great Britain went into effect.

The emperor of China died.

Race riots with lynchings of blacks and much wrecking of property occurred in Springfield, Illinois.

Ten thousand suffragettes demonstrated in London.

The first of the tunnels under the Hudson River between New York and New Jersey was opened.

The Knickerbocker Trust Co. reopened for business, following its collapse in 1907, which had caused a great financial panic and recession.

Alfred Dreyfus was wounded by Gregori, a military writer, when Zola's body was moved to the Pantheon.

King Carlos of Portugal was assassinated.

The Panama Canal was still being dug.

Harry K. Thaw, acquitted of the murder of Stanford White on grounds of insanity, was removed to an asylum.

Otto, king of Bavaria, as mad as his brother, Ludwig, was shut up in a château.

Wilhelm II succeeded to the throne of Germany.

London, with a population of 4,536,541, was the largest city in the world. Greater London, the city and suburbs, had a population of 6,581,372.

Attempts to establish the cattle industry in the interior of Africa failed because of the tsetse fly.

The Congo States, long dominated by Leopold II of Belgium, became the property of the government of Belgium. It was promised that the many atrocities committed in the past to secure rubber and ivory from the natives would be stopped.

Three thousand five hundred square miles of unexplored land in southern Nigeria were opened up under British government control. This was the result of a report turned in by Lieutenant E. A. Steel of the Royal Artillery, based on his four years of travel. (Steel had made the survey that John Clayton, thirty-two years before, had been ordered to make.)

Pius X issued his encyclical on Modernism.

The Lusitania, during a day's run, averaged 25.66 knots.

The pensions of veterans' widows were raised from eight dollars to twelve dollars a month in the U.S.A.

An announcement was made in March, 1908, that Teddy Roosevelt was to head an African expedition outfitted by the Smithsonian Institution.

On November 1, 1908, 150,000 cars were in actual use in the U.S.; 757 motor taxicabs were in New York City by September 1.

Both houses of Congress passed a law to regulate child labor in the District of Columbia as a model for other states.

A Maxwell touring car, four-cylinder, thirty horsepower, of the five-bearing crankshaft type, sold at $1,750.

The Electro-Chemical Ring Co., 1225 Monroe Street, Toledo, Ohio, advertised that its electrochemical ring, worn on the finger, could cure diseases caused by acids in the blood. (The sufferer would be cured in from one day to two weeks *after* the ring commenced to work.) The curable diseases included: Bright's disease, diabetes, chlorosis or "the green sickness," painful and excessive monthly periods, uremia, syncope, epilepsy, nervous prostration, nosebleed, internal hemorrhages, gout, lumbago, stone in the bladder, gallstone, ulcers, varicocele, deposit on the teeth, and rheumatism.

About early April, 1908, Bukawai kidnaped Tibo for ransom. Tarzan did not know this. He was hanging around the village and waiting to play one of his grisly trickster jokes. But the unceasing wailing of a woman in a hut got on his nerves. He determined to plunge in among the blacks, create a panic, and throttle the wailer. The mourner turned out to be Momaya. Tarzan could not understand her, but he knew something was wrong, and he spared her because she was Tibo's mother. On leaving the village, he saw the tracks of Bukawai, Tibo, and the two hyenas. The end of this adventure was the rescue of Tibo and the exposure of Rabba Kega, the village witch doctor, as a fake.

Burroughs, throughout all his books, Tarzanic or non-Tarzanic, is very skeptical of the motives and sincerity of witch doctors, savage or civilized. He suggests many times that a lust for power and money is what motivates most clerics. Of course, he had no way of knowing the thoughts of Rabba Kega or most of the other priests he describes, so we are free to credit them with the loftiest of motives if we wish. Tarzan's experiences, however, were to lead him to much the same conclusions as his biographer's.

A few weeks later, late April, 1908, Tarzan was knocked unconscious when lightning toppled the tree that was his refuge during a storm. This was the first of many similar accidents in which he was knocked out. But this time he did not lose his memory. Bukawai found him and took him prisoner, carrying him to his cave. Tarzan, recovering, got loose from his bonds and left Bukawai tied to a tree and at the mercy of his two hungry hyenas.

In May, 1908, Tarzan introduced an innovation to the tribe. He showed them how to set up a sentinel system against the mangani-eating leopards. This may have been one more thing to arouse Kerchak's jealousy and anger. We don't know. It's a curious omission, but not once in the twelve tales of Volume VI does Kerchak appear in person.

Another strange omission is Tarzan's bow. Not until the last adventure does he seem to have it with him. Yet there were many times when he could have used his arrows to get him easily out of a bad situation. It may be that Burroughs only wrote of certain adventures which coincided with the times when Tarzan happened to be out of arrows. Still, it is strange that he did not pick off Mbonga's men from the trees outside the village. Perhaps this was too easy to be much fun. Also, Tarzan does not seem to have been intent on exterminating the villagers. Once he had avenged Kala, he killed only when one of the natives got in his way or threatened him in some manner. He was not vindictive.

Tarzan stole a lion's skin with the head still attached from Mbonga's hut. He intended to play one of his devilish tricks on the mangani with it. (The skin, by the way, must have been brought by Mbonga from his original country. We are sure that there were no lions in the jungle of Tarzan's home territory, that every time Burroughs speaks of a lion he is referring to a leopard. The lion skin of Mbonga enables us to posit that the blacks came from the savanna or more-or-less open grasslands.)

Tarzan took Manu along with him on this particular caper. Manu the monkey sometimes told him where game was, and he was rewarded by Tarzan breaking the shells of nuts Manu couldn't open or by Tarzan scaring off Manu's worst enemies, Histah and Sheeta. Another reward, which Burroughs doesn't mention, is that Tarzan refrained from eating Manu.

The youth, grinning under the lion's head, pretended to be Numa attacking the mangani. He was sure that the scatterbrains had forgotten his sentinel system. But he found out, the hard way, that they had remembered. And he also found out that Manu and Taug and Teeka and some others were truly his friends. Tarzan swore that he would never again play a practical joke. Never? Well, hardly ever.

Chapter 9 of Volume VI, "The Nightmare," is a puzzler. It begins with Tarzan being very hungry because the grass-eaters of the plains had died off from a sickness. This could have been the rinderpest, which was brought into the equatorial west coast during the late 1890s and early 1900s. There were no plains near Tarzan's home grounds, of course, but the leopards of the grasslands, finding meat scarce, had come into the rain forest. And they, with the forest predators, had cleared out the game.

So Tarzan's belly was rumbling.

He watched his old enemies, the gomangani. They had found an elephant dead of sickness, a week rotten, and they were feasting. Tarzan did not know about these circumstances. All he knew was that he was hungry. He waited impatiently until most of the villagers were sleeping off the orgy of meat. Then he dropped into the village and took a piece of elephant from a stew pot. He was forced to kill an old man to do so, and, before leaving, stuffed the body in the pot. He tried the native beer, made from bananas or millet, and spat the foulness out. That men would drink this gut-wrenching stuff increased his contempt for them.

Tarzan ate the rank meat in a tree and then tried to sleep. But his stomach was unused to meat that had been rotting for almost a week. He got sick, though he did not vomit, and he had a series of vivid and terrifying nightmares. A lion chased him, and he climbed to an impossibly high point on a tree, and a great bird carried him off. He escaped, only to awake. He had had his first dream.

This is the strangest thing about his dreams. All men dream, perhaps even inchoately and blindly in the womb. If a man says that he has not dreamed the night before, he means that he does not remember them. If he really did not dream, he would go mad.

We can only conclude that Tarzan was so free of neurosis, of psychic disturbance, so healthy, in short, that his dreams had never penetrated into the conscious. Until now. And then his sickness was physical, not mental.

What the dreams signified, we cannot guess. He fell asleep again, and the lion and the bird were followed by a gigantic snake with the head of the old man Tarzan had put in the cooking pot. Was this latter vision caused by shame? It does not seem likely. What was there in his conditioning to cause him shame at having played another trickster joke on his enemies? Or could he have picked up shame, unconsciously, from his reading? Perhaps he learned there that good men did not kill old men unless they were threatened by them.

Tarzan, tired, thirsty, unsettled, went the next day to the cabin. There he rested, and there he enjoyed his greatest pleasure, reading. And there he encountered his second Bolgani, the gorilla. This one, like the first, had been seized with that jungle madness that has, so far, escaped the observations of the primatologists. (But we must remember that not much is yet known about the lowland gorilla in his natural habitat.)

Tarzan thought that this hairy monster was just another dream. His failure to distinguish between reality and unreality almost cost him his life, as it has done to many men, to whole peoples. Of one thing concerning the experience, Tarzan was sure. Never again would he eat of the flesh of Tantor.

As we shall see, he never broke that vow, but he did, once, kill some elephants.

In July, 1908, during the dry season, Teeka was kidnaped by an alien mangani, Toog. He was a big young bull from another tribe who had been run out when he challenged his old king. In abducting Teeka, he hurt her baby, Gazan, and left him behind. Meanwhile, Tarzan had found, without knowing what they were, a handful of rifle cartridges in the cabin. He stuck the pretty yellow objects in the pouch he had lately been carrying suspended from his knife belt, and he wandered off. Presently, he and Taug were tracking down Toog.

Tarzan and Taug found the female and the abductor with his tribe. There was a fight in which the two rescuers would have been killed. However, Teeka, ignorantly but effectively, found a way to use the cartridges. And so Tarzan, once again, was saved by the technology his father had brought to this jungle.

The incident called "A Jungle Joke" takes place in late July, 1908. Tarzan was a full six feet three inches now and weighing 230 pounds. He had "the grace of a Greek god and the thews of a bull." Burroughs stresses again and again his apollonian proportions, his resemblance to the leopard, not the lion. Undoubtedly, he was the strongest man in the world, yet he did not look like the human hippopotamus who can back-lift (off a trestle) 3 tons, or 482¼ pounds in the clean and jerk, an overhead lift. He could do the same, though much more easily, and yet he had the swiftness of foot and the endurance in running long distances that the hippopotamoid weight lifter does not have. Without shoes, he could broad-jump 30 feet. He could dash 100 yards in 8 seconds and do the 1500 meters in 3 minutes. He could clear the high-jump bar at 9 feet or more and could throw the javelin almost 400 feet. He was to lift a small lion (350 pounds, estimated) above his head and throw it 10 feet over a barrier.

(It is possible, and perhaps even probable, that Burroughs was exaggerating Tarzan's physical abilities. Burroughs does not give the above figures; these are my guesses based on what he says about Tarzan's athletic prowess. Even if the ape-man's feats were not quite as Herculean as Burroughs indicates, he would still be the greatest strong man and all-around athlete of modern times and perhaps of all times.)

He is physically ready to go out into the larger world, but he is not quite emotionally ready. He has yet to learn several vital lessons. By now he is using his clamshell to cut his hair short in back. This is more comfortable and also avoids its tangling with the vegetation. He is shaving now, using the keen-honed edge of his father's knife to scrape off the hairs every day. Apparently, this daily task is not troublesome; his beard is not heavy. He was not a hairy man. If he had been, he would have shaved the hairs off his chest, too, but Burroughs makes no mention of this. Tarzan has taken to shaving because it makes him look less like the mangani, toward whom, at this time, he felt somewhat alienated and contemptuous. Also, he had the example of the clean-shaven young tarmangani in the photograph he had found in the cabin. And, despite his hostility to Mbonga's people, he did identify them as MEN, and they scraped off their beards.

Tarzan was indeed magnificent. He looked like the hero of classical myth, and, like them, he had been hidden in a far-off corner. He had been biding his time until he had fully developed his powers. Then he would come out to astonish the great world and perform feats of wonder and be the savior of peoples. He was like Hercules, Samson, Theseus, Achilles, Hiawatha, Gilgamesh, Finn MacCool, and the young Arthur. Burroughs may or may not have been consciously aware of the similarity of young Tarzan to the heroes of old. But there is no doubt that in his unconscious, where artistry is born, where archetypes live, he was aware. He was reporting on the last of the heroes, the final great son of Mother Nature, her gift to the twentieth century, and her reminder that the demigods were not yet all dead.

Tarzan, roaming around, came across the blacks again. He watched them prepare a cage-trap for lions. When he saw his chance, he captured Rabba Kega and put him in the trap instead. The lion came, saw, entered, conquered, and that was the end of Tarzan's old enemy. But the natives hauled the lion inside their village to torture it. Tarzan got an idea for another trickster joke and took from a cache a lion head and its attached skin. (Burroughs says earlier that it was stolen from Mbonga; here, he says it was stolen from Rabba Kega. Perhaps this was a second skin, the first being destroyed when Tarzan was almost killed while playing a joke on the great apes.) And while we're leaving Rabba Kega, whom we'll see no more, it's time to speak of his name. It's unlikely that Burroughs knew his true name; but, as with Mbonga, he gave him one. Burroughs was thinking of the historical Rabba Kega, a powerful chieftain of the Unyoro tribe of East Africa. Sir Samuel Baker, codiscoverer of the Nile source and a missionary, A. B. Lloyd, have described him.

Tarzan crept into the village at night. Covered with the skin, roaring like a lion, he appeared before the natives. Believing that the lion had escaped, they fled into their huts. By the time they ventured out, Tarzan had released the real lion. Now the warriors were convinced that it was their two-legged old enemy hiding under the skin. They found out their error bloodily and too late. And this time they were convinced that the "devil-god" could change his shape.

Tarzan's baiting of Mbonga's people has been condemned by some. But this is an overreaction to, and a confusing of, the present white-black situation in America with Tarzan's situation. The facts are that Tarzan was not the white conqueror who inhumanly exploited the blacks for his own profit. In this case, the natives were the invaders. They were cannibals, and they would have tortured, killed, and eaten him just as they would anyone not of their own tribe. Mbonga's people, as has been indicated, were probably not fleeing from Leopold II's oppression. They were probably an interior tribe who had been pushed southward by the invasion of the black Fan (or Fang or Fon). These warlike cannibals had been moving down from the north into Gabon since the early nineteenth century. They had massacred Mpongwes and other less belligerent people. The end effect of this was that the tribes pushed out by the Fan in turn pushed other tribes out, if they could manage it. Whatever the reason for Mbonga's people coming into this area, it was not from a desire for peace. And there could never be anything but war between these people and Tarzan after one had killed his beloved mother.

There was no racial prejudice on Tarzan's part. He was not conditioned to regard skin color as an index of human worth. He was probably one of the few whites in the world who possessed no racial prejudice. How could he? He had never known any other race. He would have greeted the invaders as just MEN, if he had been given a chance.

And, as we shall see, the time was to come when Tarzan would accept blacks as readily as he accepted whites. Perhaps he accepted blacks more easily, since most of the villains he encountered were whites.

Tarzan's trick with the lion skin recalls the shape-shifting powers of the Trickster of primitive man's tales. The world over, primitive man, or preliterate man, as the anthropologists prefer to call him, has stories of the Trickster. He is often a character in a sacred mythology of a people. He is often the culture hero who has brought the arts of living to men. Psychologically, the trickster role projects man's weaknesses onto a smaller creature. This creature, defeating his more powerful enemies, enables the listener to identify with him. Generally, though the Trickster may himself be amoral, stupid, and even antisocial, and sometimes of an appallingly ravenous sexual nature, no sympathy is given to the persons tricked. Sometimes, the tricks succeed; sometimes, they fail. Sometimes, the Trickster is evil; sometimes, a bringer of great gifts.

Anansi, the Spider, is the hero of an enormous body of west African Trickster tales. Hare, who became Brer Rabbit in North American Negro folk tales, is the best known Trickster in East Africa.

The Trickster is noted for his feats of strength in the mythology of almost all peoples from the ancient Greeks to the Polynesians and the American Indian Winnebago and Sioux and Tlingit, from Hermes and Odysseus and Autolycus to Maui-of-the-thousand-tricks and Wakdjukanga, Iktomi, and Raven. But in west Africa the emphasis is on the victory of cunning over force. However, sometimes, the tricks backfire. Stories like the Tar Baby incident make Brer Rabbit or Hare appear anything but clever.

Note that African stories stress food while Western (European) stories often stress sex. Whatever is lacking is the thing most talked about.

Karl Kerényi says that the god Hermes, like every other trickster, operates outside the fixed boundaries of custom and law. And Paul Radin says that the adventures of Hare are of two kinds. The first deals with his *self-education*, his progress from immaturity to maturity, from insecurity to security. The second deals with his endeavors to make the earth habitable for man and with the establishment of man's customs.

Tarzan was a trickster. But, flesh and blood, he lacked certain features of the mythological creature. He was not stupid or greedy or lacking in the better feelings of humanity. But he did have the Trickster's liking for a cruel joke on those who would do him evil.

In his youth, Tarzan was a trickster (though he did not lose this trait entirely in later life). Then he became a hero. Paralleling this was his simultaneous evolution from ape to man. He could do both at the same time. As we shall see, he had a dual nature.

The last story of Volume VI is fiction.

Tarzan Rescues the Moon could not have happened. It takes place in 1908. In it, a full eclipse of the moon occurs. At this time, or at any time from 1907 through 1909, no such eclipse, partial or full and observable from the equator in Africa, happened. So this story is one of a number of fictional or part-fictional tales that Burroughs wrote about Tarzan. I believe that Burroughs wrote this story to present an extended view of Tarzan's attitude toward cosmology and theology. He was still an animist at this time (perhaps he never freed himself entirely of animism). Tarzan's reaction to an eclipse of the moon could illustrate his views on such things. The incident where Tarzan spared the life of a warrior of Mbonga because he admired the man's courage was true and was put into the story of the eclipse. But the rest was not.

In the tale, a monster, a celestial Numa the lion, is eating up Goro the Moon. Tarzan shoots his poisoned arrows at the shadowy lion, and the mangani are awed when they see the black belly of the great sky-Numa give up the Moon. They look upon Tarzan as a superior being.

Burroughs had forgotten that Tarzan would undoubtedly have read about eclipses and would have known what was happening. But the way Tarzan handled the situation is valid. Tarzan would have shot arrows at the sky-Numa just to impress the great apes. It would have been one more good joke. And even if he hadn't been aware of the true cause of eclipses, Tarzan would have been as skeptical as Burroughs said he was about the efficacy of his arrows. Tarzan had a view of religious explanations of natural phenomena that would have sent him to the stake if he had been born at an earlier time and in the civilized world.

Chapter Nine

(Last part of I–11 and through I–20)

Kingship and Love

Kingdoms are but cares.

—Henry VI

What heart could have thought you?

—F. Thompson

Kerchak's increasing jealousy of Tarzan would have reached blow-out pressure long before August of 1908 except for several things. One was that he had seen what the knife could do. Another was that he had seen what the poisoned arrows could do. A third was that Tarzan spent little time with the tribe since Kala's death and so was not around enough to enrage Kerchak past endurance.

But, one day, Kerchak's patience, and his mind, snapped.

Tarzan had killed his first lion (a female) and boasted of it, of course. Holding up the skin of Sabor, he cried out that no one else of the tribe had ever killed a lion. He said more and doubtless would have gone on if Kerchak had not suddenly gone mad. Tarzan took to the trees, but, at Kerchak's challenge he came down. Why put off the inevitable any longer? He would never be readier to face the gigantic old male. Besides, he had been bragging too much. He did not want to slide back down the scale of the pecking order because he'd let Kerchak bluff him out. For a minute, he was tempted to use his bow on Kerchak, but he decided that if he did he would never know his own potentiality. Besides, the apes would not regard the use of the bow as being quite cricket. No, he would fight Kerchak with only his knife and his quick human wits.

And so the changeling came into the kingship of the tribe. But he found that he who is obeyed by everybody must also serve everybody. This became wearisome and time-consuming. Also, Mbonga's people were out looking for a new site for their village. Their probes into the forest resulted in the killing of many of the great apes and the driving away of game. The mangani decided to move away from this troublesome area. Tarzan, however, did not want to be too far away from the cabin. He abdicated after a few more months (end of January, 1909).

Before handing over the crown, he had to battle Terkoz, son of his foster father, Tublat. This time, Tarzan did something unusual in the tribe's history. He spared Terkoz, though he was later to wish he had not been so merciful.

Tarzan convalesced for ten days afterward. Terkoz had torn him up in a number of places and ripped off a section of scalp. Tarzan got the scalp back into place, and Teeka, at his directions, stitched it up painfully but effectively with the pincers of army ants. He had seen this method used by some of the blacks, and so he owed another debt to human technology. His wounds would have put most humans into the hospital for months, but he had the amazing recuperative powers of a wild beast. Even so, the healing left a scar starting above his left eye and running across the top of his head, ending just above the right ear. The rest of his life, whenever he was angered, that scar would turn into a red lightning steak.

On the fateful day of February 2, 1909, a Tuesday, Tarzan visited the village again. This time he took a doeskin breechcloth from an unlucky warrior named Mirando and put it on. He did this because he wanted to look as much as possible like a MAN. More than ever, he was conscious of the difference between himself and the mangani. He then returned to the seashore. There he halted, astonished and delighted, though his joy was shot with apprehension. That he did not rush out to greet the white men shows us that he had learned the lesson given him by the black men. And it was well that he was cautious. Otherwise, he would have been shot down, another victim of first contact with civilization.

Tarzan had seen pictures of sailing ships before. But they had not prepared him for the reality of the barkentine, moored in the landlocked harbor, so enormous and stately and awesome. However, it was the small boat on the beach and the people by it that magnetized him. There were ten men there, arguing. Presently, Tarzan witnessed his first murder. Snipes shot King in the back and took over the leadership of the mutineers of the *Arrow*.

"They were evidently no different from the black men—no more civilized than the apes—no less cruel than Sabor."

This was a judgment that Tarzan was to give many times. Again and again, Burroughs records that Tarzan scorned the hypocrisy, hatefulness, greed, and savagery of all the races of mankind. But the whites were to get by far the greatest share of contempt and loathing.

Tarzan had no idea of what was happening on the beach. He could not know that the *Arrow* had been chartered in England by a Professor Porter for a wild treasure hunt. But the sixteenth-century map had proved genuine, and the island, of the Cape Verde group about five hundred miles off the coast of west Africa, disgorged a huge oak chest. It contained gold coins which made it so heavy that four men could hardly carry it. The crew, even more villainous than the *Fuwalda*'s, killed the officers. The leader, King, like Black Michael, spared the passengers' lives. Finding a lonely but excellent harbor, King had moored there. He had intended to leave the passengers here and notify the authorities of their location via the mails. He had been the only man who knew how to navigate, and he was dead now.

After the small boat returned to the ship, Tarzan looked into the cabin. He was furious. It had been ransacked. He penciled a warning note and stuck it on the door. It was his first communication with the whites, the tarmangani, and it was no love note. It began: THIS IS THE HOUSE OF

                           TARZAN, THE KILLER . . .

and it ended: TARZAN OF THE APES.

The legitimate objection to this is that Tarzan knew nothing of the connection between sounds and their symbols. How would he know how to print T-A-R-Z-A-N, a great-ape name, since he had no idea that T, for instance, stood for an alveolar stop, or plosive, in English?

Even if he had known, he might have been at a loss. The great ape *t* might have been dental or retroflex, aspirated or unaspirated.

The difference between such *t*'s might have been phonemic, that is, they might have changed the meaning of a word. Thus, the *tar* that had a slight puff of air following the *t* might have a different meaning from the *tar* that had no aspirated *t*. *Tar* (white) would not have the same meaning as *t*ʰ*ar*. Whether this is so or not, we do not know. Burroughs only skims the surface of mangani speech.

The truth is that the ape-man did not write his name as *Tarzan*. Instead, he wrote WHITE SKIN, a literal translation of *tar* (white) and *zan* (skin). But Burroughs did not wish to slow the story with an explanation of this. He reported that Tarzan could write his own name in English letters and then went on with the story.

Hiding in the nearby bush jungle, Tarzan watched the two boats discharge fifteen seamen and five passengers. Curiously enough, four of the passengers were related to him, though in differing degrees.

The old man wearing a frock coat and a silk plug hat was Professor Archimedes Quintus Porter. His first name came from his father's admiration for the great Greek, and his middle name came from his being the fifth (and only surviving) child. His best friend sometimes called him "Ark." He was a history and theology teacher in the Women's College of Baltimore, Maryland, established by the Methodist Church in 1885 and now known as Goucher College. He came of ancient English stock. The many branches of the Porter landed gentry bear three church bells on their arms, and the professor's own branch had for a crest a portcullis. He was descended from people who had lived in the South a long time, but we know that the flintlock of his Puritan ancestors hung above his mantel. Thus, his earliest American ancestor was a New Englander who left to settle near Baltimore for one reason or another.

One of his distinguished ancestors was Endymion Porter, a poet and a patron of the arts in Charles II's time. One of the professor's Yankee relatives was Commodore David Porter, who commanded the frigate *Essex* on her famous expeditions during the War of 1812.

The professor was very fond of the works of another relative, the novelist Jane Porter (1776–1850), and especially of her *Scottish Chiefs*.

A distant cousin was Noah Porter, the famous Yale educationalist and metaphysical writer.

Professor Porter was seventy years old and so absent-minded that unkind people might have said that he was on the verge of senility, if not already over it. An explanation for his unworldly and even "metaphysical" behavior was in the bottle he carried in his rear pants pocket under the tail of the frock coat. This was not hard liquor, because the professor was a devout Methodist and a sworn teetotaler. However, having suffered from dandruff at one time, he had purchased a bottle of Sandholm's Eczema Lotion and Dandruff Remedy. Always neglectful of practical matters, the professor had not read the instructions on the label. So, instead of applying it externally to his hair, he drank it. That it was 40 per cent alcohol and that he was addicted to it might account for his acting as if he were always in a fog.

The professor, when in his late forties, had married Jane Carter Lee of Richmond, Virginia. Her father was a cousin of Robert E. Lee and descended from Light-Horse Harry Lee's father.

The professor had borrowed ten thousand dollars from a Robert Canler to finance this expedition.

The other old man was Samuel T. Philander, also seventy years old and of Baltimore. (I do not know what the T. stands for.) His childhood nickname was "Skinny." He was the professor's secretary and companion, was an ex-history teacher, and was hired by the professor's daughter because he needed more income than his pension allowed. It was true that her father could use someone to guide him around, but she could have made a better choice.

A very fat black woman, dressed in a bright and varicolored Mother Hubbard, was the forty-year-old Esmeralda Porter. She had taken care of the professor's daughter ever since his wife's death, at the age of thirty-five, shortly after bearing the child. Esmeralda was, no doubt, comical and ignorant, and Burroughs has been criticized for making her a stereotype of the uneducated, superstitious, easily frightened, and often hysterical black female. But Buroughs only recorded what she was. People forget that stereotypes have their genesis in reality; the prejudicial part enters when the small stereotype is imprinted on everybody belonging to the group, when a little mud is used to smear many. Moreover, the critics overlook that Esmeralda had a warm and compassionate nature. And, if she had been incompetent, she would never have been allowed to become a mother-substitute for the professor's daughter. She is seen under conditions which would have made most Western females, black or white, hysterical. She did not normally behave as she did on the expedition. Otherwise, the woman she had raised would not have been so tough and self-controlled.

Also, two white men, Porter and Philander, are even more comical figures than Esmeralda, and they have far less excuse for their behavior.

Esmeralda's father had been captured in 1823, at the age of ten, off the coast of Río Muni and taken to Maryland, where he was sold into slavery. He was a Waziri, and Tarzan himself may have been descended from the Waziri through the wife of Captain Bob Singleton (see Addendum 3, extracted from Burke's *Peerage*).

The tall young man in white ducks was William Cecil Arthur Clayton. He was almost nineteen and was the son of the sixth duke of Greystoke. He was Tarzan's second cousin. As the eldest (or perhaps the only) legitimate son of the duke, he had an honorary title. This was Lord Exminster, his father having been created Marquess Exminster by Queen Victoria.

William was handsome and had money in his own right inherited from his mother, who had died in 1908. (It has been said that she was the original of the Dark Lady of the Towers portrayed in Watson's story of the blackmailer, Milverton. There is no doubt that she was the younger sister of the woman G. B. Shaw calls Henrietta Jansenius in his *An Unsocial Socialist*. See Addenda 2 and 3.)

William Clayton had no idea, of course, that his second cousin, the rightful heir to the Greystoke titles, was watching him from behind a cover of leaves. Still mourning for his beloved mother, he had met the Porters in London and joined their expedition. He knew them because they were related through the Rutherfords. A younger son of a Baron Tennington had emigrated to the colonies and married a daughter of Cecil Calvert, second Baron Baltimore of Baltimore, who founded the colony of Maryland. Their daughter married a Porter. Though this relationship was somewhat thinned by time and distance, the Porters had kept in contact with the Rutherfords and Claytons. William Cecil had thought that the expedition would help him get over his grief for his mother, and when he saw Jane, he was sure he was going to.

The nineteen-year-old girl who stepped off the boat was Jane

Porter. She was strikingly beautiful, had long yellow hair which fell to her waist when unpinned, had bluish-grey eyes, and was left-handed. She wore a white pith helmet and a white ladies' waist of taffeta silk with a high standing collar and the front tucked over. This, with the swelling-posterior skirt, gave her whole figure a peculiar broken appearance. Her white Melton-cloth walking skirt was ankle-length and flared out at the bottom with a graduated flounce. Under the walking skirt was an underskirt of mercerized sateen, also flounced, and trimmed with three fluted ruffles. Under the waist should have been a corset protector and a four-hook short summer corset, and under everything should have been the heavy underwear and the heavy stockings that the well-dressed and modest maiden wore. But Jane had been perspiring, perhaps even sweating, because of the tropical heat, and she knew that it would be hotter on the land. She had taken them off in her cabin before coming out to be marooned on this desolate coast.

Jane had been a tomboy, had gone with her father on some of his scientific expeditions during the summer vacations into the West, and was, generally, tough and strong-minded.

She loved deeply only two people in the world: her father and Esmeralda. She had come along on this dangerous trip over her father's objections. She had insisted that he needed someone to take care of him. He had given in but had demanded that she bring along a chaperone, Esmeralda. Jane had been happy when the treasure had proved not to be just a con man's carrot. Robert Canler, forty years old, had already asked her to marry him and been turned down. But if her father could not repay the ten thousand borrowed from Canler, she would have to marry him; it was the only way to pay him back. Queen Victoria had died in 1901, but her spirit still ruled.

Tarzan could not keep his eyes off her. He had seen the pictures of white women in the books, but the reality was the difference between the promise of the kingdom of heaven and its actual coming. He thought that her clothes were ridiculous, but they did make her body a mystery and hence even more exciting.

We have no data about her figure then, but measurements taken at a London shop twenty years later, when she had not lost or gained a pound, are: height, 5 feet 7 inches (tall for those days); bust, 38; waist, 19 inches; hips, 36 inches.

Tarzan was soon forced by events to quit looking at her. Today and tomorrow, February 2 and 3, were to be very busy for everybody and especially for Tarzan. He saved his cousin, William Cecil, several times. He saved the professor and his secretary when they were lost in the jungle. He saved Jane and Esmeralda that night by dragging a lioness (or leopardess) out of the cabin window and breaking her neck with a full nelson. The rescuees, however, were quite bewildered by his activities. They thought that two men were mysteriously involved. There was the writer of the note on the door, the White Skin of the Apes, who never appeared. And there was the wild white giant who could not speak any civilized tongue and who disappeared after his rescues.

The party soon determined several things. The skeletons were those of William Cecil's cousin, his wife, and his baby. They had found Clayton's name in some books and a ring on his bony finger which bore the oldest crest of the Greystoke arms, a Saracen's head.

It is strange that Tarzan had never removed the ring, but we know that he paid little attention to the bones. The dead were dead. But if he had taken the ring and then compared its crest to that in the Greystoke arms in Burke's *Peerage*, he might have grasped, though dimly, that he was a member of that illustrious house.

The professor and Philander did observe later that the skull in the crib was actually an anthropoid ape's (or, more probably, a subhuman's). But they said nothing to the others about this.

Tarzan had followed the *Arrow* along the shore as it left the harbor. He knew the party on land was not going any place, and he was curious about the ship. He had seen the smoke of a ship on the horizon and the *Arrow*'s putting about and launching a boat some miles north of the cabin. He watched the sailors bring in the treasure chest and bury it. He watched the *Arrow* sail away to escape the approaching French naval vessel. Tarzan then dug up the chest and reburied it in the natural amphitheater where the mangani held their orgiastic Dum-Dum. Returning to the cabin, he stole a letter which Jane had written though she doubted that her best friend, Hazel Strong, would ever get it.

He wrote under Jane's signature:

I AM WHITE SKIN OF THE APES

and he stealthily returned it to Jane's desk through the window.

Two days later, March 5, a Friday (the goddess of love's day),

Terkoz, expelled from the tribe as a troublemaker, lusting for a female, came across Jane Porter.

Burroughs, be it noted, says that the great apes had a mating season. This is interesting, since the higher apes, like humans, seem ready to mate the year around. And if, as suspected, the mangani were more hominid than simian, they would not have had sexual seasons. Evidence from other volumes of the epic indicates that they were always ready, and quite often eager, to mate. Burroughs attributed a mating season to the mangani because, when he wrote the first two books, he did not know much about them.

How did Terkoz know Jane was a female? He had never seen a white female before, or, as far as we know, a black female. Jane's clothes would have hidden the obvious.

For an answer, we must consider what she was doing. Jane and Esmeralda had wandered into the jungle looking for fruit. But they would have been happy to bathe if they had found fresh water. Burroughs is discreet about this; Jane may have been in a condition in which even a great ape would recognize her sex. That we know the gorillas do not abduct women for sexual purposes, or for any purpose, doesn't mean, however, that Terkoz would not. He was a sentient being, closer to man than to the gorilla.

It is possible that Jane was fully clothed and that Terkoz detected her femaleness by a similarity of body odor to the females he knew. If this were so, then the mangani are a species very close to mankind.

Whatever happened, it is best to go along with the implicit description of her as fully clothed. Terkoz did carry her off, and Tarzan did track them down and rectify his error in showing mercy to Tublat's son.

And Tarzan?

"He did what no red-blooded man needs lessons in doing. He took his woman in his arms and smothered her upturned panting lips with kisses."

Love at first sight and under rather strange circumstances.

How did Tarzan know that Jane's people kissed to express affection, love, and passion?

He had read books. And kissing must have been part of the affection pattern of the mangani. Kala was a stern disciplinarian, but she also gave Tarzan love, and petting and kissing were her expressions of this.

After yielding to his first impulse, Jane fought him off. Tarzan then carried her off deeper into the jungle, but not to a "fate worse than death," and only for a day's idyl in a place "older than Eden." That night, before they went to sleep, Tarzan gave his knife to Jane. She understood and was touched. He was telling her that he meant her no harm and that she could use the knife on him if he tried to enter the bower he had built for her. The gesture was similar to that of the medieval knight who placed a sword between himself and his chaste lady love. Tarzan was chivalry reborn, to some extent, anyway. If his behavior on this occasion and others to come seems too noble to be true, remember that he was being guided by what he had learned of idealistic moral conduct in his books. Like Don Quixote, he believed what he read. Moreover, his behavior was probably reinforced by the unwritten code of the mangani. They demanded, and got, because they were a very small, closely knit group, behavior that conformed to the ideal. It is true that their ideals were few and much simpler than man's. But their sexual code had certain resemblances to those that Western society professed. A mangani might abduct an alien female by force and bring her to his tribe to live. But he was also sexually jealous; his system of social conduct demanded instant retribution when his "rights" were violated.

Moreover, Tarzan was in love, and he was anxious to please. He was dealing with a creature whose background differed to a deep degree, and he had to be careful what he did. He could only follow the rules he knew from his reading.

At the next sunset, Tarzan returned Jane to the cabin. He kissed her, and she told him that she loved him. From far away came the sound of firing, and in the harbor were two ships, the *Arrow* and the French warship.

Neither knew it, but the French ship had caught up with the *Arrow* and its few starving survivors. Hearing of the marooned party, the Frenchmen had come to rescue them. When told that Jane had been carried off, they formed a rescue party under Lieutenants Charpentier and Paul d'Arnot. The party had been ambushed by Mbonga's men, and this occasioned the sound of the firearms Tazan heard. Reluctantly, he left Jane and went off to the conflict.

Chapter Ten

(I–21 through I–28)

Renunciation

My mother was an Ape.

—Tarzan

D'Arnot was captured and taken to Mbonga's village, where he was tortured as an appetizer for the feast to come. Tarzan rescued him and took him into the jungle to nurse him for a few days. Meanwhile, the French sailors had come back in a larger party and had killed every male in the village, believing that d'Arnot had been eaten.

However, earlier Burroughs says that you can still (1912) see the pot of food left out daily by the villagers for Munango-Keewati. If this is so, enough males must have escaped to return later and re-establish a viable community. We hope that Tibo and his mother, Momaya, were not victims of the retaliation.

Returning, the French looked for the treasure, failed to find it, and sailed away with Jane and the others. And so Tarzan got d'Arnot back to the cabin just too late.

The Frenchman was Tarzan's first, and forever his best, human friend. He communicated with the ape-man through printed English. In this series of notes, Tarzan is supposed to have written mangani words and Jane's name. It's obvious that Burroughs put the mangani words in to add a Tarzanic flavor. Where Burroughs says Tarzan gave Terkoz's name, Tarzan actually wrote the English translation of it. And he did know how to write "Jane Porter" because he had seen the signature on her letter to Hazel Strong. He had seen samples of signed letters in the novels in his father's library.

The two found a message from Clayton and one from Jane in the cabin. It was evident that neither knew that Tarzan, the note writer, and their wild-man benefactor were the same. Jane's note asked the mysterious writer, Tarzan, to tell the wild man that he was always welcome in Baltimore.

The two men left the cabin about April 16, 1909, a Friday, and arrived at a settlement about May 14, a Friday. This was a French mission and native village, Lambaréné. During the trip, d'Arnot read John Clayton's French diary and saw the page where Tarzan's baby fingerprints were inked. The two came, about six weeks later, June 26, a Saturday, to a small port at the mouth of a wide river. This was Port-Gentil at the issuance of the Ogouée (Ogowe, Ogobay) River. This is now the chief port and industrial city of the present nation of Gabon. Its population in 1960 was twenty thousand. In those days it was even less.

What is strange is that the two took a month to get to their first human habitation and two months to get to Port-Gentil. If they had followed the coastline northward, they would have come to a small native village (present Iguéla) in about thirty-one miles as the crow flies. They didn't, so they obviously struck inland. And here something happened which Burroughs omits to narrate. Even if they had gone north and inland in a straight line (as near straight as jungle travel permits), they would have arrived at the Ogowe River halfway between Port-Gentil and upriver Lambaréné, after about ninety-five miles (again as the crow travels).

I believe that the two were sidetracked, perhaps held prisoner by cannibals, and thus sent off their main path. The Catholic mission they encountered was far inland, at Lambaréné itself. A little above here was Adolinanongo, a small hill on the banks of the Ogowe where Trader Horn had established his post in 1875. Horn had left about 1884, and Albert Schweitzer would not arrive until 1913 to build his house on the hill.

Tarzan and d'Arnot had then gone down the Ogowe to Port-Gentil. At its mouth, Tarzan would have seen what was left of the island where his mother's uncle, George, was buried. By then the sea would have washed it away, since Trader Horn said the grave was about to disappear when he inspected it in the late 1870s. George's head was even then missing, having been stolen by witch doctors to make powerful magic. Tarzan's cousin, Nina, would have been the wife of a great landowner in Peru. (For George T——'s relationship to Tarzan, see Addendum 2.)

Forced to wait a month for a vessel to France, the two chartered an old tub and went back down the coast to dig up the treasure. During their stay, Tarzan earned his first money, a wager of ten thousand francs, by going into the jungle armed only with a rope and a knife and returning with the great cat he had killed on his back.

Circa July 31, the two arrived in Paris. Here d'Arnot took Tarzan and his diary to a high police official. He also learned that Jane had gone to America and William Clayton's father had died. His cousin was now the seventh duke of Greystoke. Whether he would remain so depended upon the baby fingerprints in the diary matching those of Tarzan's. A final verdict would have to be delayed until the police expert returned. Tarzan went on to America without waiting for him.

The final scene of Volume I of the Epic takes place on a farm outside a little Wisconsin town. This was Milton Junction, on the Chicago and North West Railroad line and not too far away from (appropriately enough) Janesville. Here Jane had gone to get away from Robert Canler, who was pressing her to marry him, now that her father's treasure had disappeared. William Clayton had come there in a huge touring car. Canler followed a week later in a six-cylinder. Tarzan showed up driving a large French automobile. Clayton's car was a 1908 Pierce Great Arrow, model 48; Canler's, a model K Ford selling for $2,800; Tarzan's, a 1908 four-cylinder, 45-horsepower Delahaye.

A road census, taken in 1904, showed about two million miles of public highway in the United States. One hundred thousand miles were covered with gravel and forty thousand with macadam. There were no concrete roads. One million eight hundred sixty thousand miles were dirt. These were mud when it rained; high with snow in winter, dusty in the dry season. It seems incredible that Canler and Clayton drove from Baltimore in their cars in such a short time, especially when tires blew and motors overheated and bolts dropped out at the drop of a horseshoe. They probably purchased them in Chicago and drove out from there.

Tarzan's car was French, but that doesn't mean he brought it on the ship with him. He purchased it in Chicago, too. After a day's driving-and-maintenance lesson, and armed with a road map, he set out for Milton Junction, Wisconsin.

Events moved swiftly and grimly after Canler appeared with a minister in tow (unnecessary since Professor Porter could have married them). Jane felt honor-bound to marry Canler, though she preferred William Clayton, whom she did not love but respected.

Jane was caught in a sudden forest fire. Tarzan appeared in time to rescue her and frighten off Canler. Clayton seized exactly the right psychological moment to ask Jane to marry him. Jane had thought she had loved Tarzan, but here, in civilization, out of the place older than Eden, she was overwhelmed with realistic doubts. He was uneducated and savage; they could have little in common. And he would be far happier without her.

Tarzan handed the professor a check for $240,000, the sum the treasure chest had brought. This definitely put Canler out of the running, even if Tarzan had not come close to killing him and had been, in fact, restrained from doing so by Jane. Tarzan then asked Jane for an answer to his proposal. But she had said yes to Clayton. And now, too late, she realized her mistake. She really loved this jungle man, yet she could not go back on her word. Perhaps she was too strong-minded, too responsive to her Victorian code, but that was the way it was.

As Tarzan was sadly remembering his highest moment of happiness, when he and Jane were alone in the jungle, eating fruit and smiling at each other, he was handed a telegram.

It was from d'Arnot.

The baby's fingerprints were his.

William Clayton came in then, shook his hand, and thanked him for all he had done.

Tarzan could not bring himself to tell him that he was no longer the rightful Lord Greystoke. He could strip away Clayton's titles and lands and castles. And, worse, they'd be taken from Jane.

Tarzan did not understand that Clayton would still be Marquess Exminster and Viscount Passmore, titles bestowed on his father before he had become sixth duke. Nor did he know that Clayton had money from his mother. Not that it would have made any difference if he had known. He wanted Jane to have everything possible.

Clayton asked Tarzan how he ever got into the "bally jungle."

Tarzan replied that he was born there. "My mother was an Ape. . . . I never knew who my father was."

Thus ends Volume I of the epic. Renunciation. Self-sacrifice for love. The sadness of reality. And all this from one whom everybody, including Jane, thought was a simple jungle-man.

But he had money as a buffer for his ignorance, and he had a deep and solid self-assurance which showed through even when he was doing the wrong thing. Also, he learned surface things very quickly; he never made the same mistake twice. Despite which, he was glad to leave. On September 7, 1909, he was on the French steamer *La Provence*, bound for Le Havre, France. The trip would take six days, one hour, and forty-eight minutes, if all went as planned. Tarzan listened with some amusement and wonder as a steward told him this. One thing he would never really understand was the civilized man's attitude toward Time. In this, he would never be fully human. Though he could obey the dictates of the clock when he had to, he never respected Time.

Tarzan had not been on board long when he became involved with the de Coudes. Olga de Coude, neé Rokoff, was a beautiful twenty-year-old Russian who had married a middle-aged French count, an official of the Ministry of War. Tarzan saved the count when he was falsely accused of cheating at cards. Nikolas Rokoff, Olga's crooked brother, and Alexis Paulvitch (Burroughs' spelling), his fellow-in-crime, had tried to get the count into a position where they could blackmail him. Tarzan interfered with them again, rescuing Olga, and she fell in love with him. Nor was Tarzan unaffected by her.

In Paris, Tarzan read many books in English, learned to read French, and haunted the galleries and museums, the cafes, and the theater. He drank absinthe and smoked cigarettes. He was trying to compress all the virtues and vices he had missed for twenty years into a small package. He also closely observed everyone he met. His jungle training had encouraged this natural ability of never missing a thing. Survival had depended upon it. Here, however, knowing the rules of conduct might not necessarily mean losing one's life. But it could mean a social death. And most of the rules were unwritten and often unvoiced, so he could learn only by watching and imitating people. And here one could go wrong simply by imitating the "wrong" people. Civilization was a many-leveled and complex structure, and the rules often changed just because the situation changed, even when the same people were involved. Living in the city was not like living in Kerchak's tribe or even in Mbonga's.

He concluded that it would take all his life to get a deep understanding of civilization. Or even of rural life. Indeed, he might be too late now. And he doubted that it would be worth-while to stay in civilization.

Rokoff set a trap for Tarzan in the slums of the rue Maule. Tarzan joyfully maimed the thugs who had counted on their numbers overwhelming only one man. He, however, did get into trouble when he refused to allow the police to arrest him. D'Arnot straightened out the misunderstanding with the gendarmes, but he depressed Tarzan by telling him that Jane and the seventh duke would be married in two months. Tarzan did not have much time, however, to think about her.

He went to the small town of Etampes with d'Arnot, where he was to oppose the count in a duel to satisfy the count's honor. Tarzan had been caught in another trap set by Rokoff, this time with Olga as the unsuspecting (if not entirely innocent) bait. Tarzan and Olga were in a passionate embrace when the count, summoned by Rokoff, surprised them and challenged Tarzan. The whole affair had been set up by Rokoff, but there was no way to prove this.

De Coude, reputedly the best pistol shot in France, fired twice. But he was unnerved by Tarzan's grim and unmoving attitude. Taran refused to fire until the count had spent his three permitted shots. After discharging his pistol into the air, he begged the count's pardon. He also exonerated Olga of any blame in the affair and assured the count that his honor was still intact. Tarzan had flesh wounds in the left shoulder and left side, but he recuperated quickly. And de Coude, having become his very good friend, got Tarzan his first job, which was as a special secret agent for the War Ministry.

Tarzan's behavior in the de Coude affair has been criticized as being unrealistically noble, self-sacrificing to an extent that only Victorians (in their novels) would ever consider. But it must be remembered that Tarzan was conducting himself as he thought a man should in European society. He was feeling his way down the dark alleys of civilization, and he had as guide for his ethics only the books he had read and what people assured him were the ideals. If the code of this world demanded that he should atone for his "wrong," even if he should die himself, he would do it.

Later, he would conduct himself with a somewhat less chivalrous attitude, that is, more self-preserving. He had seen by then how hollow civilized ideals were after civilized practice had done with gnawing at them.

Disguised as an American big-game hunter, Tarzan went to Algeria. There he investigated a Lieutenant Gernois of the French Foreign Legion. Gernois was suspected of selling military secrets to a great European power. The power was unidentified by Burroughs, but, since Rokoff was involved, it could have been Russia. On the other hand, Rokoff could have been working for Great Britain (possibly directly under Mycroft Holmes). Tarzan would not have known this. And even if he had, he had not developed enough patriotism to have stopped him from working against the British. He did not think of himself as having a nationality then, unless it was that of the manganis.

In two months, Tarzan had many adventures. He was captured by his archenemy, Rokoff, but he escaped. He killed lions and fought bandit Arabs and almost joined the tribe of Kadour ben Saden. But he understood that the seemingly free nomads were, within their tribal structure, even more tightly bound social prisoners than civilized man. He, the Outsider, could never fit in.

The case ended with Gernois' suicide, and Tarzan was ordered to undertake another. He boarded a steamer at Oran to go to South Africa where he was to report for further instructions. Rokoff and Paulvitch were also aboard. They had shaved off their beards and dyed their hair a different color. Tarzan did not recognize them at first, though he should have identified their body odors. Probably, the pomades and perfumes that Russian men of the upper class used overrode the body odors. Moreover, Tarzan was still smoking cigarettes, which would have dulled his keen sense of smell.

At this time, Tarzan was traveling under the name of John Caldwell. The initials were those of his real name, John Clayton, and John Caldwell was an illustrious ancestor of his. The Caldwell arms, "sable a torn or," or a golden spinning wheel on a black field, were on the Greystoke coat-of-arms.

As John Caldwell, he met Hazel Strong, Jane's best friend. She was on her way to visit her uncle in Cape Town. She was very attracted to this quiet young man with the strange accent and entertaining stories of African wildlife. Tarzan was shaken when he learned from her that Jane really loved him—even if she were going to marry his cousin. Though neither knew it, Tarzan and Jane passed each other as their ships went through the Straits of Gibraltar. She was going the opposite way on a trip around Africa. The Porters and William Cecil Clayton had accepted an invitation to accompany Lord "Bunny" Tennington (Tarzan's first cousin on his mother's side) on the trip.

A week later, one moonless night, while Tarzan leaned over the railing, thinking of Jane, he was pitched overboard by the two Russians. By one of those coincidences that occur frequently to one born on the cusp of Scorpio and Sagittarius, he fell into the sea exactly opposite the cabin where he had been born. When he reached land, he took to the branches of the forest giants.

"With the first dizzy swing from tree to tree, all the old joy of living swept over him. . . . Who would go back . . . when the mighty reaches of the jungle offered peace and liberty? Not he."

Meanwhile, Hazel had run into Jane in Cape Town, and Jane was shattered when she saw the photograph of Mr. Caldwell, who had been lost at sea.

Rokoff, as Monsieur Thuran, had managed to become close to Hazel. She was heiress to millions, and he had great visions of what he would do with them if he married her. Baron Tennington invited Hazel and Thuran and Paulvitch along, and the yacht, named *Lady Alice* after his dead aunt, continued up the western coast of Africa. And then it struck a wreck and went down.

Jane found herself on a lifeboat with Rokoff, Clayton, and three sailors. The oars were lost, and they had no food or water. Murder was to be done, and cannibalism attempted, before the boat drifted to shore.

Tarzan wandered inland. He found Mbonga's village deserted and falling apart. (But the villagers would return and rebuild it.) He kept on in a southeasterly direction, coming at last to the more or less open savanna. He found great herds of antelope and elephant. It is doubtful that Pacco the zebra was also there, as Burroughs reported. Zebras don't exist in the French Congo. Burroughs knew this, of course, having read the works of Du Chaillu and others. But he could not resist throwing in details of "local color" that did not exist. From his viewpoint, no harm was done. Such discrepancies would convince people that the Tarzan stories were all fiction.

Tarzan, coming across a black hunter, stalked him. He wanted his weapons and his finery. But civilization had changed Tarzan. True, the man was black, and hence he was identified with the killers of his mother and other mangani. Yet, he thought, the man was not one of Mbonga's people. He had nothing to do with their enmity toward Tarzan. Why should he kill a man just to get his spear and knife? The more he considered it, the more he was repulsed by his original intent.

Then a man-eating lion attacked the black, and Tarzan reacted by roping the lion. He was tumbled out of his tree and was helpless for a moment. It was the black, Busuli, who speared the lion and delayed him. Together, the two finished the big cat off.

Tarzan was welcomed into the Waziri village. He observed that these tall handsome people were not cannibals and did not seem to be of the same physical type as the western bush Negro. Nor were they, having migrated from the land south of the present country of Mali. They spoke a Bantu language but seemed to have some Hamitic (Berber) ancestry. As Burroughs tells us many times, they were the greatest warriors of Africa, though small in numbers.

Tarzan felt an affinity for these people. A metaphysician might have explained this as due to his ancestry. Tarzan may have had Waziri forefathers. But Una, wife of Tarzan's forefather, Captain Singleton, was too far back in Tarzan's lineage. None of her genes would be present in him. It is easier to believe that he admired and respected them simply because they deserved it.

Tarzan also observed that many Waziri wore pure gold ornaments. To his questions they replied that they had gotten them from the southeast, a moon's march or more away. When Busuli's father was young, he had gone with a party looking for a better place to live, one where they would be safe from the slave-raiding Arabs. Waziri, old chief of the Waziri, verified Busuli's tale of the ruined stone city where hairy white men, wearing ornaments of gold, lived.

Tarzan went on two elephant hunts with the Waziri. These are the only recorded instances of his killing Tantor. But he kept his vow never to eat elephant meat again.

On the second hunt, the Waziri village was attacked by Arab slavers and their black eastern-Congo Manyuema allies.

Chapter Twelve

(II–16 through II–23)

The Chief, the She, the City of Gold

There are two ways to enter a tribe.

—Okeli saying

Gilgamesh harrowed the house of the dead.

—Sumerian Tale

The Waziri hunting party, with those who had escaped the raiders, lost heavily in a frontal attack on the Arabs. Tarzan talked them out of making another direct assault on the palisaded village, and he took complete command, the old chieftain having fallen. He directed the Waziri to fight as guerrillas, and he used his old trickster tactics to throw the Arabs and Manyuema into a panic.

The slavers, by the way, were a long distance from home. The Manyuema land was a large area between the northwest coast of Lake Tanganyika and the Lualaba River. This was in the extreme central eastern part of the Belgian Congo (now part of the independent Republic of the Congo). Their Arab leaders would have been from British East Africa (present-day Rwanda, Burundi, Uganda, and Kenya) or German East Africa (present-day Tanzania). Slavery was forbidden in all these territories. But it was still being practiced on a large scale in 1910, chiefly by the Arabs and certain black tribes. The captured Waziri, carrying their ivory, were to be marched across the continent northeast to the slave markets of the Sudan. At least half would have died on the journey.

But Tarzan and his warriors, shooting from cover of the jungle, dogged the caravan. Eventually, the demoralized and decimated Manyuema obeyed the voice that thundered from the bush and shot down their Arab leaders. Then they returned the ivory to the village, after which they were allowed to leave. But they had to promise they would never come back, a promise not difficult to keep.

The conquered Manyuema were conducted to the northern boundaries of the Waziri land. Why the northern when the shortest way home for them would have been from the southeastern border? Probably because Tarzan wanted them to retrace the trail they had taken with their Waziri captives and so doubly reinforce the memory of what he had done to them.

And now he joined the Waziri in the great victory dance, leaping and whirling and shouting, stomping his feet, shaking his spear and war plume of feathers, his bronzed skin sweating and shining in the light of the bonfires. Born John Clayton, he had become Tarzan of the Apes, then the forest devil-god Munango-Keewati, then M. Jean C. Tarzan, then John Caldwell, and now he was Waziri, chief of the Waziri. From king of the great apes he had climbed to chief of a tribe of black men.

Tarzan would always be the chief-in-fact of the Waziri, though he gave over the titular chieftainship to others in later years.

And now is a good time to consider a puzzling thing about the Waziri. Remote as they were, they seem to have been visited, and entertained, by a white man a year or two before Tarzan found them. It is recorded in R. L. Taylor's W. C. Fields, His Follies and Fortunes, that Tex Rickard took Fields on a trip around the world. Fields juggled, but spoke no lines, before audiences varying from German emperors to Australian blackfellows. Once, he entertained a tribe of naked Waziri.

Were these Tarzan's stalwart black fighting men? It would seem so. The only other Waziri we know of are the inhabitants of Waziristan in Asia. These are Mohammedans and far from naked. Besides, Fields was never in the Waziristan part of Asia, as far as is known. So the conclusion is unavoidable that, in 1906 or 1907, somehow or other, our W. C. Fields was in the remote and near-inaccessible French Congo region, tossing balls as only he could, and wondering if the clashing of spears by the magnificent, but fierce-looking, warriors was an indication of applause or of preparation to throw said spears. We do not know how he got this billing, what he said to his agent afterward, or how he was paid, though doubtless he pocketed a number of the Waziri gold circlets. Nor is there any doubt that he quaffed frequently from his flask of pineapple juice during his short but memorable stay among the Waziri. There is no record that anything was said to Tarzan about the visit of the American juggler. Nor would he have been too curious about him. He was planning to lead an expedition to the fabled city of gold.

Tarzan set off with fifty young men, following the directions of Busuli's father. Burroughs, however, in later volumes, gives directions that would seem to contradict those in Volume II. The discrepancies are deliberately made, of course. Burroughs had no intention of giving the world a map to the source of the greatest treasure-trove in the world. In fact, it is doubtful that Burroughs himself knew the true road to Opar. Tarzan was not going to tell anyone outside his family—and the Waziri—how to get there.

All we know is that Opar is somewhere in the mountains of central Africa in a still remote and rough area. Tarzan led his men on a thirty-day march (though it might actually have been sixty or seventy days or more). At last, they climbed the almost perpendicular crags forming the final and greatest barrier. Tarzan clawed over the top of the last cliff and stood on a small level plateau on the mountain top. On either hand were peaks thousands of feet taller than the pass through which they were entering the valley.

Looking behind, he could see the forested valley across which they had marched for days. *At the other side was the low range which marked the boundary of the Waziri country.*

The italicized sentence is taken from Burroughs' description. It is one of the many purposely misleading descriptions. If the party was still within sight of its own land, it would still be in Gabon. And if it followed the directions given, it could not be in Gabon. Nor would it have encountered the massive and high range described in Volume II. Going east of Gabon, it would have had to travel across most of central Africa to reach such mountains, which are found in the country along the eastern Congo. Other volumes narrate expeditions to Opar but start them off from East Africa, and the times given for the trips and the directions are even more confusing.

In front of and below Tarzan was a desolate valley. It was

shallow and sprinkled with dwarfed trees and stippled with thousands of boulders. These, when seen close, were often as big as small bungalows.

On the far side of the valley was a city. It was not so wide, but it was high and massive. Its walls gave an impression of ponderous density even at this distance, and above them rose thin towers, turrets, and domes. In the bright sun these were red and yellow. The distance resurrected it for Tarzan as it had been in the past, since he could not tell from there that it was partly in ruins. It looked golden and beautiful, and Tarzan peopled it in his imagination with tall and handsome men and women.

The party rested for an hour, after which Tarzan led it down the mountain and across the valley. It was almost dusk when they stopped before the towering walls. The outer wall, fifty feet high, had not fallen completely. Only the upper ten or twenty feet, here and there, had collapsed.

Tarzan's neck was cold; he felt unseen eyes watching him, eyes whose owners meant no good to the invaders.

The party camped that night outside the city. Near midnight, someone in the city screamed shrilly, terminating with a number of moans. The Waziri were brave men—except when it came to the soul-eating ghosts of their religion. Tarzan calmed them down and then got them moving in the morning. They marched for fifteen minutes along the foot of the wall before finding a way in. This was a crack about twenty inches wide. Tarzan crawled through it to a flight of concrete steps worn by centuries of usage. The steps went up and then, after a sharp turn, became a passage. Tarzan went in sideways with his Waziri behind him. The passage wound snakishly for a while before opening on a narrow court. Its other side was an inner wall as high as the outer wall. On its top were small round towers alternating with cone-topped monoliths. Some of these had fallen down, and the wall had caved in somewhat here and there, but this wall was better preserved than the other.

Another narrow passage perforated this wall. At its end was a broad street. At its other side were dark gloomy buildings of decaying granite. Trees had grown out of the detritus at the bottom, and vines curved in and out of the windows, like worms crawling out of the eye sockets of skulls.

The building opposite was not so crumbled or grown over. Its cyclopean structure was capped with a huge dome. On both sides of the yawning entrance were rows of high pillars, each topped by a great carved bird.

Through the vast square archway and the windows he saw—or thought he saw—shadows moving in the twilit interior.

But the city seemed so dead, so imbued with antiquity and decay, that living things seemed out of place here.

Yet he was aware of rustling sounds, and his neck was still cold from the ghostly thrust of hidden eyes.

He went slowly into the hemispherical interior. The floor was concrete; the wall, of granite on which weird figures of men and animals were carved. There were also tablets of gold set in the walls, and these bore in alto-relievo many hieroglyphs.

Beyond this first great spooky chamber were many others. In one he came across seven pillars of solid gold, and in another room he walked on a floor of gold.

Then a scream rang out, and the Waziris, their nerves stretched as far as they could go, broke. They fled, and Tarzan watched them go. He smiled grimly, nor was he to reproach them afterward. He knew that the fear of ghosts was very real to the African native. And though he felt no fear himself, he understood that theirs must be very deep and powerful. He knew they were as brave as any men anywhere when it came to battle with other men.

He went on from room to room, stopping before a barred door. A shriek warned him to stay out of the room beyond, but he took down the bar and shoved the creaking door open. Inside, darkness and an overpowering incense ruled. It was this burning powder that kept him from smelling the hundred hairy little men waiting for him. And so he was overpowered by hands from the blackness, though he killed and crippled many, and his hands were tied behind him and his feet tied to his hands. He was dragged out into a courtyard inside the temple, and here he saw the short-legged, long-armed, hairy-chested men with bushy masses of hair on their heads and beards flowing over their shoulders and down to their navels. The faces behind the beards were gnarly; the eyes, small and close-set; the brows, jutting bone; the noses, short and round; the lips, thick and pushed out by the apish jaws underneath the flesh. They wore leopard and lion skins around their waists and big necklaces of leopard and lion claws, and massive gold bands on their arms and legs. They carried thick warty bludgeons and long knives in belts. Their skins were white; their eyes, black; their teeth, yellow.

They spoke a monosyllabic language which he did not know.

Tarzan was left alone for a while in an inclosure formed by lofty walls at the top of which was a piece of sky. The galleries rising from the floor to near the top of the walls were soon filled by the hairy faces of his captors.

Time passed. Then the sun's first rays shone down the shaft, and the people in the galleries, their eyes on the light, chanted, and those who had come into the court also took up the chant. They began to dance, circling slowly, their thick necks bent back so they could see the sun approaching the zenith. Suddenly, they rushed on Tarzan with lifted bludgeons.

A woman dashed in with a club made from gold and beat the crooked little men back with such ease that Tarzan realized the rescue was a mock, a part of the ritual.

The woman cut the ropes from his legs and tied one end around his neck and led him across the courtyard. The men followed in a line of pairs through the winding hallways until they came to an enormous room in the center of which was a stone altar. The block was stained reddish-brown and the floor around it was also dirty with dried blood. Skulls grinned from thousands of niches in the walls.

Tarzan was led up the altar steps. The galleries filled again. Through a doorway at the east end, women slowly Indian-filed in. These had large black eyes and more intelligent and human features than the men. They wore animal skins bound about the waist with rawhide belts or gold chains. On their thick black hair were caps of gold pieces from which strings of gold pieces fell to the waist.

Each woman carried two gold cups, the purpose of which Tarzan guessed. They formed a line on one side of the altar, and the men formed a line on the other. Then the men advanced in unison, and each took a cup from a woman.

Tarzan, watching this, was waiting for a chance to escape. There didn't seem to be any; his chances were practically nil. At the same time, he was trying to figure out the population of this weird city. There were a hundred men and a hundred women around him, and about twice that on the galleries above. So far, he had seen no children or even juveniles.

The people around the altar began to chant, and from a dark passageway beyond the altar came another woman. She, it was evident, was the high priestess. (Her name was La.) She was beautiful, so much so that it seemed impossible she could be of the same stock as the others, even the more human-looking women. A mass of wavy hair shot with bronze lights from the sun half-surrounded her oval face. From under narrow penciled brows grey eyes looked closely at him. Her mouth opened as if she had gasped in wonder, but the chanting was too loud for her to be heard. A close-fitting girdle of many weird designs set with diamonds bound her waist and supported a short leopard skin. Her upper torso was bare at this time, though she did wear breastplates at times, as he was to find out. Her arms and legs were almost hidden with thick and diamond-studded gold bands. A long jeweled knife was stuck in her girdle, and in her hand was a slender wand.

Tarzan did not have time to regard her beauty very long. He was stretched out on the altar, and the ceremony proceeded. The beautiful priestess would stab him, and then his blood would be drained out into the cups held by the ritualists. They would drink him dry in this grisly communion, and afterward they would do whatever they did with bloodless corpses. But his skull would end up with the others in the wall niches.

Tarzan thought that he was done for. He thought briefly of Jane, and then he tried with all his strength to break the ropes around his wrists. Meanwhile, a brutish priest, Tha, evidently suffering from insanity, got into a dispute about his place in the blood-drinkers' line. He suddenly began knocking brains out and breaking bones with his bludgeon. The others fled at this sudden outbreak of what Burroughs called "jungle madness." Since the Oparians had interbred to some extent with the local mangani, it can be assumed that they also had the fatal gene of madness, though other explanations are possible.

The madman chased La into the dark room under the altar. Tarzan broke the ropes around his hands with superhuman effort. He ran down the age-old steps into the big low-ceilinged vault with its several dark doorways, and he pulled the madman from off La and killed him.

Tarzan had tried a number of languages on her while he was on the altar. Now he found out that she could speak mangani. Indeed, this was the normal everyday speech of the Oparians, who only used their original language in rituals. (Evidently, the ritual started the moment they had a captive.) She told him her name and said she had dreamed of a beautiful man like him all her life. She was grateful because he had saved her life, and she wanted to save Tarzan for herself, not the Flaming God. She did not fear the god himself, though she was afraid of what those who believed in him could do in his name. La, like so many priests Tarzan was to meet, was very skeptical of the existence of the god she served.

La conducted him through winding hallways to a small chamber dimly lit by a stone grating in the ceiling. This, she said, was the Chamber of the Dead, where the spirits came back and, if they foud a living person, sacrificed him. Nobody except she dared enter. He would be safe here.

La, a female Virgil leading a naked Dante into the circles of the underworld, took him into a room below the Chamber of the Dead. They groped for what seemed ten minutes along another dark winding passage. Coming to a closed door, they stopped. La opened it with a key, ushered him in, and locked the door behind him. She was taking no chances that he would leave her.

Tarzan could be as patient as a hunting lioness when he had to be. But when action was demanded, he wasted no time. Investigating the source of the moving air in the twenty-foot square chamber, he found loose stones. He lifted these out, and crawled through a narrow tunnel until he came to a hole before him. Leaning out, he could see a narrow circle of starry sky and moonlight. Below, far below, water glinted. He went back, replaced the stones in his cell wall, grinning at the thought of La's consternation when she would find that he had disappeared from a locked room. Then he leaped the fifteen feet across the shaft in a standing broad jump, crawled down another narrow tunnel, and descended about twenty feet of steps. Here another horizontal tunnel started. He unbarred a massive wooden door and entered the room beyond. He could see nothing here, but his fingers told him that there were many ingots of some metal, shaped like double-headed bootjacks, piled in this place. From the heaviness of one, he thought that it must be gold.

At the far end of the room, he unbarred another door. Beyond was a long straight passage. He knew, from the distance he had traveled, that he was out beyond the outer walls of the temple.

And if he had been going west, he was beyond the outer walls of the city, also.

In half an hour, he came across another flight of steps, leading upward this time. The concrete gave way to hewn granite. For about a hundred feet the steps spiraled, took an abrupt turn, and he was in a narrow gap between two rocky walls pressing on his shoulders. Above was the sky; before him, a steep incline. Up this he went, and came out on top of a huge granite boulder.

A mile away were the ruins of Opar. In the moonlight, he examined the ingot he had brought with him. It weighed about forty pounds, and it was of virgin gold.

Tarzan went on across the valley. He appeared suddenly before the Waziri, squatting before their fires, and he said, "Arise, my children, and greet thy king!"

The Waziri greeted him joyfully but also with shame, saying that they had intended to come after him in the morning, even if it meant fighting ghosts. He led them back to the treasure chamber, and then they set out, each man with two ingots, or a total of four thousand pounds of gold. After a journey of thirty days (or so Burroughs says) they were back in their country. Here Tarzan led them deep into the mangani country before sending them back to their village. He buried the ingots in the Dum-Dum amphitheater and went on to the coast. And there he saved Jane and Clayton by throwing a spear at a lion that was about to attack them. Just as he was going to step out and reveal himself, he saw Jane and Clayton embrace. Clayton was actually trying to hold Jane from falling to the ground because of her weakened condition, but Tarzan could not know that. Enraged, he aimed an arrow at Clayton. But he restrained the impulse, and, sadly, he went off without telling them who it was that had saved them.

Jane and Clayton, however, could have used his help. They were close to dying, and Thuran (Rokoff) was sick with fever in the little hut they had built. A few miles to the north, the other survivors of the sunken yacht were safe and healthy, camped at the site of the old cabin.

Chapter Thirteen

(II–23 through II–26)

Journeys' End

Atlantis has her sons and daughters.

—P. Lambert

Better than finding ancient Atlantis with
all its treasures is finding true love.

—P. J. Finnegan

Tarzan was deeply hurt, but even the wounded lover has to think
of other things than his wound. For one thing, he might not be
done yet with Opar. His Waziri had reported seeing fifty frightful
men while they were waiting for the dawn so they could go back
in after Tarzan. It was evident that the fifty were out looking for
him. The Flaming God had been cheated of a sacrifice, and they
must make good.

What he did not know was that they would find Jane and settle
for her.

One of the things that Tarzan pondered was La's story of the
origin of Opar. In the ruins of a city evidently built to hold many
more were only about four hundred to five hundred adults. He
had no idea how many children there were, but he had the
feeling that the Oparians were a dying nation and had very few
progeny. Moreover, their custom of making sacrifices from their
own number to the sun god when strangers weren't available would
eventually cause self-extermination. Tarzan had no idea how the
people fed themselves; they must have fields and some kinds of
domestic animals in the hilly country back of the city. They had

no commerce with other peoples, so most of the population would have to be busy with agriculture.

La had told Tarzan that Opar was the last of a number of cities in Africa built ten thousand years ago. These were populated by colonists from a land far away, beyond the seas. Opar and her sister cities had mined gold for the great mother island-state, but, one day, travel and communication between Opar and the mother country ceased. Ships went out, but they found only the sea where once had been a mighty land. The waters had swallowed it up in a mighty convulsion.

After that, it was all downhill for the colonies. One by one they succumbed to the black hordes from the north and the south, and then only Opar was left. And though it was, until now, safely hidden, it was dying.

Burroughs says that the mother land was Atlantis. But this is only a guess on his part. La never called it Atlantis. La's story contains as much of legend and myth as the story of Atlantis that the Egyptian priest told Solon and which Plato reported. There is no evidence at all that there was a continent in the Atlantic Ocean which sunk ten thousand years ago. Nor is there any evidence that man was in anything but a savage state ten thousand years ago.

Yet, there may well have been an "Atlantis." It would not be where Plato located it nor would his estimate of its time of existence be correct. It would be the ancient civilization of Crete, part of which was the island of Santorin, about seventy-eight miles from Crete. This island, the southernmost of the Sporades group, is notable for violent volcanic activity even in historic times. Evidence advanced by Professor Galanopoulos, Director of Seismology for Greece, indicates that this island may have been the religious center of the ancient Minoan civilization. Santorin blew up circa 1450 B.C. The explosion not only covered, where it did not destroy, the temples and houses on Santorin, but it created a great tidal wave, or tsunami, which roared across the sea to Crete, being sixty feet high when it struck and destroyed the Minoan civilization.

Professor Galanopoulos believes that Solon erred in translating the figures given him by the Egyptian priest for the time of destruction of Atlantis. Plato, who passed on that account of his collateral ancestor Solon, gives 9500 B.C. But the Egyptian sign for 100 was mistakenly translated by Solon, and perpetuated by

Plato, as 1000. Considering the time when Solon was told about Atlantis, and the error in the translation, the time was actually 1450 B.C. This agrees with the carbon-14 dating given the explosion by the scientists today.

Other evidence ties in Plato's detailed description of Atlantis to Santorin and Crete.

Thus, if Opar's homeland was the Santorin-Cretan state, it would have been destroyed about 2,360 years before, not 10,000. The Oparians were as prone to myth-making as the outside world, and additional evidence for that is La's tale of the destroying black hordes. In 1450 B.C. it is doubtful that there were many, and perhaps there were no, Negroes in central Africa. The sub-Saharan part of the continent was very thinly populated by Bushmen, Hottentots, and pygmies. The great Negro migrations into central and south Africa did not begin until about the first centuries of the Christian era and were still going on in the late eighteenth century in south Africa. As we have seen, the Waziri were the last people to leave the Bantu homeland in the upper Niger country.

Negroes are, theoretically, the latest race to be developed in Homo sapiens, and no one yet is certain where they came from. If they originated in Africa, how did they get to New Guinea and Melanesia without leaving traces of their passage behind them in Asia? And if they developed in New Guinea, or possibly in south Asia, how did they get to Africa with no evidence of their migration?

Atlantis can't be dismissed as mere myth. The Egyptians were not the only people to know of it. Its story was current in folk legends along the Atlantic seaboard from Gibraltar to the Hebrides and among the Yorubas of west Africa. If it was not Crete and Santorin that formed the basis of this legend, then it might have been the civilized people living in ancient times to the west of Lake Tritonis in Libya. Water swept this civilization away, either from a catastrophic rainfall such as caused the floods that destroyed much of Mesopotamia (and gave rise to the story of Noah), or it was a high tide with great winds such as washed away much of Holland in the twelfth and thirteenth centuries and formed the Zuider Zee.

Whichever event happened, there is strong evidence that there was an "Atlantis."

After giving all the above, I regret to say that Santorin-Crete could not possibly have been the Oparian mother-state. Even the highly developed civilization of the Minoans could not have penetrated into inland central Africa, built the massive city and dug the mines, and then opened and kept open the extremely long trade routes to the Indian Ocean and up the African coast to the Mediterranean. Besides, the Oparians obviously have no Minoan origins in their cultural features. And there is La's story that Opar was on, or near, the great sea.

A theory advanced by John Harwood and Frank J. Brueckel, however, satisfies most of the criteria established by La's story.

In the first place, La herself never calls the mother-city Atlantis. This name comes from Burroughs' inference. It is true that the old Englishman in Volume IX (*Tarzan and the Golden Lion*), speaks of it as Atlantis. It's reasonable to suppose that he made the same mistaken inference or that Burroughs did not report his words accurately.

If La's story is anywhere near true, the mother-city was at its peak of glory and grandeur when Near Eastern man was just beginning to grow crops and domesticate animals and settle in small villages. The pre-Oparians were probably Cro-Magnons who founded the first civilization about ten thousand years ago. At this time, as geological evidence suggests, a vast inland sea spread over almost all of what was the Belgian Congo and French Equatorial Africa in 1912.

To the north was another huge and shallow inland sea. The relatively small remnant of it is today Lake Chad. Ten millennia ago, the Chad Sea covered an area as large as, if not larger than, the Caspian Sea of several centuries ago. The Sahara was not then a desert but was a green plain with many rivers and trees and much animal life only found today south of the Sahara.

Brueckel and Harwood postulate a single continuous body of water formed by the two seas. This would have extended from central Sahara down to Katanga and northern Rhodesia. The two seas may, however, have been separated by an easily traversed, or canalized, strait. In any event, they suppose a large island near the northern shore of the great and shallow northern sea. For convenience, I'll call the mother-city of the island Chadea and the single great sea the Chadean.

Chadea is what Burroughs called Atlantis.

Chadea established a number of colonies, including the city of Opar. The latter was the only one to survive when the great earthquakes and consequent tsunamis tumbled and crushed and deluged the others. It was left standing, and the jungle soon surrounded it, and the degeneration of the citizens began.

If this happened about 10,000 B.C., or perhaps even earlier, then the black hordes which La claimed threatened Opar would not have existed. It would be thousands of years before any Negroes penetrated into this section of central Africa.

This is easily accounted for. At one time in Opar's decline, after the waters had cut channels out of the basins and had drained out to the ocean, some black invaders did give the city some trouble. The story of this became magnified and distorted with the passage of millennia.

Burroughs also says that the Oparian males were apish in bone structure, although the women were splendidly human. He accounts for this with a story of a mixture of mangani and human genes. The custom was to kill all females with simian characteristics and all males who looked too human. I doubt that this form of genetic selection would have done anything except reduce the population even more than sacrifice to the sun.

Brueckel and Harwood account for the brutish features of the male by postulating a sex-linked gene complex. An abnormal Y chromosome could have spread through the isolated and inbred Oparians. It may have come from hybridization of Oparians with neanderthals or an even earlier type of man. These would have been in the area around Opar in the beginning. These may have been enslaved by Oparian humans and freed later on.

The intelligent Bolgani that Tarzan was to encounter later (Volume IX, Golden Lion) could not have been true gorillas or even great apes. They were undoubtedly the dwindling remnants of a pithecanthropoid species; they had enough intelligence to emulate their long-dead masters in working in gold. But their second contact with a true man, Tarzan, in this case, was to end in their extermination.

Tarzan was also to be involved with the degenerate black slaves of the Bolgani of the Palace of Diamonds. That is, he did if they were not an exotic element added by Burroughs. According to Harwood and Brueckel, the mountains around Opar could be relatively abundant in uranium salts and so have caused mutations among the originally quite fine human specimens of the slave-miners.

That is possible. It is also possible that the pithecanthropoid Bolgani had fathered enough hybrids to have established the low-browed long-armed traits of the gomangani slaves. The small brain power of the slaves may not have been due to genetic factors, though. It may have resulted from the cultural environment. The Bolgani kept the blacks in a terrible state of fear and awe and weeded out the intelligent among them.

A strong objection to the theory about the Negro slaves of the ancient Oparians and Bolgani is that Negroes were not in central Africa at the required time. It's not necessary to postulate that the Oparians ever had black slaves. But where did the pithecanthropoid Bolgani of the Palace of Diamonds get *their* Negro slaves?

I suspect that these were not true Negroes but a separate race, like the Hottentots and Bushmen. They would have been con-temporaries of the Hottentots and Bushmen who preceded the true Negro in central Africa. If this is so, then they may have been used as slaves by the Oparians, too. But after Opar was isolated, they either fled into the jungle or were absorbed into the Caucasoid population. It is also possible that the ancestors of the slaves of the Bolgani were, in fact, Hottentots or Bushmen. The simian traits were derived from hybridization by their masters.

Before I go on to other matters, another puzzling feature of the Oparians must be dealt with. That is the absence of bows and arrows among them. These are unknown also among the peoples whom Brueckel and Harwood speculate are descended from refugees from sunken Chadea. The Cathneans, Athneans, Xujans, and Kavurus, whom you'll meet later, don't have bows.

My theory is that these peoples refused to use the bow because of some religious tabu. This existed from the beginning of Chadean culture. It has persisted since, even in the cultures of descendants remote in time and distance from the original great mother-state.

As for the loot, three trips would eventually be made to Opar, though not all the looting was done by Tarzan. The gross amount taken out would be approximately $3,617,241.60, figuring at the pre-1934 value of gold, if John Harwood's estimates are correct. The first visit got Tarzan over a million dollars, on which he probably never paid any tax.

Tarzan, on his way back to the Waziri after seeing Jane and

Clayton, came across his old mangani tribe. He decided to stay with them. At heart, he was a mangani, not a man. The Waziri were too far up the ladder of evolution for him. Even the seemingly static mangani, however, suffered change. Their chief had fallen off a broken limb to his death. This would have been Taug, his old friend. And since Teeka is not mentioned, it is safe to surmise that she, too, was dead. Nature offered a certain kind of freedom, but there was nothing soft about Her.

Tarzan had difficulty meshing back into the old life. His conscience hurt him because he had allowed his jealousy and anger to make him abandon Jane. One day, by accident, a mangani told him about witnessing Jane's abduction by Oparians looking for Tarzan. He set off at top speed for Opar through the trees where the closed canopy was thick enough to bear his weight and on the ground when it was not. How he rescued her, and La's grief at his leaving her, are detailed in Volume II.

Tarzan and Jane returned to the hut and found that Thuran had abandoned Clayton, who was dying of a fever. Tarzan's cousin confessed that he had known all along that Tarzan was the true heir to the lordship of Greystoke. He had read the telegram when it had dropped out of Tarzan's coat pocket in the Milton Junction railroad station.

At the cabin of his birth, Tarzan and Jane, with four Waziri carrying Clayton's corpse, met Tennington's party. Rokoff had found his way to the party but had said nothing about his desertion of Clayton. He tried to shoot Tarzan, but Tennington knocked the gun aside, and Rokoff was taken into custody. D'Arnot's ship had stopped off to look the cabin over again, and the French had discovered the Tennington party.

Professor Porter, an ordained minister, married his daughter to the new Lord Greystoke. Hazel Strong and Baron Tennington were married with them. And so Tarzan, on the stern of the small French warship, watching his Waziri shake their spears in farewell, tells Jane, "I should hate to think that I am looking upon the jungle for the last time, dear, were it not that I know that I am going to a new world of happiness with you."

By which we know that Tarzan's English was considerably more fluent than that of a year before, that he was still inclined to a form of speech he had learned from Victorian novels, and that he had renounced the jungle forever.

Chapter Fourteen

(Between II and III)

The Great Trek and the Elixir

> The god Ruwa had decreed that men should change
> their skins like the snake and become young
> when they had attained a great age.
>
> —Djaga tale, Kilimanjaro

> I will eat of it and return to the condition of
> my youth.
>
> —Sumerian tale of Gilgamesh

John Clayton, Lord Greystoke, lived in England for a while after
marrying Jane. This was his first time on the island, yet he was
expected to take over duties and obligations and generally behave
as if he had been born and raised there. He had much to learn, so
much that he thought he could never do it. But Jane, her father,
and the Tenningtons helped him. He also got a man-servant, Jervis,
who instructed him in many things that a mere servant could not
have been expected to know. It was Jervis who later became the
foreman of the Greystoke plantation in Kenya. He was of the same
splendid caliber as Bunter, the servant of Tarzan's cousin, Lord
Peter Wimsey. If Burroughs had written any volumes dealing with
Greystoke's domestic adventures, we may be sure we would have a
portrait of Jervis to equal Sayer's Bunter.

Tarzan spent much time in the Greystoke house in London, and
he even joined the Stylites and Linguist's clubs. He led a quiet
life, however, partly due to his own tastes and partly to avoid
publicity. Jane had told him that if the full story of his life came

out, he would be hounded forever by journalists, movie men, cranks, and nosey Parkers of all types. At her suggestion, he spent some of the Oparian gold on well-chosen people, and his story was suppressed. It was impossible to keep it altogether from the press, since the heir of a dukedom doesn't pop up from nowhere and escape all notice. But much was kept hidden, and some was distorted, and no one outside his immediate circle of friends knew that he was Tarzan. Nor did anyone ever find out who the duke really was when an American writer got hold of his story. Burroughs respected Tarzan's wishes and presented only a partial story and put in more than enough romance and fantasy to convince many that it was really fiction.

Milord Greystoke did not sit in the House of Lords until late 1912, and his maiden speech, like so many of his, was short and to the point. Thereafter he stayed away from Parliament. He had enough trouble governing the affairs of his own estates.

He visited the ancestral mansion and castles, of course. He stayed at Westerfalcon Hall of Chamston-Hedding, North Riding, Yorkshire. He inspected the ruined castle of the barons of Grebson of Grebson. He visited the family tombs outside the ruined church of the deserted village of Grebson. He looked at the stone effigies of his medieval ancestors in their armor. His father-in-law pointed out their differences. Those lying with their legs crossed did so to indicate they had been on the Crusades. Those with their feet on lions had died in battle. Those with effigies of hounds had died in peacetime.

Professor Porter knew more about his son-in-law's ancestors than his son-in-law or his English relatives. He showed him the Greystoke section in Burke's *Peerage* and told him many things that Burke had not included.

"Outside of the royal family, nobody has a more illustrious lineage, my boy," the old man said. "Nor can His Majesty trace his forebears as far back as you can. You have many heroic men in your family tree. You also have some rotten apples. But, then, what family doesn't, even the noblest? Or perhaps I should say, especially the noblest?"

Tarzan saw the arms of his ancestors, their effigies and tombs and monuments, and the paintings in Westerfalcon Hall, Brecon-castle in Wales, and Pemberley House in Derbyshire. His ancestors looked down at him, and he returned their gazes impassively.

There was the pale face and big curved nose and long bright red beard of his great-uncle, the sixth duke. There was his grandfather, the fierce old individualist and nonconformist whom Shaw called "an unsocial Socialist," though the painting was of him as a young man, and he looked quite handsome with his reddish-brown beard and keen grey eyes. By his side was the painting of Athena Darcy, the fifth duke's wife. She was so beautiful that it was difficult to believe that she had gotten old and died. Her skin had a bright olive tone and seemed to have golden mica in its composition. Her eyes and hair were a hazelnut color, and her upper teeth, displayed in a smile, were like fine Portland stone, though they sloped outwardly enough to have spoiled her mouth if they had not been supported by a rich underlip and a finely curved impudent chin.

"Frederic Leighton did superbly well when he painted her, dontcha know?" Bunny, Tarzan's cousin, had said. "Seems to me, by the way, that you've inherited her skin color. And, speaking of old Leighton, you should see sometime his portrait of your distant cousin, Sir Richard Francis Burton. Hangs in the National Gallery, dontcha know, and if he were twenty years younger and didn't have that beastly mustache and forked beard and the ghastly old cheek scar, he and you could jolly well pass for twins, what? Except you're not so grim, old fellow."

"Your grandfather caused your beautiful grandmother much unhappiness," the professor said. "Though she knew what sort of wild radical he was when she married him; she knew he'd left his first wife, her own cousin, and she'd died of a broken heart, or so some say. She tried to keep up with him, even lived with him in the East End mews, but she couldn't see bringing up her son—your father—as a workingman's son. So she left her husband and went back to Westerfalcon Hall, and they seldom saw each other again. Shaw remarked that your grandfather said that he was 'just mad enough to be a mountebank.' He was mad, all right, but I don't know about his being a mountebank. What did he have to gain by giving up his life as a noble and making his own living as, among other things, a cabdriver? He was doing it for a Cause, true, but he embittered and grieved his wife and made his son hate him. Very strange man. And then there's his death, as strange as his life."

"Yaas," Bunny drawled. "He was murdered, dontcha know?

Caused a frightful row then, and I heard his cousin, the Great
Detective, was called in. But nothing official ever came of it. However, when your cousin William died, we found among his father's
papers some letters and notes that seem to clarify matters."

Tarzan's interest rose when he learned that his father and mother
had been involved. In fact, he had been, too, though he was
present only as a passenger in his mother's womb.

His father's diary had given the details of their trip on the
Fuwalda and their marooning after the mutiny. His father had had a
high opinion of Black Michael, the mutineers' leader, because he
had saved their lives. Also, Black Michael had promised to tell
the authorities where the Claytons were, so they could pick them up.
But the wreckage of the *Fuwalda* had been found on St. Helena,
and it was presumed the ship had gone down with all hands.

This, however, was not entirely true. The ship had been sailed
to the island of St. Helena, where Black Michael cut off some
pieces of the vessel and cast it ashore. His plan worked, because
when the wreckage was found some months later, the authorities
believed that the ship was lost at sea. The *Fuwalda* had then been
sold to a smuggler in Dakar. He, in turn, had agreed to slip them
through illegal channels into England. But Black Michael knew
that as long as any of his shipmates were on the loose, he would
be in danger of being betrayed by them. If he had had any doubts
to begin with, they had been dismissed by the drunkenness of his
companions. They were bound to talk, sooner or later. And he
was already in hiding from others and could not afford to be
doubly imperiled.

He arranged with the smuggler to get rid of his companions.
Whether the mutineers were sold into slavery in interior Africa, or
had their throats cut, was not known. In fact, the fate of the other
mutineers was only surmised from what was known of Black
Michael's efforts after he got back to England.

Black Michael kept his word—to a certain extent. He did notify
an authority that he knew where the Claytons were. But the authority
was the fifth duke of Greystoke, John Clayton, father of the man
stranded on Gabon. For fifty thousand pounds, Black Michael
would give the father the proper latitude and longitude. The duke
apparently lost his temper and attacked Black Michael, who had
met him in his lodgings in Marylebone Borough. The duke was a
powerful man, but he was fifty-four years old and had been driving

a cab for eight years, an occupation not suited for keeping a man in top condition. The very powerful Black Michael was forty-four years old and had been working as a common seamen for some years. Moreover, he carried a knife, and Clayton was unarmed. Black Michael left a dead man behind him; he made sure of that. The eccentric duke was a very stubborn and unreasonable man, and he would have told the authorities everything.

Black Michael thought that the duke's younger brother, who would now become the sixth duke, might be more reasonable. Black Michael would give William Cecil Clayton two propositions. First, he would ask for money for revealing the location of the sixth duke's nephew. His grace might refuse to do this. Under cover of rejecting dealings with criminals, he could act morally and at the same time assure that he would keep his titles and estates. In which case, Black Michael would demand money for *not* telling the authorities.

The sixth duke, however, was an honorable man. He agreed to pay the sum to Black Michael, even though it meant that he would lose much. The life of his nephew and his wife were more important to him than all the honors and estates, of which, however, he had plenty in his own right. The seaman, playing a dangerous game, allowed his greed to get the better of him (especially since he had enough money to comfortably keep him the rest of his life). He asked for seventy-five thousand pounds.

This angered the duke, who, after all, came of a stubborn breed. Moreover, though he had clashed with his brother, and even tried to get him certified insane, he felt strongly about his death. And he had guessed that Black Michael was the murderer. So he hired several private detectives, but not, alas, the best in England. They were to trap the blackmailer murderer. But he got away and apparently gave up further interest in the Claytons.

(For the theory that Black Michael was the same as the Black Peter Michael Carey described by Watson, see Addendum 4.)

The sixth duke never told the authorities about Black Michael. He could not afford any prying into his affairs by the journalists or police, since he had an illegitimate son who had fled the country because he was wanted for complicity in murder. No doubt, the duke had aided his beloved son in his escape.

Very probably if he had thought that there was a good chance of finding his nephew, he would have acted even if the consequences would be injurious. But nothing was to be gained as long as Black Michael could not be found.

Tarzan delved into his ancestors and the duties he would have as lord of many lands and tenants. Much was expected of him; his life would be taken up with petty details if he handled his business personally.

He went down to Pemberley House, near Bakewell, which he had inherited from his dead cousin. (He was to sell it later, and it was torn down sometime in the thirties.) He also visited his relatives, including those at Sigerside and Tennington, and he made at least one visit to his relative the second duke of Westminster, at Chester as noted in *Tarzan the Terrible*.

He toured much of England. He loved the Lake District, when it was not raining, and enjoyed his stay with his relatives, the Howards. These were the occupants of Greystoke Manor, and, like him, descended from the de Greystocks of Cumberland. But he was appalled by the grey, grimy, dismal factory cities of Manchester and Liverpool. What he learned of the lives of the factory workers enabled him to understand his grandfather's strong reactions. But he had no desire to emulate him. Why didn't the workers change things for themselves? Why didn't they just rise up and kill their overlords? He would not put up with such a life, if such could be called a life.

"The workingman's conditions are far better now than they were when your grandfather was a young man," Jane said. "And they are better because of what men like your grandfather did."

"It takes too long," Tarzan said, wrinkling his face with disgust. The odors of industry would kill him off if he stayed long in their neighborhood.

"They are civilized, and you are not, my jungle man," Jane said. "Besides, if they did sweep out into the streets, and if they killed the police and the soldiers, instead of being killed, then they would take away your titles and your lands and your money."

Tarzan shrugged. If that happened, he would go back to Africa. He wished—almost—that that would happen.

He had been born and raised without a past, and, suddenly a great burden of history and duties was strapped upon him. He did not like it, and if it had not been for Jane, he would not have wasted another day in getting out of England. But, for her, he would shed his ape-man self as Histah shed his old skin.

He was very intelligent and adaptable. Still, the habits of twenty-one years could not be dropped as easily as an opera cloak. There was the time when he and Jane were walking on the vivid green lawn before Westerfalcon Hall, just after the rain had ceased and the sun had come out again. He had squatted down to pluck a blade of the grass and look at the glinting drops of water on it. Jane was talking merrily of the peculiar behavior of one of Tarzan's eccentric cousins, when she suddenly stopped. He looked up at her and saw that her face was pale and twisted. With one hand, she pointed at him.

He stood up, swallowed the worm, and said, "What's the matter?" Not until then did he realize what he had absent-mindedly done.

It was some time before he had retrained himself so that, when in a "civilized" environment, his "civilized" self took over. He had to create a dual nature for himself and to teach each the proper "signals" for taking over from the other. Meanwhile, it was not easy. The customs of the mangani regarding eating, excretion, sexual matters, and an endless etcetera, often differed widely from civilized man's. He did not understand why Jane and others were so repulsed or even horrified by certain of his actions and reactions. He thought of differences among peoples as being, basically, interesting, not disgusting. Still, civilization had many things which appalled and repulsed him, so it was only natural that he should, in turn, sometimes appall and repulse the civilized.

But Jane was intelligent, and she loved him deeply, and she knew that he was not really happy here. Jane arranged for secretaries, solicitors, and business managers to remove from him all but the inescapable duties. And she told him that she would be happy only if he were happy. She proposed that they return to Africa to live.

His birthplace, Gabon, was too unhealthy for her and the new baby, due about May 20, 1912. But the high plateau of interior Kenya was cool and healthy. They could buy land there and establish a plantation near the savannas. There would be great herds of antelopes, zebras, elephants, prides of lions, and lone leopards there. And they would also be near the mountains of the west, where the rain forests were and where gorillas, and possibly the mangani, roamed. Tarzan could bring his black tribesmen there, and they would rename the territory Uziri, the land of the Waziri.

Tarzan did not argue with her. He believed that she meant what she said, and he was right in doing so. He left Jane in London with Baron Tennington, Hazel, Professor Porter, Mr. Philander, and Esmeralda. She would have plenty of company.

Back in the jungle of the Gabon, Tarzan felt as happy as Puss with a new supply of catnip. He wandered around for a while and then looked up his old tribe of mangani. It was while he was with them that he got the idea of taking them on the great trek across central Africa to East Africa. Normally, he would have had trouble in getting them to leave, but the survivors of the people of Mbonga had come back, and the dead warriors had been replaced by a group of fugitive slaves adopted into the tribe. Since the natives had renewed their war against the mangani, the mangani were willing to listen to Tarzan. He wanted to take them with him for, it must be admitted, partly selfish reasons. He would settle them in the Ruwenzori, the Mountains of the Moon, or the Uganda mountains, and thus he'd be able to visit them from time to time.

Removing an entire tribe from French Equatorial Africa, taking it through the Belgian Congo and the German East African territory, and settling it in British territory could have led to international complications. But Tarzan had learned the value of money early, and he spread enough around to various officials so that the authorities back in Europe heard nothing to trouble them. Or, if they did, they could be pacified with gold, too.

He paid for the passage of the Waziri and the mangani on a ship down the coast to the mouth of the Congo River (originally called the Zaire). They took several boats up the great stream, bypassing Stanley Falls and others on foot where necessary. Leaving the Congo, they progressed southward in a great curve on the Lualaba River in eastern Congo, using dugouts where larger boats were unavailable. (It was during this trip that some of the Waziri became reasonably proficient in the mangani speech.) Near the present village of Poma, the two tribes cut straight across the jungle, through the territory of their old enemies, the Manyuema. They crossed the mountains between Lake Kivu and Lake Tanganyika and then walked through the northwestern corner of German East Africa, south of Lake Victoria. (This lake, by the way, is about the size of Ireland or the state of Illinois.) It was during this time that Tarzan learned his excellent German. The long, and, it must be admitted, rather peculiar, safari passed through what is now Serengeti National Park, through the Masai tribes, and on up to western Kenya.

Jervis had built a low rambling bungalow in the heart of Uziri and laid out the fields where coffee, maize, and sisal were to be grown. (But not by the Waziri men, who, like their enemies, the Masai, were too proud to work as laborers. The field hands were imported from coastal tribes.) South of the land of the Waziri was a chain of rough and precipitous mountains. At its foot was a great plain where immense herds of antelope and zebra roamed and where the giraffe and the elephant were numerous and where the lion, the leopard, the hyena, and the wild dog preyed each in his own fashion. Here, too, was the buffalo, more dangerous than the lion, as Tarzan himself admitted. The plantation was several days' journey from the railhead. The first locomotive had reached Lake Victoria (Victoria Nyanza) on December 26, 1901, and the permanent railroad was completed by March, 1903. The railways, by doing away with transportation of goods by men, helped kill off the slave trade. It also ended the raids of the Masai, who had terrorized a good part of western Kenya. Despite this, there were many native wars and several uprisings in the years to follow.

Tarzan led the mangani (with a Waziri guard) to the forest of the Uganda highlands. Here he said hail and farewell to them. He would see them again, more than once, though not always in the same place. Apparently, the tribe, once having tasted travel, desired more. They were to move around for great distances in the future.

Tarzan then set out for his plantation to check on its progress before going on the railroad to Mombasa and from thence back to England.

During his return trip, while he was still in Uganda, something happened that was so important he delayed his journey for over a month. He saved a witch doctor from a lion, and the grateful man told him that he would share with him a great secret, in fact, the greatest secret in the world. This was a treatment which would keep Tarzan young forever, barring accident, homicide, or suicide.

Tarzan was skeptical. The doctor asked Tarzan how old he thought he was. Tarzan said that he seemed to be in his twenties. The doctor then took Tarzan to his village and asked the chief, a very old man, how long he had known him. The chief said that he had known him all his life and that no one knew how old the doctor really was. But the doctor had known Tippoo Tib's grandfather.

Tippoo Tib was the chief Arab trader of the eastern Congo area and an associate of Stanley. He was born in the 1840s or possibly the 1830s. Thus, if the witch doctor knew Tib's grandfather, he was living circa 1790 or even earlier.

Tarzan accepted the offer to share in the "perpetual youth." The process required thirty days of drinking vile brews, going through many religious rituals, and being transfused with several quarts of the doctor's blood. Tarzan regretted having let himself in for the tedious business, which was probably all nonsense. Still, he couldn't afford to take a chance that the doctor wasn't telling the truth. His claim did seem to be valid. But only Time would tell. If he didn't age, then he would, indeed, be immortal. Or, at least, would live far longer than most mortals.

And so Tarzan, without knowing the chemical make-up of the liquids he had drunk, went back to Uziri. After checking on the progress there, he left Jervis in charge and took the train to Mombasa on the coast. From there he took a ship back to England and to Jane, who was expecting a baby.

Chapter Fifteen

(III)

The Beasts

Who can talk to the animals is second only to Mulungu.

—Waziri saying

Burroughs was being satiric when he titled Volume III of the biography *The Beasts of Tarzan*. Though there is much about the animal allies of the ape-man in it, the savagery is mostly in the human beings. Burroughs makes evident the difference between beastliness and beastness.

In May, the first rainy season of the Kenyan highlands is at its height. The Claytons had left their Uziri plantation two months earlier to avoid the rains, not for themselves but for the sake of the baby. Little John Paul was born May 20, a Monday, 1912, at Greystoke House in Carlton House Terrace in London. Though the greatest physicians of England were available, the baby was ushered into the world by the hands of Esmeralda and Tarzan himself. To him, birth was as common as death, and he had seen so many accouchements that he felt quite qualified. Jane was healthy, the antiseptic rules were observed, and, after a labor without anesthetic, the baby was eased into the world from the womb.

A month later, Tarzan took a trip to Paris to visit his old friend, d'Arnot. There he got two pieces of bad news in rapid succession. His old enemy Rokoff had been given a life sentence to be served in a French military prison, but he had escaped. And while Tarzan was digesting this sour news, he was handed a telegram from Jane. Young Jack had been kidnaped.

Tarzan sped home, but Rokoff had set his traps well. Both Tarzan and Jane became prisoners on Rokoff's ship. After three weeks, Tarzan was marooned, naked and unarmed, on an island. As the ship sailed away, Tarzan saw Rokoff holding his baby Jack high above him. The note Rokoff had given him told of what the Russian, aided by Paulvitch, planned for his son. Rokoff also had plans for Jane, but these, he said, he would leave to Tarzan's imagination.

He could do nothing about Rokoff, so he set out to explore his island. That it was fairly large was obvious, since it supported lions and leopards and a small tribe of great apes. It was out in the sea opposite the mouth of the Ugambi River. This could not be Burroughs' name for the Gambia, which flows 450 miles through west Guinea and the Senegal into the Atlantic in Gambia. There are no large islands, such as Tarzan was left on, off this part of the west African coast. Evidence (a British sloop-of-war cruising the coast) indicates that this was British territory. The Gambia must have been one of the many mouths of the Niger River. The islands off its mouths do not hold lions or great apes or large antelopes. But it is evident that a ship carrying the big cats, antelopes, and a dozen great apes to zoos was wrecked on this island. The beasts got loose, and the crew rowed away or were killed by the cats and the apes. If Tarzan had been marooned there a few months later, he would have found the big animals dead, having starved or killed each other.

He established, for the first time, a friendship with Sheeta, the leopard, whom he rescued from a fallen tree. And he made a lifelong friend, and admirer, of Akut, a very intelligent mangani. Another addition to his strange crew was Mugambi, chief of the Wagambi of the land of Ugambi, far up the river. Mugambi and his men had landed on the island, and only Mugambi had survived when the blacks attacked Tarzan's crew. But he was spared, and he became a lifelong friend of the white demon-god of the forest.

Jane enlisted the sympathies of the Swedish cook of the ship, Sven Anderssen. (From the -sen, he was probably a Swede of Danish descent.) Sven was a repulsive-looking man, but his ugliness concealed a beauty of heart. He got Jane and the baby out of the ship, and they fled up the Ugambi with Rokoff and party in pursuit.

Meanwhile, Tarzan, Mugambi, Sheeta, Akut, and twelve great apes managed to get to the mainland. After many adventures, Tarzan found Anderssen. He was dying, having sacrificed himself that Jane and the baby might get a chance to escape. In a very moving description of Anderssen's death, Burroughs brings out the patheticalness and also the nobility of the ugly cook.

Jane had discovered, shortly after leaving the ship, that the baby was not hers. She had no way of knowing that Jack had been replaced by another baby, but Rokoff apparently thought it was hers. The baby died of a fever, and she sorrowed over it, yet she was glad that it was not little Jack. Nor did she tell Rokoff that someone had tricked him.

As she found out later, Paulvitch had learned the lessons of treachery and unfaithfulness so well from Rokoff that he had double-crossed him the first chance he got. But his confederate in London had, in turn, double-crossed him, for money, of course. Jack was already home and in the care of Esmeralda.

The hunt after Rokoff was long, and Tarzan was often frustrated. But the arch-villain met a horrible death, though not a useless one, since he provided a meal for Sheeta. Paulvitch escaped, and he was to reappear again in Tarzan's life—perhaps.

Jane fell into the hands of mutineers from another ship, the *Cowrie*, but Tarzan rescued her and snapped the neck of her would-be rapist. He was tired of letting off evil men only to have them return more evil for his mercy. Three days later, the *Cowrie* met the British coastal cruiser, *Shorewater*, and Tarzan and Jane went on it to civilization. They landed at Dover in late September, 1912.

Mugambi was to remain with Tarzan (he had saved Tarzan's life) and he would be initiated into the Waziri tribe later.

Tarzan and Jane had received the news, via wireless, that their son was safe in Greystoke House, but they were impatient to hold him again. At least, this is what we are told in Volume III, but there is a reasonable doubt that events happened exactly as reported.

Chapter Sixteen

(IV, 1–12; XX)

Problems

What the left hand gets, the right hand loses.

—Waziri saying

One day, God asked the first human couple if they
wanted the death of the banana or the moon.

—Madagascar tale

Volume IV, *The Son of Tarzan*, was one of my favorite Tarzan
stories when I was a lad. At the age of fifty-three, I haven't
changed my opinion. It's a rattling good story even if it is not
quite true to life. Burroughs has mixed much fiction with the fact.
But, first, the tale of Tarzan's son as Burroughs tells it.

Young Jack is on vacation from school (undoubtedly the Priory
School near Pemberley House, Derbyshire). Whether this is a
regular vacation or a special one, perhaps caused by the death
of the school head, we do not know. Jack is ten years old and
strong enouch to subdue and tie up his private, and very harassed,
tutor during his "jungle games." Jack has inherited his father's
cravings for the savage life, according to his mother, Jane. She
comments on Tarzan's struggles to repress his desires for his old life.

Tarzan replies that such a thing can't be transmitted, and he is
right, of course. Jack is only acting as any normal boy with a vivid
imagination would act. That he is about twice as strong as most
boys his age is due to heredity. Jack wants to go see a trained
great ape, Ajax, at Gatti's-under-the-Arches at Charing Cross. Tarzan

forbids him. Jack says he'll go anyway and take his punishment. Tarzan smiles at this; the boy has his spirit and his honesty.

What Tarzan doesn't know is that his old enemy, Paulvitch, has been picked up by sailors off the Ugambi. After ten years of disease starvation, and torment in a cannibal village, Paulvitch is half-mad. He is so changed in appearance that Tarzan won't recognize him, and he is vengeance-bent. Rokoff's fate has taught him nothing about the futility of revenge.

Since the end of Volume III, *The Beasts of Tarzan*, took place circa September, 1912, Volume IV has to begin circa September, 1922.

Paulvitch, calling himself Sabrov, picks up Akut on the island where Tarzan left him. He names him Ajax and takes him to London with him. The *Marjorie W.*, the ship on which Paulvitch sailed, is a vessel chartered for a scientific expedition. It is strange that the zoologists aboard do not recognize Akut as belonging to a hitherto unknown species of primate or as a hominid. Perhaps one did but was too scientifically cautious to bring Akut to the attention of the world. However, Paulvitch claims Akut as his own property, and he permits no one to examine him too closely or to take Akut away from him. As for Akut, he accompanies Paulvitch because he is looking for Tarzan, and Paulvitch seems to be a vehicle for this search. Akut easily learns the tricks taught him by the Russian, and he becomes a great music-hall success.

Meanwhile, Sheik Amor ben Khatour has abducted Jeanne, seven-year-old daughter of Captain Armand Jacot of the French Foreign Legion. The sheik doesn't want her for ransom; he wants to keep her for revenge. He calls her Meriem, and, in time, she forgets French and her real name. Ben Khatour is making her life a hell in revenge for her father's failure to save ben Khatour's nephew from hanging. At the time Akut goes to London, Meriem is ten years old.

Jack falls in with Sabrov (Paulvitch) and Akut. Sabrov tries to kill Jack to avenge himself on Tarzan, but Akut kills Sabrov instead. Jack and Akut flee with Akut shaved, dressed up, and heavily veiled as Jack's crippled old grandmother. They take passage to Africa, and there stop off in a hotel in the port of Duala, then a part of the German Kamerum. It is not known how Jack and Akut got passports. Jack, however, has access to much money and he knows, even better than his father, what money can do. No doubt, being a very capable young person, he gets forged passports in the Lime-house district.

He is traveling under the name of Billings. Did he pick this name because he had heard it only recently, when his father told him the story of his life? And Jack remembered Captain Billings of the *Fuwalda*?

A crook by the name of Condon enters their room to steal their money. This had already dropped out of Jack's pocket into the sea, unknown to him. Akut kills Condon. Jack, believing himself doubly a murderer and penniless in a foreign land, takes to the jungle with Akut. Eventually, he rescues Meriem, and they wander the jungles for six years.

Jack and Meriem are sixteen years old when Volume IV ends and they get married. She had forgotten her real name when she had been separated from Jack (now calling himself Korak, mangani for "Killer"). Lord and Lady Greystoke were taking care of her on their Kenyan plantation and, in fact, were raising her as their own. Then Korak was found by Tarzan and reunited with his parents. Later, in London, Jacot, now a general, visits the Grey-stokes because His Lordship has been recommended as *the* African authority by Admiral d'Arnot. (This d'Arnot is the father of Tarzan's good friend.) Tarzan looks at the photograph of the seven-year-old girl, sees something familiar in it, and brings in Meriem. There is a happy reunion.

The next two volumes following *The Son of Tarzan* in sequence of events are *Tarzan the Untamed* and *Tarzan the Terrible*. Jack, or Korak, joins the British Royal Air Force at some time in World War I. He is at the battle of the Argonne, in October–November, 1918, and the following year he shows up to rescue his parents after traversing half of the worst part of Africa alone.

There is a strange time-expansion in Volume IV, *The Son of Tarzan*. How could Tarzan's son be born in 1912, run away in 1913, battle mangani, lions, black warriors, Arabs, and such, and, in 1918, fight on the Argonne front?

Various explanations have been offered. That Burroughs wrote Volume IV in the period from January 21, 1915, to May 11, 1915, is, however, the central and insurmountable fact. Everything in *The Son of Tarzan* had to take place before January, 1915. And we know, from Volumes VII and VIII, that the events of Volume IV had to take place before World War I started (August, 1914).

What we must not forget is that there is a fictional Tarzan and a real-life Tarzan. The fictional story is based on the man who does exist, but it contains omissions, additions, distortions, and romanticizations. Burroughs was, first and last, a storyteller, and he was under no obligation to present the strict truth. On the contrary, he had explicit orders from Lord Greystoke to make the life fictional here and there. Hence, the world got the chronologically impossible Volume IV and its sequels.

No harm was done by this. As fiction, the books are exciting. Those who are aware that they are not entirely true do not reject them. They enjoy the fiction, even knowing what is really taking place. They enjoy the books as both fiction and biography and are able to dissociate the two without strain.

As a reading of Addendum 2 will show, Tarzan's second cousins, Hugh Drummond and his younger brother, John, were orphans. Hugh was twenty at this time (1912). John was fourteen and a care to his brother. Hugh could not supervise his brother's behavior nor give him the affection he needed, since he was off on an adventure at that time.

John was tall and abnormally strong, like his brother, who would (in 1919) break a half-grown gorilla's neck with his fingers in his first recorded adventure. Unlike Hugh, John was handsome. Unlike blue-eyed Hugh he was also grey-eyed and looked much like his Clayton cousins. Jane, who was tenderhearted, easily talked Tarzan into adopting the orphaned John, and John loved the idea of having them as parents.

Sabrov, as Starr and Harwood suggest, could not have been Paulvitch. He was actually a man named Sabrov. At no time did he tell anyone that he was Paulvitch. Burroughs assumed this for the story purposes. It was much more satisfying to show Paulvitch getting it in the neck (literally) through the very means he was using for his revenge. The real Paulvitch, we may be sure, perished in the jungle in which he had intended to abandon Jane to a cannibal's mercy. Moreover, Tarzan would have recognized Paulvitch's body odor if he had been Sabrov.

It is true that Sabrov wanted revenge because "Tarzan had ruined him." But this ruin was Akut's refusal to go on the stage again after he found Tarzan. Sabrov blamed his loss of livelihood on Korak and Tarzan. Burroughs, of course, ignored young Jack, Tarzan's real son, in Volume IV.

John Drummond, hereinafter called Korak to distinguish him
from Tarzan's real son, did rescue Meriem from the Arabs. She had
been, as Burroughs says, their prisoner for three years. But she was
twelve or thirteen at this time. This would still make her thirteen or
fourteen when she was rescued by Tarzan a year later. However,
she had undoubtedly matured swiftly during her time in the jungle
and probably could pass for sixteen years of age in 1913. She
would not have forgotten her French or her identity in three years
unless she had gone through some very traumatic incidents. The
kidnaping and the brutal treatment she received (softened in Burroughs' version) caused an amnesia.

While Korak was still lost, Lady Jane took care of Meriem, and
Tarzan supervised the plantation. But the inevitable time came
when he felt that he had to get out into the wilds and become
Tarzan of the Apes again. Also, he told Jane that he still had not
given up hope for finding their adopted son. He would roam about
and seek for new clues.

The early months of 1913 were occupied with this search. During
this time, he had some adventures chronicled in Volume XX, many
years after they occurred, as *Tarzan and the Forbidden City*.

This story, like *The Son of Tarzan*, is part fiction and part fact.
Unlike the story of Korak, however, it seems to be mostly fiction.
It originally appeared in *Argosy* magazine, May 19, 1938, as *The
Red Star of Tarzan*. There is no doubt that someone other than
Burroughs wrote this or else rewrote it. The style is different; the
author is ignorant of past events in Tarzan's life; he portrays
Tarzan as more like the movie Tarzan than the true Tarzan. He
describes things that could not have happened. And there are other
problems with this volume. The writer does not seem aware that
"Kreeg-ah!" in great-ape speech is a warning, not a demand for, or
admission of, surrender. Lal Taask, a Hindu, swears by Allah, the
Mohammedan god. The mangani encountered are abnormally
belligerent. References to Baby Face Nelson and Dillinger, and the
type of airplane used, indicate the story occurs in 1934 or somewhat
later.

The book version is a hodgepodge, as if Burroughs, or someone,
had rewritten the magazine story but had done so very carelessly.
There is some evidence that the book was written as a basis for a
movie script. When it was published years afterwards, it was up-
dated with topical references. However, according to Vernell Coriell,

Hulbert Burroughs told him that it was possible that his father did not write the story at all. He may have hired a ghost writer to do it from an idea provided by Burroughs.

Be that as it may, in 1934-36 Edgar Rice Burroughs, Inc. did syndicate two radio serials titled *Tarzan and the Diamond of Asher* and *Tarzan and the Fires of Tohr*. The former was finally published in *Argosy* as *The Red Star of Tarzan* and in book form as *Tarzan and the Forbidden City*. All evidence indicates that Tarzan may have been in central Africa on a jungle vacation at the time this adventure was supposed to have occurred, but, otherwise, none of the events in Volume XX happened.

There are some good things about Volume XX. I especially like the ironic ending of the quest after the great treasure and Tarzan's final comment:

"Men are strange beasts."

In 1912, one of the few who knew Tarzan's real identity would have sent him a copy of the October *The All-Story Magazine*. This showed a wild-eyed man holding a spear in the background and, in the foreground, a muscular blond white man with his right arm around a lion's neck and the left hand bringing a big knife down toward the lion. In the lower right-hand corner of this stimulating scene: *Tarzan of the Apes, A Romance of the Jungle*.

The magazine (selling for only fifteen cents) contained the first version of the first volume of the biography of the ape-man. We do not have on record Tarzan's reactions when he read the story. No doubt he was puzzled, and perhaps angry, because of the errors and the wrong guesses in it. He was especially disturbed by the references to Sabor, the tiger. There are no wild tigers in Africa. And, in fact, Burroughs was so widely criticized for this zoological anomoly that he changed the tiger to a lioness for the hardcover version, which appeared in 1914. This explains why the lion family alone, in the epics, has different names for the male and female of the species. Numa the lion and his mate, Sabor.

What nobody realized was that Burroughs could not have made the error unless he did so on purpose. He had read the book by Stanley in which Stanley says there are tigers in south Africa. But a reading of other authors would have corrected this. In the case of *Tarzan of the Apes*, he went too far in trying to give the impression that he was writing fiction. People thought he was an ignoramus, and this would never do.

This and other discrepancies were explained to Tarzan through correspondence and, later, in person when Burroughs and Tarzan met. (The correspondence, by Tarzan's request, was not kept in Burroughs' files.) By then, Tarzan's only reaction to the books was amusement and a certain respect for Burroughs' storytelling powers. His main reaction to the Tarzan movies was, first, disgust, and then laughter.

Chapter Seventeen

(V; IV, 13–27)

The Waters of Lethe, the Jewels of Opar

A wound reveals the true man.

—Waziri saying

Dug out of the earth by man, they have sent many
a man into the earth.

—V. Oesterroecker

Tarzan returned about November, 1913, to his plantation to report
no success in his search for Korak. He had not been home long
when a French hunter, a M. Jules Frecoult, visited them. The
Frenchman was, in reality, a Belgian murderer and army deserter,
Lt. Albert Werper. Captured by a bandit Arab, Achmet Zek, he
had joined Zek's band. Zek then told him his plan to kidnap
Tarzan's wife and hold her for ransom. To do this, he needed a
European.

Werper overheard Greystoke tell his wife that they were financially
ruined. One of their business managers had been dishonest, and
the Greystokes were wiped out. He had to go to Opar again.
Three days later, he set out with fifty Waziri. That Burroughs
says they set out for the southeast means nothing. Any directions
and time of travel involved with the city of Opar given by Burroughs are purposely misleading.

Werper sent a message to Achmet Zek and followed Tarzan at a
discreet distance. His mental tongue slavered at the thought of the
wealth at the end of the trail.

Tarzan was happy again. He had taken his clothes off, and he
looked forward to several months of a relatively free life. Even this,

however, was not the full liberation he desired. He would be using a bow to bring down game instead of leaping on it with his knife. And he cooked his meat because the Waziri were less savage than he and would be disgusted to see him eat it raw.

"It was a woman's love which kept Tarzan . . . to the semblance of civilization."

But the call of the wild was too insistent, and he went out one night to make a kill as the precivilized Tarzan would have done. He killed a lion that had mauled an old witch doctor, and the man, before dying, warned him that a god greater than Tarzan would strike Tarzan down.

"Turn back, Munango-Keewati!" the old man said.

The doctor was one of Mbonga's people, a colleague of the late Rabba Kega. Since Opar is a long way from Mbonga's village, the old man must have fled to this area when the French sailors killed most of the males in the village. He fully expected Tarzan to slay him after he had the lion, and he was surprised that the devil-god had changed. His prophecy was made in gratitude, but, as Tarzan expected, it was false. He had little faith in priests of any kind. Part of this attitude no doubt derived from the histories he had read in his father's library; part, from a naturally skeptical mind.

Tarzan went on, sneaked into Opar, and brought out forty-eight ingots for his Waziri to carry. Werper followed him in when he was on his next-to-last trip. An earthquake or a cave-in of tunnels tumbled a stone on Tarzan's head and knocked him out for a while. (Perhaps the witch doctor did not prophesy falsely, after all. The Creator of earthquakes was the one greater than Tarzan who was to strike Tarzan down.)

During this time, Achmet Zek's raiders carried off Jane, leaving behind many of their own dead and many Waziri dead. But Mugambi, the giant black whom Tarzan had met after being marooned by Rokoff, followed the bandits, even though he was wounded.

Tarzan, mentally an ape-man again, escaped from the treasure chamber. He had forgotten everything that had happened after 1908. La of Opar thought he had returned to her, but he rejected her. Never one to suffer a slight, La ordered him killed. Tarzan fought his way out, Werper following. Later, Tarzan brought from his belt-pouch a handful of the huge cut diamonds he had taken from deep in the tunnels of the city. Werper waited for his chance and stole them.

It would be a long time before Tarzan recovered from his amnesia. This incident and a number that followed where he lost his memory indicates a deep-seated desire to return to the precivilized ape-man state. But his strong self-healing powers always brought him back out of the earlier self.

After many adventures, La captured Tarzan. She was going to sacrifice him to the Flaming God. However, if he would only tell her he loved her and promised to stay with her, she would find a way to save him. All that night, she begged him to love her. The account of her burning caresses and kisses and the frenzy of her passion is discreetly, but provocatively, told. Whatever Tarzan's physical response, he could not be blamed by even the most demanding of moralists. He did not remember Jane, and he was tied up and unable to resist anything that La did to him. But something kept him from telling her he loved her. Why he did not do so in the simple interests of self-preservation is a mystery. Possibly, being in an early mangani state, he did not know what love was. On the other hand, La was speaking to him in mangani, so she must have used the word for love, or mangani equivalent, if it exists.

"And Tarzan, untroubled by thoughts of the future, slept peacefully in La's embrace."

There is no doubt that La, like two other women in his life, played the role of the classical seductress to his hero. The seductress was that archetypal female who appears in so many dreams of men (according to Jung) and in so many myths of the hero and in legends and fairy tales. She existed as flesh and blood, of course, just as Tarzan did. But as he was the last of Nature's attempts to copy man's myths, so La was Nature's incarnation of the seductress. She was Nimue, Morgan le Fay, She-who-must-be-obeyed, Melisande, Circe, Calypso, Lilith, and a score of others.

How Jane got away from her captors, how Mugambi found her, how Tarzan regained his memory, and how Werper made compensation are all in Volume V. Eventually, Jane and Tarzan got their treasure and rebuilt the burned-down plantation. And Tarzan invested the gold after a deep investigation into the honesty of the investors to whom he was entrusting his fortune.

About February, 1914, Meriem was saved by Tarzan from rape by a poacher-bandit, Sven Malbihn. Tarzan did not kill him, con-

tenting himself with running him out of the territory. As he told
Muviri the Waziri, a new law had come in. It was not as in the old
days.

Tarzan took Meriem home, where Jane took care of her as if she
were her mother. Meriem knew only Arabic and mangani, but
there was no reason for her to bring up the great-ape experience.
Otherwise, Tarzan would have known that Korak was alive. Her
description of Korak and Akut would have left no doubt of that.

A visitor, the Honorable Morison Baynes, tried to run away with
Meriem. He intended to seduce her, but she fell into the hands of
Hanson, a trader. He was really Malbihn, who had insinuated himself as a guest at the Greystoke's for a while. He had shaved off his
beard, and he bathed frequently. Tarzan did not remember his
body odor because he had been with the man only for a few minutes
a year before. Meriem did not recognize him until too late.

One who did not fail to remember him, however, was Tantor.
Years before, Malbihn had killed his mate. Tantor, following
Korak into the Swede's camp, recognized him and took vengeance.
Meriem and Baynes were captured by the old sheik, Amor ben
Khatour. Korak, trying to rescue her, was captured and tied to a
stake. Tantor, after wreaking destruction upon the Arabs, lifted
Korak and the stake and carried him off. But the elephant could
not untie Korak, and Meriem, trying to do so, was charged by
Tantor. Then Tarzan dropped out of the trees and stopped Tantor.
Akut appeared, and the mangani, Tarzan, Korak, and Meriem
were reunited.

And, as Korak said, renouncing his wild life, "There is but one
Tarzan, there can never be another."

Korak and his mother had a tearful meeting. Later, Korak and
Meriem were married (even if she were only sixteen), and the
couple, with their parents, the Greystokes, went to London. It was
here that General Jacot came to Lord Greystoke and was rewarded,
a few minutes after stating his quest, with his daughter. That
Captain Jacot is, four years after his daughter's abduction, a
general, is due to Burroughs. He promoted him solely to give the
reader a sense of the passage of six years. However, Burroughs'
promotion was valid in that Jacot did become a general before
World War I ended.

A month later, Lord and Lady Greystoke returned to British
East Africa, leaving Meriem and Korak to visit her parents in

Paris. Meriem's mother was the lovely Englishwoman, Suzanne Fogg. There is some evidence that Suzanne was the daughter of the late Phileas Fogg of No. 7, Saville Row, Burlington Gardens, London, and of the late Aouda Jejeebhoy, a Parsee of Bombay. (I should say, she was the daughter of the man on whose trip Verne based his *Around the World in Eighty Days*.)

Some have speculated that Meriem and Korak were too young to rush into marriage unless they had an urgent reason. But, as far as we know, the two had no children until 1921. Jane may have had something to do with urging that their union be made legal. Though George V was king, his grandmother's influence was still strong; the storms of World War I had not yet battered it down. On the other hand, Jane was realistic-minded, and any faint traces of prudery in her had been knocked out since she had set foot in Africa. It seems more likely that it was love only that made the two lovers hurry into matrimony.

While in Africa, the Greystokes had been visited by two Americans, Barney Custer and his sister, Victoria, from Beatrice, Nebraska. Their mother had been a Rubinroth of the royal house of the little sovereign state of Lutha, on the Austrian and Serbian border. Burroughs relates Barney Custer's adventures prior to this time in the first part of *The Mad King*. Barney's mother's mother was a von Ruderfurd, a German form of the Scots-English name Rutherford. Several branches of this border family had migrated to the German states in the sixteenth century. In Samuel Rutherford's *Examen Arminianismi*, published at Utrecht in 1668, his name is changed into Rhetorfortis and was further changed by his continental contemporaries into Retorfortis. Among the Scots settlers in Prussia before 1644 the name appears as Routherfurd, Ritterfart, Rudderfoord, Ruthyfurd, Rwthirdfurde, and other variations. The first duke of Greystoke had married a Rubinroth (see Addendum 3), and a number of the younger branches of the Claytons had married their German Rutherford cousins.

The Mad King is not to be taken literally. It is as much a romanticization by Burroughs as his Tarzan chronicles. What really happened is that Barney Custer visited his relatives in Carinthia, a mountainous area of southern Austria, bordering on Italy and Serbia (as the "Kingdom of Lutha" did in *The Mad King*). Carinthia had become a duchy in 976 A.D., but when the line of Carinthian dukes died out, it became part of a large but short-lived state ruled by Otokar II of Bohemia. In 1276 Rudolf I of Habsburg became its ruler. In 1286 he gave it to the count of Tyrol. In 1335 the Habsburgs took Carinthia back again and kept it until 1918.

Barney Custer got into some kind of trouble during his visit. The details are still largely unknown, but he seems to have become embroiled in a plot to revolt and form an independent state with the Rubinroths as the rulers. Serbia was to aid the Rubinroths in return for support of Serbia against Austria.

It seems to have been true that Custer did have a close physical resemblance to the chief of the revolutionary party, his cousin. No doubt, as in *The Mad King*, he doubled for his cousin in order to confuse the Austrian authorities and the Carinthians who were pro-Austrian. The similarity of *The Mad King*'s plot to that of *The Prisoner of Zenda* is close, though *The Mad King* is more than just an imitation. Apparently, the Englishman whom Anthony Hope Hawkins calls Rudolf Rassendyll, the earl of Burlesdon's, brother, became involved in Carinthia in the early 1890s. That time, however, it was a Habsburg, the natural son of an Austrian duke, who was the head of the revolutionists.

The late General H. P. Flashman, however, in the second volume of his recently published papers, *Royal Flash*, New American Library, maintains that Anthony Hope Hawkins got the idea for *The Prisoner of Zenda* from his own experiences in 1847–48 in the duchy of Mecklenburg-Strelitz. (Flashman calls this duchy Strackenz in his papers for some reason. Perhaps the editor of the papers, George Macdonald Fraser, renamed it for publication, though I do not know what personal or political repercussions he feared.)

Since things often occur in threes, it's possible that *Royal Flash*, *The Prisoner of Zenda*, and *The Mad King* were just instances of history more or less repeating itself. There were due exaggerations and falsifications by the various authors, of course.

If Barney Custer was related to the American general of the same name, he never mentioned it.

The story of Barney's sister, Victoria, in *The Eternal Lover*, is a strange one. It is so dreamlike that I am convinced that most of it is Victoria's fantasy. Barney stated that he was worried about his sister's sanity, and he had good cause. To most people, at most times, Victoria would have appeared to be a well-balanced American girl. But she had a near-psychotic horror of mice and earthquakes and a neurotic aversion to getting married.

The Eternal Lover is concerned with Lord Greystoke only in that it enables us to learn what he and his family were doing at a certain period of his life. What chiefly interests us in *The Eternal Lover* is the brief appearance of the "youthful Jack" during an earthquake.

Tarzan's son was born in 1912, so, in 1914, he would not be "youthful." This adjective is usually applied to that period between childhood and maturity. It's possible, however, that Burroughs was not being exact in his choice of adjective. And Webster's does admit that a youth can be just a young person with no specification as to age. The child was undoubtedly the son of Tarzan and Jane. Korak and Meriem were not mentioned as being at the plantation at this time. It seems unlikely that, if they had had a child, they would have left him in Africa while they went to Europe. And if they had been little Jack's parents, they would have been very youthful, too-youthful, and too-soon, parents.

Chapter Eighteen

(VII)

War and Freedom

Which if not victory is yet revenge.

—J. Milton

All time was his and all Africa.

—E. R. Burroughs

England entered the war against Germany on midnight of August 4, 1914. A few days later, three German officers and a company of black soldiers crossed the western part of the border between German East Africa and British East Africa. They were Hauptmann (Captain) Fritz Schneider, Leutnant Obergatz, and Unterleutnant von Goss. They were lost, but they eventually came through the jungle east of the isolated Greystoke plantation. They were welcomed by Lady Jane, whose husband was in Nairobi on business and who had no idea that war had been declared.

The three officers, after accepting Lady Jane's hospitality, suddenly attacked. They killed her bodyguards and servants, crucified Wasimbu, son of Muviro, against a wall, burned buildings, and created all the destruction they could. They also burned a native woman's body beyond recognition after putting Lady Greystoke's ring on the corpse's finger. Schneider took from Jane the diamond-studded locket enclosing the cameos of Tarzan's father and mother. Then the three, with Jane and the survivors of their company, hurried away to join the army around Mt. Kilimanjaro. They said nothing to the higher officers of the killings beyond reporting that they had been forced to shoot a few natives in self-defense. They did present Lady Greystoke as their prisoner, but, to their surprise and intense discomfort, they were greeted with consternation and severe reprimands. The German High Command in East Africa, despite what Mr. Burroughs thought in his reaction to propaganda about German atrocities, would never have considered taking Lady Greystoke as a prisoner. But now that she was theirs, she was an embarrassing problem. The commander was about to order her released when he got word from Germany to keep her a prisoner. Why is not known, but the best guess is that some high officials had heard about the treasure of Opar. Or they knew that Tarzan had access to a source of great wealth. Thus, they hoped to pry the information from her or, if not from her, her husband. She was taken across the border into the Congo Free State by Obergatz to ensure that nobody would determine her location.

Tarzan did not find out, until long after, that Schneider had played a trick on him. Schneider had done this to inflict pain upon the English pig, Greystoke. But he said nothing of this or his other atrocities to his superiors. If he had, he and his two fellow officers would have been shot by the next day.

There are criminals in every army. But these three were practically the only ones among the whites of German East Africa, as far as we know. Their general, von Lettow-Vorbeck, was a man of irreproachable morals and highest character. He conducted himself as a Christian and a German soldier was supposed to do in theory. He won the respect and admiration of his British enemies. He was probably the greatest guerrilla commander of World War I, but he was unlucky enough to be on the losing side and he lacked a Lowell Thomas to publicize him. Otherwise, he would have gotten his rightful praise as greater than Lawrence of Arabia. With a handful of white officers and noncoms and a few thousand black troops, he pinned down a quarter of a million British and Allied men very much needed in Europe. When the war was over in Europe, he had to be begged to surrender. Part of his success was due to his treating his native soldiers as "fellow Africans," not subhumans.

Schneider, von Goss, and Obergatz were three rotten apples in an otherwise fine barrel.

Tarzan, hearing in Nairobi that war had broken out, hurried home as fast as he could. He took the train out from Nairobi and then dropped off and proceeded on foot southeastward. He wolf-trotted most of the way across the plains and the broken country.

His tireless Waziri, like the Masai, could eat up fifty miles a day on the savanna when burdened only with weapons. Tarzan, when pushing, could cover seventy-five miles from dawn to several hours past dusk on relatively flat country.

Still, it took him two days from the railway because of the very rugged country. He was beginning to tire at the end of the second day, and so he slept that night. In the morning, after shooting an antelope with an arrow, and eating several pounds of it raw, he continued. He reached the plantation in midmorning, but, long before, he saw the smoke still rising from the barns.

He found the charred corpse of the woman with the hair, fingers, toes, ears, and nose burned off. If it had not been for the ring on a finger stub, he would not have known that the corpse was Jane's. Sadly, he buried her and the bodies of the Waziri who had died defending her. Then he opened some fresh graves by the bungalow's ruins and identified the insignia on the askaris' uniforms. Now he knew where to look for the murderers. He took an oath to himself to hunt them down, not to stop until the last one was dead. In that moment of cold fury and resolve, he reverted to the ape-man almost completely. He shed his clothes, wearing only a loincloth. He carried his father's hunting knife on his left hip, his bow and quiver slung across his shoulders, a long grass rope over his chest and beneath one shoulder, and a heavy war spear in one hand.

On the second day, he was in German East Africa. By this, we know that the Greystoke plantation must have been about 150 miles from the border, if he went on a straight line to it. On the other hand, Burroughs deliberately misleads us about times and distances, and the Greystoke plantation may have been closer or further away than he tells us.

By the fourth day, Tarzan could hear the cannon booming around Kilimanjaro. This mountain, the highest in Africa, towered 19,340 feet above sea level. Kilima Njaro, the "little mountain" of Jaro, was a volcanic cone on the borders of the British and German possessions. In Upper Pleistocene times, its glacier cap went down to the 11,000-foot level, or 9,000 feet above the round at its base. In Tarzan's time, the ice had retreated to the 15,000-foot level. In a hundred years from now, it will be gone entirely.

The base was semiarid, but there were jungles on the highest peak, Kibo, perforated only by elephant and buffalo trails. The area between Kilimanjaro and the perpendicular blue Para Mountains to the south formed a relatively narrow gateway into German East Africa. The British would have to penetrate that gateway, but, first, they had to repel the German invaders.

Burroughs says that Tarzan found a small British army facing a German horde. Actually, the reverse was closer to the truth. At this time, some bands of commandos under Captain Tom von Prince were operating around the mountain. (Later, von Lettow-Vorbeck would threaten Mombasa.) Von Prince was half-Scotch, still had his British nationality, and had been a German soldier since he was turned down by the British Army. He was leading a bunch of white gentlemen-farmers and black soldiers on raids into enemy territory.

Burroughs reports that regular troops with machine guns and artillery were here at this time. It is probable that Burroughs was economically combining two or more conflicts in which Tarzan was a peripheral, but extraordinarily effective, combatant. The description of the battles around the Para, or Pare, Mountains sounds as if they were those fought when General Smuts' forces arrived to bolster the Allied forces. But this was after February, 1916.

Whatever the time, or priority of battles, we know what Tarzan did. He terrorized the black askaris and the white officers, killing quite a few. He stopped a major attack by his guerrilla sharpshooting and by letting a lion loose in the German trenches. He slipped into the heart of the enemy forces, leaped into a room filled with officers, and carried off Schneider. A Schneider, anyway. He had wondered how Schneider had been promoted to major so soon. Later, he found out that it was Captain Schneider's brother that he had left to face a hungry lion. No matter. To Tarzan, all Germans should be dead. He tracked down von Goss and exacted vengeance in sight of the 2nd Rhodesian Regiment. This would be after March 6, 1916, when a full-scale battle was raging for possession of Kilimanjaro.

At the end of this March, the rains began. The roads became impassable, and the fords were swollen. Nevertheless, Smuts pursued von Lettow-Vorbeck, though, if he had known how horribly his army was to suffer, he might have quit. It was Tarzan who shot Lieutenant-Colonel von Bock during the battle around Kondoa, though British Intelligence kept this quiet.

Finding out that Schneider was at Wilhelmstal, the summer

capital, Tarzan started toward there. On the way, he fell in with
Bertha Kircher, the beautiful young woman whom he knew to be a
German spy. He took Jane's locket from her after discovering that
Schneider had given it to her to identify herself to General Kraut.
(If this Kraut was von Lettow-Vorbeck's aide, he would have been
Major Kraut.)

The woman knocked Tarzan out with a pistol and took off.
He followed her to Wilhelmstal, where he found her with Schneider.
Tarzan spared her without knowing why. He attributed his re-
luctance to kill a woman to the decadent influence of civilization.
Later, he admitted that he had a hard time hating her, though it
was his duty to do so.

Tarzan decided to return to his natal country on the west coast
before returning to England to pick up his six-year-old son. The
war in East Africa would soon be over; he wasn't needed any more.

In this, he was mistaken. This was September, 1916, but the wily
German general would keep on fighting very effectively until November, 1918. However, it was true that he would be unable to
invade British East Africa. If Tarzan had stayed there and con-
centrated his attacks on the guerrilla troops, he might have shortened
the fighting by two years.

He wandered toward the west, somewhat to the south of Lake
Victoria. He started across a desert and almost died of thirst, but
he caught Ska, the vulture, as the big bird swooped over what it
believed was a corpse. The blood and the stinking tough meat kept
Tarzan alive a little longer. And then it rained.

Before this he had come across the bones of a giant in armor
which the Spanish, or Portuguese, of the sixteenth century wore.
Beside the sword and the ancient harquebus was a metal cylinder
enclosing a map and a parchment in what seemed to be archaic
Spanish script. Tarzan put the cylinder in his quiver and went on.

Tarzan entered a more humid area and soon found Bertha
Kircher, who was a prisoner of black deserters from the German
Army. Once again, Tarzan played the Trickster. The terrorized
soldiers fled to a village, where Bertha killed her would-be rapist
and escaped. She came across Tarzan making the reluctant acquaint-
anceship of a tribe of mangani. Its king, Go-lat (Black Nose),
challenged Tarzan. He used his knowledge of jujitsu to great advantage, completely subduing Go-lat. Bertha was discovered while

watching the scene, but Tarzan saved her by declaring that she was his mate.

Enter Lieutenant Harold Percy Smith-Oldwick, Royal Air Service pilot. The lieutenant was on a mission far to the west. He was investigating a report that the Germans had landed a large army on the west coast and were now marching through Portuguese territory toward German East Africa. How the Germans could have sneaked a large army past the British fleet, and why they would waste sorely needed men on such a wild venture, were questions that really did not need answering. Probably the Germans had put the rumor out. But the British High Command could not afford to ignore it, so they sent a plane out.

Smith-Oldwick's engine stalled; he landed safely; he was captured by Numabo, chief of the Wamabo. Tarzan was also captured by Numabo, escaped, lassoed the plane as it was taking off and climbed up the rope and threw Usanga, the ex-sergeant, out, while Bertha took over the controls.

Tarzan's feat of lassoing the plane is similar to the classical myth in which a god ropes a great flying monster. Usanga had forced Smith-Oldwick to teach him how to fly. Usanga was not nearly ready to solo, but he believed he was, and so he flew off with Bertha, who would be number one of the twenty-five wives Usanga planned on having after he became a great king. Smith-Oldwick was to be killed after Usanga left. But Tarzan climbed up the rope and gave Usanga a chance to fly without wings. Bertha, fortunately, was a pilot and so she returned the plane to the ground, bringing the plane back among the natives advancing to kill the Englishman. The impact did not break the wings or the propellers of the fragile machine, and the girl and the lieutenant flew off. However, they were forced to land again, and Tarzan, having seen them go down at a great distance, went after them.

Tarzan, Bertha, and Smith-Oldwick eventually ended up in the city of Xuja in a valley in the desert. Xuja was the remnant of an old civilization which had not quite completely fallen apart yet. Possibly, the Xujans were descendants of refugees from sunken Chadea. Most of the citizens were competent much of the time, but they were also often mad. (In which they differed little from civilized people elsewhere.) Their insanity was rapidly killing them off, and it came close to doing away with the three strangers. The Xujans worshiped parrots and raised lions for food, sentinels, and trackers. They held prisoner an old Englishwoman, a missionary's daughter, born 1837, and in Xuja for sixty years. She had seen the decline of her captors, though she had no explanation for their mental instability. Perhaps they cooked their food in lead vessels and so suffered from lead poisoning, as the Roman aristocracy did.

Tarzan and his two companions got away, though not before Tarzan was almost killed due to his inept swordsmanship. Just as they were about to be dragged down by the pursuing lions, they were saved by British soldiers. Tarzan, however, was severely wounded by a thrown spear.

Back in H.Q., Tarzan found that Bertha Kircher was in reality an English Intelligence agent. She was the Honorable Patricia Canby, the daughter of a baron or a viscount. Burke's *Peerage* contains no Canbys, and a letter to the British Intelligence about her identity has resulted in one short communication: *The information is not available.* It surely would be no breach of security to reveal Canby's true identity now, and if she is still alive she could provide many details which Burroughs skips. No doubt, the British Intelligence has its own reasons for this secrecy. This, of course, is one of the many points I could have cleared up if "Lord Greystoke" had granted me more time.

From Colonel Capell, Tarzan obtained Fritz Schneider's diary, which Bertha (Patricia) had taken off the officer's body after Tarzan killed him. Tarzan discovered that Jane had not been killed, but no one knew what had happened to her.

Tarzan heard that Patricia and Smith-Oldwick were going to be married. He congratulated them and then set out to look for Jane. And here Volume VII ends.

For the scholar, the main problem with *Tarzan the Untamed* is: Is Jane dead or not?

The hardcover book edition, first published in 1921, says that she was not burned at Greystoke plantation.

Originally, the first part of this volume appeared in *Redbook Magazine* as a novelette. And Jane was definitely killed in it. On rewriting this part for the hardcover book, Burroughs made her death uncertain, revealing in the last part that her death was a fake.

Was Jane really killed, and did Burroughs resurrect her for fictional purposes? Or did Tarzan find out that he wasn't the only trickster in the world?

Did Tarzan, as some have suggested, marry Meriem when Korak

was killed in the war? And did she play the part in the latter volumes that Burroughs attributes to Jane?

Jane lives. The truth is that when Burroughs first wrote the series of stories which were to become Volume VI, he had just discovered that an enterprising newspaper reporter was on Tarzan's track. The identity of "Lord Greystoke" was on the point of being revealed to the world. The world would know that Tarzan was not a fictional character after all.

To throw smoke in the reporter's eyes, Burroughs killed Jane off in the magazine story. Thus, the reporter would not be led to a married couple then living on a plantation in western Kenya. The reporter, at that time, would soon have been at Tarzan's doorstep. What would have happened to the reporter we don't know. But we do know that Tarzan values his privacy highly and that he sometimes has a hot temper. We also know that he had considerable money, and it may have been the reporter's intention to permit himself to be bought off. It is more likely that Tarzan would have told him that he needed killing, but, if he kept silent, he would live.

We will never know what would have happened, because the reporter died while traveling in Kenya toward the plantation. Thus, Burroughs no longer had to worry about him.

One scholar has said that it was Burroughs' mother who talked him into bringing Jane back to life in the Tarzan stories. She may have urged him to do so, but he would have done so, anyway. And the very fact that he was treating Jane as if she were a character in a story, instead of the flesh and blood person we know she is, would convince many that she was indeed fictional.

Another question unresolved in Volume VI is what happened to the lost city of Xuja and its inhabitants. Once the British Army knew of its location, Xuja was doomed to invasion. After the war, an expedition would have visited it, and we surely would have had articles in the learned journals and an entire issue of *National Geographic* devoted to it.

Something happened to Xuja before the British could get around to investigating it. The files of the War Ministry on certain events of World War I are inaccessible even at this late date except to a few in the proper positions. "Lord Greystoke" himself revealed to me in the interview that the British expedition found only burned ruins in the valley in the desert and a few bones. Some fierce native tribe had evidently invaded, looted, and burned it.

The parrots, monkeys, and lions that had been the allies of the mad Xujans were also gone, presumably killed or driven into the desert. For some reason which even "Lord Greystoke" did not know, the War Office clamped a tight security on the whole valley. And, now that Kenya is no longer a British possession, the native government seems to be averse to lifting the lid. Or, perhaps, there is something of value there which the government would just as soon the outside world did not know.

Whatever happened, Xuja is one with Nineveh and Babylon now, and the lizards crawl through the ruins and the owl sits on a crumbled tower.

I was surprised when I found out that Xuja had actually existed. I could believe in one lost city, Opar, but more than one? No. "Lord Greystoke" stated that there was a Xuja, though it was not quite as large or the people as civilized as Burroughs depicted.

Since then, I have restrained my skepticism. After all, in my fifty-three years, I've seen many theories of scientists disproven and many things scoffed at turn out to be true.

Remember the okapi. Remember Miss Goodall's meat-eating chimpanzees.

1919: THE WORLD

The total world population, according to 1918 estimates, was 1,692,604,366.

The king of England was still George V; the prime minister, David Lloyd George.

Woodrow Wilson was President of the United States.

Congress (and the majority of U.S. citizens) rejected the League of Nations covenant.

"Spanish" influenza, starting in 1918, was still raging over the world and would kill fifteen million before it was done. Many a soldier who had survived four years of the bullets and diseases of the "War to End All Wars" died of the flu.

The approximate number of deaths during the war due to fighting were: Germany, 1,900,000; Russia, 1,700,000; France, 1,400,000; Austria-Hungary, 1,000,000; United Kingdom, 750,000; Italy, 500,000; Turkey, 400,000; Serbia, 400,000; U.S., 115,000. Disease, as usual, had taken far more than bullet and shell.

The Kaiser of Germany had gone into exile in Holland; Czar Nicholas of Russia and his family were shot by the Bolsheviks; the Austro-Hungarian Empire had fallen apart and its emperor, Charles, went into permanent exile; despite the Armistice, Turkey and Greece were to fight for four years more; Japan felt its military muscles growing, having experienced victory against its Western enemies; women were used for the first time in great numbers in factories; the world had changed enormously.

In Africa, the German South West and East African colonies had become British. The Kikuyu of East Africa were organizing against the white masters. One result of the war in Africa was that the black soldier knew that the white man could be beaten and that the country itself was the black man's greatest ally.

Despite the increasing population, there were still many thousands of square miles in Africa where no white man or black man, except for a few pygmies or Bushmen, had ever been.

Chapter Nineteen

(VIII)

Guru

Tarzan . . . playing a lone hand against creation.
. . . he who will may always pass. . . .

—E. R. Burroughs

In 1916, Tarzan left Canby and Smith-Oldwick to look for Jane.
During October, 1918, he returned for a short while to civilization.
In Nairobi he learned from a high official, who was also a good
friend, that Korak was flying on the Argonne front. The war in
German East Africa was far from over, but Tarzan was not interested
in that. Despite von Lettow-Vorbeck's successes, he was bound to
be run to earth sooner or later, or so the British officials claimed.
And there were rumors that the German High Command had sent
feelers out for an armistice.

Tarzan set out again on his quest, this time into a different area.
The chronology given above is contradicted by Burroughs' statements in Volume VIII, *Tarzan the Terrible*.

"Two months . . . had passed since Tarzan . . . learned from
the diary of the dead German captain that his wife still lived."
But Burroughs often purposely collapsed or expanded time, as we
know. Tarzan could not have learned about his son's presence at
the Meuse-Argonne operation if he had not come back to civilization for at least a short while in the September-to-October period
of 1918.

During the two years' search for Jane, he had found himself in
the neighborhood indicated on the map by the bones of the sixteenth-century Spaniard. Since a scholar had translated for him
the old Spanish writing, he knew what to look for. Unfortunately,

we don't know about this adventure. While I could easily make
up a story to fill the gap, I am sticking strictly to biographical
facts. Or, if I make surmises and deductions, I label them as such.

Intelligence had finally found out that Leutnant Obergatz, with
Jane and some black troops, had gone into the Congo Free State.
Tarzan crossed a waterless thornbush steppe and came to a great
morass entirely surrounding a mountainous country. This was infested with poisonous snakes and giant reptiles.

The latter were unknown to the white man, though they appeared
in the scary tales of the black tribes just outside that area. These
creatures were the survivors of the dinosaur age, the huge reptiles
which natives variously called, depending upon the language, *mokéle-
mbêmbe*, or *mbokälemuembe*, or *coje ya menia*, or *dilali*, or *morou-
ngou*, or *gassingrâm*. There is also the great hippopotami-swallowing
snake called *diba*, or *badigui*, or *ngakoula-ngou*, or *songo*. There
are also the *lukwata* to consider, the *dingonek*, the *lau*, the *chipekwe*,
the *nfezu-loï*, the *lepata*, and the *isiququmadevu*. There are the
monsters mentioned by Trader Horn: the *jago*, the *nini*, and the
amali. There is the creature with an un-African name, the *sirrush*,
the dinosaurian beast portrayed on the Ishtar Gate of ancient
Babylon. This animal was either captured in interior Africa by
the Babylonians or purchased by them from natives, according to
speculations by Willy Ley and others. They have produced enough
evidence to conclude that this heraldic-looking creature probably
existed in historic times and was captured in African swamps and
brought to Babylon by King Nebuchadnezzar's men. A few still
existed in early 1919 when Tarzan entered this dismal swamp surrounding the mountain which the peculiar aborigines called Father
of Mountains. On the basis of a few survivors of Time, Burroughs, using poetic license, filled this area with many prehistoric
beasts, reptiles, and several species of tailed men. Here, Tarzan supposedly found some unknown genera of big cats and some spotted
lions.

By the end of January, 1919, he still had found no trace of
his wife. But he had become friends of two tailed men of different
races (in Burroughs' novel but not in reality, of course). One was
Ta-den, a hairless white; the other, Om-at, a hairy black. Both
spoke an unknown language. However, it was evident that at some
time in the past they had had extensive contact with the mangani.

Their speech contained a small number of loan words from the great apes.

This was Pal-ul-Don, or Land of Men. Also in the valley were the *waz-ho-don*, black-white hybrids, and the *tor-o-don*, or beastlikemen. The latter were as intelligent as the mangani. More so, since they had domesticated, or at least were able to control, the *gryf*. This was a huge triceratopslike reptile on which the tor-o-don rode. Tarzan, watching rider and mount, learned how the almost brainless and vicious-tempered beasts were controlled. Later, he used this knowledge to his advantage.

In one of the most interesting, and exciting, volumes of the jungle Epic, Tarzan moves like a god searching for his abducted goddess. Burroughs exaggerated, and even added things that did not exist in reality, but, as a novel, *Tarzan the Terrible* is very satisfying and is, in every sense, superbly Tarzanic.

Whatever the truth, Tarzan had a great adventure. And this volume, like so many by Burroughs, affords him a chance to be satiric. Burroughs has unfortunately been put down by some intellectuals, or by those who have not bothered to read all of him, and so his excellent satire, some worthy of Voltaire and Swift, is overlooked. It is time that this and his other virtues are brought to the notice of critics and the public. Burroughs has his faults as a writer and he is by no means a "great" writer. But he is more than just an adventure writer.

Tarzan became known in this land, with good reason, as Tarzan-jad-guru—Tarzan the Terrible. Eventually, he became known as Dor-ul-Otho, that is, the Son of God. This was not the first nor the last, time that he would be a god, though this is the first time he was called God's son. And, like other divine saviors, he was accused of being a blasphemer and a false god. Unlike his predecessors, he escaped martyrdom. And he truly saved the people who had worshiped him and then fallen away from him. He did this, it is true, only by being saved by his son, Korak. So it may be said that Korak was the grandson of God and God's savior, though Tarzan never made any claim that he was truly God. He just did not contradict the assumptions of the aborigines.

Moreover, he refused to stay and rule as God. As other, more mythical deities, or those more remote in time, have done, he appointed a human being as king, as his vicar. With Korak and Jane, he rode away on the back of a monster out of the prohuman past, a beast such as appears in Revelations. First, though, before making his ascension, he abolished human sacrifice, reminding us of the Central American god, Quetzalcoatl, who had also forbidden this ritual.

As for his vengeance on Leutnant Obergatz, that had been taken care of by Tarzan's son. Obergatz had claimed to be the Great God, and he was about to stab Tarzan and Jane with the sacrificial knife when lead from Korak's Enfield shattered his golden divinity.

When Tarzan was imprisoned by a man who wasn't sure that Tarzan was not a god (thus recalling other gods of ancient myths and their imprisonment by humans) he looked out through a window upon the valley of Pal-ul-Don. And there he had a vision which was truly prophetic, sadly prophetic, of what was to happen, not just here, but throughout Africa.

". . . What a paradise! And some day civilized man would come and—spoil it. Ruthless axes would raze that age-old wood; black, sticky smoke would rise from ugly chimneys against that azure sky; grimy little boats with wheels behind or upon either side would churn the mud from the bottom of Jad-in-lul, turning its blue waters to a dirty brown; hideous piers would project into the lake from squalid buildings of corrugated iron, doubtless, for of such are the pioneer cities of the world.

"But would civilized man come? Tarzan hoped not . . . God grant that it never would. Perhaps He was saving this little spot to be always just as He had made it. . . ."

Tarzan *did* have this vision, and his thoughts were much as Burroughs reported. He *did* find Jane and Obergatz in the valley. He *did* find the last of the sirrush, but not the gryf, in the swamps. The natives were, however, not tailed. They were tall blacks with an obvious Hamitic admixture in their ancestry. There was a single family which did have tails several inches long. This freakish mutation occurs sometimes among individuals of all races. Undoubtedly, the caudally equipped family suggested to Burroughs the idea of a whole species of whites and blacks differing from other human beings only in having long prehensile tails.

The natives *were* going to sacrifice Tarzan and Jane after finding out they weren't really gods, and Korak *did* rescue them.

When I heard this during the interview, I said, "What about Cathne and Athne?"

"True enough," he said.

"But . . . ," I said.

"But they've been massacred and the cities stripped of their gold and ivory. At least, so I heard from one of my Abyssinian friends."

"And Nemone?" I said.

"Nemone! It's all over with. But she won't die. Burroughs saw to that. She'll live on in his book."

Chapter Twenty

(IX; X)

The Lion and the Ants

The lion is great, but it is the ant who picks his bones.

—Akuba saying

Time was when Burroughs' great apes were said to be impossible. They could not exist if only for the reason that they ate meat. It was well established that all of the great apes, gorillas, chimpanzees, orangutans, and gibbons were pure vegetarians.

Then along came Jane Goodall with her five-year observations of chimpanzees in the wild. Their diet was so close to that of the mangani that Burroughs, not Goodall, might have written that report. And chimpanzees kill antelopes and baboons for meat and use simple tools.

Similarly, the great golden lion of Tarzan's, Jad-bal-ja, was deplored by the critics. No lion could possibly be so tamed. Volume IX, *Tarzan and the Golden Lion*, was poppycock!

Then along came Elsa of *Born Free* by Joy Adamson.

And so we hear no more of "impossible" lions.

Tarzan, Jane, and Korak, returning in early 1919 from Pal-ul-Don, came across a dead lioness with a spear through her and her jaws locked on the head of a dead black hunter. Nearby was the sole survivor, a male lion cub still in the nursing stage.

The defiance of the little lion and its plight aroused Tarzan's empathy. He suddenly decided to raise it, though Jane and Korak doubted that it could be done. Besides, why raise the beast as a pet only to be forced to put it in a cage when it became big enough to be dangerous? Tarzan said that Jad-bal-ja (Pal-ul-donian for "the Golden Lion") would never attack a human being unless he, Tarzan, ordered him to do so. Or in self-defense, of course. Perhaps others might fail in this training project, but not he. He was half-beast himself, and he could speak in a language a beast could understand.

Moreover, this lion was more intelligent than Jane and Korak thought. They would soon see that. Korak bet him a hundred pounds that he'd fail; Tarzan accepted. And he continued his daily training of Jad-bal-ja.

From March, 1919, to March, 1921, Tarzan spent most of his time on or near the plantation. The Waziri had rebuilt the plantation, and Jervis did most of the supervising. Apparently, Meriem made at least two long trips to Paris during this time. Her son, John Armand, was born at her parents' home, Cadrenet Château, Normandy. Tarzan's son, John Paul, and his tutor accompanied her.

Jad-bal-ja grew into a huge, black-maned, yellow-haired, green-eyed beauty, a terrible and awe-inspiring beauty. He had been taught how to hunt by the master huntsman, Tarzan himself, and thus was more efficient than a wild lion. He would kill an antelope and, though hungry, would not eat until Tarzan gave the word. He would obey commands to sit, to heel, to leap for the throat of a dummy, to do everything that Tarzan ordered. Tarzan was his master, the beloved master, since he gave the lion a constant affection along with the strict discipline.

In London, Flora Hawkes, a former houseservant of the Greystokes, met with five men. One was Esteban Miranda, a young Spanish actor who closely resembled Tarzan. Flora had found him and trained him, since he was the pivotal role in her plan. He had listened to Tarzan's voice on records and could imitate it exactly. He was in love with Flora and was very jealous, though she was still only second in his affections. Esteban loved Esteban most of all.

The others were Bluber, a former German citizen who was financing the expedition; two English ex-pugs, Throck and Peebles; and Kraski, a Russian dancer. They were meeting to make final arrangements for an expedition to loot the city of Opar. Flora Hawkes had the map showing the route to the fabled city of gold and diamonds. She had eavesdropped on her ex-employers for several years and from the pieces she overheard, she had put together the maps. Bluber and Miranda would go first to a designated spot to set up a camp for the safari personnel and the supplies. The two Englishmen would meet them there later, and Flora and Kraski would arrive last.

In the final stage, Miranda would shave off his whiskers and start playing Tarzan. As the ape-man, he would smooth their way past natives who might otherwise give them trouble. Miranda, however, objected to Kraski's being with Hawkes, but he finally—and sullenly—agreed.

In 1921, the Greystokes were suffering financially. Their wealth had been reduced to almost nothing. During the war, Tarzan had sent orders to Meriem in Paris to contribute most of his money to the British and French governments for the Allied cause. The rebuilding of the plantation had been costly, and now he had to set out again for Opar. He left Korak and the lion behind with Jane, taking fifty Waziri with him. On the way, he came across animals slain with machine-made arrows, including a great ape, Gobu. While tracking down the mysterious killer, he met a band of twenty mangani. In Kerchak's day, this tribe had numbered about seventy, but it was dwindling away swiftly. In another thirty years, or perhaps even less, the tribe would be gone. And so would the other tribes, of whom there could not be more than two or three, each no larger than this one. It was no wonder that, with their rarity, they had not been discovered by science.

He approached them, expecting to be received as one of them after a certain amount of challenging and of identifying. But this time they drove him away, saying that he had killed Gobu. Angry and puzzled, he left, and then he came across the tracks of a large safari, evidently headed toward Opar.

At the plantation, Jane received a telegram saying that her father was very ill in London. She left with Korak for Nairobi. While they were gone, Jad-bal-ja escaped from his cage and set out on the trail of his master.

Tarzan confronted the stranger whites in their camp. Miranda was not there, and Flora was in her tent. This was fortunate for the party, otherwise Tarzan would have known at once that something unsavory was being planned. Flora, however, remembered that, though Tarzan no longer drank liquor, he did love a cup of coffee now and then late at night. She sent Kraski out with a knockout pill to drop into the ape-man's coffee. Tarzan drank it and quickly passed out.

While he slept, the Hawkes party broke camp and fled with no attempt to kill Tarzan. There were too many witnesses to try this. If word ever got out to the Waziri that he had been murdered, they would track down and massacre the entire party, and, if they failed, Korak would not. Besides, except for Kraski, none of them were cold-blooded murderers. They only wished to go as swiftly as possible to Opar, loot it, and continue on across central Africa to the west coast, where they could embark for England and be rich and happy forever after. And so it was that one of the troll-like sentinels of the city of Opar reported to Cadj, the high priest, La's mate, that strangers were approaching.

"It has been many moons since the great tarmangani who called himself Tarzan of the Apes was among us," said Cadj.

Many moons indeed! It was in 1914 that Tarzan had last left Opar, promising to return before the rains to make sure that La was not being harmed because she had permitted Tarzan to escape the sacrifice to the Flaming God. Seven years had passed, and everybody, including the broken-hearted La, had thought he was dead. The Oparians, of course, knew nothing of the Great War which had interfered with Tarzan's promise, nor of his quest for Jane, or of the labor and time involved in rebuilding the plantation.

Cadj, looking out across the valley, saw Tarzan and his blacks. Or he thought he did. In actuality, the big white man in the leopard-skin loincloth was Esteban Miranda.

Cadj said he was going to kill Tarzan, and a little grey monkey that had been eavesdropping hurried off to warn Tarzan, who was the friend of Manu, the monkey.

This particular Manu is a problem to the scholar. He apparently belongs to a species unknown to science and one that has no business even being in Africa. He is a migratory monkey, and he can hang from a tree-branch by his tail. Zoology is unaware of the presence of migratory monkeys in the Dark Continent. This, of course, does not mean that such do not exist, since science is also unaware of the mangani, which do exist, and science scoffed at the reports of the okapi until it was found in the Ituri Forest in 1900.

But prehensile-tailed monkeys are confined, as far as is known, to the New World. This particular Manu was either a member of a very rare species or it was a South American individual that escaped from a scientist who had brought it to Africa for experimental purposes. A third, and most probable, explanation is that Burroughs, who supplied the details for the adventures outlined to him by Lord Greystoke, had forgotten that prehensile-tailed monkeys are exclusively New World.

Manu, believing Miranda to be Tarzan, warned him about Cadj. Miranda did not understand him, of course, nor did he even know that the monkey was attempting to speak to him. Miranda was pretending to have had an accident such as had once happened to Tarzan. He claimed to have lost his memory and so could not speak Waziri. His Waziri felt sorry for him. They were deeply grieved when their Tarzan fled like a coward from a rhinoceros. He had indeed suffered a pitiable change.

Cadj set out with a party into the jungle and found the real Tarzan still sleeping off the drug. He tied him up and started the sacrifice there and then, a procedure forbidden to any but the high priestess. La, warned by Dooth, a priest, got to Cadj in time to stop him. Tarzan was taken into Opar, but Dooth told La that Cadj and Oah, a priestess, were plotting against her. The only way she could save herself was to sacrifice Tarzan with her own hands.

Since the front exits were being watched, Tarzan and La escaped out through a secret back exit. They went up into the hills, where they found a tribe of very primitive black-skinned people. These were not true Negroes, differing from them as much as Hottentots and Bushmen differ. They were the abject slaves, the cattle, in fact, of a group of half-human, half-gorilloid hybrids. These peculiar Bolgani wore garments encrusted with diamonds and lived in a huge castle occupying fifteen or so acres. The castle itself was of granite covered with mosaics of gold and diamonds. The ancient Oparians had built this structure, and now the Bolgani lived in it and were ruled by a great lion, Numa. Of course, he who spoke for Numa had the real power.

(The theories explaining the strange hybrids, and the equally strange discrepancy between the male and female Oparian, are given in chapter 13.)

Tarzan was to have many adventures and to come close to death many times while he was in the Palace of Diamonds. He found an old Englishman who had come to Africa with Stanley when he was a boy (circa 1879). He had been a prisoner in the Palace most of his life. Tarzan, aided by the old man, led a revolt of the blacks against the Bolgani and killed their lion emperor.

During a moment when it looked as if the Bolgani would be victorious, Jad-bal-ja appeared. He had trailed his master to this remote place, and now he ravaged among the Bolgani.

Jane Clayton had not gone to London. At Nairobi a telegram informed her that her father was out of danger. She returned to the plantation but became alarmed because her husband was far overdue. She set out with fifty Waziri to find him. She would be separated from them, be abducted, and have to fight off a rapist and escape through many dangers before she saw him again. The readers of Volume IX will be entertained by the perils, the intrigues, the double-crosses, the accidents, fortunate or unfortunate, and the "gang aft agleying" of the best-laid plans of the Hawkes gang, the Arabs, and other evil men trying to get their hands on Jane and the treasure of Opar. The reader will be entertained whether he is reading this volume as biography or, as I understand some do, as fiction. He will see how the golden lion saved his master from Cadj, and how Tarzan left La secure on her throne once again. This time he set up a bodyguard of a hundred Bolgani for her, though they were to melt away in a few years.

The reader will see how Jane mistook Miranda for Tarzan, and the results thereof. He will see how Miranda, playing Tarzan, overdid it and became convinced that he was indeed Tarzan. He will see what happened to Kraski when he stole a bag of diamonds from Tarzan. He will see what happened to Flora Hawkes and how she came back into the service of the Greystokes, who forgave her. He will see how Jane had her heart broken by a man she believed was Tarzan and how she was eventually reunited with her husband.

Tarzan thought that the golden lion had killed Miranda. But the Spaniard escaped with the bag of jewels which he had taken from Kraski. He was, however, captured by the people of Obebe, a cannibal chief of the Ugogo River. Obebe, believing Miranda to be Tarzan, wanted to kill and eat him. The witch doctor, Khamis (a most un-Bantu name), insisted that their captive was the river-devil, who had taken on Tarzan's shape. If they tried to kill him, Khamis said, they would all suffer dreadfully. So Miranda was kept chained up in a filthy hut while Obebe and Khamis disputed over his true identity.

Volume IX ends about November, 1921. Volume X, *Tarzan and the Ant Men*, begins a year later. Miranda was still a prisoner, captive of the superstitions of the chief and the doctor and of his own belief that he is Tarzan. But Uhha, the fourteen-year-old daughter of the witch doctor, became curious about the prisoner. Miranda, mad but crafty, told her that he was the river-devil and was permitting himself to be held prisoner only to test Obebe's people. He who was his friend and arranged his escape would be the savior of his people.

Uhha stole from Obebe the brass key to unlock the iron collar around Miranda's neck. Miranda forced Uhha to go into the jungle with him to keep him company. The two were at that moment only twenty miles from Tarzan and eighty miles from the Greystoke plantation, though neither knew this. The two went along the eastern edge of the Great Thorn Forest for some days. Then Uhha stole Miranda's pouch of jewels after hitting him on the head, and she ran away. But not far. A hungry lion killed and ate her. Miranda awoke, but he did not know that Uhha was gone or that his diamonds were missing. The blow on the head had completed the disintegration of his mind. He was a living robot, stumbling along and babbling in his native tongue as if he were a child—which he was—and sometimes quoting in English whole pages of Shakespeare, the sense of which he did not understand.

Eventually, he was found by Usula, a Waziri, and brought back to the plantation. Korak despaired over his father's idiotic condition —he was fooled, too—and he sent for a great surgeon.

The doctor operated on the supposed Tarzan and then the doctor and the Greystokes waited for ten days to find out if the operation had been successful.

The day that Miranda had escaped from the village of Obebe, Tarzan soloed. He had been fretting for some time because two of his Waziri could fly and he, their chief, could not. So he had gotten his son, Korak, to instruct him, and today he was going up alone whether or not his son thought he was ready. Jane was in London. Meriem was at the plantation with her husband and Tarzan's grandson, Jackie, one and a half years old. Jackie was attended by his unnamed "perspiring governess." Esmeralda is not mentioned here or in any of the succeeding volumes. She was only fifty-three in 1922, and it doesn't seem likely that she would be away from little Jack unless something grave had called her away. This could only be Professor Porter's ill health, which would

mean that she was nursing him in London. But when her services
were no longer required, she would hasten back to the plantation.
The only family she had was the Greystokes.

It is also in Volume X that we learn that Korak was a flier.
Until the publication of this volume, scholars had assumed that
Korak was an infantryman because he was on the Argonne front
in 1918. It is true that he had enlisted in the Hallamshire Rifles.
But he transferred to the Royal Flying Corps and in 1918 was
an ace in what was now called the Royal Air Force. He was,
in fact, a member of the famous Tiger Squadron (No. 74), com-
manded by the great Mick Mannock until his death. During the
Argonne operation, however, Korak had been attached to an
American unit (as his father was to be in World War II).

There are speculations that Korak was the Lt. John Clayton
who attended the services for Baron von Richthofen on November
19, 1925, when his body was brought to Germany for a final burial.
However, research has established that the John Clayton mentioned
in Floyd Gibbons' *The Red Knight of Germany*, New York, 1927,
was an officer in the U. S. Army Aviation Corps.

Before Tarzan took off over Korak's protests, he was asked by
him what he would do if he had to land and had no mechanic
to fix the engine.

"Walk," Tarzan replied.

He never used two words where one would do; he had a very
practical attitude toward all problems.

He flew for an hour and a half in a straight line, exulting in
this device which, noisy though it was, yet enabled him to feel
as if he were an eagle. When he reached the Great Thorn Forest,
he was unable to resist his curiosity. This growth was only a
hundred miles from his plantation, yet he had been unable to
penetrate the barrier of thorns and see what was inside. Now he
could do so. He dipped down into it and flew around, rubber-
necking like any tourist. The forest was off the southwest coast
of Lake Victoria, between the lake and the present Serengeti
National Park. And yet it was as isolated as if it were on the
moon. (It does not exist now, having fallen to the flame thrower
and the ax of the white settler and the local natives.)

Tarzan's plane skimmed over the tops of the tall trees inside
the thorn walls. The top of one caught a wing and swung the
plane around, and it crashed down through the branches. Tarzan

was hurled out, hitting branches on the way down, breaking some, bouncing off others, and then he hit the ground so hard he was knocked out.

Here began a very strange adventure. He was captured by a huge brutish Caucasian woman who, unlike her sisters outside the thorn forest, was without speech. Perhaps it was this handicap that made her kind so mean and so tyrannical. In her cave-dwelling society, women were the heads of the family. It is true that they didn't wear the pants but only because none of them had ever heard of pants. The females of the Alalus would delight the members of today's Women's Liberation movements. In their crude culture, women used men only as sexual objects. In fact, they had to chase the poor male down and drag him into their caves after stunning him with a bludgeon. However, Tarzan was not the physically inferior Alalus male, conditioned to run until caught and then cower helpless while waiting to be raped and possibly eaten. He got away, and he taught a young male the use of bows and arrows and how to stand up against the females. This male organized his fellows into an aggressive band which beat up the females and reversed the situation. The man was now triumphant; female brutality had been replaced with male brutality.

The greater part of Volume X, however, is not concerned with the Alalus but with Tarzan's adventures among the white pygmies, the Minunians. These were a highly civilized people of whom the tallest was eighteen inches high. They rode a form of the tiny royal antelope, fifteen inches high at the withers, and they lived in a marvelous dome-city resembling ant colonies.

Beginning with the Alalus, Volume X leaves biography and becomes romance. Beginning with the Minunians, it becomes science-fiction.

Evidently, Burroughs did not feel that the plane crash and the Miranda story were enough to make a complete novel. Besides, he had been wanting for some time to write a satire. And what better vehicle than the ant men, the Minunians? Just as Jonathan Swift had put Gulliver among the Lilliputians so he could illuminate the pettinesses of mankind, so Burroughs put Tarzan among the Minunians. Nor does Burroughs suffer much by comparison with Swift, unless his lack of savagery and hatred and his compassionate laughter are faults.

In his satire, Burroughs is closer to Voltaire or Rabelais than

Swift, though his story is completely lacking in the earthiness of the latter. Burroughs laughs; he does not snarl.

Tarzan and the Minunians remind us of Hercules and the pygmies. Nor would it be too difficult to believe that the Minunians, if they existed, were the real basis of the Greek legend. The shortest adult recorded is a Dutch midget, Pauline Musters, who measured 23.2 inches tall and weighed nine pounds. Just possibly, a group of such midgets might have transmitted, through mutated genes, their tiny stature and so founded a nation. And this nation may have sought out such a place as the Great Thorn Forest where they would be safe from the giants.

But even if I could believe this, I could not believe that a Minunian scientist could invent a pill which would reduce the six-foot-three inches of Tarzan to eighteen inches. Such a feat would require enough energy to suck the sun of its energy and turn it into a dark and cold ball. Thus, I'm forced to regard this part of Volume X as science-fiction.

But it is a good story, a first-rate satire, and excellent science-fiction. This tale of the very little people with very big names (Komodoflorensal, Elkomoelhago, Zoanthrohago, etc.) is always a pleasure to read. And the fact that it is fiction accounts for a discrepancy that has long bothered scholars. Tarzan, in Volume X, is an excellent swordsman, having been taught by that great rapier artist, d'Arnot. In an earlier work, Volume VII, he is a poor swordsman. In a later volume, X, he is again a poor swordsman. Burroughs, writing his fiction, forgot that Tarzan was inept with a sword and gave him a skill which, in reality, he did not have. We may be sure, however, that sometime before World War II Tarzan did take lessons and became quite proficient.

Whatever adventures actually befell him after he taught the Alalus boys a successful militancy, he got out of the Great Thorn Forest. Then he was captured by Khamis, who thought he'd retaken the river-devil. Tarzan was thrown into the same hut in which Miranda had been kept. When he refused to tell what had happened to Uhha—because he did not know—he was threatened with torture. Khamis meant to put out Tarzan's eyes with a red-hot iron, but Tarzan broke his bonds. And then it was as if a mad hero of old had broken loose, Hercules from his ropes, or Samson from his chains. Tarzan raged like an elemental force, like a true demon. And, once again, though he was so heavily outnumbered

that he could have been overcome, he was helped by the superstitions of his enemies. The villagers, believing that he was really
a devil and was now out to get revenge, fled. Tarzan threw Khamis
into the air and through the roof of Obebe's hut. Obebe, mistakenly
thinking it was the devil coming after him, stabbed Khamis to death.

When all was quiet, the natives came back to the village and
Obebe came out of his ruined hut. And Obebe cried out that he
had been right.

"The creature was not the River-Devil—it was Tarzan of the
Apes, for only he could hurl Khamis so high above his head that
he would fall through the roof of a hut, and only he could pass
unaided over our gates."

Thus, Tarzan became a greater god than even a river-devil.

Be it noted that Tarzan had saved several witch doctors from
death but that most usually came to grief when they tangled
with him. Tarzan had little use for priests of any kind unless
they were sincerely lovers of God and men.

He hastened back to the plantation, arriving just in time to
stop Jane from accepting Miranda as her husband. The Spaniard
fled into the outer darkness. Burroughs does not say what happened
to him after that, nor did I have time to ask Lord Greystoke
about him in our very brief meeting.

Chapter Twenty-one

(XI; XII; XIII)

Lord of Many Places

Where the lion is, there is his kingdom.

—Waziri saying

Volume X, *Tarzan and the Ant Men*, ends circa December, 1922. Volume XI, *Tarzan, Lord of the Jungle*, takes place from June, 1926, through March, 1927. The three and a half years between Volume X and XI are not accounted for. No doubt, Tarzan spent part of it in west Kenya and part in England. He also toured some areas in Europe, because we know from Volume XII that he had been in Rome. During this time, he continued his self-education, which included learning to read classical Latin. He also continued his work on the mangani grammar and dictionary. This will not be released to the world until Lord Greystoke is certain that he will be safe from its attendant publicity.

On this fateful morning in June, 1926, Tarzan was on a vacation from civilization in a jungle near the southern border of Abyssinia. He was dozing and daydreaming on top of Tantor. Then man entered, and, as usual, ruined peace and contentment and pleasant reveries. Two Arabs and their black slaves, hunting elephants, saw Tantor. One fired, Tantor bolted, and Tarzan, sitting up, was knocked unconscious by a tree branch. The Arabs tied him up and took him to ibn Jad, their sheik. The sheik's brother, Tollog, advised that Tarzan be killed secretly that night and his body buried where no man would find it. Tarzan called Tantor, as he had done in the past and would do again in the future. Tantor wrecked the camp, hurled Tollog onto the top of a tent as he was about to stab Tarzan, and carried Tarzan off into the jungle.

This time, Tarzan could not break his bonds, and there were no monkeys to bite them apart. Tantor grew thirsty and hungry and on the fourth day he left Tarzan to fill his belly.

Tarzan thought, "He is gone. I cannot blame him. Perhaps it is as well. What matter whether it be today, tomorrow, or the day after that death comes to me?"

This was Tarzan's never-changing attitude. He would not, it was true, welcome death. He would fight with everything he had against it. But he was not afraid of the great darkness. Everybody had to die, sooner or later.

He lay helpless while the insects crawled over him and bit him. He was annoyed by them, but he had become immune to their poisons through a lifetime of inoculations. And this, by the way, answers a certain critic and his comments. The critic, after a short trip to Africa, wrote that Tarzan could not have swung on vines through the jungle. He knew, because he had pulled on a vine in an experiment, and the insects swarming on it had bitten him so virulently that he had been unable to hang on to the vine.

Meanwhile, of course, monkeys used this vine and did not seem to be bothered by the insects, but on this the critic did not comment.

Tarzan, like the monkeys, was partially immune to the insect bites. However, he would never have swung on the vine in any event. This method of travel is an invention of those who wrote the movies about Tarzan. Nowhere in any of the twenty-four volumes of the biography is there a mention of vine-swinging by him. If the critic had read the books, he would never have made his erring observation.

However, to be fair and truthful, it must be admitted that Burroughs does exaggerate, at times, the ability of Tarzan to travel through the trees. Weight is weight, and gravity looks aside for no man or beast. Young gorillas speed through the branches, but the older and heavier gorillas spend most of their time on the ground. Not for them the fun which the lighter chimpanzees and monkeys enjoy in their arboreal world. And Tarzan, though only half as heavy as a large adult male gorilla, still carries about 235 pounds. He cannot, being of so much flesh and blood and bone, compete with the squirrel or the small simian.

Nevertheless, when he is in the closed-canopy rain forest, where there are several levels of thick tangle, he can use them as highways

and as stations for arrival and departure. No other man could go as
swiftly or as surely; so we do not have to discount his feats of tree
travel entirely, by any means. The episode in Volume I, where he
carries Jane off from a forest fire by swinging through the Wisconsin woods, is, we must admit, one of the places where Mr.
Burroughs' imagination triumphed over reality. Doubtless, Tarzan
did carry Jane off on his back, but he was running on the ground.
That no one else in the world could have traveled so swiftly or so
easily should have been enough to satisfy Burroughs. But his hero
was more than just a hero, he was a god. Nor was Burroughs
obligated to stick to the facts. Still, I wish that we had a motion-
picture record of Tarzan actually traveling through the middle
terrace. Though no chimpanzee or gibbon, he would be seen as
progressing breath-takingly fast through the closed-canopy upper
levels. No other acrobat could keep up with him or would care to try.

Tarzan lay helpless on the jungle path, and presently the manganis did come along. They formed a fairly large group, being
composed of several bands that had united. Toyat, their king, was
going to kill Tarzan, but Tarzan called on the gratitude of several
whose lives he had saved. They became his champions and released
him. For a while, he lived with the manganis and was content.

But, once again, the dreams, greeds, and lusts of men interfered,
and Tarzan became involved. The Arabs of ibn Jad sought the
fabled leopard city of Nimmr with its great treasures and the most
beautiful woman in the world. James Hunter Blake, a rich young
American, an eight-goal man in polo and a fencer, and his older
friend, Wilbur Stimbol, an arrogant New York stockbroker, fell out
and split up. Blake was to end up in the valley of Nimmr as a sort
of Connecticut Yankee in King Arthur's African Court. And ibn
Jad and company would find Nimmr, its teasures, and its fabulous
woman.

Tarzan saved a gorilla from a python and Stimbol. (For gorilla,
read baboon. Gorillas don't live anywhere near Abyssinia.) Stimbol
became Tarzan's enemy. When Tarzan was knocked out by a fall
during a storm, Stimbol tried to stab him, but the gorilla stopped
him.

The Valley of the Holy Sepulcher, the source of the fable about
the city of Nimmr, was in a mountain range in southern Abyssinia.
It seems to be somewhere between the Omo River and Lake
Margherita. It was at this time held by two opposing forces, both

of which had continued a form of twelfth-century West European feudal society. Both were descended from two shiploads of English knights and Cyprian women wrecked on the African shore. These knights had accompanied Richard the Lion-Hearted in 1191 on his crusade against the Saracens of Jerusalem and elsewhere. One company had been commanded by a Bohun; the other, a Gobred. Searching for Jerusalem, they found this valley, which Bohun declared the Valley of the Holy Sepulcher. As a sign that the crusade was over, his men removed their red crosses from their breasts and put them on their backs. But Gobred said that they had not reached the Holy Valley, and his men kept their crosses in front. And so the valley was divided between the Fronters and the Backers.

Gobred built a castle and a city at the valley entrance to keep Bohun from leaving. Bohun, at the valley's other end, built a castle and a city to keep Gobred from pushing on. Blake happened on the city of Nimmr, where he fell in love with the fair Guinalda, the local Helen of Troy. Blake was accepted as a knight when he told the naive citizens that his father was a thirty-second degree Mason and a Knight Templar. Blake kidded the knights throughout the book.

Burroughs compresses the real-time element in this volume and ignores the linguistic difficulties. The English of the early twelfth century was much more archaic than that described by Burroughs. The arbitrary date of 1100 A.D. separates Old English from Middle English, but early Middle English was much more unintelligible to modern speakers than Chaucer's, which was based on the London dialect of circa 1400 A.D. Blake would have taken several months to gain even a modest fluency in early Middle English. It is likely that the ancestors of the valley-dwellers were not English but Norman. Very few knights of Old English descent accompanied Richard I on his crusade. This does not matter from the viewpoint of learning the language. Blake, if he knew modern French and classical Latin, could have mastered Anglo-Norman as quickly as, or perhaps even more quickly than, early Middle English.

Another problem with this narrative is the title which Tarzan gave the people of Bohun when asked if he was a noble. He replied (according to Burroughs) that he was a viscount. If he did, he would have gotten blank expressions. The title of viscount is derived from *vice-comes*, meaning, in ancient England, a sheriff of a county. Viscount did not become a grade of the peerage until

February 12, 1440. Burroughs says in a number of the volumes that Tarzan is a viscount, and so he undoubtedly is one. But he was, as we know, far more. Still, it would not have done much good to tell his captors that he was a duke, since this did not become an English title until 1337, when King Edward III created the title of duke of Cornwall for his eldest son, Edward the Black Prince.

However, either of Tarzan's other two titles, earl or baron, would have satisfied his questioners. These are very ancient ranks in England.

At the annual Great Tourney, which began the first Sunday in Lent, Blake distinguished himself with lance and sword. During the jousting, Bohun broke the truce by abducting Guinalda. Blake rode off after him to rescue her. Tarzan and Blake fought in the battle that ensued, though neither knew the other was present. It was during this conflict of armored knights and armored horses that Tarzan performed a feat which none of his illustrious ancestors, including William Marshal, earl of Pembroke, and Norman of Torn, the greatest of all medieval fighters, could have duplicated. He threw his heavy war lance as if it were a Waziri spear, and it went through the shield and armor of his foe. Then Tarzan fought with his sword, winning three encounters by luck, agility, and main strength, not his bladesmanship. Afterward, he shucked off his hot and imprisoning armor and ran off with his rope and knife.

After many adventures and close brushes with death, Blake won his fair Guinalda; the evil ibn Jad and his Arab band were defeated; Zeyd, a young Arab friend of Tarzan's, killed his murderous rival, Fahd, and won his Arab girl; Jab-bal-ja appeared in time to help Tarzan bedevil the Arabs as they carried off their loot.

It is worth noting that Tarzan was distantly related to Prince Gobred. The original Gobred had been a bastard son of Henry II, from whom Tarzan was descended (see the Greystoke Lineage, Addendum 3).

Most of Tarzan, Lord of the Jungle is a fictional distortion of actual events. According to "Lord Greystoke," he did encounter two wealthy American hunters. "Stimbol" was deserted by the natives, and "Blake" did turn out to be something of a "hero." There was a valley which had protected two Coptic-speaking Caucasoid tribes from the outside world, though not from each other. They had been influenced in the remote past by Crusader elements, which meant that they had not entered the valley until the medieval period. They wore chain armor and used shields, swords, and long spears. They did have gold mines, which provided the metal for ornaments. The Arabs did invade the valley. "Lord Greystoke" and "Blake" did get involved and take part in the fighting. There was a "Guinalda," a beautiful woman though not nearly as fair as Burroughs described her. "Blake" did take her back to civilization, where she was killed by a hit-and-run driver.

"Where are the people of the Leopard City of Nimmr today?" I said. "Why haven't they been discovered?"

"Smallpox," he said. "There were no survivors."

I was silent for a few precious seconds. I said, "I prefer Burroughs' version."

He smiled, and he said, "He knew what he was doing."

Volume XII, *Tarzan and the Lost Empire*, begins about June, 1926, and ends circa March, 1927. This is the first of many adventures in which Nkima, a very little monkey, appears. He spends much time riding on Tarzan's shoulder, playing the same role that Socrates' invisible demon played. Nkima is also a great comic figure, and if he had not existed, Burroughs would have had to invent him. Whereas Jad-bal-ja is a simple and elemental force, Nkima is a complex and quite human, all-too-human, person.

It is in this volume that we first meet Doctor von Harben, a German medical missionary from the Urambi country, a few marches to the west of Tarzan's domestic domain. The doctor and his daughter, Gretchen, appear in *Tarzan and the Tarzan Twins*, but that work is entirely fictional (which Burroughs admits) and not considered in this study. The doctor was distantly related to Tarzan through the Prussian Rutherfords and the first duke of Greystoke's wife, who was descended from the von Harbens. The missionary was looking for his son, Erich, an archaeologist and linguist who had become lost in the Wiramwazi Mountains. By now Tarzan had gotten over his antipathy to Germans and was very good friends with many. They were not all Schneiders, von Gosses, or Obergatzes, by any means.

Tarzan and Nkima went looking for Erich and eventually ended up in the same place as he. This was a valley occupied by the descendants of a Roman cohort which marched south from Egypt to escape the wrath of Emperor Nerva (died January 27, 98 A.D.).

In this green and wet valley, the Roman soldiers, and the Caucasian slave girls picked up on the way, built a city, Castra Sanguinarius. Later, a civil war resulted in another city, Castrum Mare, being built on the other side of the valley. Erich von Harben came to Castrum Mare and Tarzan to Castra Sanguinarius, and they went through many perils before getting together. They found a small ruling class of whites, a larger middle class of mulattoes who were common soldiers and merchantmen, and, most numerous, a black servant-and-slave class. The language was descended from the Roman Latin of the first century A.D. but had many loanwords from the local Bantu dialect. Linguists the world over are waiting for the day when von Harben will release his grammar and dictionary of this unique language. And classical scholars are still eagerly anticipating publication of the other treasures he brought out of the valley with his beautiful wife, Favonia. These are manuscripts of hitherto unknown works by Vergil, Cicero, Julius Caesar, and Juvenal, and Latin translations of lost Greek works.

Tarzan was forced to fight in the gladiatorial combats. A retiarius dropped a net over him from behind, but the ape-man tore it apart with his bare hands and seized a gladiator, lifted him into the air, and shook him to death as a terrier shakes a rat. The emperor, Sublatus, who hated Tarzan, sent in a lion against him. Tarzan killed it with a dagger as he had killed many before and would kill many afterward.

Sublatus, furious, then sent in six mangani. He did not know, though he soon found out, that Gayat and Zutho and Goyad and the others were Tarzan's old friends. They refused to fight him and went with Tarzan and his Roman friends back into prison.

Tarzan has always believed, and so far his belief has been justified, that he can get out of any prison that has ever been built. He did so, but he would have perished if it had not been for little Nkima. The monkey had gone many hundreds of miles past leopard and eagle and larger, very nasty, monkeys, and the great baboon, Tongani, whose diet is largely vegetarian but who would eat a monkey if he could catch him, and past the worst enemy of all, Histah, the snake. Despite a world which thought of nothing except catching and eating him, Nkima got to the Waziri. He showed them the way to the valley, where they arrived at a crucial moment.

Here it was ancient Roman legionary against the Waziri, the finest fighting men of modern Africa, and it was the Romans who broke. Tarzan was proclaimed as Caesar, but he turned the honor down. He gave it to his friend, Dion Splendidus, on the condition that the black barbarians of the outer marches be no longer warred upon and that all slaves be freed. Then Tarzan led his Waziri and the soldiers of Castra Sanguinarius and the black barbarians against Castrum Mare. And there he found Erich von Harben.

How much of Burroughs' version is true and how much fiction? Unfortunately, I don't know. I suspect that Tarzan may have found a mountain-isolated tribe of blacks with some ancient mixture of Caucasian genes. But I did not ask him about this. Time was too short.

Volume XIII, *Tarzan at the Earth's Core*, is canonical. That is, it was written by Edgar Rice Burroughs, but it is all fiction. It's a good thing it is. Otherwise, it would present a problem in dating. If this adventure had actually happened, it would have taken at least a year in which to occur, including the building of the great Zeppelin O-220. Volume XIII was written from December 6, 1928, through February 7, 1929. Volume XII, *Tarzan and the Lost Empire*, ends about July, 1927, but Volume XIII begins January, 1927, or even earlier. We know this because the O-220 could not have been built in less than six months, and it took off on its maiden flight on a clear June morning, 1927. There are other dating problems which we don't need to go into. The above is enough. Besides, it was no coincidence that Burroughs' phone number was the same as that of the Zeppelin.

Moreover, if the Earth were really hollow, and a large polar opening to it did exist, modern science would have established these facts long ago.

Volume XIII is all fiction, though very good fiction, and knowing this does not interfere with the enjoyment of reading it. The book is, in essence, a story of Tarzan going to Heaven. This world inside our world is wild and free with great jungles and beasts that have become extinct on the outside. It would be Tarzan's Happy Hunting Ground if it existed, and he would have left it only long enough to get Jane and his son, Jack, and perhaps Korak and Meriem and their son, and then return to it. And we would not have had Volumes XIV through XXIV. At least, they would not be in their present form.

Pellucidar, the vast prehistoric world deep beneath our feet, is a dream of a world such as Tarzan would call Paradise.

1929: THE WORLD
(with some 1928 events)

The total world population was 1,906,000,000 (according to the May, 1927, estimate). Every day, 150,000 were born and 100,000 died.

Calvin Coolidge was President of the U.S.A.; Herbert Hoover, the President-elect.

The king of England was George V; the prime minister, J. Ramsay MacDonald.

In the U.S., prohibition was the big problem for the federal government, which spent $177,716,860 in 1928 to enforce the Volstead Act.

Benjamin Purnell, sixty-six, king of the "House of David," a religious cult with headquarters in Benton Harbor, Michigan, died. He left word to his followers to expect him to rise on the third day. "—but he didn't."

In Sierra Leone, Africa, 250,000 Negro domestic slaves were freed by British government decree.

Ruth Brown Snyder and Henry Judd Gray were electrocuted at Sing Sing for the murder of her husband.

Radiotelephone service from the U.S. to Germany was inaugurated.

All women employees of the German postal system had to wear service skirts at least eight inches below the knee.

Nicaragua guerrillas ambushed and killed five U. S. Marines and wounded eight.

Mayor Thompson of Chicago and six associates were found guilty of conspiring to defraud the city of $1,732,279.23 to finance their political machine. The defendants were ordered to make a complete restitution.

France returned to the gold standard.

The king of England, George V, signed a bill giving voting privileges to women twenty-one or over.

Herbert Hoover accepted the Republican presidential nomination.

The Briand-Kellogg treaty for renunciation of war was signed by fifteen nations, including Germany, the U.S., Great Britain, and India. French Communists demonstrated against the treaty.

Commander Byrd left New Zealand for the Antarctic.

The ninth Olympic games were held at Amsterdam, Holland.

Supersonic waves were produced by an electrically driven crystal at 406,000 cycles per second.

Hafnium was found in the sun's spectrum.

Professor Thomson reported that electrons might be waves resembling light or radio waves.

The newest art in the movies was "the talkies."

Things had never looked so good.

Chapter Twenty-two

(XIV–XIX; XXI; XXIV; XXIII)

Hail and Farewell

Stated in direct terms, the work of the hero . . . is to slay the dragon.

—J. Campbell

Once again, and for the last time recorded by Burroughs, Tarzan returned to Opar.

Between July, 1927, the end of Volume XII, and January, 1929, the beginning of Volume XIV, *Tarzan the Invincible*, is a year and a half. During this time, Tarzan, except for a few brief jungle vacations, was at the Greystoke plantation or at Chamston-Hedding. Then, restless again, he decided to visit the great apes. He had no sooner found them than Nkima, his monkey Hermes, riding Jad-bal-ja, arrived. Nkima bore news of a very large party of blacks headed by some white men and a woman. Tarzan investigated, since this was his domain and all intruders had to explain their presence.

Volume XIV is the story of a plot by Zveri, a Russian agent, to rob the city of Opar. Ostensibly, the loot was to go into the Communist treasury. But Zveri planned to use the money to stir up rebellion among the blacks all over the continent and make himself emperor of Africa, Peter I. Zveri was not what his Communist allies, the Mexican Romero, the Asiatic Indian Jafar, the Filipino Mori, or the American Wayne Colt thought he was. Nor was Colt what he seemed, since he was an intelligence agent for the U.S.A. Zora Drinov, the beautiful Russian Communist who seemed to loathe all capitalists, was in actuality the daughter of an aristocrat who had been murdered, along with his family, by Zveri.

Zora was only waiting her chance to avenge her family. That she could be the true Anastasia, the daughter of the tsar, doesn't seem likely. The tsar had five children who were killed by the Bolsheviks. Zora stated that only her older brother and sister were murdered.

Tarzan saved Colt's life with an arrow from the jungle when Jafar tried to knife Colt because he had saved Zora from rape by the Indian. Later, Tarzan played one of his trickster jokes by throwing Jafar's body down from a tree among the conspirators.

In Opar, Dooth, who had once helped La against Cadj, had conspired with Oah, a priestess, to put La in prison. Tarzan was seized when he appeared in Opar and was placed in a cell. But he bent the iron bars with his hands, tore them from the sockets, and escaped. After freeing La, he found out what had happened in Opar. The hybrid bodyguard that Tarzan had set up for her had deserted her and gone into the jungle to build a new city for themselves. Oah, whom La had spared even though she had collaborated with Cadj, had talked the not-too-bright Dooth into revolting against La.

La still loved Tarzan, and in her forthright manner told him so. Tarzan was troubled by this. He told her not to speak of it. She replied that she liked to speak of it. It gave her sorrow to do so, but it was a sweet sorrow, the only sweetness she had ever had in her life. Love was a gift of the gods, and sometimes it was their reward to humans and sometimes it was their punishment. Her love for Tarzan was hopeless, she knew, but without it she had no reason to live.

Tarzan and La became separated. She fell in with Jad-bal-ja, who conceived a strange affection for her. She also ran into Wayne Colt. After many months and adventures, Zveri paid the highest price for having killed Zora's family, and Zora and Wayne decided to get married. Tarzan had foiled Zveri's plot to start a war between France and Italy and to ignite a native revolution throughout Africa. Tarzan also set La on her throne again. He asked her if she liked Colt, since he was hoping she would find a mate who could make her forget him. La said that she liked him very much but not in the same way she liked Tarzan.

Tarzan touched her shoulder in a half-caress and murmured, "La, the immutable!" And then he tossed his head as if to shake out all sad thoughts. "Come," he said, "the Queen is returning to her throne."

These are the last recorded words he ever spoke to La.

Hail and farewell, La!

At this time you were thirty-nine years old but still as youthful and as beautiful as when Tarzan, stretched out on the bloody altar of the Flaming God, first saw you. And it could be that if it had not been for Jane, he would have taken you as his love and his mate. But Tarzan was steadfast. Once sworn to fidelity, he would never break his oath. He could be tempted, we know, he could feel himself weakening. But he was inviolate in his central being, and he never completely succumbed. And yet he must have been very sad when he left you. It hurt him to know that you were so terribly hurt.

Volume XV, *Tarzan Triumphant*, takes place from January through April of 1930. Most of the action is in a valley in Abyssinia (Ethiopia). This was inhabited by a people who called themselves Midians, though they were not of that Semitic tribe but were actually descendants of Ionian Greeks of the time of Paul of Tarsus. They had a strange quasi-Biblical civilization with two contending groups, one of which was largely epileptic.

In this valley, Tarzan met Lady Barbara Collis, daughter of the first Earl Whimsey, and, hence, Tarzan's cousin (see Addendum 2). Tarzan pretended to be Lord Passmore, a title which had become extinct when his cousin, William Cecil Clayton, died. Lady Barbara fell in love with LaFayette Smith, a young geologist studying the great rift valleys. Another American intruder, Danny "Gunner" Patrick, ex-Chicago ex-gangster, fell in love with Jezebel, a beautiful blonde Midianite of the healthy group. The Russian agent, Stabutch, and the bandit Capietro met deserved ends, and this adventure ended happily.

Unless . . .

"Gunner" Patrick and Jezebel were going to California to buy a garage and a filling station. This borders on the tragic, but there is the possibility that Patrick changed his mind and went elsewhere. Still, Patrick and Jezebel would, today, be approaching the age of retirement. Perhaps they will soon be free of the man-swarm and the noise and the smog. But there must have been many times when they longed for the wide open green spaces, the quiet, and the exhilarating fresh air of that lost valley in Abyssinia.

Volume XVI, *Tarzan and the City of Gold*, begins in the middle of September, 1930, and ends in the middle of November,

1930. The first chapter is as fine a piece of poetry and of exciting adventure as Burroughs has ever done and is mostly true.

Tarzan was investigating a bandit gang, some of whom had made the fatal mistake of attacking him. He was trailing "man, the archenemy of all created things." Tarzan could define man as such, since, at this time, he thought of himself as a beast. He always thought this when he was out in the wild, wearing only a skin loincloth and carrying his primitive weapons. To Tarzan, intellect aside, most beasts were superior to man. As for intellect, man used it mainly to satisfy his greed and his hates and his lusts and to foul his own nest.

Tarzan rescued a strangely dressed white man from the bandits, not because he was concerned about the man but because he was curious. This deed led Tarzan into a valley where descendants of ancient pre-Mycenaean Greeks had built a civilization of two opposing cities, Athne and Cathne. (Or they may have been descended from refugees from sunken Chadea.) The elephant-men and the lion-men they called themselves. They were right to do so since these two animals formed the respective bases of their cultures.

Here Tarzan met and conquered the boastful Hercules, Phobeg, whose crime was that he had stepped on God's tail. And here he met Nemone, the very beautiful but mad queen of Cathne.

Nemone was shadowed by a strange and sinister secret and a psychic link which made the fate of Belthar, the god-lion, hers. Nemone was one of the few women who attracted Tarzan far more than was good for him. In fact, he would have fallen this once if he had not been repelled by her insane cruelty. She attracted him even more than La had.

In the end, having rejected her love a number of times, he was sentenced to be the quarry in a Great Hunt. Belthar, the god-lion, was the hunter. Tarzan ran as only he could. But, realizing that he could not outrace this great beast, bred for both swiftness and endurance, he turned to face it. He would try to get on its back, but that would only delay the inevitable. Without a dagger, he could not do much. This male lion was too huge and too powerful for him to have broken its neck with a full-Nelson as he had broken the neck of the big cat that had been after Jane in his father's cabin.

And then furred lightning broke out of the tall grasses along the river's bank. A giant, black-maned, golden-pelted lion, Jad-bal-ja, leaped upon Belthar. He had been trailing Tarzan for a long time and had been sleeping nearby when the crowd's noise woke him up. Now he tore into the god-lion, and they fought to the death, Belthar's death.

Nemone drove her dagger into her heart and fell across the body of the beast whose destiny was hers. The crowd went to free Nemone's brother, Alextar, from his prison, leaving their dead queen for the hyenas and the vultures. It was Tarzan, the beast-man, who gave her the burial the humans had denied her. He offered a prayer for this tormented creature whom he had come so close to loving. And then he turned away and slipped with the lion out of the bright African moon into the shadows, as dark as his sorrow for Nemone.

Volume XVII, *Tarzan and the Lion Man*, starts out in early 1931. The story proper does not begin until late that year. At this time, Tarzan was loafing in the shade of a tree with the Golden Lion when he heard the rifle shots.

"Tarmangani!" he murmured. And then, "I shall have to look into this matter, perhaps tonight, perhaps tomorrow!"

Tarzan was floating in the beasts' sense of timelessness, and he felt like sleeping at that moment.

Nearby, a safari had just defended itself against an attack by Bansuto cannibals. The whites in the safari were here to make a picture about a white youth who had been raised in Africa by lions. Obroski, its athletic male star, just happened to resemble Tarzan closely. This similarity of appearance caused a number of mistakes, comical and tragic, before Obroski came to a bad end.

Hollywood does not fare well in this volume. Burroughs did not care for many aspects of "tinsel town," and this adventure of Tarzan gave him a chance to show it with its facade collapsed. As Rhonda Terry, understudy for the egotistical Naomi Madison, said, "It's Hollywood—we all try to be something we're not, and most of us succeed only in being something we ought not to be."

After Tarzan had saved the movie company from being wiped out, he traveled to Hollywood. He went as plain John Clayton, and just for the hell of it, tried to get the lead role in a new Tarzan picture being cast. But he was turned down as not being the type.

Mr. Clayton, checking out of the Roosevelt, asked the desk clerk if he could give him some information.

"Certainly; what is it?"

"What is the shortest route to Africa?"

Tarzan was never really happy unless he was in the jungle. And, unlike most men, he did not have to stay in a place where he was not happy.

Before we leave Volume XVII, we note that, in this adventure, Tarzan kills the duke of Buckingham and Henry VIII is killed by a lion. How this came about, the reader of this volume may find out.

I'm afraid that most of *Tarzan and the Lion Man* is fiction. Research indicates that there was no such movie being made in Africa in 1931. Also, a second double for Tarzan seems to be too much of a good, or bad, thing. And the scientifically impossible tale of the old man in the hidden valley and the genes he had dug up from Westminster Abbey make this chronicle highly suspect.

Another fact which categorizes this volume as mostly fiction is the amusing tale of Lord Greystoke's tryout for a movie role. He would have arrived in Hollywood too late to try out for *Tarzan the Apeman* (starring Johnny Weissmuller) and too soon for *Tarzan the Fearless* (starring Buster Crabbe). Tarzan did visit Hollywood, but events did not occur as Burroughs describes them in his satiric anti-Hollywood novel.

The adventure of Volume XVIII, *Tarzan and the Leopard Men*, is basically true. It took eleven days, beginning in January, 1931. Tarzan became involved with the natives' fight against the sinister *Anyoto* (Leopard) society in the area around the eastern edge of the great Ituri Forest. He seems to have quelled their activities for a while, though one of the worst outbreaks of the society occurred three years later in this area. Tarzan lost his memory again for a while and was regarded by some of his native allies as Muzimo, a ghost.

This name, by the way, is very close to the Swahili *mzimu*, an ancestral spirit. Obviously, the natives in this area were Bantu speakers.

That Tarzan suffered amnesia again is one more evidence of his deep-seated desire to rid himself of his civilized persona. Nkima was also regarded by the natives as a spirit, the ghost of the grandfather of Orando, a Utengi. Nkima played a prominent part in Tarzan's battle against the Leopard Men. Tarzan, without his father's knife, which was a human heritage, and without his animal helpers—

Nkima, Jad-bal-ja, Tantor, and others—would have died many times. On the other hand, no one but he could have used any of these with such great effect.

Tarzan and the Leopard Men is perhaps the closest of Burroughs' novels to the reality. It is also the dullest, though I found it much more interesting reading at the age of fifty than at fourteen.

Volume XIX, *Tarzan's Quest*, begins in the Savoy Hotel, London, May 1, a Monday, 1933. Jane was having lunch with Lord Tennington and his wife, Hazel, before she left for Africa to rejoin her husband. An old acquaintance happened to come in and join them. She was the former Kitty Krause of Baltimore, a sixty-five-year-old woman with a young fortune-hunting husband, the Russian Prince Sborov. Kitty was desperately looking for youth, and now she was off to seek a witch doctor who was supposed to have the secret of eternal youth. Jane accepted Kitty's invitation to fly to Africa in her private plane, which was piloted by an American. It was the pilot, Brown, who had told Kitty about the witch doctor. And so, on a Wednesday, May 10, the plane left Croydon Aerodrome with the Sborovs, their maid Annette, their man-servant Tibbs, Jane, and Brown. It crashed in the jungle, and this accident would lead to Kitty's murder and, finally, to the very real pills which would stop aging.

Tarzan's Quest is an exciting adventure and is the first volume in the biography to give anything like a three-dimensional portrait of Jane. In the end, on a Friday, June 23, 1933, Tarzan, Jane, Brown, Annette, Tibbs, and Nkima got equal shares of the elixir-pills stolen from the Kavuru. Since Tarzan did not need them, he gave his share to Jad-bal-ja. The Golden Lion was fourteen years old in 1933, very old for a lion, and would soon have died if it had not been for the pills.

Tarzan gave them to the lion because he needed them at once. He was not neglecting his son and his family. They, too, would come in for their share of immortality. He sent some of the pills to a man who could analyze and synthesize them if anybody could. And his American surgeon cousin undoubtedly could. Tarzan then had an unlimited supply and, as payment for his cousin's services, told him what the pills were for. That is why his cousin and his five comrades have not aged since 1933.

At this time, Jane was forty-three years old, though she looked ten years younger. Tarzan seemed to be about twenty-five years old, so there was not too great a discrepancy in their seeming ages.

It was a wise decision on the part of the five humans not to give the world the secret of the Kavurus. As Brown said, "Most everybody lives too long anyway for the good of the world—most of us ought to have died young. Suppose Congress got hold of 'em?— just think of that! Not on your life!"

Volume XXI, *Tarzan the Magnificent*, begins on a Friday, June 1, 1934, and ends on a Friday, September 7, 1934. Tarzan had been asked by Haile Selassie, emperor of Ethiopia, to investigate a rumor that a European power was trying to start a rebellion. (The trouble was caused by Italian agents under the orders of Mussolini.) Tarzan's mission was sidetracked by the Lord Mountford mystery and the strange and sinister Kaji diamond. Before the affair was over, Tarzan had come close to being killed many times, and he had become involved with the people of Athne and Cathne again. Alextar, Nemone's brother, had turned out to be as mad and as cruel as she. Eventually, Tarzan got the great diamond Gonfal to his home in Kenya and buried the huge emerald of the Zuli for safekeeping. His final words in this volume were to the American, Wood, and his lover, Gonfala (the long-lost daughter of Lord Mountford).

"You and Gonfala should have enough [wealth] to get you into a great deal of trouble and keep you there the rest of your lives."

Tarzan did not refuse to use money or to go after it, because he knew how vital it was if one lived in civilization. But he also knew that he who had it was not necessarily happy.

"Tarzan and the Jungle Murders," Part III of Volume XXIV, *Tarzan and the Castaways*, is an interesting adventure. Tarzan was every bit as keen in solving a mystery as his English cousins, Holmes and Wimsey, or his American cousins, Wolfe and Savage. This piece of detective work by the ape-man involved a sense which he possessed to a degree that his civilized relatives lacked. It took place from September 7, a Wednesday, 1938, through September 29, a Thursday, 1938.

Part II of Volume XXIV, "Tarzan and the Champion," is entirely fictional and is Burroughs having fun.

Volume XXIII, *Tarzan and the Madman*, covers events from June 1, a Thursday, through June 25, a Sunday, 1939. In this, Tarzan became God Himself, according to some of the people he found in this remote valley in Abyssinia. Tarzan was not fooled by this title, of course, and he shed his divinity as quickly as possible. He was caught in a weird civilization, in a castle held by descendants of Cristoforo da Gama, brother of Vasco da Gama, and his soldiers. He also found a man who thought he was Tarzan. Rand, recovering from his insanity, remembered his identity and the strange wager that had gotten him into such trouble.

On the way back from the lost land of Alemtejo and his brief stint as God, Tarzan was injured. His basic tendency to reject his later civilized self was manifested again. He roamed the forest as a truly "wild man" until he was caught by two old enemies, Nadalo and Abdullah Abu Néjm. He killed three men with his bare hands before being subdued and put into a cage. The Arab then took him to Mombasa and sold him, as arranged, to a German, Krause. Krause had chartered a Norwegian tramp steamer, the *Saigon*, to take his cargo of wild animals to the States. Krause also planned to exhibit the crazy white in his cage as a "wild man."

While the *Saigon* was in the South Pacific, war was declared on September 3 between Germany and her two old enemies, France and Britain.

What really happened after that must be winnowed from the fictional parts of Part I of Volume XXIV. After the account of the lost Mayan civilization is removed, those interested only in the biographical facts may read how Tarzan tricked and outfought his enemies. His memory had been regained shortly after the *Saigon* left Mombasa, and the iron bars of the cage, though thick enough to withstand the efforts of most men, were easily bent by Tarzan.

For three and a half years afterward, he was to be John Clayton, Lord Greystoke, and not Tarzan. He got back to Kenya, kissed Jane good-bye, and flew to England, where his son Jack, Korak, and Korak's son had already enlisted. Here he entered the R.A.F. He became, in time, a group captain, the English air force equivalent of an American colonel. He flew a number of bombing raids over Europe, though, given his temperament, we should have expected him to be a fighter pilot.

In late 1942, he was transferred to the Far East theater. There he managed to visit for a few days with his Waziri, who were with those Kenyan forces sent to this area to fight the Japanese. He was in on the tenth Air Force B-24 bombing raids on Bangkok and various enemy sites. In November, 1943, the Tenth joined General

1943: THE WORLD
(From the 1944 *World Almanac*)

The total world population, based on 1939 data, was an estimated 2,169,868,000.

F. D. Roosevelt was President of the United States.

George VI was king of England; his prime minister, Winston Churchill.

Hitler held most of Western Europe and a good part of Eastern Europe, but he had lost northern Africa. Japan held an enormous area in east Asia, southwest Asia, and the Pacific. Before the year was over, much of this territory would be regained by the Allies.

Advertisement: YOU MAY BE SITTING PRETTY NOW, BUT AFTER THE WAR, WHAT?; LaSalle Extension University and Correspondence Institution, Chicago, Illinois, *World Almanac*.

Among new inventions were: (1) a cheaper safer hand grenade the size and shape of a baseball which used centrifugal force to set off the fuse; (2) the use of solid strands of nylon-type plastic in tires to replace cotton and rayon cords; (3) the hope for the conquest of venereal disease by penicillin was expressed because of reports of cures of syphilis and gonorrhea by this safe and potent chemical from molds; (4) a major factor in causing sterility and stillbirths was traced to incompatibility of parents with regard to a newly recognized blood factor, Rh.

Undernourished children scored as much as 14 points higher in IQ tests after being given an adequate diet.

The Brooklyn Syndrome, a chip-on-the shoulder defensiveness of men from crowded districts of some large cities, as well as some rural districts, was identified and differentiated from the psychopathic personality.

Chapter Twenty-three

(XXII)

Exit Tarzan, Smiling

When the half-gods go, men arrive.

—P. J. Finnegan

Now, that which he had lost he had regained.
That whch he loved most. Freedom.

—Tarzan

"Tarzan says that it does no good to hate. . . ."

—Corrie van der Meer

Tarzan and the Foreign Legion, Volume XXII, begins on March 13, 1942, when the Japanese paratroopers landed at Palembang, Sumatra. Sumatra was the largest island of the Netherlands East Asia possessions (later to be part of the Republic of Indonesia). It is 1,069 miles long and 246 miles at its greatest width. It lies off the southwest coast of the Malayan peninsula, running generally southeast to northwest. Almost as large in area as Spain, it is very mountainous in the west with great areas covered with dense jungle. The equator splits it almost in half.

A Dutch rubber planter took to the hills with his family and two Chinese servants. Two years later, only the daughter, Corrie van der Meer, and Sing Tai, a servant, were alive. They were high in the remote mountains, staying with a native chief. And then they were betrayed, Sing Tai was bayoneted, and Corrie was marched off to the Japanese post.

In January, 1944, a B-24 Liberator bomber took off from its

base in India. Its mission was not to bomb but to photograph enemy installations or anything suspicious along the west coast of upper Sumatra. Aboard were eleven men. These included Staff Sergeant Joe "Datbum" Bubonovitch, a Brooklynite of Russian descent; Staff Sergeant Tony "Shrimp" Rosetti, a Chicagoan of Italian descent; Captain Jerry Lucas, part-Cherokee, of Oklahoma City. With them was Group Captain John Clayton of His Majesty's Royal Air Force. (Burroughs calls him Colonel, doubtless for the convenience of his American readers.) The Englishman was along as an observer, having been attached to the U.S.A.A.F. of the Eastern theater for some months in this capacity.

These men, together with others that would join them in their tremendous odyssey—Corrie, Sing Tai, Dutch guerrillas, and a beautiful Eurasian, Sarina—would form the "Foreign Legion." Rosetti was suspicious of Clayton, because the late great Mayor Bill Thompson of Chicago had hated Britishers and especially the sinister George the Third. In time, Rosetti would go from suspicion and repressed hostility to outright admiration, if not worship, of the Englishman. And when he found out that "George the Thoid" was really a German, he relaxed his attitudes toward England in general.

It is difficult to recognize in the group captain our Tarzan. He is affable and gregarious, even passing out cigarettes to the others and inquiring about their backgrounds. He looks as if he is twenty-five, though he was fifty-five, of course. There was nothing as yet to reveal him as anything but an R.A.F. officer and not even the "dook" that Rosetti said he was.

But, when the plane was shot down, he parachuted into the jungle and there threw away everything except a web belt and his hunting knife. (It's presumed the knife is his father's, though Burroughs never says so.) That he made a loincloth of parachute silk is significant. In his last adventure, he reverted to the ape-man. But he didn't wear leopard or deer skin. He wore silk from a modern technological device. He had stepped upward in his evolution. At least, he is marked with "civilization"; the silk cloth is a badge.

He was happy. Without transportation except his feet and hands, in a jungle over sixteen hundred (airline) miles from the nearest Allied base, surrounded by enemies, he was happy. He had shed his uniform, which, though it had been worn proudly, was bondage in both symbol and reality. As the rain beat on his naked body, he restrained his yell of exultation only because he was in enemy territory.

But the country, though not Africa, was *his* country. He was like a fish here, a shark, while all other men, Allies, Japanese, or even natives, were as divers, men out of their element.

After locating Bubonovitch, Rosetti, and Lucas, he set out. It wasn't long before he was their unquestioned leader. Clayton taught them what he knew about survival in the jungle. But between them and him was this difference. They just survived, and they longed for the day they could get out of the terrible jungle. He flourished, and if it had not been for his duty, he could have stayed in Sumatra a long time.

His lessons included the eating of raw meat. This demanded swallowing whole small pieces, not chewing them. Rosetti asked Clayton where he had learned this. Clayton replied, "From the lions." This confirmed Rosetti's belief that the Englishman was crazy, though he had to admit to himself that they all should be as nuts.

Clayton found the wounded Sing Tai. Learning that Corrie had been taken by the Japanese, he entered their camp and cut a sentinel's throat. He carried off the girl, and the party continued their odyssey. But they were not by any means to see the last of the Japanese. Lucas, whose girl had written him a Dear John letter telling him she was marrying a 4-F, pretended indifference to the beautiful Dutch girl. He was through with women. But he was attracted despite his misogyny, and, when she was taken away by some Sumatran collaborators, he was deeply affected. Corrie, however, escaped, only to be confronted by a hungry tiger. Clayton dropped from a tree onto the big cat, killed it with his knife, and then gave the victory cry of the bull great ape.

Jerry Lucas suddenly knew who Clayton was.

"Lord Greystoke—Tarzan of the Apes!"

Rosetti's jaw dropped.

"Is dat Johnny Weissmuller?"

No one appreciated this remark more than Clayton. He had laughed every time a new Tarzan movie came out; they were so untrue and unrealistic. (Despite this, he couldn't resist seeing every one that came out and had even purchased the first one, starring Elmo Lincoln, 1918, to show for his private amusement.)

However, for a few seconds after the victory cry, he was the primordial mangani, and he looked at the humans with suspicion. Then he quickly regained his "second self," as Burroughs called it. His dual nature enabled him to pass easily from Clayton, Lord Greystoke, to Tarzan, son of Kala, and back again. But there was no doubt which was his pristine person and which he preferred. Tarzan was truly the untamed, and if he appeared to be a highly cultured and even well-read and informed man when in the cities, he was only wearing the persona. The wild beast lurked behind the mask; it could be dropped more quickly than a false face at a carnival.

To think, Rosetti told himself, that he'd ever be running around the jungle "wit Tarzan of de Apes." But he found out that Tarzan, though essentially as undomesticable as Sheeta, was in many ways more "civilized" than he. Rosetti wanted to kill all the natives who had abducted Corrie. But Tarzan said he killed only for food and defense. This he had learned from the beasts.

"Those who kill for any other reason, such as for pleasure or revenge, debase themselves."

But Tarzan had not in any way gone soft. The captured leader of the collaborators knew this. He had looked into the tall man's grey eyes and seen the eyes of a tiger.

Later, Tarzan told the party that he could remember feeling hatred or having killed for revenge only once. That was when Kulonga killed his foster mother, Kala. But he was very young then and Kala was the only creature in the world that loved him or that he loved. He had never regretted this killing.

Tarzan was forgetting what he had done when he thought Jane had been killed by Schneider and his men. Nevertheless, his basic statement was true.

In several of the epics, Tarzan is reported as speaking lovingly, tenderly, of Kala. It is fitting that in this last recorded adventure we should know that he has not forgotten her. It has been thirty-seven years since that terrible day on which she died, but Tarzan still thinks of that great, hairy, brute-faced, long-fanged creature as beautiful and precious and he thinks of her often. But he does not suffer from neurotic grief; her memory does not cripple him.

Later, Tarzan came across an elephant. It was, of course, of the smaller Asiatic species, having small tusks and ears and with the same number of toes on fore and back feet. But it was as much Tantor as its cousins in Africa. It understood, though it could not speak, some of the mangani language. (Tarzan believed that this speech was understood by all the more intelligent animals of the world.) Tarzan "talked" to Tantor and then departed, reluctantly. Tantor was always his best friend among the beasts. Between him and the great grey dreadnaught of jungle and savanna was a vibration of sympathy, perhaps of empathy. He and Tantor could be together, loaf, invite their souls to their heart's content.

As Tarzan told his friends, Tantor had saved his life on more than one occasion (three, to be exact). Whenever he came across Tantor and wasn't pressed by business, he tarried with him, even if only long enough to speak a few words and pet him.

The "Foreign Legion" pushed on. The country was so rough that Rosetti said that God must have been practicing when He made it. Tarzan, following strange tracks, met a group of orangutans. He saved one from a python, but a belligerent young ape, Oju, forced him to fight. Tarzan got a half-Nelson on him and pressed his knife point against his side. Oju said, "Kagoda!" But, as with Terkoz many years before, Tarzan would have done better to have killed his antagonist then and there. He went on, though he would have liked to stay with these mangani who looked so much like the comic-strip Jiggs. We don't have to accept Burroughs' account of the ability of the orangutans to talk. Nor should we accept his account of the abduction of Corrie van der Meer by Oju as anything but fiction. Burroughs must have put in this scene to "spice" up the story or because he thought his fans would be dissatisfied without it. The story, however, does not need it. And the book, with the exception of the orang speech and the abduction, is very close to the reality.

A little later, Tarzan was captured by a band of white criminals. A captive, Tak van der Bos, freed him. Tarzan killed a sentry, took his rifle, and the two escaped into the tiger country.

Before the "Foreign Legion" reached the southern end of the island, its members had many adventures. The reader may enjoy these in detail in Volume XXII. Some revealing things must be noted here, however. When identifying himself to a band of suspicious Dutch guerrillas, Tarzan did more than say he was John Clayton of the R.A.F. He told them he was Tarzan. One of the Dutchmen confirmed his claim, remarking on the scar on his forehead gotten in the battle with the gorilla when he was ten. (It was, however, Terkoz who'd ripped the scalp open.)

And Captain Jerry Lucas was to remark that the Tarzan books had strongly influenced his life.

So Tarzan, flesh and blood, had also become a well-known, and even influential, figure of literature. Though still living, he had passed into folklore and myth, became a hero and a demigod.

Yet despite his great superiority, making him an Odysseus and a Hercules, he is shown as having become more human. He even makes jokes and kids around with the men. His trickster role has been shed. Now, when he dogs the enemy, he does so with grim efficiency. He is all business, the "red business," as Whitman called it. No more does he terrorize by plucking an enemy from his fellows with a rope around his neck and then placing his severed head on the trail ahead of the band. Now, he shoots from the jungle cover, one, two, three. All business.

Still, he finds time to make friends with Tantor and the monkeys. One, Keta, travels with him through the forest and even accompanies him when the Legion sails for Australia on a proa. Keta reminds him of Nkima, whom he hasn't seen for years. And Keta reminds him also of his beloved Africa. When will he see it again?

It is during this journey that Tarzan reveals that he has a prolonged youth. He tells the group about the witch doctor who had known Tippoo Tib's grandfather. The doctor, grateful because Tarzan saved him from a lion, gave him the immortality treatment. And Tarzan also told them about the pills obtained from the Kavuru.

"Would you want to live forever?" they asked him.

He replied that he would as long as he did not have to suffer from old age's infirmities.

One objected that his friends would be gone. Tarzan replied that he would miss them, but he was constantly making new friends. This statement tells us that Tarzan was not only well adjusted to the harshness of reality, but he was thoroughly human. A pure demigod does not make friends.

However, Tarzan continued, his chances of living forever were very slight. With the type of life he led, a bullet would get him or a lion or a buffalo.

"Death has many tricks up his sleeve beside old age."

True. But, human though he was, Tarzan had a force about him that moved him into the superhuman. This force twisted the paramagnetic lines of the fields of probability. Odds might seem to be a hundred to one against him; in the last few seconds, they always became one to one or less, in his favor. Born on the cusp of Sagittarius and Scorpio, he had a double insurance for coincidence and favorable situations occurring in his neighborhood. Where he was, they seeded, sprouted, and bloomed.

Still, Death would win in the end.

He did not worry about it. When the time came, it would find him fighting with every atom of his mighty strength and will. And if he yelled during the battle, he would not do so with terror or panic. It would be with defiance, with the cry of the great ape attempting to scare Death.

The Legion went on over the mountains and through the dense jungle at an average of five miles a day—when they were traveling. Tarzan was captured by the Japanese, and Keta, the monkey, fled to Rosetti. The Chicagoan couldn't understand him, but he knew that something bad had to have happened to Tarzan. The Legion investigated, ambushed the Japanese, and rescued Tarzan. Once again, Tarzan was saved by an animal helper.

Rosetti and Sarina, the Eurasian, fell in love. Sarina, who spoke much better English than Rosetti, corrected his grammar and pronunciation. Lucas and Corrie van der Meer fell in love. But war cares nothing for lovers, and, when the Legion sailed toward Australia, it was blown out of its boat by a Japanese merchantman.

Here Tarzan made his last recorded kill, a shark. It was significant that it took place in the ocean, the womb of life. This is not the end of Tarzan and his adventures, Burroughs seemed to be saying to his readers. Tarzan, his father's knife in hand, kills the monster of the deeps, the terrifying killer. And in so doing, he is reborn in the great womb. He will continue through life, even if his life is no longer narrated by Burroughs. Burroughs knows he himself is mortal, but Tarzan is, in one sense at least, immortal.

The party is rescued by a monster from the deeps, another great grey killer. But this is an English submarine, and they set out for Australia.

Tarzan's last words are directed to Rosetti.

"What do you think of the British now?"

"I love 'em," Rosetti says.

The last description of the ape-man takes two words.

Chapter Twenty-four

Tarzan and the Monomyth

O God, Beast, Mystery, come!

—Euripides

Having established how human Tarzan has become, we now demonstrate that he is still like a demigod. Though he is not a semidivine being, since he is as much flesh as you and I, his life has many parallels to the central characters of myth, legend, and fairy tale. As we have said before, Tarzan was Nature's last creation of a Golden Age man. He has traveled on the path of the mythological hero. His life has been, as Joseph Campbell says of all heroes, "a magnification of the formula represented in the rites of passage: *separation—initiation—return*: which might be named the nuclear unit of the monomyth."

Campbell says earlier: "A hero ventures forth from the world of common day into a region of supernatural wonder: fabulous forces are there encountered and a decisive victory is won: the hero comes back from this mysterious adventure with the power to bestow boons on his fellow man."

Tarzan was the lost or abandoned or abducted heir to the throne or the ducal crown (or even a godship). He was in this respect like Oedipus, Theseus, Moses, King Sargon of Argade, King Chandragupta, Pope Gregory the Great, the Abraham of Hebrew legend, Romulus and Remus, Telephus, Zeus, and many others.

Tarzan was also the changeling of so many tales. Kala the great ape left her dead baby in the cradle when she took the infant Lord Greystoke. The mortal who is the twin of the immortal is Kala's dead baby. Hercules and his mortal brother, Iphicles, and Castor and his mortal twin, Pollux, resemble Tarzan and his dead ape twin in this respect.

Kala, of course, played the same part that the wolf-bitch did for Romulus and Remus, the doe for Telephus, and the goat, Amalthea, for the infant Zeus.

Many of the heroes were, as infants, unpromising. Tarzan, whom the great apes thought was retarded, and whom Tublat wished to kill, was an unpromising hero. Others were King Arthur as a young boy, the Little Tailor of the fairy tales, and the Pueblo Indian Water Jar Boy.

.But the unpromising infant reveals in time that he is precociously strong and clever. Hercules in his cradle strangles a snake sent by Zeus' wife to kill him. The infant Polynesian hero-trickster, Maui, ropes the sun and slows it down so his mother can have time to cook his meals. The Hindu god Krishna kills a goblin woman with poisoned breasts while he is still nursing. The Irish hero Cuchulainn becomes a berserk warrior at the age of four.

Tarzan, being of the same protoplasm as human beings, developed much more slowly than the mythological heroes. But at ten he was as strong as the average man of thirty, more agile than any Olympic athlete, and had killed his first monster, the mad Bolgani.

The folk and fairy tales of talking animals are of ancient origin and worldwide. Tarzan's great apes are not really such, however. Despite a bestial appearance, they are true sentients, symbol-users. In the same way, dolphins, if they are found to possess a genuine language, must be reclassified as sentients or sapients. They will be animals only in the sense that human beings are animals.

The gorillas and monkeys, however, are able to communicate to a limited extent, and elephants, lions, and leopards can understand Tarzan even if they cannot reply in anything but signals.

The stories of the Animal Helpers have come true in Tarzan's case through the media of Tantor, Sheeta, Jad-bal-ja, some other lions, and some monkeys (especially Nkima). Tarzan's freeing of a lion from a trap in Volume VII and its helping him later on recalls the story of Androcles and the lion.

Many legends and myths tell of the magical gifts left to the infant by dead or departed parents or by supernatural beings. For Tarzan, these would be his father's books, the hunting knife, and the rifle cartridges he found. The books enabled him to become more than just a wild man of the jungle. They prepared him for the great world outside Kerchak's territory and gave him a knowledge and a wisdom he would otherwise not have developed. The hunting knife recalls the sword that Aegeus, Theseus' father, left for him under a rock. With this sword, Theseus hacked a bloody way through all the evil men and monsters on the road to Athens. Without his father's knife, Tarzan would have died at the age of ten and many times thereafter. The cartridges which Tarzan found and which Teeka used to save his life are "magical" gifts. And, in a sense, his father's diary, written in a mysterious language, was also a magical gift. It bore the infant Tarzan's fingerprints and so proved his right to the title.

The Trickster role of Tarzan has been fully described, including the shape-shifting parallels. However, under the metamorphoses of Tarzan we must include his many names and titles. Besides being Tarzan of the Apes and John Clayton, Lord Greystoke, he was Munango-Keewati, the forest devil-god, M. Jean C. Tarzan of the rather large estate of Africa, John Caldwell, Waziri, Tarzan-jad-guru, Dor-ul-Otho, Caesar, Big Bwana, River-Devil, Greater-than-Mulumbe, Muzimo the ghost, Daimon, and Lord Passmore. If Volumes X and XXIV are real biography and not fiction, then he was also the Giant and Che, Lord Forest, a Mayan demon.

Tarzan fights the evil magician of legend and folk tales in the persons of Bukawai, Rabba Kega, and the majority of the medicine men he encountered. And, like many heroes, he sets out in quest of God, first, among his books, then among the mangani, and finally among the people of Mbonga. But he failed each time to find God, nor is it recorded that he continued his search in civilization.

The unpromising hero and the revenge of the son of his father's killer are combined when Tarzan slays Kerchak and becomes king of the people who rejected him.

Like many culture heroes, Tarzan is an inventor. He invented—reinvented, rather—the grass rope and the running noose. He invented wrestling, as Theseus was said to have done. While fighting Terkoz, he conceived the full-Nelson on the spot.

The hero rescues the maiden and slays the dragon, as Perseus, Hercules, Marduk, and so many others have done. Tarzan rescued Jane from the lioness and from Terkoz (who might be regarded as a symbolic satyr) and from many men, beasts, and monsters while she was a maiden and afterward.

Like Odysseus, Tarzan was to wander far and wide and encounter many perils and seductresses before finally coming home to his wife. Tarzan, however, made many such odysseys, while the great Ithacan made only one.

Aeneas, Odysseus, Gilgamesh, Maui, Orpheus, Hercules, Beowulf, Väinämöinen, and many others went into the underground (or underwater) world, into Hell. The Eskimo hero Raven, Jonah, and Hiawatha were swallowed by monsters of the deep. The Irish Finn MacCool was gulped by a monster called the *peist*; Maui, by his great-great-grandmother, Hine-nui-te-po. These descents or swallowings are supposed to symbolize death or annihilation, and the escapes are the rebirths of the heroes. Tarzan's descent into the ancient and perilous underground of Opar was for him a form of death and rebirth. It enabled him to find the inexhaustible golden treasury, a form of the Finnish Sampo. And he became, in one bound, a new person, though in a material, not spiritual, sense.

His first Oparian experience made him a new person in the sense that he would henceforth be an independent being in civilization if he cared to live in it or near it. He had the wealth to guard him from all material cares in the outside world. Moreover, his descent into the underworld and his emergence can be considered as a spiritual birth in one sense. He was tempted by the seductress, La, and did not fall.

The theme of the Seductress or Temptress occurs many times in myth and legend. Odysseus had his Calypso and Circe; Samson, his Delilah; Merlin, his Viviane; Arthur, his Morgan le Fay; Gilgamesh, his Ishtar. The main temptresses for Tarzan were Olga de Coude, La of Opar, and Nemone of Cathne. However, only one of these, Nemone, was evil, and she was not morally responsible, being mad. Jane was also a temptress, since it was because of her that he became "civilized." But even Jane's spell on him was not overly powerful. If it had been, he would not have spent so much time without her in the wilds. Jane, however, knew when to bind and when to loose. Tarzan was happy with the way matters were arranged, and if Jane was discontent she never said so—to the best of our knowledge.

The hero has to make a self-sacrifice if he is to advance spiritually. Tarzan's consisted of refusing to claim his title when doing so would have meant a great loss for Jane.

The theme of the World Redeemer, the Savior of the People, is repeated many times in Tarzan's life. He saves Opar, the mangani, the Waziri, Pal-ul-don, Castra Sanguinarius and Castrum Mare, Athne and Cathne, the Utengis, the black slaves of the Bolgani, the people of Midian, of Almetejo and Zuli, and the slaves of the Kavuru. He saved the world from a possible world war when he ruined Zveri's plans, though this only put off the inevitable for a few years.

Tarzan's encounters with the boastful strong man of Cathne, Phobeg, and with others recalls Hercules' combat with the earth-giant Antaeus, and with Eryx in Sicily, and Theseus' with Sciron, Sinis, and Procrustes.

The boon that the hero may bestow on his fellow man is, in Tarzan's case, the Kavuru youth-elixir pill. If Tarzan had given this to the world, he would have brought about the end of aging. And then the rate of population increase would have accelerated even more and with an accompaniment of far greater pollution and other problems. But Tarzan refused to open this Pandora's box for Earth, and his decision was quite wise.

Tarzan's boon was the withholding of the boon.

Another classical theme prominent in Tarzan's career was that of the Master Thief.

Hermes was the patron god of thieves, being himself a great one almost from birth. Autolycus, Hermes' son and Odysseus' grandfather, was also noted for his nocturnal projects and especially for his rustling of Sisyphus' cattle. His name meant "Very Wolf" or "Lone Wolf," and, in this respect, too, he resembled Tarzan, who was a lone wolf. Odysseus, as we know, was also a great thief.

Tarzan's thefts began with the stealing of arrows and other weapons and body decorations from the people of Mbonga. His greatest feat, however, was the stealing of the gold and jewels from the underground treasury of Opar. It is true that the Oparians had no idea that their city contained such wealth. Nor would they have had much use for the treasure if they had known of it. Nevertheless, from a "civilized" or legal viewpoint, it was their property, and Tarzan was a burglar. He also stole the giant Gonfala diamond and the great Zuli emerald.

But what he did was on such a scale and under such circumstances that his deeds, like the heroes of old, were above the bounds of morality. Moreover, all the people from whom he stole were out to kill him before he had an idea of taking their property. Thus, it can be successfully pleaded that he was justified. He was merely emulating civilized nations, which consider it morally justifiable to take the property of the people with whom they are at war.

Tarzan's harrowing of Opar is like that of Hercules' and Theseus' of Hell. And his threading of the dark underground maze of Opar reminds us of Theseus' penetration to the center of the Minoan labyrinth. In this respect, La may be considered an Ariadne. And in another incursion into Opar, Tarzan, rescuing Jane, is like Orpheus bringing Eurydice out of Hades. But, where Orpheus failed, Tarzan succeeded.

Another classical theme is the Lethean. It can be said that Tarzan drank of the waters of the river of Lethe many times (three, to be exact). His frequent losses of memory make this an unforced parallel.

Besides descents, heroes have, from time to time, made ascensions. Hercules, Castor and Pollux (according to one account), Abraham, Elijah, and others have been drawn up to Heaven. Tarzan's ascension occurred when, as Dor-ul-Otho, the Son of God, he left Pal-ul-Don on the back of the monstrous reptile, the gryf.

In this connection, his son Korak played the classical role of the Messenger of Death for the Great God. He arrives just in time to save his parents by killing the false god, Obergatz, with means that seemed godlike to the Pal-ul-donians.

The African, Tarzan, had a career much like that of the North American, Hiawatha.

But first we should clarify that Longfellow's poem is really about that Algonquin trickster and culture hero, Nanabozho. Longfellow took his data from the scholar Henry Schoolcraft Rowe, who made a great and famous goof in confusing the Iroquois hero Hiawatha, who actually lived, with the Algonquin hero. But, in other respects, Longfellow's characters are valid enough. In this comparison, we'll keep Hiawatha's name, but we'll really be speaking of Nanabozho.

The human parents of Tarzan, like Hiawatha's, are absent. Tarzan's are dead; Hiawatha's mother is dead and his father is gone. Both heroes are raised by a nonhuman; Tarzan, by the great ape Kala; Hiawatha, by Nokomis, daughter of the Moon.

Both Tarzan and Hiawatha know the language of the animals.

No one is so swift of foot or such an archer as Hiawatha; the same is true of Tarzan.

Hiawatha fights his father. Tarzan, in a sense, does the same when he fights his foster father, Tublat. However, Mudjekeewis, Hiawatha's father, after being defeated by his son, sends him out as a slayer of monsters and wicked magicians and as a cleanser of the earth. Tarzan performs the same feats as Hiawatha but his occurred as an accidental byproduct of his wanderings or because his wealth attracted criminal men.

Hiawatha had his superhuman friends and allies, Kwasind the Strong and Chibiabos the Singer. Tarzan's human friends were not of heroic stature, but his animal allies could be considered as fulfilling the roles of Hiawatha's great friends. Jad-bal-ja, and the Sheeta who killed Rokoff, and Tantor are Kwasinds, though they cut a larger figure than the Algonquin Hercules.

Nkima, the monkey, is like Adjidaumo, the squirrel, who helps Hiawatha, especially in getting out of Mishe-Nahma, the monstrous sturgeon who swallowed Hiawatha. The sea gulls who also aid him in escaping the great fish's belly recall the other monkeys and beasts Tarzan summoned from time to time to help him.

Hiawatha kills Megissogwon, the evil magician who slew the father of Nokomis and infected the people of Hiawatha with deadly fevers. Mama, the woodpecker, aids Hiawatha in his battle with Megissogwon. Tarzan killed Kerchak, who had killed Tarzan's father, though without the aid or advice of anybody else. But there are other adventures in which Nkima and other monkeys, like the woodpecker, provide help.

Tarzan, like Hiawatha, regards the serpent as the spirit of evil. And Tarzan, like Hiawatha, is one with Nature.

The ape-man's career as a hero fulfills most of the transformational criteria established by Campbell and other mythographers: the Primordial Hero and the Human, Childhood of the Human Hero, the Hero as Warrior, the Hero as Lover (but not the Hero as Emperor and Tyrant), the Hero as World Redeemer, and the Hero as Saint (in the sense that he doesn't care for the outside world of civilization).

The final chapter of this biography tells of the Departure of the Hero, which is the last of the transformational criteria.

Chapter Twenty-five

The Rest Is Silence

Kindle, as I, his lamp, and from the
  parchment
Shaking the dust of ages, will transcribe
My chronicles.

—A. Pushkin

Edgar Rice Burroughs did start to write Volume XXV of Tarzan's biography. But the Ender of Tales visited him, and so we shall have no tales by him of what happened to Tarzan after 1944.

Tarzan was discharged after the war. He returned Keta to the Sumatran jungle. Nkima would never accept another monkey pet of Tarzan's, and Tarzan would not care to hurt Nkima's feelings.

Tarzan had a joyous reunion with Jane, his son Jack, Meriem, Korak, and his grandsons, John Armand and John. All of them except little John had served in the war against Germany and Japan. Of the men, John Armand was the only one who had not risen high in rank or received many medals. But he was actually an espionage agent who spent most of the war in France, Germany, and Norway under various disguises. Like his uncle, Captain Hugh Drummond, he was a master at make-up, though, unlike his uncle, he seems to have been a superb linguist.

In 1946, those who knew Tarzan's real age and did not know of his immortality treatment thought it queer that he looked so young. What, then, would he do in, say 1971, when he was eighty-three? Once others really believed he had the secret to prolonged youth, they would be like hungry hyenas. They would try to capture him so they could torture the information from him. Or they would seize Jane to use as a lever.

This may have happened; this may be one of the adventures Burroughs did not get to report.

Thus, Tarzan had to arrange a false death, not only for himself but for Jane, John Paul, Korak, and Meriem. Young John Armand would then become the ninth duke of "Greystoke." He would know where his parents and grandparents would be, of course. And the time would come when he would have to arrange his own "death," providing that the real article did not occur.

Where would Tarzan live then?

The Mau Mau uprisings (1952–1956) would have made life exciting and dangerous in Kenya. The Waziri would not have aided their enemies, the Agikuyu, of course. Tarzan was a white but not, in their eyes, a *real* "white man." He had always treated them as men, not as inferior natives or blacks. They were not his physical or mental equal, of course; no one, black, white, yellow, or brown, was. But he was their Tarzan.

The Mau Mau rebellion would have given us another volume in the biography. Some time afterward, Kenya became ruled by the blacks, as was inevitable. Tarzan could have stayed in his plantation if he had become a citizen of Kenya. Losing his titles of nobility would not have stopped him from doing this. He could easily have renounced them or given them to his son or grandson. But he could not stay in Kenya. Too many were wondering about his youthful appearance. And too many were investigating the source of his wealth. Tarzan did not flaunt this; he lived moderately. But men had ways of finding out that he could get gold when he needed it. The Kenyan leaders could bring against him the full force of their army and air force if they wished. He had to leave, and he had to do so soon.

He arranged the report of his death. He also arranged for new identities and papers. He arranged, in fact, for a dozen identities and purchased a dozen homes and estates in a dozen countries around the world. London and Paris, however, were out. He and Jane had too many friends and acquaintances there, even though they had always led quiet lives and shunned publicity.

Tarzan took a farewell tour of Kenya. What he saw saddened and angered him but strengthened his intention to leave. The old and beautiful animal life was dying out. The great herds of antelope and zebra were gone. The giraffe, the elephants, the lions, the leopards were numerous only in the national parks. And there the poachers were helping them along to extinction.

Herds of cattle were taking the place of the many and varied animals. A dull uniformity of cows was ruining the savannas; the cattle had dislodged the many species, each holding its niche in the ecology, each now gone and their functions in balancing Nature not replaced. The savannas would be a desert waste in a few decades. Then the cattle would die, and the native herdsman would starve. And the life would be gone except for a few trees in the wind-carved land and the lone vulture, the little fox, the rodents and the lizards. This might take fifty years, but it was coming, was coming.

Tarzan went into the rain-forest mountains of eastern Congo. The gorillas were few. They would be extinct by 1990, at the very latest.

He searched long before finding any mangani, a single family, a male, two females, and three children. He knew none of these; all his old friends were gone. And even this pathetic little family would be gone before another five years. One of the babies was dying of disease; the mother was too old to have any more children. Disease, hungry leopards, the press of the exploding black population would get them.

Tarzan was touched with sorrow. But he knew that the mangani were doomed before he had been born. Their population had dropped to a point below the vital level in the late nineteenth century.

He went into the great deep dark Ituri Forest. This had been reduced considerably since he had first entered it. Ax and fire, wielded by the natives, had felled great tracts. But there were still vast tracts where none but the pygmy lived or even ventured briefly. Here Sheeta prowled in quest of Wappi and Horta, and here Tarzan would roam for another fifty years before it became too small and crowded. Perhaps. Things were changing so fast he might not have even that time.

There was still his homeland, Gabon. This was very thinly populated and much of it was still rain forest. The Gabon gorilla would last longer than his eastern Congo highland cousin, and there might be a few mangani deep in the interior.

Still, he could only take a vacation there now and then. Jane couldn't live in the Ituri or Gabon. Both places were just too unhealthy for her. Moreover, she was civilized. The tree house in the jungle, which those bad movies of him had invented, was not for Jane.

So Tarzan and Jane went to their mansions near New York City and San Francisco and Guatemala City, their house in the Colorado Rockies or the Cumberland country of England or in New Zealand or their mansion on a jungle-covered mountain just outside of Rio de Janeiro. Or their house in the Kashmir mountains of India or the Swiss Alps or any of a score of other estates.

Now and then, Tarzan would have to leave civilization. He would kiss Jane and take off, and in the jungle he would renew his soul and his strength with the animals and the trees, avoiding man as much as possible. For Tarzan, no matter how skillfully he conducted himself in civilized society, was still the essential Outsider. He was the Insider only when among the trees that had given birth to the first men—and to him. There he was a beast and a demigod, the foundling who had become the lord of the green domain.

Before leaving with Jane for one of their new homes, Tarzan made a last trip to Opar.

It was evident that Opar would soon be "discovered." He had reports that it had been photographed several times by planes, and he heard that the native government in whose territory it was intended to send a helicopter and a crew in to explore. None of the reports said anything about the roofs being covered with gold.

Tarzan set out for Opar at once, traveling swiftly on foot as only he could, while a hundred Waziri trailed along behind him. He was clad only in a leopard-skin loincloth and was armed with his father's hunting knife (now well worn) and a bow and quiver of arrows. This time he did not take it easy nor allow himself to merge into the beast's one-dimensional view of Time. He had business to transact.

The sky was cloudless, and the moon was full when he came to the ancient valley. Across its bare boulder-strewn floor was the city. As always, it was silent and brooding. But, while he neared it, he did not have that feeling that eyes were watching him. Or that the silence had been made only to be broken. This time, this time, what waited for him? His heart beat faster; his throat narrowed. He was not afraid, because he did not know what fear was. But he felt pain. Pain for what? He did not know. Perhaps for the life that would never be there again.

His forebodings, his imaginings, were soon verified. The gold and the diamonds were still in the vaults, waiting for hands to brush off the dust of millennia and to carry them off. The underground corridors and chambers were empty, if he did not count the bones of men. The rooms under the domes and the spires were empty. The hieroglyphs on the wall still held their secrets. The courtyard with its bloodstained altar was empty.

Here and there were a few skulls and bones, all gnawed and scattered about by rats.

Tarzan felt like calling out, "La! La!"

But he didn't. Not at first. He knew that she was not here, at least not in living form, and he had never been one to waste speech.

But he was, after all, human. And so, within a few minutes, his deep voice rang out.

"La!"

Under the brightness of the great African moon, his voice soared out again.

"La!"

Monkeys and parrots and other birds screamed their fright and their protest.

He waited until they had settled down, and he called the last time.

"La!"

The monkeys and the birds shrilled, and then they became quiet. The moonlight was bright, but it made the shadows even darker. The shadows seemed to have absorbed Time, to have been stained by many thousands of years. Where the moonlight was warm, they were cold. The skulls in the shadows gleamed palely and seemed to waver, as if they were under moving water.

Tarzan was silent thereafter. He buried the bones, the heavy leg bones and bar-browed skulls of the men and the lighter bones and smooth-browed skulls of the females. He looked for evidence of the cause of death, but he found none. He also inspected the jeweled garments still on the female skeletons. None bore the distinctive clothing of the high priestess of Opar.

Had she died and been thrown to the lions in the pits? She would be, if still living, fifty-nine years old. And though she did not seem to have aged at all when he had last seen her, she was as subject to aging as anyone else. If she had anything like the Kavuru pill, she had not told him. And surely she would have done so since she had offered him everything she could think of to keep him. Perhaps, grieving for her lost beauty and her lost Tarzan, she had killed herself? Or had she gone into the jungle to look for him, either voluntarily or else fleeing from treachery by the successors of Cadj and Oah?

He would never know.

The Waziri arrived five days later, carrying ropes and shovels and picks and crowbars and large boxes of dynamite. By then Tarzan had decided that there was an easier way to hide Opar's existence than by covering it with rock. He had studied the terrain with the eye of the natural engineer (after all, his father had been one), and he found another way. There was a river that ran nearby which could be diverted into the valley if a canal were cut. It would take several months, and he would have to send back for much more blasting powder.

He and the Waziri buried most of the ingots and the jewels in a place not likely to be found. Later they would come back and get it. They would take some of the ingots and jewels with them. These would be sold from time to time on the black market, and the money was to be put into the tribal treasury. It would be spent for education and medical treatment and farming and husbandry equipment. The gold now buried would be split between Tarzan and his family and the tribe.

But there was much work to be done. The city of Opar had to be taken apart. The gold had to be stripped from the roofs and melted down. The great blocks of stone had to be tumbled down the cliff face. Tarzan toiled with the rest, lifting massive squares of granite that four Waziri could not lift although they were very powerful men. With every stone pushed over the edge of the cliff he felt as if another block of his life were falling away, as if his past were being dismantled.

But he was not one to get stuck in the past; he was as free of neuroses as it was possible for a man to be and still remain human. He worked on, and within two months the entire city was spread out over the valley floor. In another month, the digging of the canal was finished, and the earth dam blocking the flow of the river in its bed was also completed, and then the waters gushed out over the valley. They spread out at first but soon were channeled in the trough at the deepest part of the valley. Within this the ruins of Opar lay, and within three days they were entirely covered.

The earth dam was strengthened even more, and vegetation was planted on it. And then the work of covering up the mine shafts in the hills began. This finished, the huge castle of the Bolganoids had to be leveled.

Tarzan had gone up to it a few days after exploring the city of Opar. He found the place deserted; the black natives who had lived there were gone. Apparently, they had packed one day and left. There was nothing to indicate why. But it was nothing unusual for whole groups in the central African jungles to get up and move out. Nor was it unusual for tribes to disappear from the ken of men with no clue as to what had happened to them. They were just gone.

The city of the gorilloids was much smaller than Opar and much easier to take apart and hide. It was torn down, and its blocks were dragged down the hills and cast over the edge into the river. The mine shafts were covered over, and traces of the work removed as much as possible. The jungle itself would do most of the covering up.

The gold in the mines would be discovered some day, though Tarzan believed it would not be for some time yet. This was a very remote and not easily accessible place. If affairs could be arranged, Tarzan might set up a dummy corporation under native directorship and "accidentally" discover the gold and mine it. Of course, there was always the high probability that the government would seize it for itself. But that would have to be chanced when the time came.

Tarzan, however, in destroying the city and the castle, had also preserved them. He was aware of their scientific importance, so he photographed every square inch before touching them. He measured everything, and he removed the hieroglyphs from their pillars and took them with him. Someday, the true location of Opar could be revealed to the world. And then archaeological books would be written, and scientists would come to whatever museum would house the records and the hieroglyphs. But that was in the far future. Immortals needed much money, and Tarzan knew the value of gold. He would keep the secret as long as he could.

The time came to leave.

The Waziri had marched off, singing under their burdens.

Tarzan stayed behind. The sky was clear tonight, and there was another full moon.

He stood on the edge of the wide valley, looking across the wide muddy stream.

Beneath it lay Opar, one with the sunken cities of Chadea and Atlantis.

Crocodiles had moved in. A great bull was bellowing on the banks below him. A small herd of hippos was rollicking above Opar. He waved good-bye to the city and to La, wherever she was. Good-bye to La. Good-bye also to Gimla the crocodile and Duro the hippo. They wouldn't last long, either. They had been here for millions of years before Opar, millions of years before the first true man walked across the steppes of Africa. But their days were numbered. The hunters were too many; every day thousands of new mouths were born and had to be fed. The hunters were slaughtering Gimla and Duro for the hides and the meat. And though this was a place difficult to reach, it would be reached. And the crocodile and the hippo would not last then.

He turned and trotted away. He was thinking that, perhaps, mankind would have perished in its own poisons before that day came. A few men would be left, of course. Men were too tough to be entirely killed off, barring a nuclear war. But if outraged Mother Nature, violated Mother Nature, retaliated, then Man would become few again. His cities would be crawled over by the lizard, and the owl would sit on the trees growing from their ruins. The survivors would be savages. Earth would begin to heal herself. And perhaps there might be enough elephants, monkeys, antelopes, buffaloes, leopards, lions, and, yes, even snakes, still living to re-populate the savannas and the woods.

The trees would green the earth again. The earth would be, if not as wealthy and as beautiful in life as it had been, still wealthy and beautiful enough. And he would, if he were lucky, be here to enjoy it, to loaf, to invite his soul, to have adventures, to talk with the beasts and those men worth talking to. Pass the time of day and of eternity with them.

If not, so be it.

The tall, bronzed, black-haired, and grey-eyed man, more Apollo than Hercules, disappeared into the green chambers.

The forest god's skin gleamed as he crossed an open space, and the moonlight seemed to bless him.

ADDENDUM 1

A CASE OF IDENTITY

or

The Adventure of the Seven Claytons

by

Professor H. W. Starr

This article originally appeared in the *Baker Street Journal*, New Series X, i, January, 1960. Professor Starr, a well-known critic and scholar, is the author of two books, *Gray As a Literary Critic* and *A Bibliography of Thomas Gray*, co-editor of the definitive edition of Gray's *Poems*, and editor of Gray's *Elegy*, Twentieth Century Interpretations series. He was an English professor at Princeton and Temple Universities. He is a member of the Sons of the Copper Beeches, a Philadelphia-based Scion Society of the Baker Street Irregulars, was its Headmastiff for many years, and has also been a contributor of articles to the *Burroughs Bulletin*. However, at the time he wrote this, he was not aware of the existence of organized Burroughs groups or of publications devoted to the works of Burroughs.

A CASE OF IDENTITY
H. W. Starr

There is, in the Sacred Writings, a question of identification, which to the best of my belief, has been neglected by the students of the Canon. This is the peculiar problem of John Clayton. To solve it we must begin by examining the brief career of a certain English nobleman who himself does not appear in any of Dr. Watson's cases, although other publications concerning his son of the same name have attracted much attention. The only published account of his life, by an American author, appeared shortly before the First World War. It is, according to the writer, based upon family diaries and official records then in the possession of the British Colonial Office.

This nobleman is John Clayton, Lord Greystoke,[1] but the author adds that this designation is not quite the correct one, a point which will be discussed later. Greystoke is described as "above the average height . . . his carriage that of a perfect, robust health, influenced by his years of army training. Political ambition had caused him to seek transference from the army to the Colonial Office." He seems to have been almost immediately "commissioned to make a peculiarly delicate investigation of conditions in a British west coast African colony from whose simple native inhabitants another European power was known to be recruiting soldiers for its native army, which it used solely for the collection of rubber and ivory from the savage tribes along the Congo and the Aruwimi." In May, 1888, he sailed with his wife, formerly the Honourable Alice Rutherford, from Dover. Since they had been married three months, their wedding obviously took place in early 1888. In June they arrived in Free-

---

[1] For accounts of the "Greystoke" family, as cited herein, see E. R. Burroughs, *Tarzan of the Apes* (New York, 1914), pp. 1–5, 38, 220, 236–39; *The Son of Tarzan* (New York, 1917), pp. 16, 54; and *Tarzan and the Ant Men* (New York, 1924), p. 18.

town and chartered a small sailing vessel, the *Fuwalda*, which was to take them upon the last leg of their journey.

For some twenty years, this was the last heard of the Greystokes, the vessel, and its crew. However, the Colonial Office documents we have mentioned reveal that the crew of the *Fuwalda* mutinied, murdered its officers, and marooned Lord and Lady Greystoke upon the west coast of Africa at approximately 10° south latitude. The Lady Alice was pregnant at the time, and a son was born, either late in 1888 or in early 1889. The boy was named John, after his father—and this is significant, for a later account of the Greystokes published in 1917 reveals that when, many years afterward, this son became a father, he too named the oldest child John. A still more recent account mentions the fact that this child also, when he had reached maturity and married, named *his* son John. Hence we have a reliable record of four generations of male Claytons, each named John. The conclusion is inescapable: John was the name invariably given to the oldest Clayton son, and the probabilities are overwhelming that the father of the marooned Lord Greystoke bore the name John Clayton.

There is one more fact which is of major importance. The Greystoke documents make it clear that John Clayton, Lord Greystoke, had a younger brother who succeeded to the title after John's disappearance. This younger brother had a son, William Cecil Clayton, who in 1909 was in the neighborhood of nineteen or twenty years of age.

Finally, it should be mentioned that in the second of the Greystoke publications discussed here there appears a passage which connects the fortunes of this family with the Canon, and which leads to the suspicion that the American author was not wholly unaware of the connection:

> Herr Skopf . . . was baffled. He had never heard of Sherlock Holmes or he would have lost no time in invoking the aid of that celebrated sleuth, for here was a real mystery . . .

If our curiosity is aroused by this puzzling little passage and we leaf through the consecrated pages of Watson in search of a name similar to Greystoke, we of course stumble across ". . . the case . . . of the Abbey School, in which the Duke of Greyminster was so deeply involved" (*The Adventure of the Blanched Soldier*). The passage is recognized by all Sherlockians as a reference to *The Adventure of the Priory School*. Now we know that, when necessary, Watson could be most discreet, and there were few of Holmes's cases that required more discretion than the kidnapping of Lord Saltire, heir to the Duke of Holdernesse.

Undoubtedly, the first precaution that was taken was the substitution of fictitious titles for the ones actually borne by the duke and his son. We should note that the family name of the duke is never mentioned. However, *The Adventure of the Blanched Soldier* is one of the two related by Holmes himself, and here, through either carelessness or indifference, he has let slip the correct title—Greyminster.

Another significant point is that the American who wrote up the misfortunes of John Clayton made at least a cursory attempt to obscure the identity of the nobleman. We may be certain that the names "John Clayton" and "Alice Rutherford" are authentic. Even a glance into Burke's *Peerage* or *Landed Gentry* will show us that the Claytons and Rutherfords are distinguished English families. Obviously no man in his right mind would try to disguise the identity of a nobleman by giving him the name of a different but equally prominent family. The writer would naturally manufacture a name which was *not* listed by Burke. Like most Americans, he thought of members of peerage in terms of their titles. The family name of a nobleman seldom occurs to us. Hence, it would seem sufficient to the author to alter the title alone. The oldest son of a duke is commonly known as Lord Blank, but the "Blank" is not the proper noun that appears in the title of the duke; the son of the Duke of Holdernesse, for example, is Lord Saltire, not Lord Holdernesse. Thus, the narrator of the Greystoke material very probably substituted a fictitious title derived from the first syllable of the title borne by Clayton's father. Clayton's real title was possibly some such designation as "Lord Stoke Poges"—although I shall not insist upon the validity of this specific example.

As our next step, let us examine in *The Adventure of the Priory School* the brief sketch of the Duke of Holdernesse—for to avoid confusion we shall continue to refer to him by that title. He is described as the sixth duke, as being since 1900 the Lord Lieutenant of Hallamshire,[2] and as the father of an only child, Arthur, Lord

---

[2] Hallamshire is an imaginary county but was the name of an ancient lordship. It has not had any official use in recent years. What careful, though futile, precautions Watson took to hide the identity of this great man!

Saltire, whose mother he married in 1888. These details are portentous. Holdernesse, of course, could not have been John Clayton, for Lord and Lady "Greystoke" did not survive to return to England; but it is very likely indeed that he is the younger brother of John Clayton. (Incidentally, both brothers were married in 1888, perhaps in a double wedding.) Nor do we have to seek very far for evidence of this identification. The younger brother of Clayton not only succeeded to the title, but also had a son, William Cecil, whose age corresponds very closely to that of Lord Saltire. This seems too close a correspondence of facts to be mere coincidence.

Since we have formed this hypothesis, we must seek in the Canon itself for a link which may act as confirmation. Is there, for example, any reference to John Clayton? There is. In *The Hound of the Baskervilles* the driver of the cab in which Stapleton trails Sir Henry and Dr. Mortimer is John Clayton, of 3, Turpey Street, the Borough. If this man belonged to the Greyminster family, he must have been an elder son, for he bears the name of John, which we have already established as traditionally reserved for the first son. But he appears at 221B in 1889 and remarks that he has been driving a cab for seven years. Consequently, it is impossible for him to be either "Greystoke" or "Holdernesse." Indeed, if he is connected with this family, there is only one person he can possibly be—the *fifth* Duke of Greyminster, father of the two Clayton brothers. He, of course, must have died before Holmes encountered his son, for *The Adventure of the Priory School* occurred during or between the years 1900–1903, and by that time the younger son had inherited the title.

There are a few minor details which would tend to confirm our identification. The only description Watson gives of the cab driver's appearance is "a rough-looking fellow." This is not a term that would ordinarily be applied to a small and insignificant man. Therefore, the cabman was probably fairly tall and muscular. Here we should pause to note evidence of a family resemblance. The father of Lord Saltire is described as "tall and stately," and "Lord Greystoke," like most of the males of his line, we know was robust and above the average height.

Another curious detail should be observed. In his conversation, the cabman does employ the words "gent" and "toff"; but his language, although far from Chesterfieldian, is by no means the illiterate speech we should expect from a London cab driver of the eighties.

These are, admittedly, rather slight grounds on which to base our assumption, although their cumulative weight is considerable. Unfortunately, they do not answer the obvious objection to our theory. Why should the fifth Duke of Greyminster spend seven years working as a London cabby? It cannot be denied that—until the recent emergence of the welfare state—few members of the British peerage have taken up the profession of cab driver. But this obstacle is not as insurmountable as one might think. Let us consider the probable age of John Clayton in conjunction with certain developments that took place in Victorian England.

If "Lord Greystoke," when he sailed from Dover in 1888, was still a young man—about twenty-four or -five, let us say—the approximate date of his birth was 1864; and we may reasonably assume that his father was a young, and possibly enthusiastic, man at that time. The year 1864 is an important date in social history, for it was then, in London itself, that the first International Workingmen's Association was founded by Karl Marx. And only three years later Marx published *Das Kapital*. Think of the impact of these events upon a young and enthusiastically idealistic aristocrat!

There was indeed a strong and aggressive social consciousness among many of the British intellectuals during the following years. In the 1880's, for example—the years during which Clayton took up cab driving—innumerable socialistic pamphlets poured from the pens of William Morris and his fellow radicals. All of these must have made a marked impression upon Clayton. But what could a British nobleman do to further the cause? He could not sell his vast estates and devote the proceeds to the advance of Socialism or Communism, for the estates were entailed. There was one thing, however, he could do: he could abandon his enormous wealth and live solely upon his own earnings as one of the underprivileged masses—a magnificent gesture! Unquestionably, John Clayton was one of the forgotten pioneers of social enlightenment; one of those enthusiasts who carry the principles of class equality to such an extreme that they refuse to live in, perhaps even to acknowledge, the class to which their birth entitles them. And in passing we might note that this rebellion against the *mores* of society was very likely inherited by his famous grandson, John Clayton

III, who, as the reader is doubtless aware, is well known for his frequently expressed contempt for the petty conventions, hypocrisy, and pusillanimity of our effete twentieth-century civilization.

It is an axiom of scholarship that "a hypothesis has met its supreme test when it solves not only the problem which it was designed to cover, but also the cognate problems that arise during further investigation." Let us see what cognate problems our hypothesis has solved.

In the first place, many readers have been rather startled by the irritable and belligerent attitude of the cab driver. Until Holmes soothes his ruffled feelings, his manner is far from that which we should expect a cabby to adopt in the presence of so august a figure as the Master. Yet this attitude is in no way unusual if our hypothesis is accepted. First, the fifth Duke would certainly not be humble, and—most important of all—in 1889 he must have been tortured by anxiety. His charming daughter-in-law and his older son, the handsome and promising "Greystoke," by far the more attractive of the two brothers, had both apparently vanished from the face of the earth. Under such circumstances, patience and conciliation would be the last thing we could expect from this man.

Our second problem is just as satisfactorily disposed of. The abnormal dread of publicity on the part of the "Duke of Holdernesse" in particular and the Greyminster family in general is a little hard to explain: for example, why this reluctance to acknowledge openly the real story behind the disappearance of the "Greystokes"? "Holdernesse," we know, had had an illegitimate child, James Wilder; he had been separated from his wife; his heir had been kidnapped, and an innocent man murdered in the course of the crime. These facts related by Watson are embarrassing enough, but they do not quite account for the Greyminster sensitivity. Let us, however, look at the picture we have uncovered. The fifth Duke had blossomed forth a rampant Socialist or Communist, had turned his back upon his own class, and had become a cab driver. Probably, he had hideously humiliated his snobbish younger son by turning up at the double wedding of 1888—one of the great social events of the season—dressed in a hackman's outfit and preaching inflammatory communistic doctrines in the lingo he had acquired during six years of cab driving and more than twenty years of radical political activities. Is it any wonder that the Greyminster family exerted pressure on the British Colonial Office not to publicize even the "Greystoke" mishap?

A third question to which our hypothesis provides an answer is that raised by *The Adventure of the Empty House*. Here Holmes informs Watson that during the period of his supposed death (1891–1894) he "paid a short but interesting visit to Khalifa at Khartoum." Of course, all Sherlockians are aware that during this time the Khalifa was not at Khartoum; so why did Holmes lie? We must remember that after the Reichenbach episode there was only one person who was aware both of Holmes's survival and of his hiding place. That person was Mycroft—and of Mycroft, Holmes said ". . . occasionally he *is* the British government." When "Lord Greystoke," who was to make "a peculiarly delicate investigation," disappeared, the Colonial Office would naturally feel it necessary to call in a master of "delicate investigations" to find the vanished nobleman. Doubtless, Mycroft as ʾa last resort called upon his brother. However, after so many years even the great Sherlock could not possibly discover the whereabouts of the "Greystokes"; and this is very likely the reason that Holmes—never the most modest of men and rather sensitive about his few failures—was reluctant to explain to Watson the real reason for his presence in Africa.

When a problem is as simple and straightforward as this one, a summary seems scarcely necessary; but in conclusion I think we may safely say that the hypothesis with which we began has justified itself, and that it had led to these sound conclusions: (1) that John Clayton, cab driver, is John Clayton, fifth Duke of Greyminster, father of the "sixth Duke of Holdernesse" and of John Clayton, "Lord Greystoke"; and (2) that the kidnapped "Lord Saltire" is William Cecil Clayton, seventh Duke, first cousin of John Clayton III, "Lord Greystoke," eighth Duke of Greyminster—popularly known as *Tarzan of the Apes*.

Addendum 1 contains the ingenious and delightful article by Professor H. W. Starr titled "A Case of Identity, or The Adventures of the Seven Claytons." This must be read first to understand Addendum 2. Starr's article is the springboard from which I have dived into deep waters.

Before delving into the Sherlockian Canon and the Tarzan Epic, hybridized for the first time by Professor Starr, I will state what I intend to do, or will attempt to do, in this "recasing."

One. I maintain that Starr is essentially correct in his article but that some of his conclusions have to be revised. Starr has opened a door to a mansion of many more rooms than he thought. Or, perhaps, he's raised the lid of a very big can of very big worms. But I prefer the first metaphor, unless you use "worm" in its early meaning of "dragon."

Two. I maintain that Watson, Doyle, and Burroughs used a form of coding to identify certain characters of the Holdernesse-Greyminster-Greystoke family. This family is generally referred to as Greystoke to save space, the reader's eyes, and to preserve Burroughs' traditional usage.) This coding was also used as clues to direct the scholar through Burke's *Peerage* and *Extinct Peerage* and many other works, both fact and fiction. This coding was not direct and often was deliberately tenuous and leads the researcher through circuitous trails.

The reader has by now an idea of what occurred in the case Watson calls *The Adventure of the Priory School*, even if he has not read the original. A more detailed summary is given here so that readers unacquainted with the original may know it (and perhaps be interested in reading the original). Also, a summary is necessary so that the code words used by Watson may be italicized. The reader will then understand thoroughly what I am explaining.

Watson and Holmes are visited by a Dr. Huxtable, owner-supervisor of the Priory School. This is a distinguished preparatory school for the sons of the wealthy and is located in *Hallamshire*. Hallamshire is, in the story, a still viable political district, though, in actuality, it is an extinct lordship. When it flourished, it included parts of Yorkshire and Derbyshire, taking in Sheffield, Doncaster, Barnsley, and Rotherham and other towns. Dr. Huxtable tells Watson and Holmes that the ten-year-old son of the sixth duke of *Holdernesse* has been kidnaped. The duke wishes no publicity, nor has he notified the police. The son is only referred to as Arthur or Lord *Saltire*.

The sixth duke of Holdernesse (whom Holmes refers to in another case as *Greyminster*) is *Baron Beverley*, and earl of Carston, Carston *Castle*, *Bangor*, *Wales*. He has a residence on *Carlton House Terrace*, which comprises two blocks of houses on the north side of the Mall, a very exclusive place.

The sixth duke is married to Edith *Appledore*, who is separated from him and living in the south of France. As it turns out, she is doing so because of the presence in the duke's house of his young secretary, James *Wilder*. The young man is actually the duke's oldest, and his illegitimate, son.

The duke is upset because Huxtable has called in Holmes, but he agrees to hire him if he remains discreet. However, when Holmes discovers the body of Heidegger, Lord Saltire's German teacher, the affair becomes the business of the police. The murderer is caught through Holmes' detecting. James Wilder, though not the murderer, is the instigator of the kidnap plot. Wilder intended to restore Arthur, Lord Saltire, to his father only if the duke would break the entail, that is, make Wilder his rightful heir. Wilder had nothing to do with the murder but was, of course, by law, an accomplice.

The duke pays off Holmes, and Wilder is supposed to leave at once for Australia to seek his fortune. The duchess is coming back from France for a reconciliation.

Legally, Wilder should have been apprehended by the police and charged with a hanging offense. But it is evident, as will be seen, that he escaped, and, as far as we know, the actual murderer was never brought to trial. We can only surmise that he died in jail shortly after being arrested, or that he escaped and Wilder's part in the case was suppressed.

As we shall see, James Wilder's son, born off the shore of Andros Island, the Bahamas, was to become very famous.

Three. The Edith Appledore who married the sixth Duke and was Lord Saltire's mother was the unnamed lady who shot down "the worst man in London" in Watson's *The Adventure of Charles Augustus Milverton*.

Four. Holmes and the Greystoke family had a closer relationship than that indicated in the Priory School case.

Five. Mr. Baring-Gould states in his *Sherlock Holmes of Baker Street* that Holmes and Challenger are first cousins. This can be shown as valid, though the relationship is not through Holmes' father. Not only that. Sir Percy Blakeney (the Scarlet Pimpernel), Dupin, Sherlock and Mycroft Holmes, Professor George Edward Challenger, Raffles, Tarzan, Korak, Doc Savage and his comrade, Monk Mayfair, Ludwig Horace Holly, Nero Wolfe, Lord Peter Wimsey, Lord John Roxton, Denis Nayland Smith, Richard Wentworth (the Spider), Kent Allard (the Shadow), G-8, and "Bulldog" Drummond are closely related. Of the nineteen named, be it noted, thirteen had grey eyes.

Six. George Bernard Shaw wrote a somewhat romanticized novel about the fifth duke of Greystoke (whom he calls Sidney Trefusis). Included in the novel were Edith Appledore's older sister and her cousin, who was Tarzan's paternal grandmother. The fifth duke's sister is mentioned therein.

Seven. A part of the genealogy, the hard core, as it were, will be demonstrated by textual evidence. Other relationships will be shown as necessarily existing because of similar physical and temperamental qualities that must come from a common descent. I will fill these slots with people for whom the genetic and chronological evidence is of the strongest. It's necessary to do this because a certain amount of inbreeding had to occur to bring out certain recessive genes. These genes bore the superheroic qualities of most of the men mentioned above. Anyone who writes of these has to be a creative mythographer, and that is what I propose to be. But the distinction will be made between relationships supported by textual evidence and those created to fill necessary genetic and genealogical slots. Also, there will be unavoidable repetitions, because the reader will need to be reminded of identities and descents in this complex family tree. To help the reader, a genealogical chart is provided. (See the endpapers inside the covers.) The numbers in parentheses in the text correspond to those in the endpapers.

Eight. I'll give my theory about the single cause of this nova of genetic splendor, this outburst of great detectives, scientists, and explorers of exotic worlds, this last efflorescence of true heroes in an otherwise degenerate age. But on to the revisions of Starr's theory.

Starr agrees with Burroughs that William Cecil Clayton (61) was first cousin of Tarzan (83). This means that the sixth duke of Greystoke (40) would be the younger brother of Tarzan's father (65). But Tarzan's father was a "young nobleman" when he married in 1888. If he were at most thirty years old, his younger brother (who later became the sixth duke) would be at most twenty-nine in 1888 and so born in 1859.

Yet Holmes' reference book states that the sixth duke (40) was a Lord of the Admiralty in 1872. At the age of thirteen?

An investigation of the Admiralty of 1872 uncovers no one likely to be the sixth duke. Nor would Watson have given the exact date. He was anxious to conceal the peer's true identity. But we may be sure that he held a position of similar importance around the early seventies and so, in May, 1901 (the date of the Priory School case), was not a young man. The sixth duke was at least thirty years old around 1872, which would make him born, at the latest, in 1842. He could not have been the younger brother of Tarzan's father, who was probably born around 1862. He would have been Tarzan's great-uncle, the younger brother of the fifth duke, John Clayton (43), the cabdriver questioned by Holmes.

Burroughs was as determined as Watson and Shaw to hide the real identity of this noble family. He purposely altered many facts in his biography. He knew very well that William Cecil (61) was first cousin to Tarzan's father (65).

Shaw knew the fifth duke (43) well, of course. He doubtless worked with him at committee meetings, demonstrations, and the writing, printing, and distribution of literature written by Clayton, William Morris, the Webbs, Marx, and others. Shaw, in fact, wrote Clayton's story as a novel. This was An Unsocial Socialist, first published in 1884 in the Socialist magazine, To-Day. The publication of this probably caused a break between Shaw and Clayton.

The novel takes place in 1875-1876 (according to Shaw). Its protagonist is Sidney Trefusis (43), who is about thirty years old. Trefusis, by the way, is the family name of the existing Barons of Clinton (see Burke's Peerage), but apparently Shaw's Trefusis was not the baron of Clinton.

According to Shaw, Trefusis' father (20) is a commoner, a Manchester bagman who has become a millionaire cotton-spinner. Jesse Trefusis (20) has married the daughter of a baronet who exploits his tenants as his son-in-law does his factory workers. Sidney (43), revolted by the treatment of the workers, becomes a Socialist. He deserts his bride and disguises himself as a common workman. Henrietta, his first wife, is the daughter of John Jansenius (19), a wealthy Jew converted to Christianity. Jansenius is the guardian of his sister's daughter, Agatha Wylie (44), who marries Trefusis (43) after Henrietta dies.

Shaw took care to keep from being sued by the Greystoke family when he wrote An Unsocial Socialist. His story is set ten years later than the real events, which occurred circa 1861–1862 in view of what we know about Trefusis' (Clayton's) real age. Shaw also made Trefusis only the grandson of a baronet, not a duke himself. He slipped up, however, in revealing that Trefusis' mother was a Howard. This, by the way, may account for the resemblance of the sixth duke (40) to Henry Fitzalan-Howard, fifteenth duke of Norfolk. This resemblance was noted by Michael Harrison in In the Footsteps of Sherlock Holmes. Note also that the sixth duke strongly resembles his nephew, Lord John Roxton (81), and Lord Rudolf Rassendyll.

John Jansenius (19) had another daughter, Edith (39), born circa 1866 after the events described by Shaw. She would be the Edith Appledore mentioned in Holmes' reference book as Sir Charles Appledore's daughter. Sir Charles (John Jansenius) was knighted only a few years before the Priory School case.

John Jansenius (19) was the son of Mr. Karoly (1), a Hungarian Jew. John was also the brother of Julius Higgins (22), who had changed his name after settling in Ireland. He invited his brother John and his sister (Shaw's Mrs. Wylie, 23) to follow him from Szombathelny, Hungary. They did so, but decided they could do better in England.

Watson gave Jansenius (Karoly) the name of Charles Appledore for two reasons. The Karoly reminded him of Carolus, hence, Charles, and Jansenius had built the apartments Watson called the "Appledore Towers" in The Adventure of Charles Augustus Milverton. In this building, Milverton was justifiably (if unlawfully) killed by Jansenius' youngest daughter (39). Watson recognized her and learned her identity when he and Holmes saw her photograph in an Oxford Street shop window shortly after the murder. This explains why he used the code word "Appledore" when mentioning her in the Priory School case.

John (Karoly-Appledore) Jansenius (19) had a sister, Shaw's Mrs. Wylie (23). She was, in reality, Mrs. Agatha Darcy, having married a Fitzwilliam Bennet Darcy (24). He was a member of the same family, the Darcys, of which the actual earls of Holdernesse (see Burke's *Extinct Peerage*) were the most prominent. The issue of this marriage was Athena Darcy (44), whom Shaw called Agatha Wylie. She married John Clayton (Shaw's Sidney Trefusis), the fifth duke of Greystoke (43). Watson gave the sixth duke the title of Holdernesse as a code word because of his close associations with the Darcys.

Pemberley House, as located by Jane Austen, is obviously on the same place as Watson's Holdernesse Hall. The estate had been in the possession of a branch of the Darcy family for centuries. The sixth duke had, in fact, only recently purchased it from a Darcy. The fifth duke, his brother, had married a Darcy who had lived on the estate when a little girl. The Darcys and the Claytons had a common origin. As Jane Austen in her *Pride and Prejudice* points out, the Darcys of Pemberley House were an ancient and honorable family but untitled. This branch, thus, must have been descended from a younger son of Norman de Areci, who held thirty-three lordships in Lincolnshire at the date of the Domesday Book. But the mother of Fitzwilliam Darcy (5) was the sister of a Fitzwilliam, Earl L———. (For L———, we can read Lambton, Jane Austen's name for Bakewell, Derbyshire. The real lord of Lambton is the earl of Durham, Viscount Lambton. D'Arcy is an old secondary family name among the Lambtons. See Durham, Burke's *Peerage*.)

The earl of Bakewell was not related to the earls of Fitzwilliam of Northampton and Ireland. He was of that branch of the family closely related to the now extinct Baron Greystokes of Cumberland. (See H. N. Nicholas' A *Synopsis of the Peerage of England*.) This Fitzwilliam branch even had the same coat of arms as the Cumberland Greystokes, probably from Rauph Fitz-William, the lord of Grimthorpe. His father had married a Greystoke, and so he came into the Greystoke barony when his uncle died. Fitzwilliam Darcy (5) was therefore entitled to bear the arms of the ancient Greystokes through his mother. The Claytons bear the Greystoke arms through two lines: the Grebsons and the Darcys.

We may dismiss Shaw's picture of Sidney Trefusis' father (20) as a commoner and bagman. He was, in fact, the fourth duke of Greystoke. The fourth duke inherited the title and some estates but little money, his father (2) having gambled it all away. The fourth duke made his fortune, however, through the exploitation which Shaw describes.

It's worth noting that Holmes was involved with six members of the Greystoke family. These were the sixth duke (40), his illegitimate son, James Wilder (63), and his legitimate son, Lord Saltire (61), in *The Adventure of the Priory School*; the fifth duke (43) in *The Hound of the Baskervilles*; the sixth duke's estranged wife (39) in *The Adventure of Charles Augustus Milverton*. If Starr is correct, Holmes may have been investigating the disappearance of the fifth duke's son (65) and his bride (66) in Africa during the Great Hiatus.

Most of Watson's and Doyle's writings preceded the publication of *Tarzan of the Apes* in 1912. Burroughs was familiar with them. He did not connect certain adventures of the Canon with his "Greystokes" until he first learned about Tarzan early in 1911. Like Watson and Doyle, he disguised the noble family. But he was also unable to resist coding so that it would be possible for some astute (and lucky) researcher to track down the truth. Perhaps these three should have resisted the temptation. But they were human, and they believed that their systems were so obscure and complex that, by the time they were decoded, all the principals would be dead. (At that time, Tarzan had not revealed that he had been given the elixir of prolonged youth by a grateful witch doctor.)

I was started on the trail by Starr's article, by noticing that Tarzan (83), Holmes (73), and Challenger (68) had grey eyes. I also discovered that, in the original manuscript of *Tarzan of the Apes*, "Greystoke" had been "Bloomstoke." Later, Burroughs crossed out "Bloom-" and substituted "Grey-."

Is there a connection between the wandering jewgreek of Dublin, whose story is told by James Joyce, and the wandering ape-man of the rather large estate of Africa?

The publication dates of *Ulysses* (1922) and of *Tarzan of the Apes* (1912) would seem to sever these ties. Surely, Burroughs could not have known about Bloom unless he had read Joyce's work. Nevertheless, I propose to show a definite connection between the two, not only in story but in blood.

(As an aside, Joyce used the verb "sherlockholmesed" in *Ulysses*, and I am presently looking for references to Tarzan and the Greystoke family in *Ulysses* and *Finnegans Wake*.)

Both Watson and Burroughs were Joycean in the multileveled (or many-armed) codes they used to conceal, and also to reveal, certain places and people. An investigation into both Bloomstoke and the later Greystoke, for instance, led me in several directions, yet all roads ended up at the same place.

Burroughs removed the "Bloom-" for esthetic reasons, among others. Greystoke is more aristocratic-sounding than Bloomstoke. Also, he may have thought, wrongly, that the "Bloom-" would make the truth too evident.

Burroughs had also intended to use "Bloom-" to point at Doyle. Thus, the scholar would eventually go to Watson and so to the Priory School case and so to others. The *Encyclopaedia Britannica* says of Doyle, "In 1902 a knighthood acknowledged his work with the Langham field hospital in *Bloem*fontein. . . ." (Italics are mine.) Bloemfontein is in South Africa. (Tarzan's grey-eyed cousin, A. J. Raffles, died near Bloemfontein during the Boer War.) Tarzan was born in Africa, and the sixth duke's nephew and son died there. Indeed, as we'll see, the uncle (49) of Tarzan's mother (66) died in the same African country, Gabon, as she.

Admittedly, this coding of Bloom into Bloem is a very slight, almost ectoplasmic, spoor to lead one to Doyle. But if this particular lead had escaped my notice, Bloom would have led me on another and more productive trail. An excursion into Burke's *Peerage* revealed no Blooms or blooming names (Blomefield, for instance) which could be linked up with Watson's or Burrough's noblemen. But a bloom is more than a flower. It is a noun and a verb, and it means flower, plant, or bouquet, to shine out or flourish, a wrought iron mass from the forge or puddling furnace, a *bar* of iron or steel hammered or rolled from an ingot.

A sniffing down the tracks of all these definitions (and mutations thereof) resulted in nothing until I tried all the titles beginning with *Bar-* in Burke's *Peerage*. Barbour through Barwick turned up Barrington.

The first Viscount Barrington, John Shute (d. 1734) inherited the considerable estate of John Wildman. The second and third viscounts bore the surname of Wildman. The greatest of all "wild men" is Tarzan, of course, and he is also a viscount, if Burroughs told us the truth. But there was nothing in the genealogy of Barrington to indicate that the viscounts were Tarzan's ancestors.

However, a further study enlightened me. The Wildmans were connected to Tarzan through the mother (41) of the illegitimate son of the sixth duke (40). In Watson's story, the son's name was James Wilder (63). Watson changed the son's name only slightly when he wrote *The Adventure of the Priory School*, perhaps through carelessness or through an unconscious desire to reveal the identity of the duke. In any event, Watson never dreamed that an American writer would be adding a code to his (Watson's). In *The Adventure of the Priory School*, the duke does not say what James' mother's name was, but it's evident that it was Wildman and that she was related to the Viscounts Barrington.

Neither Watson nor Burroughs could have known what their common clue would lead to. Both were apparently unaware of what had happened to James Wilder. Or, if they knew, they had no reason to think that James Wilder's son (82) would some day be a giant figure in the annals of crime fighters and great scientists. In *The Adventure of the Priory School*, the duke had indicated that James Wilder was going to "seek his fortune in Australia." Well he might, since to stay in England would subject him to trial for murder as an accessory, and he probably beat the police by a few hours, if that, getting out of the country. Holmes seemed not at all interested in bringing Wilder to justice. Perhaps he did not like to arrest a relative.

In *The Adventure of the Blanched Soldier*, which occurred in 1903, Holmes mentions that he was clearing up the Greyminster case. I suggest that this meant that the sixth duke had hired Holmes again to find out what had happened to his beloved first son. It's doubtful that Holmes left England; he probably employed foreign detectives for this fairly straightforward job. These discovered that Wilder had married, had a son one year old, had struck it rich in Australia almost at once, and had migrated to America.

James Wilder (63) had been conscience-stricken by the results of the kidnaping of his half-brother (61). He resolved to make amends. He would use his fortune to raise his son to "travel over the world and fight evil wherever he found it." The son would be trained from the age of two to be a physical, mental, and moral superman. (Fortunately, the child had the genetic potentialities to be a superman.) The son was probably born in January or February, 1902. But he may have been born before *The Adventure of the Priory School* occurred. James was indeed a "wild man" and may have inherited his aunt's and father's tendency to illegitimate love. In fact, the sixth duke, having heard he had a grandson, may have set Holmes to locate him.

In 1932, a pulp-magazine writer, Lester Dent, using the "house" name of Kenneth Robeson, wrote the first of 181 volumes of a somewhat romanticized biography of James Wilder's son. Dent called the subject of his biography Doctor Clark Savage, Jr. (82). Doc Savage was worthy to stand beside Tarzan and Holmes, and those who know his story are aware that he shares many characteristics with them. (But his eyes are brown and contain weird-looking gold flecks; they lack all grey.)

Doc lived not too far from his relative, Nero Wolfe (87), in his study-laboratory-operational headquarters on the eighty-sixth floor of the Empire State Building. Neither, as far as we know, ever met.

The name of James Wilder's (Wildman's) mother was, I believe, Patricia Clerk (or Clarke) Wildman (41). Doc's beautiful young Canadian cousin was named Patricia. It's likely that her father, Alexander Wildman, named her after his beautiful young sister who had died so soon after bearing a child of the sixth duke's. Wild(er)man's mother was also descended from the old and honorable family of Clarke (some branches of which spell it Clerk or Clark). The motto of the Clarkes is "Free for a blast" and their crest is a demihuntsman blowing a horn. (See Burke's *Peerage* and *Landed Gentry*.)

The Clerk (or Clark or Clarke) family originates from a Scotsman, Alanus Clerk (meaning clergyman), living circa 1349. His family estate of Pennycuick was held by a singular tenure. Its owner was bound to sit upon a large rock called the Buckstane and give three blasts on a hunting horn whenever the king came to hunt upon the Borough Muir near Edinburgh. Hence, the crest and the motto in the arms of this family. They are singularly appropriate for Doc Savage, who was a great huntsman in the fields of science and criminology and always ready for a "blast," though his blasts did not involve debauchery.

James Wild(er)man's mother was a direct descendant of Micah Clarke, the Puritan yeoman (born 1664) whose biography Doyle wrote in *Micah Clarke*. Rufus Tucker, in his *Genealogical Notes on Sherlock Holmes*, maintains that Sherlock's great-grandfather (11) married a descendant (10) of Micah Clarke. This is correct in my view. She was the aunt of James Wild(er)man's grandfather. He married Mavice Blakeney (21), a daughter of Sir Percy Blakeney, baronet, known as the Scarlet Pimpernel (6).

Lester Dent, the biographer of Doc Savage, was aware of the real identity of Doc Savage's father. Dent also knew Wildman's reasons for dedicating his infant son to an unceasing battle against crime.

I quote from the footnote to page 21, "The Black, Black Witch," *Doc Savage* Magazine, March, 1943. "First, something happened to Doc's father—Doc had never known exactly what it was that led him to make a remarkable decision, the decision, that, shortly after birth, Doc should be placed in the hands of scientists for training. This training lasted nearly twenty years. . . ."

Doc knew, but just did not admit knowing, what caused his father's decision. But he would have found out what it was. Doc, like so many of his relatives—Sherlock Holmes, Tarzan, Challenger, and others—had an intellect like an anteater's tongue: long, sensitive, and poking into every dark hole and crevice, catching the termites of fact.

Doc Savage's mother, who died so young, was Arronaxe Larsen (62). Through her, Doc inherited the rather strange gold-flecked eyes. Two branches of her family account for these. One, curiously enough, was founded by Chauvelin, the Scarlet Pimpernel's most unrelenting and dangerous antagonist. Thus, Doc was descended from both Blakeney and his Gallic nemesis. Chauvelin, as we know, had peculiar yellow eyes. He married a second cousin, whose eyes were also of a pale gold, and their son, Jules, married his first cousin, Norma. Their daughter, Marie, married Ned Land, a very powerful French-Canadian harpooner. He named his only child Arronaxe in honor of his scientist friend. Arronaxe married a Norwegian sailor (of Danish descent) but was deserted by him long before her daughter, Arronaxe, was born.

There is little doubt that Arronaxe's father was Wolf Larsen, the sinister Nietzschean captain of the schooner *Ghost*. His story has been relayed from Humphrey Van Weyden via Jack London. Doc must have inherited many of his physical and mental qualities, though, fortunately, not his amorality.

Wolf Larsen, according to Van Weyden, was a great man *in potentia*, a genius who never arrived. Though entirely self-educated, he invented a starscale so simple that a child could navigate a ship. Like Doc, he was very handsome. He had tremendous physical strength, an awesome tigerish personality, and a scary elemental force which seemed to radiate from him—when he let it loose.

Larsen's eyes were large and handsome; they were of a baffling protean grey which ran through many shades of colorings, which were never the same, like intershot silk in sunlight. A number of times, Van Weyden mentions their *golden glints* or *golden gleams*. His skin, like his grandson's, was a beautiful dark bronze. And, like his grandson, he rarely laughed. All powers, says Van Weyden, all potentialities seemed his. Can anyone doubt that Doc Savage was descended from him?

Out of Lord Saltire's kidnaping and Heidegger's murder great good came. Doc Savage literally saved the world many times from criminal geniuses who matched Moriarty in his abominable evilness and hellish intellect. And Doc has rehabilitated many criminals and set them on the straight and narrow. He has done this by operating on their brains in his New York upstate "college," excising the memory, and training them for virtue and a vocation. Doc never asked the criminals' permission, it is true, so he was acting illegally and tromping on the criminals' civil rights. But Doc never doubted that he was doing right, and the results have vindicated him.

What I have to demonstrate next contradicts, I'm sorry to say, some of Baring-Gould's statements in his *Sherlock Holmes of Baker Street* and *The Annotated Sherlock Holmes*. Baring-Gould believed that Holmes' mother was Violet Sherrinford, daughter of Sir Edward Sherrinford. He also stated, giving no evidence whatever, that Holmes and Challenger were first cousins. However, it is difficult to believe that such a learned and authoritative man as the late Baring-Gould would state something as a fact unless he had good reasons. His death may have prevented him from giving us the facts. I will be glad to supply them, though I anticipate disagreement. But disagreement is the heartbeat of scholarship.

Baring-Gould based his statement that Holmes had an older brother Sherrinford on Doyle's notes for A *Study in Scarlet* (see page 11, *The Annotated Sherlock Holmes*). Doyle was not only Watson's agent but sometimes his editor, and this note reveals that he played a big part in the selection of Holmes' first name for the somewhat fictionalized biographies of the Greatest Detective. "Sherrinford" was suggested, but evidently Watson decided to use Holmes' real first name after all. On this evidence, Baring-Gould decided that, in a sense, Sherrinford was Holmes' older brother and that the name was used in honor of the father of Holmes' mother.

However, we know from Burroughs' first Tarzan book that the Honorable Alice Rutherford (born circa 1868) was Tarzan's mother. The "Honorable" indicates that she is the daughter of a baron or viscount. Evidence from Volume II of the Epic (*The Return of Tarzan*) indicates that she was very close to the parents of Lord Tennington, who married Hazel Strong, Jane's best friend. She was so close to and remembered so tenderly among the Tenningtons that the conclusion is inescapable that she was the sister (66) of Tennington's father (not shown on the chart). Thus, the family name of Lord Tennington would be Rutherford. This ancient and honorable border family has many representatives in Scotland and England and at least one member distinguished in physics.

It has been suggested that Doyle's biographies of the famous, or infamous, zoologist, physician, and spiritualist, Professor Challenger (68), were fictitious. It has been said that the character of Challenger was based on Doyle's teacher at Edinburgh University, a Professor Rutherford. And it is true that Challenger and Doyle's teacher were remarkably similar in physique, coloring, and bearing (or overbearing). But this is due to a close consanguinity. The two were similar but not identical, so similar that Challenger's real name must be Rutherford.

Challenger would be one of Alice Rutherford's first cousins. There is no evidence that he was heir to the title of Tennington, so his father must have been a younger brother of Alice's father (46). He settled in Largs, Scotland, where George Edward was born in 1863.

Doyle, when asked by his client, Watson, to give Sherlock Holmes a fictitious first name, immediately thought of Rutherford. In fact,

Holmes' parents (51, 52), before deciding to name their youngest son Sherlock, had considered naming him Rutherford.

Whatever pressures were brought to bear or whatever influenced them, Doyle and Watson abandoned Rutherford as a first name for Holmes in his literary appearances. This name, by the way, comes from the Old English *hrythera ford*, meaning "horned cattle of the ford." Doyle and Watson knew this, and this name suggested Sherrinford, a shallow place in a stream where sheep are sheared. But this name, too, was rejected.

Thus, the name of Sherlock's mother was Violet Rutherford, not Sherrinford. Her husband's mother *was* the sister of Horace Vernet and the daughter of "Carle" Vernet, both of whom were famous French artists (see the *Encyclopaedia Britannica*). Holmes, Challenger, and Alice Rutherford were first cousins, all descended from the Rutherfords. Tarzan has many French ancestors, though not through the Vernets. This is fitting. He was born in a French possession, French was his first spoken human language, his best friend was Captain Paul d'Arnot of the French navy, his first employment was as a French secret agent in Africa, and his son married the daughter of a French nobleman and general.

I postulate also, in order to fill a slot, that Holmes' mother, Violet Rutherford (51), had a sister, Lucasta (54). She was the mother of Honoria Lucasta Delagardie (77), who was the mother of Lord Peter Wimsey (90). The evidence for this will be given after considering some other "family" members.

There is much evidence that Nero Wolfe (87) is Holmes' son by Irene Adler. He would, thus, be the second cousin of Tarzan (83) and of Enid (85), Challenger's daughter. It is worth noting that Wolfe's eyes are brown, unlike his father's, which share the color grey with Tarzan's and Challenger's. (In *The Lost World*, the professor's eyes are said to be blue-grey, but in three others of the Explorations they are grey.)

One of the five men who helped Doc Savage in his incessant battle against evil was Lt. Col. Andrew Blodgett Mayfair (84), nicknamed "Monk." Even if we did not know that Monk was a Rutherford, we could guess it at first sight. His physical and personality characteristics are such that we could not escape the conclusion that he was a close relative of Professor Challenger. He wasn't his son, of course, because the professor had only one child, Enid. And he wasn't his brother because of age disparities (Monk was born circa 1890). Also, Monk was American to the point of painfully embarrassing vulgarity and deliberately substandard speech. But there can be no doubt that he was the son of Challenger's sister Melissa (67), who married an American.

Consider Monk: "Only a few inches over five feet tall, he weighed better than two hundred and sixty pounds. He had the build of a gorilla, arms six inches longer than his legs, a chest thicker than it was wide . . . he grinned with a mouth so very big it looked like an accident."

We know the professor's striking resemblance to the ape-man who captured him in Maple White Land. And in more than one place in the Explorations, Challenger is compared to a simian. Monk is consistently described as gorillalike or baboonlike in the Savage Sagas.

Monk's character is also Challenger's, though he does not have a "Jehovah complex." He is just as extroverted and belligerent, though more pleasantly so. He is, like Challenger, ecstatic when in a hand-to-hand encounter against great odds. Despite his low and slanting forehead (in this and his rusty-red hair he differs from the professor), he is one of the world's greatest industrial chemists. Thus, he shares the propensity for chemistry with Holmes and Savage. His eyes are blue-grey.

It's worth noting that Ludwig Horace Holly (69), the narrator of Haggard's She, must be a Rutherford. He looks remarkably like Monk and Challenger. He has grey eyes and an ugly gorilloid face, an iron and abnormal strength, and considerable intellectual powers. In She, he is referred to many times as "Baboon."

It is true that Holly claims to have no living relatives. This statement, however, is just the result of a soured and essentially nongregarious, even antisocial, nature.

Lord John Roxton (81) is first met in Doyle's The Lost World. He is the third son of the duke of Pomfret. Since he was forty-six years old in 1903, the year of The Lost World, he was born in 1857, six years before Challenger, three after Sherlock. He resembles Holmes and, even more, Lord Peter Wimsey. His restless reckless eyes, however, are not grey but a cold light-blue. Like every one of the men mentioned so far, he is a great hunter. (Some hunt men only; others, both men and beasts.) Lord John's hair is gingery, resembling the sixth duke's (40). His overall physical resemblance to Wimsey is too close to be a coincidence. And, chronologically, he could be Wimsey's uncle. (Wimsey was born in 1890.)

It can't be denied that Lord Peter Wimsey's father, the fifteenth duke of Denver (78), could have been born circa 1857. Nor can it be successfully denied that D. L. Sayers (biographer of Wimsey) and Doyle could have used different titles when writing of the same noble family (respectively, Denver and Pomfret). The dukes of this family are for this reason titled Pomver in this book.

There is textual evidence that Wimsey was related to Challenger not only by blood but by marriage. Wimsey's mother (77) was of the vigorous French-English strain of the Delagardies, according to a biographical note by Wimsey's uncle, Paul *Austin* Delagardie (76). (See *The Dawson Pedigree*, D. L. Sayers, Harper & Row, retitled *Unnatural Death*, Avon edition.) In Doyle's *The Lost World*, Chapter 3, Malone describes Mrs. Challenger (75) as more French than English in her type. She speaks English as a native, which she is, but Malone implies she is of French descent. And Challenger's chauffeur-butler is named *Austin*.

Could this Austin be a poor relative of Mrs. Challenger, perhaps her uncle? Austin, the middle name of Wimsey's uncle, might have been a family one, his mother's. Her younger brother fell on evil days (perhaps even was a convict, since he has the aura of one as described by Doyle). Mrs. Challenger (75), a half-sister of Paul Austin Delagardie (76) and full sister of Honoria Lucasta Delagardie (77), took Austin in as a servant. Challenger's inability to keep a servant was notorious, but Austin proved to be of strong stuff. Working for the stormy professor was better than being in jail.

An objection to the genealogy could be based on a remark by Paul Austin Delagardie, Lord Peter's uncle. In his biographical sketch of his nephew, he says that the only sensible thing Peter's father ever did was to bring the vigorous English-Gallic blood of the Delagardies into the ancient and exhausted Wimsey stock. Obviously, this isn't true. Joane Clayton (59), Peter's paternal grandmother, brought very vigorous blood into the Wimsey veins, even if the results weren't manifested until Peter was born. Moreover, the Blakeneys and Rutherfords, ancestors of Lord Peter through his mother, can't be ignored by an objective genealogist.

The truth is, judging from Uncle Paul's character, that he was very prejudiced *against* the Wimseys and *for* the Delagardies. He refused to consider that any good could come from the former.

Indeed, Lord Peter may have absorbed some of this attitude from his uncle. He says (*Clouds of Witness*, D. L. Sayers, Harper & Row) that his detective instincts come from the Delagardies. It is true that his mother's grandfather, Paul Honoré (35), was an identical twin to Charles Dupin (37), father of C. Auguste Dupin (57). He follows this with a quote from his mother, in which she allies *mother* wit with Sherlock Holmes. (Here the duchess was referring slyly to a common descent for Peter and Holmes.) The detective instinct did, in truth, come through Lord Peter's mother. But was it from P. H. Delagardie (35), identical twin of the great Dupin's father (37)? Or was it from the Scarlet Pimpernel (6), from whom she is descended by way of (27) and (36)? Sir Percy Blakeney, though not a detective, must have contributed the genius for disguise that distinguishes his descendants, most notably Savage, Drummond, Wentworth, Holmes, and Wimsey. Nero Wolfe, on at least one occasion, has shown the same genius.

The families of Clayton, Blakeney, Rutherford, Holmes, Delagardie and Drummond produced four distinct somatic male types. There is that of the near-giant, superhumanly strong, and very handsome Doc Savage, John Drummond, and Tarzan. (Bulldog Drummond is a variant; he is ugly.) There is that of the tall and obese but very strong Mycroft Holmes and his nephew, Nero Wolfe. There is that of the extremely short, gorilla-bodied, and simian-faced Monk Mayfair, Professor Challenger, and Ludwig Horace Holly. There is that of the tall, lanky, aquiline-faced but wiry muscled Sherlock Holmes, Lord Peter Wimsey, and Lord John Roxton. All are very courageous, even fearless, and most are endowed with a detectival genius. Raffles (71), it could be said, had the genius in reverse.

Several members of these families so far not described are mixtures of two of the four types.

G-8, Richard Wentworth (the Spider), and Kent Allard (the Shadow) are mixtures of types one and four above. G-8, the flying ace and secret agent for America in World War I, is ambiguously described as neither too short nor too tall. He was handsome, grey-eyed, and very powerful. Richard Wentworth (92) was five foot eleven, had a superb physique, could run the hundred-yard dash under ten seconds at the age of thirty-seven, and was very handsome and grey-eyed. Kent Allard (also a World War I ace and a spy), who was the real Shadow (not Lamont Cranston), was tall, but we can't be sure that even the few details we do have about his appearance described the true Allard. His physical prowess was near-superhuman. All three, G-8, Wentworth, and Allard, were masters of disguise. Like their relatives Holmes, Savage, Wimsey, and Drummond, they were quick-change artists unsurpassed. (It's worth noting that Wentworth, like Holmes and Savage, was a violin virtuoso. And Wimsey's musical abilities are well described by Sayers.)

We do know what the Shadow looked like when he wasn't pretending to be Lamont Cranston or Phineas Twombley or a thousand others. We know this because we know what Wentworth looked like when he was not in one of his thousand disguises. He looked remarkably like Kent Allard and G-8.

Consider. He carries two big handguns and wears a mask and a cloak and slouch hat with a big brim when he is either the Spider or the Shadow. He has no compunctions about taking the law into his hands. (Neither did Holmes, Raffles, Mayfair, Savage, Tarzan, Challenger, or Drummond.) His burning eyes are powerful, indeed, overwhelming, whether he is G-8, the Shadow, or the Spider. In fact, the almost supernatural magnetism of the eyes are described again and again in much the same language by their main biographers, Page, Hogan, and Gibson. And the Spider and the Shadow operated in the same period, beginning about thirteen years after G-8 ceased his activities, shortly before the end of World War I. G-8, whose name was actually Richard Wentworth, spent some years recovering from a breakdown caused by his terrible and unceasing war experiences. In the eighteen months that the U.S. was officially in the war, G-8 had at least 110 adventures. (His first recorded adventure indicates that he had been busy for some time previously.) G-8 never had a chance to recuperate; any leaves he took resulted in being involved in something deadly almost at once. And if G-8 did not begin his activities as the dreaded U. S. Intelligence agent and flying ace until his country had really launched its forces, his exploits were compressed within a year or less.

(G-8, by the way, was the greatest ace of World War I, far surpassing von Richthofen's score of eighty. But, to preserve his identity, his record could not be revealed.)

There is strong evidence that the never-ending pressure on G-8 was enough to cause even a superman to have a mental breakdown.

His reports of his adventures (put into third person by Robert J. Hogan) indicate an increasing tendency to fantasy. After the horrifying case detailed in "Wings of the Death Tiger," *G-8 and His Battle Aces* magazine, June, 1944, G-8 was hospitalized. After, or perhaps during, his long convalescence, in which he attended college, he originated the two roles in which he would fight criminals of all nationalities, not just German war criminals or Allied traitors. The roles of the Spider and the Shadow may have been consciously created. But it is more likely that the mad genius of Wentworth, the Spider, was unaware that he was also Kent Allard, the Shadow.

The complete splitting of personality, or, rather, the generation of a second full personality, excuses Wentworth's simultaneous intimacy with Margo Lane and Nita van Sloan. He was not double-dealing in the sense of being unfaithful. As the Spider he had never heard of Margo, and as the Shadow he knew nothing of Nita. No wonder, then, what with his two love lives and his two crime-fighting careers that "Never was there rest for the Spider." The same could undoubtedly be said of the Shadow.

Wentworth's surname was not derived from the family name, but from the title of his ancestors. His grandfather, according to my researches, was Byron Noel-King, twelfth Baron Wentworth (60). The twelfth baron was the elder son of the first earl of Lovelace and of Ada Augusta (38), daughter of Lord Byron, the poet (18). The twelfth baron died unmarried at the age of twenty-six in 1862. The mother of his natural son was Joane Clayton (59), sister of the fifth and sixth dukes of Greystoke. As wild and unconventional as her older brother, and as passionate as her other brother, Joane fell in love with the twelfth Baron Wentworth and bore him a child. But she soon found they were incompatible, and, like her brother's mistress, Patricia Clarke Wild-man (41), she refused an offer of marriage. (The fifth duke, in Shaw's book, speaks of his sister as "common." He had no right to cast stones at anyone, however.)

The son was named John Byron Wentworth (81) and was adopted by the fourteenth duke of Pomver when the duke married Joane. (It is said that Joane named her son Wentworth to offend Noel-King's relatives, who had insulted her publicly and had tried to get her ostracized from the society of her peers.)

John Byron Wentworth was the man Doyle called Lord John

Roxton, third son of the duke of Pomfret. In a sense, he *was* the third son, since Joane's husband had two sons by her before he adopted John. The duke's eldest son (78), of course, became the father of Lord Peter Wimsey (90).

Lord John Roxton (John Byron Wentworth) briefly married Rhoda Delagardie (80), a sister of Lord Peter's mother and of Challenger's wife (75). Rhoda emigrated to America with a good settlement, where she married again, but not before bearing Richard Wentworth (92) circa 1895. We do not know anything about Richard's childhood, but, as stated, he operated as G-8 for the American Intelligence during 1917–1918. Later, as the Spider, he claimed to have been an Army infantry colonel, not an aviator. But he would have pretended this to conceal his role as the supposedly dead G-8.

G-8 had a batman, a Sergeant Battle, an ex-actor and make-up man. Wentworth, as the Spider, had a manservant, Ram Singh, who helped him in his exploits. Ram's relationship to Wentworth is similar to that of some of Wentworth's relatives and their servants. Wimsey had his ex-batman, Bunter; Bulldog Drummond, his ex-batman, James Denny; Nero Wolfe, his Archie Goodwin, who was a servant in many senses though much more than that, of course. C. Auguste Dupin had his Hyacinthe. Tarzan had his Jervis, but he didn't figure much in Burroughs' Epics.

It is time to talk of Chevalier C. Auguste Dupin (57). It would be gratifying to put him in a slot where he could be the genetic ancestor of all the detectives and heroes whom we have mentioned and of some yet to be mentioned. Unfortunately, this can't be done. But if he is not the genetic father of all great detectives, he is their literary father.

To show the Chevalier's position (everybody's in this framework, in fact), it's necessary to go back to 1795. Five married couples and a brother of one of the wives were riding in two coaches past Wold Newton, Yorkshire. They were on the way to a visit with relatives at Rayleigh. A meteorite struck only twenty yards from the two coaches. (A monument on the spot where it hit may be seen today in this northeastern corner of England.)

In the first coach were the third duke of Greystoke (2) and his pregnant wife, Alicia (3), sister of the eleventh Baron Tennington; the eleventh baron, George Edward Rutherford (8), and his pregnant wife, Elizabeth Cavendish (9), related to the duke of Devonshire;

Honoré Delagardie (14) and his pregnant bride, Philippa Drummond (15). Honoré, with his coachmen, Lupin (16) and Lecoq (17), had been smuggled out of England during the Terror by Sir Percy Blakeney (6), of Starr Hall, Durham County. Closely related to Marguerite St. Just, Sir Percy's now-dead wife, and to the Rutherfords and Drummonds, Delgardie had stayed with the three English families and ended by marrying a Drummond. Also in the huge first coach were Fitzwilliam Darcy (5), wealthy nephew of Earl Bakewell, and his wife, Elizabeth Bennet (4).

In the second coach were Sir Percy (6) and his second wife (7). She, like all the other women in the coaches, was in the common eighteenth-century condition of pregnancy. She was Alice Clarke Raffles, sister of Violet Clarke (10) and great-aunt of A. J. Raffles (71), famous cricket player and gentleman burglar. (His cousin, Lord Peter Wimsey (90), was as famous a cricketer.) Alice Clarke Raffles was a cousin to Sir Thomas Stamford Raffles, founder of Singapore, which makes me wonder if she also was not related to that young Stamford who introduced Watson to Holmes.

With the Blakeneys was Sir Hugh Drummond, baronet (12). His wife was Georgia Dewhurst (13), sister of the Antony Dewhurst who was a prominent member of the League of the Scarlet Pimpernel. Their son John Drummond (33) was to marry Oread Butler (34) of that distinguished family of Charleston, South Carolina. Doctor Siger Holmes (11) and his bride, Violet Clarke (10), were with them. Doctor Holmes was related to the third duke and the Drummonds, though the direct line of the Holmeses had never been anything but country squires.

The bright light and heat and thunderous roar of the meteorite blinded and terrified the passengers, coachmen, and horses. But they recovered quickly, thanking God that they were unharmed by the near-hit. They never guessed, being ignorant of ionization, that the fallen star had affected them and their unborn.

Philippa Delagardie gave birth to twins, Paul Honoré (35) and Charles (37). (There is textual evidence for the existence of both; their twinship is created to fill a necessary genetic slot.) Several years later, the parents being accidentally killed while visiting Paris, the twins were adopted by relatives named Dupin. On reaching maturity, Paul returned to England, reclaimed his birthname, and married Marguerite (36), a daughter of Sir Percy.

Francis Delagardie (55), son of Paul Honoré, married twice. His first wife was Enid Austin (56), whose brother was Challenger's servant. Francis and Enid had issue: Paul Austin Delagardie (76).

Francis married, secondly, Lucasta Rutherford (54), the twelfth Baron Tennington's daughter. Her mother was Serena Blakeney (27), daughter of the Scarlet Pimpernel. Francis' and Lucasta's daughter, Honoria Lucasta (77), married Gerald Wimsey (78), fifteenth duke of Pomver.

If Gerald Wimsey and Lord John were the first and third sons of the fourteenth duke of Pomver (58), who was the second son? For the answer, we go to Burroughs *Tarzan Triumphant*. One of its heroines is Lady Barbara (91). She is the daughter of the first earl of Whimsey (79). The first earl is a distiller of fine whiskeys and a prominent contributor to the treasury of the Liberal party in England. Born in the middle 1860s, he was the second son of the fourteenth duke of Pomver. As the second son, he would be legally a commoner. But, as many younger sons of peers have done, he earned a title of his own. His family name was also his title, as often happens.

If this were so, why was Barbara's family name given by Burroughs as Collis? The answer is that Wimsey (or, as Burroughs spells it, Whimsey) married a Collis. She was the daughter of a very wealthy noble. Wimsey, as sometimes happens in the peerage, took her name also. Burroughs gave only half of the hyphenation, thinking, I suppose, that he could disguise Barbara's true identity in this manner.

As noted, Lucasta (54) married Francis Delagardie (55). Violet (51) married Siger Holmes (52), and their two famous sons and grandson we know.

John (47) married Dorothy Swinton of that eight-hundred-year-old distinguished Scots family. Their son was George Edward, whom Doyle called Challenger. (As an aside of genealogical and literary interest, Burke's *Landed Gentry* states that Sir John Swinton, twenty-fifth of that ilk, had a daughter, Jean, who married a Professor John Rutherford. Jean and John were the grandparents of Sir Walter Scott, the author.)

Venetia (48) married, firstly, a Mr. Holly, a musician and lover of Beethoven. Their son was Ludwig Horace Holly (69). Ludwig was the scholar, African explorer, and guardian of Leo Vincey, the beloved of She-who-must-be-obeyed of the fabled city of Kôr.

Venetia (48) married, secondly, William Drummond (53). Their son was Roger (74).

The twelfth baron's eldest son, George (49), was somewhat of a black sheep. Rusticated at Oxford, he went to the west coast of equatorial Africa as a trader. He married a Portuguese-Icelandic girl, an octoroon, from Principe Island. He had three boys and one girl, the youngest child. George's mother kept writing him, begging him to come home. But Africa held him until he was poisoned by a witch doctor, a few days before his father, the twelfth baron, died. George was buried on an island off the mouth of the Ogowe River, Gabon. His head was afterward removed by witch doctors to make powerful magic. His oldest son joined the infamous bandit Josef Cariella, and he was killed by a British patrol on the Lake Chad road in the north Niger. The other boys died in unknown circumstances. George's widow, the octoroon, married a witch doctor. George's daughter, Nina (70), was raised as a priestess, a veritable white goddess, by the devotees of the god Izaga.

When about seventeen years old, she ran off with a young English trader and his wealthy Peruvian friend, a school chum. Later, she married the Peruvian and went to his country to live. We know all this because Trader Horn describes it in his biography, edited by Ethelreda Lewis. The twelfth baron's son (49) was the Honorable George T——, whose ill fate Alfred Aloysius Horn describes. Horn stated a number of times that George T—— was of a prominent noble family of England. Horn refused to reveal George's true identity to spare the feelings of the family. The T——, however, was not the initial letter of the family *name*. Horn used the initial letter of the family's title, Tennington.

Dr. Albert Schweitzer, in his *African Notebook*, Henry Holt, 1939, states that his home was on the site of Horn's old trading post above Lambaréné, on the Ogowe River. Schweitzer says that, in the main, Horn's book is true, although Horn (like Burroughs and Watson) would deviate from the strict truth now and then for the sake of a good story. Schweitzer does not believe that George T——'s daughter was a virgin priestess, since the natives of that area did not believe in virginity.

She may not have been a virgin, but Little Peru married her, and Latin-American aristocrats were very particular about such matters.

George T——'s beautiful daughter had dark auburn hair and

looked much like La of Opar, except that her eyes were blue and La's were grey. Schweitzer refers to her, not as Nina, but as "Lola." Why did he make this mistake? Was it because he knew her real name, which Horn gave as Nina? Did she furnish the basis for Burroughs' La of Opar? Did Burroughs chop off the Lo- when he wrote of her?

I don't think so, since La of Opar is an actual person, not a fictional character. There was no need to present her under a false name. But the slip of the pen by the good doctor does reveal to us George's daughter's real name.

George died in the lifetime of his father, and thus the next oldest son, Edward (46), became Baron Tennington.

Sir Percy Armand Blakeney (25) (the Scarlet Pimpernel's son) married Alexandra Grosvenor (26) related to the duke of Westminster. (Tarzan, in *Tarzan the Terrible*, speaks of having visited the duke. His relative was the second duke, Hugh Richard Arthur Grosvenor, lord-lieutenant of Cheshire.)

Sir Percy Armand's daughter, Marguerite (45), married Edward Rutherford (46), thirteenth Baron Tennington. One of their daughters, Alice (66), married John Clayton (65), in 1888. Challenger's sister Melissa (67), married an American, Blodgett Mayfair, and their son (84) was the world-famous industrial chemist and joyous free-for-all mayhemmer and brawler, Monk Mayfair, Doc Savage's friend and aide.

The "Bloom-" which Burroughs deleted from the original manuscript of *Tarzan of the Apes* is a truly Joycean clue, a many-armed signpost. It has led us to a number of trails, and this time it goes to the Bloom we rejected on first consideration.

Shaw's Jansenius, Watson's Appledore (19), was born John Karoly. His brother, Julius (22), went to Dublin from Szombathelny, Hungary, at the invitation of Rudolph Virag. Virag was a relative who had settled in Ireland after living in Vienna, Budapest, Milan, and London. (Like Odysseus, he was wont to wander.) Virag's name, in Hungarian, meant "flower" or "bloom," so he anglicized it to Bloom. Julius Karoly (22) changed his name to Higgins. His second daughter, Ellen (42), married the much older Rudolph Virag Bloom, and their son, Leopold (64), became the basis of a character in a somewhat strange novel titled *Ulysses*. Tarzan (83), the wandering ape-man of the large estate of Africa, a lord of England and the Lord of the Jungle, was second cousin once removed of Leopold Bloom, lord of little but his own fantasies, but nevertheless a courageous and intelligent man, the mundanely heroic and wandering jewgreek of the geographically restricted but psychically enormous estate of Dublin. Bloom, be it noted, was married in 1888, the same year his cousin, John Clayton, married Alice Rutherford.

It is strange that Burroughs knew of the existence of the Blooms at least ten years before *Ulysses* was published. He must have learned about the Jewish cousins of the dukes of Greystoke when he was researching Tarzan's family tree. It amused him to use "Bloom—" as a clue even though he changed his mind later on about it. It's doubtful that he knew anything beyond the dates of birth and the livelihoods of the Higginses and the Blooms. He would have known nothing about the character of Leopold Bloom, and if he had he would never have considered Leopold as the protagonist of a novel. But the cousin of Tarzan and Lord John Roxton was, in his quiet way, a hero, and of a scientific bent, as so many of his English and American relatives were.

Burroughs knew of Tarzan's relationship to Holmes, but he would not have known much about Denis Nayland Smith (86). Smith's first case did not come to public notice until 1913. Yet, if Smith was not too young to have been born in 1854, it wouldn't be beyond reason to think he was Holmes come out of retirement. Smith, unrelenting foe of the insidious Doctor Fu Manchu, is tall, of spare physique but powerful muscles, has grey eyes, smokes a big pipe of shag tobacco, has for a close companion and sometime biographer a medical man, Doctor Petrie, and has a manner of speaking which often resembles Holmes'.

Smith could easily be the nephew of Holmes (73). And Holmes, in *The Adventure of the Copper Beeches*, makes a somewhat ambiguous reference to a sister. Actually, the wording "a sister of mine" could indicate that he had more than one. Thus, I am placing a character for whom there is some textual evidence in the slot as Smith's mother. She is the aforementioned Sigrina Holmes (72), who gave birth to Denis in 1880.

Watson, as we know, connected *The Adventure of the Priory School* and *The Adventure of Charles Augustus Milverton* by a code word—Appledore. Edith Jansenius (39), wife of the sixth duke, is the woman who killed Milverton in the Appledore Towers. (Her father, as we know from Shaw's *An Unsocial Socialist*, had

widespread financial interests. He built and named the luxurious
Appledore Towers.)

Milverton's murderer is described by Watson in such a way that
it is obvious he is trying to say, without saying it, that she is of a
wealthy Jewish family. She had been married to a gentile nobleman
who died of a broken heart (probably in 1886, given the chronology
of the Milverton and Priory School cases). She had refused to
pay blackmail, and so "the worst man in London" had revealed
to the nobleman that his wife had been involved romantically with
(according to some authorities) the Prince of Wales. Two years
later, she married the wealthy and distinguished younger brother
of the fifth duke.

Edith's child, William Cecil Arthur (61), was born in 1891.
(He was named after her older brother —— see *An Unsocial Socialist*.) In 1899 (probably January), she was separated from
her husband and living in the south of France. But she traveled
quickly to London when her friend, the Countess d'Albert, told her
that Milverton was trying to blackmail her. She saved her friend
and revenged herself by emptying a pistol into Milverton. Shortly
after May, 1901, she returned to her husband.

The main objection to the above is the photograph of her
which Watson and Holmes saw in a shop window on Oxford
Street after Milverton's unlamented death. Below the photograph
was the "time-honored title of the great nobleman and statesman
whose wife she *had been*." (Italics mine.) But why wasn't she
identified as the wife of the sixth duke of Greystoke?

The answer is that she *was* so identified. But Watson concealed
this. He had given too many clues to her identity as it was.

It has been necessary to go into Edith Appledore's story because
she was intimately involved in a theory of mine. This was to explain
what Burroughsian scholars call the "Korak time-discrepancy."

The third book of the Epic, *The Beasts of Tarzan*, begins circa
June, 1912, in London. Tarzan's son, Jack, is a month old when
he is kidnaped by his father's old enemies. The baby apparently
dies of a fever in west Africa. In the end it is revealed that the
kidnapers were double-crossed by a confederate, who kept the real
heir alive in London. The fourth book, *The Son of Tarzan*,
begins in London circa May, 1913. Jack is only ten years old; but
he is strong enough to subdue his tutor in their London residence,
which is what we would expect from the son of the ape-man. He is

also attending a school, which we may suppose is Watson's Priory School (Holmes' Abbey School), though Dr. Huxtable is probably dead by now.

Jack runs away with a great ape, Akut, and disappears into Africa. He adapts well enough to be a second Tarzan, though not the equal of the first, and to be named Korak by the mangani, meaning "killer." He rescues a little French girl from a wicked French Arab chieftain, and the two grow up together in the jungle. Korak and Meriem are sixteen by the time he is reunited with his parents. Jack and Meriem, who is in reality the kidnaped daughter of General Armand Jacot, le Prince de Cadrenet, are married at the end of the book. The marriage takes place (from evidence in Burroughs' *The Eternal Lover*) in the middle of 1914.

In September, 1918, Jack is a British officer on the Argonne front (*Tarzan the Terrible*). But if he were born on May 20, 1912, he would have been only six years old in 1918.

The solution to this problem has been given in chapter 16. The "son" of Tarzan was actually Tarzan's adopted cousin, John Drummond. John Drummond was one of Captain "Bulldog" Drummond's seven siblings. He was related to the earls of Ancaster and Perth, who are Drummonds, and descended from the Scots poet, Ben Jonson's friend, Drummond of Hawthornden.

John and Hugh Drummond's grandmother (48) was the great-aunt of Alice Rutherford, Tarzan's mother, as noted. (Their mother was Lorena Ridd of Exmoor.) Bulldog's ugly face and enormous strength are traits shared with Challenger and Mayfair. But, unlike them, he is tall, about six feet, and definitely blue-eyed. His strength is quite Tarzanic. In the first of Cyril McNeile's biographies, *Bulldog Drummond* (1919), the captain kills a vicious half-grown gorilla loosed on him by the arch-villain Peterson, the "Comte de Guy." Drummond snaps the simian's neck with his fingers. This requires herculean powers even if the snapping was aided by knowledge of jujitsu. His younger brother, John (Korak), was as strong, if not stronger, and, moreover, was handsome, even "godlike," inheriting his mother's beauty.

This strange tendency of the otherwise beautiful Rutherfords to produce an occasional simianlike male may have inspired Burroughs when he wrote of the Oparians. (There is no doubt that Opar itself existed or that it had citizens. But Lord Greystoke himself has never commented, to me, at least, on the Oparian male-female skeletal discrepancies.)

La of Opar, the priestess who loved Tarzan so madly and so futilely, has many resemblances to the ᐧ She-who-must-be-obeyed described by a Rutherford, Ludwig Horace Holly.

Bulldog Drummond is obviously a Rutherford, and there is textual evidence that he and his brother John are closely related to Tarzan. In *The Black Gang*, London, 1921, are two references to Bulldog's cousin, Lord Staveley. And Bulldog's servant, Denny, comments that Lord Staveley is in central Africa again. The reference, of course, is to Tarzan's real son, Jack, the *honorary* Earl Staveley. He would be nineteen years old at this time and off to see his parents during school vacation. This was, however, during the events of *Tarzan and the Golden Lion*, which means that he may not have found them at home.

The code word *Bloom*, as we've seen, led us on three different and fruitful trails. But what about Watson's duke of *Holdernesse* and lord-lieutenant of *Hallamshire*? What about Burroughs' *Grey-* in Greystoke or Holmes' *Grey-* in Greyminster? What about *-stoke* and *-minster*?

"-stoke" leads to many places and people, but one path is through Burke's *Peerage* and *Extinct Peerage*. This leads to the original and nonfictitious de Greystocks, barons of Greystoke, who were ancestors of the Howards and of the Claytons. Stock, or stoke, means a stick, a pole, a tree stump, and so on, Webster's dictionary giving twelve primary meanings. Investigation of one meaning led to the noble families of the Poles and de la Poles and branched out into many families through their marriages. "Munster" is a phonetic variant of "-minster" (as a code word), and this leads to the earl of Munster (nothing profitable here). But, considering the variant of "-minster," we come to the baron of Inchiquin, an O'Brien, descended from Brian Boru, Prince of Thomond (North Munster).

"-minster" is a multidirectional signpost pointing to the barons of Leominster, who were also the earls of Pomfret (both titles being extinct now). Fermor, the original spelling of Farmer, was the family name of the earls of Pomfret and barons of Leominster. It pleases me to believe that I am distantly related to Holmes and Tarzan.

Another "-minster" takes the researcher to the marquess of Conyngham, who is Baron Minster of Minster Abbey, Kent. The Conyn-

ghams were ancestors of Holmes and Tarzan and related to the
great African explorer and linguist, Sir Richard Francis Burton.
Burton was a cousin of Siger Holmes, Sherlock's father, and he is
mentioned in *Sherlock Holmes of Baker Street*, though not named.
He was the friend involved in the dog-cart accident (outside
Karachi) which crippled Siger and forced him to leave the East
India Company army. So, in one way, Burton is responsible for the
birth of the Great Detective, he having fallen on top of Siger and
contributed to the dislocating of Siger's hip.

"-minster" also leads to the already noted relationship of the
dukes of Westminster to Tarzan. Even if we had not had the
"-minster" to guide us (not to mention the reference in *Tarzan the
Terrible*), we would have gotten to Westminster through "-stoke."
An early ancestor of the dukes, a Robert le Grosvenor, did homage
circa 1293 for his manor of Lostoke (now Allostock).

"-stoke" also leads us to another ancestor, Sir Everard Digby,
lord of Tilton and Drystoke, beheaded in 1606 for complicity in
the Gunpowder Plot, and ancestor of the present baron of Digby.
His son, Sir Kenelm, was a very learned man, called the Ornament
of England. He married a granddaughter of a Percy, the seventh
earl of Northumberland.

The great north of England family, the Percys, is arrived at as
ancestors of the Greystokes through other trails also. Holmes, in
the Priory School case, noted that the sixth duke was also Baron
Beverley. Actually, a Percy, the duke of Northumberland, was the
earl of Beverley, its only lord. Holmes probably never said this;
Watson put the words in Holmes' mouth to cover up the real title
and also to code that the duke was descended from the Percys.
From Holmes' Beverley we trace through Burke's *Peerage* and
Extinct Peerage and come to Sir Percy Blakeney. He was named
after his grandmother, who was of that illustrious family of Hotspur.
His father was named Algernon, a name traditional among the
Percys since the days of William the Conqueror.

"-stoke" also leads us to a Sir Thomas Dilke of Maxstoke Castle,
Warwick County, ancestor of the Baronets Dilke. Wentworth is a
long-persisting family name among the Dilkes, though their relationship to the barons of Wentworth is remote. It's worth noting
that the lords of Wentworth have a castle in Barnsley and a mansion
in Rotherham. These two towns, as I have said, are included in the
ancient lordship of Hallamshire.

Hallamshire and Holdernesse both lead to Elizabeth Clayton, an ancestor of the dukes of Greystoke and also of Lord Tennyson, the poet. Hallam became a family name, the poet naming his son Hallam after his dear friend who died so young. And Elizabeth Clayton's ancestors were from Winestead, Holdernesse. Watson was well aware of this and so planted these clues in his narrative of the Priory School case.

"-stoke" leads to the barons of Revelstoke. The family name is Baring (recalling again the rejected Bloom). The founder of this line married Elizabeth Grey, daughter of the second earl of Grey. This lineage leads us to the barons of Northbrook and other ancestors of Tarzan.

If the first and final letters of "Revel-" are transposed, we have "Lever-." Doctor Huxtable, in the Priory School case, boasted that Lord Leverstoke had entrusted his son's education to him. A reading of the Revelstoke lineage dismisses the idea that Watson was obliquely referring to any of Baron Revelstoke's sons. Their ages are not right for attendance at the Priory School in 1901.

Tarzan, in Tarzan Triumphant, disguises himself as a Lord Passmore. If you remember that the actual barons of Greystoke became lords of Morpeth, Northumberland, and that the lordship passed into the Howard family (earl of Carlisle), then you know why Burroughs picked this code word. Reverse and then separate the syllables of Passmore. More pass. A pass is a path, from which we easily pass to "peth." Passmore stands for Morpeth, and it opens the door for the identification of the de Greystocks and Howards—and others—who were the ancestors of the dukes of Greystoke.

Watson, when giving Holmes' listing of the sixth duke's titles and possessions, mentions the earl of Carston and Carston Castle, Bangor, Wales. Watson was tenuously referring to the duke of Greystoke's third title, Viscount Breconcastle, and to Brecon, Wales. The manner of reference is an example of what Holmes called Watson's "pawky humor." To bang something may be to break it, and this, in Watson's mind, linked Bangor to Breconcastle. Watson undoubtedly was aware of Shaw's novel, An Unsocial Socialist, and the true identity of the people behind the names Shaw used.

Watson's use of "Lord Saltire" for the sixth duke's younger son suggests that the saltire, the St. Andrew's cross, was a prominent part of the Greystoke arms. The saltire has led Dr. Julian Wolff, commissionaire of the Baker Street Irregulars, to examine the great

Neville family for candidates for the sixth duke. This being ruled out, he suggested the eighth duke of Devonshire, a Cavendish, but the family situation of the sixth duke of Greystoke seems to eliminate the duke of Devonshire.

However, the Neville-Howard-Greystock trails lead to the barons of Furnivall. (It would be tempting to consider that Watson was using Furnivall as a punning code, For Neville. But I pass on this.) The founder of this family, Gerard de Furnivall, was present with Richard I at Acre in 1191. He sounds suspiciously like the founder of the family of the dukes of Denver (Pomver), Gerald de Wimsey; Lord Peter's ancestor was also at Acre in 1191.

Moreover, Gerard's son, Gerard, became lord of Hallamshire in 1204. (Remember that Watson's sixth duke of Holdernesse was lord-lieutenant of Hallamshire.) Baroness Joane Furnivall married a Nevill, brother of the first Earl Westmorland. The Nevill arms, "gules, a saltire argent, a martlet sable for difference," is one of the ten quarterings of the Furnivall arms. And the twelfth baron married the sister of the first earl of Devonshire. Through marriage with the Howards, the Furnivalls were ancestors of the present Lord Petre, who is co-heir to the abeyant barony of Greystoke.

Sayers' Wimseys are, if not the Furnivalls, descended from or closely related to them. Moreover, Doctor Wolff was on the right track when he investigated the Nevilles and the Cavendishes for a candidate for the sixth duke.

(Inasmuch as the family name of the lords of Furnivall is now Dent, I wonder if Lester Dent, who wrote so many fictionalized biographies of Doc Savage, did not take advantage of his relationship to delve into the family records for Doc's lineage.)

A strong reason for calling the sixth duke's son "Lord Saltire" was his real honorary title. This was Lord Exminster. The "-minster" needs no comment, and it is obvious that the "Ex-" immediately summons to mind the X, which is the shape of the saltire.

Watson may also have called Arthur "Lord Saltire" because the saltire is actually a prominent part of the first quartering of the Greystoke arms. The blazoning: "Argent, upon a saltire azure drinking horns in triskele gules."

The Greystokes, like the present queen of England, can trace their ancestry through Egbert, king of Wessex, to the great god Woden in Denmark of the third century A.D. (See the Royal Lineage section of Burke's Peerage and Grimm's Teutonic Mythol-

ogy, Vol. 1, Dover Books.) The founders of the Greystoke line
were secret worshipers of Woden long after their neighbors had
converted to Christianity. They used the red *waelcnotta* on their
shields with the other two colors of Woden, grey and blue, long
before heraldry became established.

Thus, Tarzan has as ancestor Woden. It would be difficult to find
a more highly placed forefather than the All-Father.

Perhaps the great god of the North is not dead but is in hiding.
It pleased the Wild Huntsman to direct the falling star of Wold
Newton near the two coaches. Thus, in a manner of speaking,
he fathered the children of the occupants. The mutated and reces-
sive genes would be reinforced, kept from being lost, by the
frequent marriages among the descendants of the irradiated parents.
And this reinforcement and reshuffling of superior genes resulted
in at least fourteen great detectives, scientists, and explorers, some
of whom bordered on the superhuman. These would be Dupin,
M. Lecoq, Arsène Lupin, Mycroft and Sherlock Holmes, Professor
Challenger, Lord John Roxton, Denis Nayland Smith, A. J. Raffles,
Tarzan, Monk Mayfair, Bulldog Drummond, John Drummond
(Korak), Nero Wolfe, Lord Peter Wimsey, Richard Wentworth
(who was also G-8 and Kent Allard), and Doc Savage.

And so these were born to create terror among evildoers and
delight among the readers of Poe, Gaboriau, Leblanc, Watson,
Doyle, McNeile, Rohmer, Sayers, Gibson, Dent, Hogan, Page,
Goodwin, and Burroughs.

What about the younger generation, the descendants of the fourteen? We may presume that, with such heredity, the sons of Lord
Peter (90) and Harriet Vane, and of Inspector Parker and Mary
Wimsey are engaged in detective work. Tarzan's grandson must be
battling wicked men in the jungle or the city. Nita van Sloan and
Margo Lane may have had sons by Richard Wentworth (92), and
these may have teamed up to carry on their father's merciless campaigns.

But there are three other grey-eyed candidates to consider. One
is Shell Scott; the second, Travis McGee; the third, Lew Archer.
Scott is strong and courageous, and his adventures are amusing. He
has created much havoc among evil men, but his detective abilities
seem to tend more toward blundering around than toward keen
deduction. Aside from the grey color of his eyes, and the chance
that he may be descended from the Scotts who were also the an-

cestors of William Sherlock Scott Holmes, he has little to recommend him.

Travis McGee seems a likely candidate. He is big, handsome, very bright, compassionate, sensitive, strong, courageous, and chivalrous. At present, however, no descent from anybody on the endpapers chart can be established. But I have hopes for McGee. In the meantime, there is Lew Archer.

Lew Archer is courageous, incorruptible, and endowed with a great detective's mind and intuitions. Moreover, as any reader of the entire corpus of Archer's adventures can testify, he is unusually sensitive, a genuine poet. One might almost think that Byron or Tennyson would have to be among his ancestors. These qualities, it is true, would not be enough to make him a candidate. But he seems to share certain mutated genes with Tarzan and Doc Savage. He has their superhuman—or subhuman—sense of smell. His nose is so extraordinarily sensitive, he claims, somewhat facetiously, to have canine chromosomes.

The only slot I can find for him is as the son of Enid (Challenger) Malone (85). Lew's real name is Malone, or else Edward D. Malone died and Enid then married an Archer. She bore Lew in 1914, or 1918, in Los Angeles. She would have converted to Catholicism before then, thus rejecting, after all, her father's beliefs in spiritualism.

Lew Archer did not follow his mother's religion; his Catholicism is compassion for human beings. And he considers only mysteries which spring from the workings of the human heart. But Enid Challenger's son inherited his grandfather's (68) strength and inquiring mind, his aggressiveness (but not to the point of also being overbearing, though sometimes approaching it), and, if not his spiritualism, his spiritual qualities.

ADDENDUM 3
The Greystoke Lineage

> Just as we have seen in the *Roland*, one good yarn deserves
> another. Poets therefore gave Charlemagne a childhood, and Ro-
> land also. Then they moved backward to give them ancestors
> whose lives made attractive subjects.
>
> —Norma Lorre Goodrich

The lineage herein is as if taken from the pages of Burke's
Peerage. The real coat of arms and lineage of "Lord Greystoke"
can't be presented here, of course. But over half of the people and
almost all of the places in the lineage are true. The others are
not really fictional; they are just disguised. Thus, Sir Oliver Tressilian,
the hero of Sabatini's novel *The Sea-Hawk*, is used as a cover for the
very real Cornish knight and Grand Armada hero who was an
ancestor of the very real "Lord Greystoke." Greystoke is also
descended from the man whom Daniel Defoe called Captain Bob
Singleton in a three-quarters true narrative. Be it noted that Sir
Nele Loring, K.G., did exist and that he was knighted on the
spot during the great naval victory of Edward III's sailors over the
French at Sluys. Doyle based his character of Sir Nigel Loring on
Sir Nele and undoubtedly knew that Sir Nele was an ancestor of
"Lord Greystoke."

Greystoke is descended from the various royal families of Great
Britain and Ireland, France, Castile, Denmark, Germany, Hungary,
et al. However, this lineage, like the history of the Greystokes in
the main text, is analogical.

For the sake of brevity and clarity, the long listings of the families
of daughters, younger sons, and remarriages have been removed.

Many of the repetitive listings of honors are also excised. The remarks in brackets are my explanatory insertions. There is no title of Duke or Viscount Greystoke, of course. "Greystoke" was used by Edgar Rice Burroughs to conceal the true title. I continue to honor this usage. The most common abbreviations used in Burke are retained; a table of definitions precedes the lineage. The blazoning of the coat of arms is described in nontechnical language at the end of this addendum, and some historical notes are added.

Abbreviations and Definitions
(In the order in which they appear)

K.C.S.I.	Knight Commander of the Order of the Star of India
V.C.	Victoria Cross
D.F.C.	Distinguished Flying Cross
educ.	educated
hon.	honorary
Capt.	Captain
G/C.	Group Captain
R.A.F.	Royal Air Force
U.S.A.A.F.	United States Army Air Force
Offr.	Officer
b.	born
s.	succeeded
m.	married
dau.	daughter
D.D.	Doctor of Divinity
Ph.D.	Doctor of Philosophy
LL.D.	Doctor of Laws
●	in the line of precedence for the title
K.G.	Knight of the Order of the Garter
F.R.G.S.	Fellow of the Royal Geographical Society
F.Z.S.	Fellow of the Zoological Society
W/Cmdr.	Wing Commander
Bt.	Baronet
G.C.B.(M.)	Knight Grand Cross of the Order of Bath (Military Division)
F/Lt.	Flight Lieutenant
A/Cdre.	Air Commodore
ca.	circa
d.	died
bur.	buried
d.v.p.	died vita patris, i.e., in the father's lifetime
k.	killed
unm.	unmarried
co.	county
K.C.B.	Knight Commander of the Order of the Bath
Lt.-Col.	lieutenant-colonel
M.P.	member of Parliament

Lord-Lieut.	lord-lieutenant (originally the king's deputy for military affairs in a county)
Chm.	chairman
Bd.	Board
Corpn.	Corporation
vice-pres.	vice-president
Kt.	knight
Pres.	president
P.C.	Privy Counsellor (member of the advisory council to the monarch)
M.V.O.	member of the Royal Victorian Order
J.P.	Justice of Peace
Col.	colonel
Bn.	battalion
Fus.	fusiliers
Inst.	institute
B.	baron (used only in Creations)
(E.)	England
E.	earl
(G.B.)	Great Britain
V.	viscount
D.	duke
(U.K.)	United Kingdom

The Duke of Greystoke (John Clayton, K.C.S.I., V.C., D.F.C.), Earl Staveley and Viscount Breconcastle and Viscount Greystoke of Great Britain, and Baron Grebson of Grebson and Baron Sallust of England; privately educ. French Equatorial Africa (Gabon);

served World War I as guerrilla (hon. Capt. 2nd Rhodesians, hon. Capt. King's African Rifles); late G/C., R.A.F. World War II, Europe, India, Burma, attached to U.S.A.A.F., Indonesia (wounded); has Croix de Guerre, Offr. Legion of Honour, Distinguished Service Cross (U.S.); b. 22 Nov., 1888; s. his cousin as 8th Duke, 1910; m. Jane, dau. of the late Archimedes Q. Porter, D.D., Ph.D., LL.D., and his wife, Jane Carter Lee, of Baltimore, Maryland, and by her has had issue,

● Sir John Paul, K.G., V.C., D.F.C., F.R.G.S., F.Z.S., *honorary* Lord Staveley, author of many works on African archaeology and zoology, educ. Eton, Cambridge, University of Stockholm, late W/Cmdr., World War II, prisoner in Germany, escaped, has Order of the Elephant of Denmark, b. 20 May, 1912; m. 3 Nov., 1942, Alice Horatia, dau. of Sir Holmes Rochester, Bt., of Thornfield, and of Alice Gridley, great-grand-dau. of Admiral Viscount Hornblower, the naval hero of the Napoleonic Wars, and has issue,

● John, b. 24 Nov., 1943

● Sir John Drummond, G.C.B.(M.), V.C., D.F.C., *honorary* Lord Breconcastle, His Grace's cousin and adopted son, educ. Grey Priors, Derbyshire, University of Paris, late F/Lt. R.A.F., World War I, late A/Cdre., World War II; b. 24 Nov., 1898; m. 26 May, 1914 Jeanne, dau. of the late General Armand Jacot, le Prince de Cadrenet, and of the late Suzanne Fogg, of Paris, and by her had issue,

● John Armand, educ. Eton, late F/Lt. R.A.F., World War II, b. 7 May, 1921, m. 1 May, 1945, his kinswoman, Hazel, dau. of Edward, 15th Baron Tennington, and of Hazel, dau. of George Strong, of Baltimore, Maryland, and Beatrice Conyngsby of London.

Lineage—Westerfalcna, b. ca. 578, son of King Aelle of Deira by Osburh, a Wessex woman, claimed descent from the God Woden through Waeġdaeg, of south Denmark, ca. 260 A.D. [See *Teutonic Mythology*, Grimm, for the divine genealogy of early English kings. The present monarch of England also claims descent from Woden; see the Royal Lineage Section, Burke's *Peerage*.]

Westerfalcna, who called himself Grǣġbēardssunu [Old English for The Son of The Grey-Bearded One, an epithet for Woden] fled after Aelle was slain and Aethelric, king of Bernicia, seized the throne. In what is now the North Riding of Yorkshire, Westerfalcna erected on a peak a wooden fort, Grebson's Hold.

Godwulf of Grebson [modern spelling], b. 1010, m. a dau. of Kormak Sigurdsson, Irish-Norwegian lord of the neighboring holding eventually known as Sigerside.

His son, Godwulf, m. a dau. of the lord of Greystoke, Cumberland.

Godwulf, Godwulf's grandson, m. ———— of Greystoke, a cousin, and fell at Stamford where the invading Norwegian, King Harold Hardrada, was killed. Godwulf's brother, Westerfalcna, who had m. a sister of his brother's wife, was also present at Stamford. He marched with King Harold of England to Hastings and was slain.

Beowulf, Westerfalcna's son, was born posthumously with his cousin, Godwulf's son.

The lordship of Grebson then passed into the hands of Rainulph FitzGilbert, brother of Richard FitzGilbert, or De Clare, who received 176 Lordships after accompanying William the Conqueror into England. Rainulph's wife dying, Rainulph m. Westerfalcna's widow, and, his six children dying in infancy, because, it is said, of a curse, adopted Beowulf as his son and heir on the condition he change his name to Rainulph FitzRainulph and swear anew devotion to Christ.

[The Grebsons were suspected of being secret worshipers of the pagan god, Woden, and, indeed, for four centuries thereafter, many Grebsons were burned or hung for witchcraft, though none in the direct line of descent.]

Thus, the Grebsons kept their lands in a time when most of the Old English lords were permanently dispossessed.

Lord FitzGilbert d. 1090, and Rainulph, succeeding, swore fealty to King William Rufus, son of William the Conqueror. He m. Erica, a grand-dau. of Harald Hardraade, while on a trip to Norway.

[This giant Norse king, one of the greatest warriors and travelers of the Viking age, is said by William of Malmesbury to have been thrown down to a lion while a prisoner in Constantinople but to have strangled it with his bare hands. If this is true, he was a fit precursor of his descendant, Tarzan of the Apes.]

Rainulph, accused of complicity in the death of William Rufus in the New Forest, was arrested in 1100 but d. under mysterious circumstances in prison. Rainulph's son, FitzRainulph, b. 1100, m. Elizabeth Dacre and by her had four dau. and a son. His lordship d. 1128 of the ringworm disease after being ill for some time.

[The "ringworm" was probably an acute form of ergotism, caused by eating meal which was ground from corn affected by a fungus disease. Ergotism was widespread during the medieval period.]

Rainulph's son, William, m. a dau. of Humbring, a priest of York, and d. ca. 1150, leaving an only son, John.

John, b. ca. 1145, had a natural son by a Welsh slave, and declared him his son and heir.

Sir John FitzJohn of Grebson was one of the few Englishmen who accompanied Richard I, the Lion-Hearted, on his crusade. John, knighted outside Acre, returned in 1199 with a Saracen bride, Ayesha, dau. of the half-Persian Abdul el Dehshetli, cousin to Saladin and descendant of both Mohammed and Zarathustra.

[The sinister crest of the Grebson coat of arms is "a spear or transfixing a Saracen's head gules." That is, a golden spear stuck through a red-hued Mohammedan's head. A Saracen's head usually commemorates an ancestor who has been on a crusade to the Holy Land. The Grebson crest is colored gules instead of the proper, or natural, color, because of Sir John's use of the severed head of a Moslem while escaping from Acre. After cutting off the head, Sir John threw it, knocked another soldier off his horse, and fled with Ayesha on the horse through the momentarily opened gates.

[It's worth noting that Tarzan's ancestor, Mohammed, belonged to the Qoreish, the dominant tribe of Mecca since 440 A.D. These claimed descent from Qosaiy, whose ancestors were, supposedly, Abraham and Ishmael.]

Sir John d. in 1220, leaving an only son,

Richard "The Black Lion," 1st Baron Grebson, so declared by a writ issued by Henry III in 1222. Richard m. Catherine O'Brien, dau. of The O'Brien of North Thomond, Munster, and returned from Ireland with her and her brother, Finn O'Brien, "The Red Bull of Munster," exiled for having killed his cousin in a quarrel. He lived on the Grebson estate until he m. Rebecca, a dau. of John Griffin, ancestor of the Barons Griffin of Braybroke Castle of Northants.

[Finn O'Brien was of those ancient and illustrious families, presently represented by the barons of Inchiquin and the earls of Dunraven and Mountearl. Through the O'Briens and the O'Quinns, Finn could trace his ancestry to Brian Boroimhe, monarch of Ireland and victor of the battle against the Danes at Clontarf (23 April, 1012), and to Cormac Cas, son of Olliol Olum, monarch of Ireland ca. 200 A.D.]

The 1st Baron at this time changed the arms on his shield, because, it is said, of a desire to impress his neighbors with his devotion to Christianity, a brother and sister having been burned for witchcraft. The former arms, one of the most ancient of record in England, "Per pile azure and argent, thereupon drinking horns in triskele gules" were changed to the present arms. The saltire is a St. Andrews' cross.

The 1st Baron's wife dying and his eight children d. in infancy, his lordship made a pilgrimage to Rome. While in Italy he also visited Florence, and from there eloped with Alessandra, dau. of Alessandro di Parco, count of Scarlassi-Longobardo. This illustrious family, now extinct, could trace its ancestry without question to Julius Caesar, who, in turn, claimed descent from the goddess Venus.

By Alessandra the baron had one son,

William, 2nd Baron Grebson.

The 1st Baron and his wife d. in 1238, presumably of poison administered by an agent of Alessandra's father.

William, 2nd Baron, m. Margery, dau. of Sir William Nevill of Stainton and grand-dau. of William Marshal, 1st Earl of Pembroke, and by her had one surviving child, a dau., Alicia.

[William Marshal, b. ?–d. 1219, second son of John le Maréchal by Sybille, sister of Patrick, earl of Salisbury, succeeded to the title by marrying Isabel, dau. of Richard, earl of Pembroke, called "Strongbow." William was undoubtedly the greatest warrior of his time and probably of the entire Middle Ages. He won every one of the five hundred jousts in which he fought and once unhorsed Richard the Lion-Hearted in a skirmish but spared his life.]

The 2nd Baron d. 1278, succeeded by his adopted son,

John Caldwell-Grebson, 3rd Baron, who, a landless knight claiming to be of Scots descent, m. Alicia in 1278, and by her had one son,

John Caldwell, 4th Baron of Grebson.

The 3rd Baron being slain during an encounter with the officers of Edward I in 1280, his son assumed the lordship of Grebson.

*[There is little doubt that the 3rd Baron was, in actuality, Richard, son of Henry III, known at one time as Norman of Torn (see Edgar Rice Burroughs' *Outlaw of Torn*). Richard, according to Burroughs, was the son of Henry III and Eleanor of Provence, though it seems more likely, from his obscurity in the historians'

records, that he was a natural son of the king. Kidnaped at the age of three, Richard was raised as "Norman" of (the ruined tower of) Torn in the hills of Derby by de Vac, a Gascon who hated Henry III, and who taught Norman to hate Englishmen. Richard, or Norman, fell in love with Bertrade, dau. of Simon de Montfort, Henry's brother-in-law and enemy. Richard fought with Simon against Henry at the battle of Lewes. The second baron of Grebson, also present at Lewes, probably knew Richard's true identity when Richard later claimed to be John Caldwell.

[Richard was recognized by Henry III as his son under dramatic and almost fatal circumstances and was reconciled with his father and mother. He m. Bertrade, but she d. in childbirth. After Henry's death, Edward accused Richard of treason, and Richard became an outlaw again. Disguised as Caldwell, he m. Alicia. But, when adopting new arms, he was unable to resist an example of "punning arms." A spinning wheel was then known as a torn, and his shield bore "Sable, a torn or," i.e., a black field on which is a golden spinning wheel. Edward, hearing of this, sent five knights to arrest him. They caught the outlaw alone, but he killed all, though he died of wounds immediately thereafter. A violet lily-shaped mark on his left breast identified him as Henry III's son.

[John Caldwell, or Richard Plantagenet, or Norman of Torn, was, through Henry III, descended from King John and the following: William the Conqueror; Hrolf the Ganger, the Viking who became lord of Normandy by the treaty of St. Clair-sur-Epte in 912; Charlemagne; Alfred the Great; Egbert, king of Wessex; Woden, the chief god of the Germanic nations. Thus, the son of John Caldwell was doubly descended from Woden.

[Tarzan is descended from a number of huge and powerful men. Hrolf the Ganger, or Walker, was so called because no horse was big enough to carry his gigantic body.]

John Caldwell-Grebson, 4th Baron, m., 1289, his cousin, only dau. of Sir Robert O'Brien-Griffin, a grand-dau. of Finn O'Brien, the "Red Bull of Munster," and had one surviving child, a son,
    Robert, 5th Baron of Grebson.

The 4th Baron, outlawed in 1296, fled with relatives and re-tainers into the hills of Derby as his father had. A great bowman, and dressed in Lincoln green, he became known as The Green Baron, or The Green Archer. The story of his long fight against Edward I and Edward II has, according to some, been incorporated into the legend of Robin Hood, along with that of Robert Fitzooth. The 4th Baron was pardoned by Edward II in 1325. The baron d. Aug. 1327 in an attempt to rescue his king, who was imprisoned in Berkeley Castle, and murdered there, 21 Sept., 1327.

Robert, 5th Baron, b. 1298, m., 1322, Katharine Drummond, a dau. of John Drummond, a son of Sir Malcolm Drummond, and she bore him

Sir John Malcolm, 6th Baron and 1st Earl of Grebson.

The 5th Baron's wife disappeared during a visit to her father in 1340, it being presumed that bandits had murdered and bur. her and her cortege. The 5th Baron d. a year later of a broken abscess in his ear.

The Drummonds, according to unvarying tradition, are of Hungarian origin, Maurice, the first of that family who settled in Scotland, having come from that country in 1066 with Edgar Atheling and Margaret, his sister, afterwards wife of King Malcolm III of Scotland. Maurice adopted the name Drummond from the Gaelic *druim* and *monadh*, that is, "back of the mountain." Maurice was the son of George, a younger son of Andreas, king of Hungary. Andreas could trace his ancestry to Árpád, the Magyar king who conquered Hungary (d. 907).

[What Burke's *Peerage* omits is that Andreas I m. a dau. of Jaroslav, the king of Novgorod and Kiev. Jaroslav was descended from the Swedish Viking Rurik (d. 870), who became king of Novgorod. The Swedish conquerors were called the Rus, or fairhaired, from which the word "Russia" is derived. Jaroslav's other two daus. m. Henry I of France and Harold Haardrade of Norway. Thus, Tarzan is descended through three lines from Rurik. Henry I of France was the ancestor of Edward III of England, whose great-grand-dau., Jane Beaufort, m. James I of Scotland. He was the ancestor of the first Duke of St. Albans (natural son of Charles II and the actress Nell Gwynn), who was the great-great-grandfather of Alicia Rutherford. Alicia m. the third Duke of Greystoke, as noted in Addendum 2. More details of this genealogy later.]

Sir John, 6th Baron and 1st Earl of Grebson, b. 1325, m. Winifrede, a dau. of Thomas, 3rd Lord Frunivall, Lord of Hallamshire, and of Joan, dau. of Sir Thomas de Mounteney, of Swinton and Scoles, and by her had one surviving child, a dau.,

Joane, 7th Baroness and 2nd Countess.

Sir John accompanied Edward III's son, The Black Prince, into France and was knighted on the battlefield of Crécy. Sir John sickened of the Black Death in 1348, but, recovering, built a chapel at Grebson and founded a priory outside Macclesfield, where he had recovered. [This later became Dr. Huxtable's Priory School, described by Dr. Watson in *The Adventure of the Priory School*.] Sir John was on the famous Burned Candlemas expedition (Jan.–Feb. 1356) with Edward III and distinguished himself at Poictiers under the Black Prince. Sir John was made 1st Earl of Grebson in 1357. His lordship d. choking on a fishbone in 1359, and was s. by his dau.,

Joane, 7th Baroness and 2nd Countess, b. ca. 1348, m. Thomas, a brother of William de Greystock, 4th Baron Greystoke, who was adopted as his son by the 6th Baron before his decease. Lord and Lady Grebson had issue, the fourth son, their only survivor, inheriting as

Thomas Ralph, 8th Baron and 3rd Earl.

Lord and Lady Grebson were murdered by their vassals during the Peasants' Revolt of 1381 and were s. by Thomas Ralph, 8th Baron and 3rd Earl, b. 1366, m. Maude, grand-dau. of Sir Nele Loring (d. 1385), and by her had, among others,

John Ralph, 9th Baron and 4th Earl.

His lordship d. of infection from a foot crushed by a horse (bur. March, 1401) and was s. by his 3rd son,

9th Baron and 4th Earl, b. 1396, m. Anne, dau. of Mycroft Holmes, of the neighboring estate of Sigerside, and of Agatha Bumppo, dau. of Sir Nathaniel Bumppo, Kt., of Winestead, Holdernesse, by whom, among others, he had a third son,

John Mycroft, who m. (banns in 1448), Maude, a dau. of Thomas, a younger brother of Henry Percy, 3rd Earl of Northumberland, and had issue of whom the third son,

John William Arthur, was 10th Baron and 5th Earl.

His lordship d. at the advanced age of 75 while accompanying Edward, Prince of Wales, to the battle of Tewkesbury, where Edward fell, and his lordship was s. by his grandson,

John William Arthur, 10th Baron and 5th Earl, b. 1449, m. his kinswoman, Margaret, dau. of Thomas, a younger son of John Talbot, 2nd Earl of Shrewsbury and 7th Baron Furnivall [and so a Neville], and Martha, a dau. of Thomas Dilke, a gentleman of

Maxstoke Castle, co. Warwick, and by her had, among others, an oldest son,

John Thomas, 11th Baron and 6th Earl of Grebson. His lordship, a devoted Lancastrian, was k. outside London 12 May, 1483, by, it is said, men of the Duke of Gloucester [who became in 6 July, 1483, Richard III], and was s. by

John Thomas, 11th Baron and 6th Earl, b. 1475, m. Jessica, natural dau. of Edmund de la Pole, 2nd Duke of Suffolk, and of Anne, dau. of Sir John Carter of Ravenspur, and had, with seven daus., a son,

John Edmund.

His lordship, being accused of treason by Henry VIII, was captured while fleeing to the coast, imprisoned, and deprived of his titles and honors. His lordship was condemned to be beheaded but d. 4 May, 1515 of a flux before the sentence could be carried out.

His son, John Edmund, b. ca. 1501, m. Ellen Washington, a dau. of John Washington of Warton, Lancashire, [John Washington was an ancestor of George Washington, first President of the United States] and had issue, with many daus., of a son,

John, b. 1531, m. 1554, a distant kinswoman, Katherine, a dau. of Morrogh O'Brien, 1st Baron Inchiquin, and had issue,

Captain John Dermod, b. 1556, sailed with Sir Richard Greville to the New World where the ill-fated Roanoke colony was founded. John returned with a woman of the Delaware tribe who d. en route after giving birth to a son,

John Richard, b. 1587, m. Jean, a dau. of the brother of Lord Ruthven of co. Perth, and of Devorgulla Drummond, and had a son,

Captain John Charles.

Captain John Dermod Caldwell-Grebson became immensely wealthy through privateering [actually, piracy] and m. four times after the death of his Indian wife but by these had no surviving male issue. The captain petitioned Her Majesty, Queen Elizabeth, to be rightfully recognized as a co-heir to the Barony of Greystoke through his descendency, this barony having fallen into abeyance through the death of Thomas, 4th Baron Dacre of Gillesland and Baron of Greystoke, and his lordship's sisters become co-heirs. This petition was never acted upon, though resubmitted in 1712 and 1750, but the family shield still bears the arms of the de Greystocks.

Captain John Dermod d. 1634 of a rupture suffered while bearing a coffin at the funeral of a friend, and left his estates to his grandson, Captain John Charles, his son having d.v.p.

Captain John Charles, b. 1607, m. 1629, Elizabeth, dau. of Sir Oliver Tressilian of Penarrow, Cornwall, and of Rosamund Goldolphin of Goldolphin Court, Cornwall, and by her had, with four daus., three sons,

1. John Tressilian, d. at 9 of a fall from a tree
2. Ralph Arthur
3. Harold Cecil (of whom more later)

[This Sir Oliver Tressilian was knighted at the age of twenty-five for sinking two ships of the Great Armada. He was with Hawkins at San Juan de Ulúa. He was a tall, grey-eyed, long-nosed man of immense strength and had a reputation as a daring privateer (Elizabethan euphemism for pirate). Captured by the Spaniards, he became a Catholic, only to convert to Mohammedanism when enslaved by the Algerians. He rose rapidly as a captain of Asad-ed-Din, Basha of Algiers, becoming known throughout the Mediterranean as Sakr-el-Bahr, the Sea-Hawk. Escaping after five years, Sir Oliver returned to England and m. Rosamund Goldolphin, related to the Earl of Goldolphin. Sir Oliver's second cousin, Edmund Tressilian, was used as a character by Sir Walter Scott in his novel *Kenilworth*.]

Captain John Charles Caldwell-Grebson was k. while serving with Sir John, first Baron Byron, at Roundaway Down, 5 July, 1643, and was s. by his second son,

Ralph Arthur, the "Hercules of Yorkshire," b. 1634, m. Ursula d'Arcy, a sister of the second Baron d'Arcy and first Earl of Holdernesse, and by her had, with other issue,

John Charles Conyers, 12th Baron Grebson of Grebson.

Ralph Arthur was famous for his strength and is reported to have been able to lift a full-grown bull above his head. Dying of a bee sting, he was s. by

John Charles Conyers, 12th Baron, b. 1668, m. Constance, natural dau. of Charles de Baatz, seigneur d'Artagnan, Field-Marshal of France, and of Dolores María Salvador, dau. of Don Esteban de Echequivarra y de Miranda, of Cádiz, Spain, by whom he had one surviving child,

Elizabeth Gracia, Baroness Grebson of Grebson.

[It's worth noting that Dolores' family, like so many noble families of Spain, could trace their ancestry back to Rodrigo Díaz (b. 1043), known as El Cid.

[It's also worth noting that Dolores' brother disappeared in Africa while with a Portuguese expedition. He was a giant of tremendous strength (his sister was also unusually large), which has caused some to speculate that it may have been his skeleton which Tarzan found in the desert in *Tarzan the Untamed*. If so, the bones were of his collateral ancestor, and, possibly, of the direct ancestor of the dishonest actor, Esteban Miranda, who resembled Tarzan so closely. See *Tarzan and the Golden Lion* and *Tarzan and The Ant Men*.]

John Charles Conyers set forth in a petition to James II that His Majesty be pleased to restore to him, and to the heirs of his body, the barony and earldom of Grebson with such precedency as John Thomas, 11th Baron and sixth Earl, his ancestor, had enjoyed.

Whereupon, His Majesty did graciously condescend, by a letter patent, dated at Westminster 10 April, 1685, to restore and confirm to the said John Charles Conyers and the heirs of his body, the barony (but not the earldom because of the limitations of the patent), and he had summons to Parliament accordingly. His lordship d. fighting for James II at the battle of the Boyne (1 July, 1690), and was s. by his only surviving child,

Elizabeth Gracia, Baroness of Grebson of Grebson, b. 4 April, 1708, m., July, 1730, after being three times a widow, her cousin, Earl Staveley, Captain John Clayton. His lordship was the grandson of the aforementioned Harold Cecil, third son of the aforementioned Captain John Charles Caldwell-Grebson, and the earl became 13th Baron by right of his wife.

The aforementioned Harold Cecil m. Chrysogon, only child of the third Earl Staveley of Staveley Hall of Islington.

[The third earl was descended from George Clayton of Grimsby co., ancestor also of Lord Tennyson, the poet, and from John, or Thomas, Horner, steward to the last Abbot of Glastonbury Cathedral. When Henry VIII dissolved the monastic orders and seized so much church property, the abbot sent deeds to twelve manorial estates to the king to appease him. These were baked into a pie to fool robbers and delivered by the steward. On the way, Horner opened the pie and appropriated the deed to the estate of Mells. Hence,

the nursery rhyme of "Little Jack Horner." See Horner of Mells
Park, Burke's *Landed Gentry*.]

Harold Cecil, on condition that he inherit his father-in-law's
wealth and title, adopted his wife's surname, and renounced his
own. The will of the third earl assured that Harold Cecil would
not be able after his death to reclaim his own name or to hyphenate
it with Clayton.

The only son of this union, John, was stolen at the age of two,
his abductors proposing to sell him, a criminal practice quite common at this time. The authorities being close on their trail, the
abductors disposed of John to a beggar woman, who, in turn, sold
him to a gypsy woman. She named him Bob (not Robert) Singleton,
the only name he knew during most of his life. The gypsy woman
being hanged when Bob was six, he was raised by various parishes.
At twelve, he was taken to Newfoundland as a cabin boy on a ship.
[Much of his life is detailed with more or less validity by Daniel
Defoe in the biography *Life, Adventures, and Piracies of Captain
Singleton*, published in 1720. The narrative, however, ends in 1711.]

At the age of 18, Singleton, marooned on Madagascar, sailed
with 24 other seamen to the coast of Africa near the mouth of the
Zambezi River. From there he began a three-year odyssey which
ended at Cape Coast Castle in what is now Ghana. This feat,
covering more than 5,000 total miles through unexplored jungles
and deserts and mountains inhabited by lions, leopards, poisonous
snakes, and cannibals and infested with malaria, tsetse flies, and
diseases of many and terrible sorts, is unmatched in history. Yet it
is ignored by most historians, probably because of the character
and reputation of this intrepid explorer. From Singleton's account,
he may have discovered Lake Tanganyika, thus preceding Sir Richard
Francis Burton by about 150 years.

Captain Singleton m., firstly, —— Walters, sister of William
Walters, a Quaker and a fellow sailor on Singleton's later exploits
in the Indian Ocean. His first wife dying soon after marriage, and
his fortune lost for a second time, Singleton sailed off the coast
of western Africa and made a third fortune. He m. Una, dau. of a
Swedish merchantman, Captain Ulf Larsson, and of Haiba, a
beautiful quadroon who seems to have been the dau. of a half-
Waziri woman and a Finno-Lithuanian, Algirdas Otava, an employe
of a Swedish slave factory and trading post.

[The Waziri, at this time, were near the coast of the Cameroons, on their way from the homeland in northern Nigeria or southern Mali. Their two-centuries-long migration represented the last great movement of Bantu speakers from the area where this language family originated. Linguistic and somatic evidence indicates that the Waziri had absorbed some Hamitic (Tuareg) words and genes before the migration.]

Returning with his third fortune, his wife, and a son, John, b. 1712, Captain Singleton settled in Islington. Having made extensive investigations on which he spent great sums, he determined that he was the abducted son of Harold Cecil Clayton and his wife, who, at the age of 87, was still living. She, having proved his ancestry by a birthmark and the few facts he remembered from his infancy in Islington, proclaimed him her son and, to strengthen the claim, adopted him. He thereupon, by royal petition, got himself and his son, John, acknowledged as in the line of heirship to the barony of Grebson of Grebson and the earldom of Staveley. The titles were not, however, officially confirmed until after the captain's death.

The captain purchased Chamston-Hedding, an estate neighboring to Grebson, and built thereupon Westerfalcon Hall (1731–2), naming it after the founder of the line. This became a family seat, Grebson Hold having been ruined when stormed by Cromwellians in 1651.

[Elizabeth Tressilian, widow of the aforementioned Captain John Charles Caldwell-Grebson, blew up the powder magazine, perishing with all defenders and most of the invaders.]

Captain Clayton (the erstwhile Captain Singleton) k. a neighbor, a Squire Holmes, who had insulted his wife because of her reputed Waziri ancestry, but the captain was acquitted on a plea of self-defense. There was bad blood between the two families for several generations, with deaths from several duels, but marriages were not infrequent between the two families at a later period.

John, the fourth Earl Staveley and 13th Baron Grebson, and his wife, Elizabeth Gracia, had issue, of whom the heir was their second son,

John Cecil, first Duke and Viscount of Greystoke.

The fourth earl d. 1749 of the pox, being survived by his wife, who was declared mad and shut up in a wing of Westerfalcon Hall, constantly attended, until death put an end to her sufferings in 1764.

John Cecil, first Duke and Viscount of Greystoke, b. 1730, m. (when he was sixteen) Hilda, dau. of Major Bolko Rubinroth of Lustadt, Kingdom of Lutha, and Julia, dau. of Dr. Wilhelm von Harben and Augusta, dau. of Baron von Ruderfurd of Cronstadt, and had issue, including,

1. Cecil Arthur, 2nd Duke
2. John William, 3rd Duke.

The 1st Duke was a child prodigy, starting to read, at the age of three, Latin, at four, Greek, and at five, Hebrew. At seven, he could play six musical instruments and composed, at eight, a number of musical pieces, including a concerto grosso which puzzled many critics but which Bach was to declare a work of genius and which he predicted would not be fully appreciated until the twentieth century. (Unfortunately, this work has since been lost.) At fifteen, the precocious 1st Duke went on a grand tour and met Hilda Rubinroth, a famous singer, thirty years old, served a year in the Luthan army as a Lieutenant, and then resigned, eloping with Hilda.

Upon returning to England, after a visit to Egypt and the Holy Lands, His Grace seemed to lose all desire to further his musical and classical genius. His Grace had access to an immense fortune, his father being one of the few who had profited by the South Sea Bubble of 1720, escaping the general ruin.

Becoming intimate with His Majesty, George II, who shared his interest in opera and was a patron of Handel, His Grace loaned His Majesty vast sums. Little of this was repaid, but His Grace could afford it, deriving his fortune from the very profitable trade in slaves and goods in Africa, the West Indies, and the North American colonies. Though he never held public office, he nevertheless had great influence on the king, and this despite a long absence from England during the French-Indian War. Also sharing George II's keen interest in military life and affairs, His Grace purchased a commission and went to the Colonies. There he was wounded in the battle in which General Braddock was k. He served in Lord Loudon's unsuccessful amphibious expedition against Louisbourg, but was with Lord Amherst in the capture of Louisbourg and the victories of Fort Ticonderoga and Crown Point.

His Grace derived much fame from the publication of his journal, *An Odyssey in the American Wilderness*, 1754, in which he described his capture, torture, and escape from the Cayugas. While being tormented, His Grace lost an eye and, after his successful flight, his right leg from an infection resulting from a dispute with a bear over a rabbit. Returning to England, his lordship saved His Majesty from a Jacobite assassin and was for this and his other services created Duke and Viscount of Greystoke (not to be confused with the extinct Barony of Greystoke, Cumberland). His Grace d. in 1765 of a fall from a horse while hunting and was s. by his son,

Cecil Arthur, second Duke, b. 1749 in New York, and d. unm. two months after his father, accidentally shooting himself while loading a pistol. He was s. by his younger brother,

John William, third Duke, b. 1750 in New York, m. Alicia, a dau. of Sir John Rutherford, Bt., younger son of Baron Tennington and of Alicia Drummond.

[Alicia Drummond was the dau. of John Drummond of Stanmore, M.P., and of Charlotte, grand-dau. of the first Duke of St. Albans, natural son of Charles II and Nell Gwynn. Charles II was descended in a direct line from Mary, Queen of Scots, from James IV of Scotland, who m. Margaret, dau. of Henry VII of England, from James I of Scotland, who m. Jane Beaufort, Edward III's great-grand-dau., from David I of Scotland, whose sister m. Henry I of England, son of William the Conqueror, and from Malcolm III, who m. Margaret, dau. of Edmund Ironside, Alfred the Great's great-great-great-grandson. It was Margaret who brought Maurice, the first Drummond, from Hungary in 1066. Malcolm III claimed descent through the kings of Dalriada to Fergus Mor MacErc (ca. 490) and Cruithne, the eponymous king of the Picts.

[Through these lines, Alicia Rutherford was also descended from every one of the dynasties of France and from royal families of Castile and Denmark.]

The third Duke and his duchess were among the party which narrowly escaped being struck by a meteorite near Wold Newton, East Riding, a monument of which may be seen today at the area of impact. The duke and his wife were lost at sea off Cherbourg, 26 Jan., 1801, leaving two sons,

1. Sir Jesse, 4th Duke

2. General Sir William (V.C., K.C.B.), 1st Bt., (author of many books and poetry), b. 1 Jan. 1799; educ. Eton; went at 18 to S. Africa, his father having gambled away everything except the family seats and lands, where, after some misfortunes, including almost dying of thirst while lost in the Kalahari Desert and

being chased by twelve natives for five days, during which he slew ten of their party, he found enough gold to make him wealthy for several years. He m., firstly, Wilhelmina, dau. of Jakobus Retief, a Boer, but she d. of a snakebite before he returned to England. On the trip home, William doubled his fortune by gambling, he having his father's love of this sport, though much more moderately. William accused another card player, Major Upwood, of cheating, and in the ensuing duel on shipboard he k. the major with a pistol shot. Being brought to trial in London, William claimed self-defense, all witnesses having disappeared when the ship docked, and he was acquitted. William thereupon wrote a narrative of his S. African travels, *Gold and a Lost Love in Africa*, from which he derived much fame and not inconsiderable royalties. William, however, discovering that his publisher and agent were in collusion to cheat him, broke both their skulls by knocking them together, he being very big and strong and, in fact, called by one journalist, "an Apollo with the strength of a Hercules." The ensuing trial and double suit against him resulted in a great loss of money to him, he being forced to pay the family of the agent, who d. a few months after the assault, despite plain evidence of his having cheated William. At this time, William had the final break with his older brother, the 4th Duke, and they were never reconciled.

Young William, having corresponded with Lord Byron, and being fired with enthusiasm for the cause of Hellenic independence, went to Greece with his good friend and schoolmate, Phileas Longferry, son of Lord Longferry of Skiddaw. William was at this time, because of his handsomeness and close resemblance to the poet, called "The Young Byron" or "George's Twin," and a famous French author was to remark on the similarity to Byron of William's son.

William Clayton and Phileas Longferry were on Chios with the Greek forces when the Turkish fleet conquered that island and massacred or sold into slavery almost all the population. Escaping, the two joined Lord Byron at Missolonghi and were present when His Lordship died. William later wrote and published a poem, *The Eagle That Shames*, which attracted considerable attention because of its protest against England's refusal to bury Byron in Westminster Abbey. Captured at the siege of Missolonghi (23 April, 1826), William and Phileas were spared in the general massacre but Phileas d. of maltreatment and a fever shortly therafter. William later escaped, diving from a ship taking him to Turkey and swimming twelve miles to the mainshore of Greece.

William m., secondly, Ermione, dau. of General Alexandros Khatamagos, but she d. shortly after childbirth of puerperal fever. Disgusted with Greek factional rivalry, intrigue, and corruption, revolted at the terrible massacres by both sides, and saddened by the deaths of his friend and his wife, William returned to England. Soon after, having arranged for the care of his daughter, Aspasia, William went to the American Rockies with the scientific expedition of Prince Peter Rubinroth of Lutha, having been invited along because of his relationship to the prince and his fame resulting from his African and Greek adventures.

William was captured by the Sioux but escaped, thus emulating the exploit of his illustrious ancestor, the first Duke. William m., thirdly, Marie, dau. of —— Grandin, a French trapper and of a Crow woman, while living with the Crows. Returning to England after his wife was drowned in a mountain stream, he wrote a best-selling narrative, *Blood and Love Among the Redskins*. Afterward, he purchased a commission as a captain of the 1st Hallamshire Rifles but later taught in the Sandhurst cavalry school. During this time, he m., fourthly, (1832), Lorina, dau. of Lord Dacre by Jane Carfax, dau. of Lord Rufton, and by her had issue,

1. Phileas, b. 1832
2. Roxana, b. 1833.

His wife divorced William in 1835 and m. Sir Heraclitus Fogg, Bt., an eccentric inventor and owner of a vast estate, Fogg Shaw, in Derbyshire. Sir Heraclitus adopted the two children, William not objecting.

In 1839, Lt. Col. Clayton was sent to India and then to China, where, as a staff member, he took part in the occupation of Hong Kong and the Opium War. William acquired a considerable fortune at this time, though its source was never known. Sir William was knighted in 1845 and thereupon sent to S. Africa, but not before having m., fifthly, Maida, dau. of Petronius van Kortrijn, a Dutch merchantman, and, she being stabbed in an altercation with her cook, Sir William m., sixthly, Maida's sister, Katrina, who d. of a fever while en route to S. Africa.

Sir William, now a colonel, was wounded (1847, despatches)

in the War of the Axe, in the Battle of Boomplaats (Aug., 1848, despatches) and in 1852 during the Great Kaffir War (V.C.), on each occasion by an assegai. During this time, he m., seventhly, Leona, dau. of Giuseppe Allendi, rancher. In 1853, he returned to England as a Brig.-Gen. and was attached to the staff of Lord Ragland. Thereupon he was sent to Crimea, his wife dying of pneumonia in England in 1854, at which time Sir William was lying severely wounded in the hospital, having been caught in the explosion of the French magazine during the siege of Sevastopol.

[The late Brig.-Gen. H. P. Flashman, in his Crimean memoirs *Twixt Cossack and Cannon*, mentions Sir William. For the book title, see *Flashman*, George Macdonald Fraser, New American Library, N.Y.]

In 1855, Sir William m., eighthly, Natalie, dau. of Prince Alexander Gromsky of Kiev, but, she disappearing shortly thereafter, Sir William had the marriage annulled. In 1857, Sir William went to Mexico City as military adviser to the Mexican Army, where he m., ninthly, Angela Bridget, dau. of General Pedro Alvarez y O'Shaughnessy, but she d. of melancholia a year after giving birth to a dau., Angela.

Resigning in 1859, Sir William returned to England to settle his dau. there and went up the Amazon with the ill-fated Sevarac Expedition. Returning in 1864, Sir William wrote a novel based on his South American experiences, *Love Is a Jaguar*, which was scorned by the critics but went into twenty-two printings. Announcing his decision to retire, Sir William purchased Sallust's House, Oxfordshire, on the condition that it revert to the fifth Duke, his nephew, or his heirs, on Sir William's death. Sir William was made a baronet of the U.K. in 1866 and m., tenthly, his housekeeper, Margaret, thirty-year-old dau. of Richard Shaw of Dublin, she bearing him a son, William, a year later. Margaret being drowned in 1869 during a picnic on the Thames, Sir William m., eleventhly (1870) his succeeding housekeeper, Martha, thirty-five-year-old dau. of the Rev. Robert Wharram of Reigate, and by her had issue,

1. Phileas Sallust, d. in infancy
2. Martha, d. of burns at age of three.

His wife dying in 1874 in the same fire in which his dau. suffered her fatal burns, Sir William, though 76, m., twelfthly, Jane, forty-one-year-old widow of Sir Charles Brandon of Brandon

Beeches, a neighboring estate [see *An Unsocial Socialist*], and by her had, to his and his wife's surprise,

Ultima, b. 1877, m., 1898, John T. McGee, an Ohio landowner visiting London.

By this time, Sir William was the object of much gossip and even caricaturing in the newspapers, being called "Wandering Willie," "Billy Banns," and "Marrying Bill," or, because of the tendency of his wives to die, "The Bluebeard Baronet" or "Gruesome Grebson."

At the age of 80, Sir William began writing his best-selling, sensational memoirs, published in three volumes in 1888, Paris, under the title, *Never Say Die*. Due to this book, Sir William was denied the title of Marquess of Brandon, which Her Majesty was considering granting him, despite his being a divorced man and once having been named as co-respondent (though not guilty). But, as he was said to have commented, "A title means nothing if no money or love comes with it." [A sentiment echoed by his great-great-nephew, Tarzan.]

At the age of 90, Sir William published the final version of poems first written in 1818–1828, *Love of War and Women*, a best seller widely denounced for its erotic content, though, from the viewpoint of a later generation, innocuous enough.

In 1899, Sir William celebrated his 100th birthday. His wife having died two days later, there was considerable speculation, some rather rabelaisian, about whom Sir William would choose for his next wife. Sir William astounded everybody by proposing to, and being accepted by, Genoa Darnley, a 22-year-old widow of unknown antecedents and distressing circumstances, who announced she was marrying for love only. [Love of what? was Frank Harris' widely bandied-about comment.] Sir William's dau. and grandchildren by Mrs. Heraclitus Fogg thereupon attempted to have him committed. Sir William, leaving his solicitors to fight for him, took his bride to Greece for the honeymoon. While there, he erected a monument to the memory of Phileas Longferry and also announced that his wife had conceived. This was followed by the famous remark that he should have named his previous child Penultima. The son was named Isaac but d. four years later of diphtheria.

At the age of 103, Sir William d. in the arms of his wife under circumstances which caused much unseemly merriment not unmixed with envy. He was bur. in the family cemetery by the ruins of Grebson's Hold below the inscription of the family motto, *Je Suys Encore Vyvant*—I Still Live.

His older brother, Sir Jesse, fourth Duke, m. Arabella, dau. of Charles Howard, third Viscount Breconcastle and fourth Baron Sallust, and of Mary, an actress of repute, dau. of Roger Kemble of Brecon, Wales, and by Arabella had eight children, of whom three survived,

1. John, 5th Duke
2. William Cecil, 6th Duke
3. Joane, b. 1836, m. 14th Duke of Pomver.

The fourth Duke became Viscount Breconcastle and Baron Sallust by right of his wife. At the time of marriage, the fourth Duke was recouping the fortunes of his family, his father having experienced great losses of money and property. [The third duke, a compulsive gambler, although a strict teetotaller and faithful husband, traveled extensively throughout Europe to the spas, where he lost most of his fortune and much property at the gaming tables. His son, the fourth duke, borrowed money with his estates as collateral and built cotton factories, from which he became very wealthy.] His Grace was M.P. for Manchester, Lord-Lieut. of Hallamshire, Chm. of Clayton Manufactories, Chm. of Bd. of Supervisors of the Trojan Mineworks and Trading Corpn., founder of The Society for the Redemption of African Heathen, vice-pres. of the Anti-Anarchist Soldiers for Albion Association, and financial advisor and main contributor to the Servants of the Queen Charitable and Educational Society of Manchester and Liverpool. The Duke was created Lord Ranger (of Clayton Deer Park, co. Perth) by Her Majesty in 1853. His Grace d. 1858 of a fall from a window in his Kensington mansion [while trying to retrieve a pound note blown by the wind from his study desk.] Her Majesty attended His Grace's funeral but rejected the petition of His Grace's younger son to permit him to be bur. in Westminster Abbey. The fourth Duke was s. by

John, the fifth Duke (author of *The Criminal Class: Our Peers; Why New Harmony Failed; Infant Mortality and Its Causes in Manchester; The Fabian Blindness*), educ. Eton, Cambridge; b. 8 Nov., 1835, m., firstly, Henrietta Jansenius (d. 1863), dau. of Sir John Jansenius, Kt. (Chm. of the Transcanadian Railway Company, Chm. Cotman's Bank, Pres. Appledore Construction and Engineering Company, Director of Peak Midlands Gas, Light, and Coke Company) and of Ruth, dau. of Absalom Rothschild of that

illustrious family, and m., secondly, Athena (d. 1894), dau. of
Fitzwilliam Bennet Darcy, of that ancient and honourable landed
family, and of Agatha Jansenius, sister of Sir John Jansenius, by
whom His Grace had one son,

John, *honorary* Lord Staveley.

[Both Sir John Jansenius and his wife claimed to be able to
trace their ancestry back to King David, circa 1000 B.C., and thus
were far more ancient in lineage than any of the other human lines
ancestral to Tarzan.]

Lord John Staveley, educ. Eton and Chatham, b. 13 Jan., 1864,
m. 21 Feb., 1888, Alice Rutherford, a kinswoman, dau. of George,
13th Baron Tennington, by his wife, Marguerite Grosvenor Blakeney, grand-dau. of Sir Percy Blakeney, Bt., and the famous actress,
Alice Clarke Raffles, cousin to Sir Thomas Stamford Raffles, founder
of Singapore, and by her had issue,

John, the eighth and present Duke.

John Clayton, son of the fifth Duke, Capt. Pioneers of the Corps
of Madras Sappers and Miners, Her Majesty's Indian Army, invalided home after mauling by a tiger, became a special Investigator-
Commissioner for the Colonial Office. With his wife, he proceeded
to the coast of West Africa, where they d.v.p., 22 Nov., 1889,
thought to have perished over a year before at sea.

The fifth Duke was murdered 21 Nov., 1889, by an unknown
assailant and was s. by his younger brother,

Sir William Cecil, K.G., P.C., M.V.O., Custos Rotulorum and
Lord-Lieut. of Hallamshire; Hereditary High Sheriff, Hallamshire;
J.P. and M.P., Chester; hon. Col. 5th Bn. Hallamshire Fus.; hon.
LL.D., Liverpool University; Lord of the Admiralty, 1872; leader
of Hallamshire Trade Mission to Canada, 1887; Vice-Pres. Bd.
Trade; Lord Privy Seal; Chief Sec. State European Affairs, 1899;
b. 2 Oct., 1836; m. 21 Feb., 1888, to Edith (d. June, 1907), widow
of Marquess Blackwater and youngest dau. of Sir John Jansenius
and Ruth Rothschild, and by her had one son,

William Cecil Arthur, seventh Duke.

[Burke's *Peerage* either ignored, or was not aware of, the existence
of an older, but illegitimate, son, James Clarke Wildman, son of
Patricia Clarke Wildman, a grand-dau. of the Scarlet Pimpernel.]

The sixth Duke, while his older brother was still alive, and
therefore he was still a commoner, was honoured by Her Majesty
with letters patent creating him first Marquess of Exminster, first
Viscount Passmore, and a baronet. His lordship purchased Pemberly

House from his cousin, Sir Gawain Darcy, Bt., who had purchased it from Fitzwilliam Bennet Darcy when that gentleman had suffered great financial reverses.

[It has been speculated that Pemberley House is the Holdernesse Hall of Doctor Watson's narrative of the Priory School.]

His Grace continued to live at Pemberley House even after inheriting the titles and estates of his brother. His Grace d. 3 Feb., 1909, and was s. by his only son,

Sir William Cecil Arthur, seventh Duke, b. 18 May, 1891, educ. Eton, Cambridge, d. unm. 1910, in Gabon, the marquessate of Exminster, the viscountcy of Passmore, and the baronetcy becoming extinct according to the limitations of heirs male of the body, and was s. by his cousin,

John Clayton, eighth and present Duke, who was discovered alive in Gabon, having been raised after the death of his parents by the aborigines.

Creation—Grebson of Grebson, B. (E.), 22 April 1222
               Grebson of Grebson, E. (E.), 1 May 1357
               Sallust, B. (E.), 15 April 1685
               Breconcastle, V. (G.B.), 16 May 1708
               Staveley, E. (G.B.), 9 May 1733
               Greystoke, D. and V. (G.B.), 12 May 1756
               Restoration, 10 April 1685, Act of Parliament

Arms—Quarterly of six: 1st, GREBSON OF GREBSON, arg. on a saltire az. drinking horns in triskele gu.; 2nd, DRUMMOND, or three bars wavy gu.; 3rd, O'BRIEN, gu, three lions passant guardant in pale, per pale or and arg.; 4th, CALDWELL, sa. a torn or; 5th, RUTHER-FORD, gu. a wild bull's head caboshed, eyes of the first, otherwise of its own kind, between the horns a wildman's head affrontée, eyes of the first; 6th, FITZWILLIAM & GREYSTOCK, barry of six, arg. and az., over all three chaplets of roses gu. *Crest*—a sleuth-hound arg., collared and leashed gu., for DRUMMOND; issuing from a cloud az. an arm embowed brandishing a sword gu., hilt and pommel sa., for GREBSON; a spear or transfixing a Saracen's head gu., for GREBSON. *Supporters*—Dexter, a wildman wreathed about the middle with oak, in the dexter hand a bow, with a quiver of arrows over his shoulder, all vert, and a lion skin or hanging behind his back; sinister, a female great ape guardant, ppr. *Mottoes*—(over the crest) Je Suys Encore Vyvant; (under the arms) Kreeg-ah!

Seats—Westerfalcon Hall, Chamston-Hedding, Yorkshire; Greystoke

House, Carlton House Terrace, London; Greystoke Plantation, West Kenya, Africa.

Clubs—Stylites; Linguist's

THE ARMS EXPLAINED AND SOME HISTORICAL NOTES:

The language of heraldry is highly technical but easily interpreted. "Quarterly of six" means that the shield is divided into six equal parts, each bearing the arms of a particular family.

Arg. is abbreviation for argent, meaning silver or gray. The basic color of the field is gray. The saltire az. is a cross in the form of an azure or blue X. Gu. is gules or red. The drinking horns are *in triskele*, that is, they form three curved or bent branches radiating from a center. As far as is known, this figure is unique in heraldry, being restricted to the Grebson family. The charge, however, is of ancient origin, being originally a symbol for Woden, or Odin, in his aspect of god of warriors killed in battle. The Old English knew it as the *waelcnotta* and the Old Norse as the *valknutr*, both words meaning "the knot of the slain." The drinking horns in triskele, or three triangles connected at the apex, are found scratched in rocks in many parts of Scandinavia and some parts of England and Scotland. Historically, the use of this symbol on the shield started with Westerfalcna, son of Aelle, king of Deira, but it probably originated with Waegdaeg, who claimed to be Woden's son.

The Drummond arms are "or, three bars wavy gules" or a golden field on which are three red and wavy horizontal bars. A bar is supposed to occupy one-fifth of the field.

O'Brien: Any beast that is "passant guardant" is walking past with its head facing the beholder. In pale means the lions are arranged one beneath the other. Per pale means the lions will be divided in color by a vertical line in the middle of their bodies.

"Sa. a torn or" means that the field is sable, or black, and the charge is a golden torn. A torn meant, in the late thirteenth century, a spinning wheel, and the torn illustrated here is an example of the archaic spinning wheel. It is also an example of "armes parlantes" or "canting arms" or "punning arms." Many heraldic charges originated from plays on the owner's name or title.

The term "caboshed," or "cabossed," which we find in the Rutherford arms, applies to the head of a beast facing forward with no part of the neck visible. *Of the first* means that the color is the same as the first color mentioned in the blazoning; colors are not to be repeated by name. *Of its own kind* is an old phrase meaning colored naturally. Affrontée means that the human head is looking forward.

Fitzwilliam & Greystock: *Barry* means that the field is divided into a stipulated equal number of equal-sized horizontal parts. *Over all* means that the charges are placed over other charges or a vari-colored field.

Dexter is the right-hand side, of course, and in heraldry the dexter is on the left of the beholder because positions are from the viewpoint of the man behind the shield. The dexter supporter of the Greystoke arms is unusual in being vert, or green, instead of ppr. (proper) or naturally colored. It was colored so in honor of the son of the Outlaw of Torn, himself an outlaw and called, in folk legend, the Green Archer or the Green Baron. The lion skin was added by the present duke in commemoration of Jad-bal-ja, the Golden Lion.

The left-hand supporter is called sinister only in the old-fashioned sense of the word. The present duke replaced the original supporter, a sagittarius, with the "female great ape guardant, ppr." in honor of his foster mother, Kala. This substitution of personal supporters in the coat of arms is not uncommon. (See, for instance, the tenth duke of Marlborough, Burke's *Peerage*.)

The upper motto, "Je Suys Encore Vyvant," is the original war cry of the Grebsons, adopted by Rainulph FitzGilbert and trans-lated from the Old English into Anglo-Norman and later put into more modern (but archaically spelled) French. It means "I Am Still Living," and it pre-echoes, as it were, the words of Tarzan in many situations where things looked hopeless.

The lower motto, "Kreeg-ah!" is, as we know, the warning cry of the mangani, and was added by the present duke.

I do not know why the Clayton arms were not added to the Greystoke shield. Perhaps the fourth Earl Staveley thought that its addition would crowd the shield and cause an aesthetic im-balance. Or perhaps he intended to do so but never got around to it, and his descendants saw no reason why they should bother with it. It is a fact that no petition to add the Clayton arms is known.

WHAT HAPPENED TO BLACK MICHAEL?

Based on an original idea by Dale L. Walker
Developed by John Harwood
Additional notes by Philip José Farmer

From all signs, Black Michael and his cutthroat crew were dead. But some events which Burroughs does not describe in *Tarzan of the Apes* indicated that Black Michael may have survived the wreck of the *Fuwalda* only to be killed in England.

Consider. A certain former captain of a steam sealer suddenly disappeared from his usual haunts in 1884. Just as suddenly, he reappeared in England in 1889, the year following the mutiny on the *Fuwalda*.

Some believe that this former sealer captain and the common seaman, Black Michael, were the same person.

Both were huge men, and both had violent tempers. The captain wore a heavy black beard; Black Michael, tremendous black mustachios.

According to some, the captain changed his name and shaved off his beard while aboard the *Fuwalda*. But he resumed both name and beard when he settled down in England with his wife and daughter. The story of his death, of his being pinned to the wall by a harpoon, and the events that followed, have been told by a Dr. John H. Watson in *The Adventure of Black Peter*.

A TENTATIVE CAREER OF BLACK PETER—BLACK MICHAEL

Peter Michael Carey was born in 1845 and ran away to sea at the age of ten in 1855 or 1856. He became a cabin boy aboard the *Sea Unicorn*[1] and worked his way up to captain by 1882.[2] He became known as Black Peter for his temper as well as for his black beard.[3]

In August, 1883, he picked up Neligan, a West Country banker, from his disabled yacht. Neligan had been on his way to Norway to sell some securities to prevent a failure of his bank. Black Peter found out about the securities and pitched Neligan overboard to get them. Patrick Cairns, a harpooner, witnessed the murder but said nothing about it to anybody at the time.

In 1884, Black Peter Michael Carey retired to live on his stolen securities. But, in some way, he learned that Cairns had witnessed the crime and was intending to blackmail him.

Cairns must have provided safeguards, such as a letter, held by a friend, which would go to the police if he was murdered. Otherwise, Black Peter Michael would have killed him. Instead, Black Peter Michael decided to get out of England for a while and so shake Cairns off his trail. Knowing that Cairns would look for him in the northern whaling-sealing fleets, Black Peter signed on as a common sailor on a southbound ship. He changed his name and shaved off his beard. Though he would have had to present papers as a deckhand, he could get forged documents easily. If he had tried to get a captain's position, he would have met great difficulties in obtaining forged papers.

We know that he used his middle name, Michael, as his first name, but what name he used as his so-called family name, we do not know. But he could not hide his swarthiness or his temper, so he was dubbed "Black" Michael by his shipmates. Character shapes destiny, as Heraclitus said, and the seaman could not escape that inevitability.

Black Peter–Black Michael may have knocked about for a while in the South Atlantic, sailing on several vessels, before he shipped aboard the *Fuwalda* in 1888.

After leading the mutiny and marooning John Clayton and his wife, he may have set sail for the nearest civilized port. The crew would have planned on scattering from there before the *Fuwalda* was missed.[4] They would have been more inconspicuous in a large port than a small coastal town.

They may have waited until it was dark, approached the port, set the ship's sails, and rowed into port in boats after abandoning the ship. The crew split up in the port, and Carey made his way back to England in 1889 and settled down in Sussex. In this out-of-the-way area, he hoped to stay hidden forever from Cairns.

The *Fuwalda*, instead of being wrecked at sea, drifted into the

South Equatorial Current. This took it out into the Atlantic, down the east coast of South America, out east into the Atlantic again, and so to its wrecking on the shores of St. Helena. Finding the wreckage, the authorities believed that the ship had gone down with all aboard, including the Greystokes, and called off the naval search.

NOTES (by John Harwood)

1. Black Peter Michael may have shipped aboard various ships before the *Sea Unicorn*. But page 666 of *The Complete Sherlock Holmes*, Garden City Publishing Co., 1938, quotes Holmes thus: "So far as I could learn he had sailed in no other ship." Would this indicate that he had worked his way up from cabin boy to captain of the same ship on which he had started? Or would it mean that it might be difficult to trace the career of a man through the lower jobs such as cabin boy and common sailor and that Holmes only looked up the records of his employment as mate and captain? The officers may have been on record at some central shipping agency, but the crew members might only be available in the logs of individual ships.

2. Stanley Hopkins, a young and promising police inspector, says of Black Peter, "In 1883 he commanded the steam sealer *Sea Unicorn* of Dundee. He had then several successful voyages in succession, and in the following year, 1884, he retired."

   What does Hopkins' first sentence mean? Was 1883 the first year he commanded the ship? Also, he had several successful voyages in succession. Does that mean he had a number of trips in a single year? Evidently, the English sealers did not go on long voyages as did the New Bedford whalers, who went out for three or four years at a time.

   Mention is made on page 655 of the above-mentioned book of ". . . a line of logbooks on a shelf." As captain of the ship he might have taken the logbooks relating to the time he was captain, but I would think they would go to the shipowners. Would a single logbook cover a year or would there have been one for each voyage?

3. Why did Black Peter Michael grow a beard again when he settled down in England? If Cairns was still looking for him after all these years, he probably would have been searching

for him in England as well as in Scotland. Besides asking
for him by name, he would have given a description, and
this would have included the huge black beard.
4. According to Burroughs in *Tarzan of the Apes*, British warships
were searching the South Atlantic two months after the disappearance of the *Fuwalda*.

NOTES (by Philip José Farmer)

1. As thorough as Holmes was, he should have located the records
of Carey's entire career. He would have found these records
in the shipowners' files, but it is possible that many of the
records were lost or destroyed. Probably, Carey stayed on one
ship.
2. Carey's first command was in 1883. And, as Harwood spec-
ulates, English (or Scotch) sealers didn't stay out as long as
whalers. The natures of the two hunts require different lengths
of time.
    Black Peter's logbooks would be those in which the captain
records a summation of events from the ship's log. These
are the property of the captain.
3. Black Peter Michael grew a beard again just because he
liked his beard. And, if he had not talked to that sailor in
London, if he had stayed out of London, he would not have
been found by the harpooner, Cairns. He thought he was safe
in Forest Row, Sussex.
    As I stated in the text of this biography, Black Michael
was probably an American or an Irishman. There is nothing
in Watson's report to contradict this, since he does not say
what nationality Black Peter Michael Carey was. The Black
Michael of Burroughs does, however, seem more humane than
the Black Peter of Watson. But it must be remembered that
Watson says that Black Peter Carey was much easier to get
along with when he had not been drinking. And Cairns says
that on his first visit to Carey, he and Carey had a reasonably
rancor-free conversation. It was during the second visit, when
Black Peter had been drinking so heavily, that he attacked Cairns
with a knife. Black Michael treated the Greystokes so well
because, one, he did have some sense of gratitude, and, two—
and this was by far the stronger reason—he planned on selling
the Greystokes' location for a great sum of money.

Starr makes an objection to the Black Peter–Black Michael theory. He does not think that there is any reason for Black Peter taking up the hard life of a common sailor again. But Hopkins says that Carey did travel for some years after retiring in 1884. Where he traveled or in what style, Hopkins does not say. I suggest that he did sign up as a common seaman on several South Atlantic ships. He did this solely to throw any pursuers off the track, and he chose the southern seas because he was not known there. Moreover, he hated the Arctic cold. And he may have hoped to run across another chance to make a fortune while he was in hiding. The mutiny occurred, and he saw his great opportunity to use the Greystokes.

I believe that Black Peter Michael deliberately chopped off some parts of the *Fuwalda* and cast them adrift off the shore of St. Helena. Harwood's theory that the ship drifted across the Atlantic and back again requires too much time. Only two months after the *Fuwalda* left Freetown, Sierra Leone, it was being looked for by half a dozen warships. And the wreckage was found almost immediately. The ship could not have drifted on the path Harwood describes in the month and a half after the Greystokes were marooned. Indeed, this time element would be even shorter, since the *Fuwalda* would have to be sailed to the nearest large civilized port first, and that would take about a month.

Be it noted also that Holmes, strong as he was, could not drive a harpoon all the way through the body of a pig. He concluded that the man who pinned Carey to the wall with a harpoon was very strong and probably a professional harpooner. Cairns was such, but he would have had to use both hands to do it. Tarzan, of course, could have performed the feat with one hand and without drawing on all his strength.

Nov. 8, a Sunday, 1835	John Clayton born at Westerfalcon Hall, Chamston-Hedding, Yorkshire.
Oct. 2, a Sunday, 1836	William Cecil, John's brother, born at Greystoke House, London.
1855	John, a student at Oxford, reads Louis Blanc's socialist works and Robert Owen's *A New View Of Society* and *Report to the County of Lanark*. He becomes a zealous Socialist and quarrels violently with his father, the fourth duke of Greystoke, about the condition of his employees and of the poor in general.
1858	The fourth duke dies; John becomes the fifth duke.
1859	John meets Karl Marx in London and reads his *Critique of Political Economy*. He becomes a fanatical Socialist but has great trouble cooperating with his fellow ideologists.
Aug. 5, a Sunday, 1860	John marries Henrietta, daughter of the banker, John Jansenius. He leaves her and takes up the first of his workingmen disguises.
Dec. 21, a Monday, 1860	Henrietta dies.

Jan., 1861	The fifth duke, under the name of Jack Cade, is put on trial for seditious libel at Old Bailey, is sentenced to six months' imprisonment, but his counsel finds a flaw in the indictment, and the sentence is quashed.
April 2, a Tuesday, 1861	The fifth duke marries Athena Darcy, a cousin of his first wife.
Jan. 6, a Monday, 1862	John Clayton, son of the fifth duke, born in a house in London's East End slums.
1867	The duchess, unwilling to raise her son in the slums, and feeling neglected, leaves her husband. She raises her son at Westerfalcon Hall and Greystoke House.
April 15, a Wednesday, 1868	Alice Rutherford, daughter of Lord Tennington, born.
March, 1868	The duke is arrested for "obstruction in an open-air meeting." The first effort by his brother to have him certified as insane fails.
1878	The duke meets Annie Besant and George Bernard Shaw, radicals.
1879	The duke, with Shaw, joins the Zetetical Society.
1880	The duke joins Marx in his work in February. In August, he bloodies Marx's nose during an argument, is arrested, but escapes with a fine. The affair is hushed up. The duke is kicked out of the International Working Men's Association. Shaw remarks, "Clayton is far too fierce an individualist, too much an anarchist, to be a Socialist." Clayton replies, "Shaw is, of course, in a position to throw bricks at glass houses."

883	John, the duke's son, enters the Indian Army, is badly mauled by a tiger, and invalided home.
1884	The duke meets William Morris, writer, poet, designer, painter, and radical. He joins the new Socialist League and resigns over policy matters. He joins the Fabian Society, quarrels with Shaw over the publication of *An Unsocial Socialist*, resigns, but does not sue Shaw.
1885	William Clayton buys Pemberley House in Derbyshire. John is arrested for rioting during a dock workers' strike but is let off with a suspended sentence. William tries again to get his brother certified.
1887	John, the duke's son, instructor at the Chatham engineering military college, obtains a transfer to the Colonial Office. William Clayton is created first marquess of Exminster, first viscount of Passmore, and a baronet.
Feb. 21, a Tuesday, 1888	The duke's son marries Alice Rutherford in a double ceremony with his uncle and Edith, a younger sister of the fifth duke's first wife. The fifth duke appears uninvited and mars the wedding.
May 11 or 23, 1888	Clayton and his pregnant wife sail from Dover for Freetown.
June, 1888	The Claytons sail on the *Fuwalda* for an Oil Rivers port.
Late June, 1888	The Claytons are stranded in the jungle of French Equatorial Africa (Gabon) by the mutineers.
Nov. 21, a Wednesday, 1888	A "great ape" attacks the Claytons.

Nov. 22, a Thursday, 1888	John Clayton III, the future "Lord Greystoke," is born a few minutes after midnight.
May 22, a Wednesday, 1889	The infant John accidentally puts his inky fingers on a page of his father's diary.
Nov. 21, a Thursday, 1889	The fifth duke is murdered by an unknown assailant in his lodgings in Marylbone Borough. His brother becomes sixth duke of Greystoke.
Nov. 22, a Friday, 1889	Alice Clayton dies. Kerchak kills John Clayton II. Kala adopts the human infant and names him Tarzan (White Skin).
Jan. 1, a Wednesday, 1890	Jane Porter born in Baltimore, Maryland.
May 18, a Monday, 1891	William Cecil Arthur, son of the sixth duke, born at Pemberley House.
July 1, a Monday, 1895	Black Michael, long thought dead, is found murdered in Forest Row, Sussex. Tarzan's cousin, the Great Detective, solves the mystery. He also uncovers evidence that Black Michael killed the fifth duke but this evidence is not released to the public.
Early Nov., 1898	Nine-year-old Tarzan escapes from Sabor by learning to swim.
Middle Nov., 1898	Edith, the duchess of Greystoke, leaves her husband and goes to the south of France to live.
Late Nov., 1898	Ten-year-old Tarzan first enters his parents' cabin; he kills a mad gorilla with his father's hunting knife.

Nov. 24, a Thursday, 1898	John Drummond, Hugh's younger brother and Tarzan's cousin, born in Drummond Hall, Eryholme, Yorkshire.
Dec., 1898	Tarzan begins to teach himself how to read and write English.
Early Jan., 1899	The duchess of Greystoke returns to England and kills the blackmailer who had broken her first husband's heart. Ironically, the blackmailer died in the very building that the duchess' father had built.
May, 1901	The sixth duke's son is kidnaped. The Great Detective solves the mystery. The duke and duchess are reconciled.
Nov., 1901	The thirteen-year-old Tarzan kills his foster father, Tublat, with his father's knife during a Dum-Dum. He begins his lifelong friendship with Tantor.
Nov., 1906	The eighteen-year-old Tarzan can read and understand almost all the books in his father's library. Mbonga's people establish a village near the territory of Kerchak's tribe.
Dec., 1906	Kulonga, Mbonga's son, kills Kala. Tarzan kills Kulonga.
Jan., 1907	Tarzan finds the diary, photograph, and locket.
Feb., 1907	Tarzan falls in love with Teeka, a female great ape, and loses her to Taug.
March, 1907	Tarzan is captured by Mbonga's warriors but is rescued by Tantor.
Nov., 1907	Teeka bears a son. Tarzan kills a nameless bull mangani.

Dec., 1907	Tarzan puzzles out the meaning of the word *God* in his father's books. He invents an ingenious method for pronouncing the let- of the alphabet.
March, 1908	Tarzan kidnaps a little black boy, Tibo, to raise as his own but compassionately returns him to his mother.
April, 1908	The horrible, but poetically just, end of Bukawai, the witch doctor.
June, 1908	One of Tarzan's many trickster jokes backfires. He finds out that Manu, his monkey friend, has courage and his mangani friends have learned the value of cooperation.
July, 1908	Tarzan eats rotten elephant meat and has a terrible nightmare. He kills his second gorilla, unsure that he is not still dreaming. Teeka throws Tarzan's father's cartridges against a rock, and the explosions save Tarzan's life. Rabba Kega, witch doctor, is hoisted by his own petard (with Tarzan's help).
Aug., 1908	"A Jungle Joke" episode. (*Tarzan Rescues the Moon*, being entirely fictional, is not included in the chronology.)
Aug., 1908	Tarzan kills Kerchak and becomes "king."
Late Jan., 1909	Tarzan abdicates the "kingship" and invents the full-Nelson.
Feb. 2, a Tuesday, 1909	Tarzan sees his first whites. He saves William Clayton from the mutineer Snipes, Sheeta, and Sabor. Using a full-Nelson, he breaks the neck of Sabor as she tries to get into the cabin after Jane.

Feb. 3, a Wednesday, 1909	Tarzan digs up the treasure buried by the mutineers and reburies it. He steals Jane's letter to Hazel Strong. The sixth duke dies in Pemberley House.
March 5, a Friday, 1909	Terkoz abducts Jane, and Tarzan kills him. The "jungle idyll" episode.
March 6, a Saturday, 1909	A French cruiser appears. Tarzan returns Jane to the cabin. Lieutenant d'Arnot is rescued by Tarzan.
March 7, a Sunday, 1909	The French sailors, thinking d'Arnot has been eaten by Mbonga's people, give no quarter to the adult males. Tarzan and d'Arnot communicate in written English.
March 14, a Sunday, 1909	The Porter party leaves on the cruiser. Tarzan and d'Arnot arrive too late.
April 16, a Friday, to May 14, a Friday, 1909	The two, traveling north, reach the village and the mission (Lambaréné).
June 26, a Saturday, 1909	The two arrive at the mouth of the Ogowe (Ogooué) River.
July 26, a Monday, 1909	The two embark for Lyons, France.
Early Aug., 1909	Tarzan's fingerprints are taken in Paris, and he leaves for America.
Middle Aug., 1909	The forest fire. Telegram from d'Arnot: "Fingerprints prove you Greystoke." Tarzan's self-sacrifice.
Late Aug., 1909	Tarzan travels from Wisconsin to New York City; sightsees.
Nov. 7, a Sunday, 1909	Tarzan sails on La Provence for France.

Jan., 1910	Rokoff's frameup and the duel with Count de Coude.
Feb. to April, 1910	The Gernois case.
Late April, 1910	Tarzan ordered to Cape Town, meets Hazel Strong on the steamer. They pass the Tennington party, going the other way.
Early May, 1910	Rokoff and Paulvitch throw Tarzan overboard. He discovers the Waziri.
Late May, 1910	The yacht, the *Lady Alice*, sinks. Jane is in a boat with Rokoff, the seventh duke, and three sailors.
Early June, 1910	Tarzan and the Waziri defeat the Arab slavers. Jane is dying in a lifeboat.
Early June to early July, 1910	The lifeboat lands five miles south of the old cabin. Tarzan and the Waziri travel to the lost city of Opar.
Early July to early Aug., 1910	La of Opar falls in love with Tarzan. He escapes, returns to the coast, saves Jane and his cousin from a big cat but leaves without revealing himself.
Middle Aug. to middle Sept., 1910	Jane abducted by the fifty frightful men. The seventh duke sickens; Rokoff deserts him. Tarzan goes after Jane.
Middle Sept., 1910	Tarzan rescues Jane, finds that she is not married and that she loves him. The seventh duke dies after confessing that he told no one about the telegram.
Late Sept., 1910	D'Arnot's ship finds the lost Tennington party at the cabin. Tarzan and Jane appear. Tennington saves Tarzan's life. Rokoff is arrested.

Sept. 22, a Thursday, 1910	Tarzan and Jane and Tennington and Hazel are married in a double ceremony.
Sept. 23, a Friday, 1910	Tarzan and Jane sail away. He has the Oparian gold, his woman, and the title of eighth duke of Greystoke.
Oct., 1910 to Oct., 1911	Tarzan and Jane live in England.
Oct. through Dec., 1911	The great trek to Kenya.
Jan., 1912	Tarzan receives the immortality treatment from the ancient witch doctor.
March to April, 1912	Tarzan and Jane at the Kenyan plantation.
Late April, 1912	They return to London.
May 20, a Monday, 1912	Tarzan's son, John Paul Clayton, born in Greystoke House, London.
Late June to late Sept., 1912	The events of *The Beasts of Tarzan.*
Sept. to Oct., 1912	Tarzan and Jane in London. Tarzan and Jane adopt Tarzan's second cousin, the orphaned John Drummond. Tarzan makes his maiden, and only, speech in the House of Lords.
May to Nov., 1913	First part of *The Son of Tarzan.*
June to July, 1913	Tarzan searches for Korak (John Drummond). During this time, the events, if any, of *Tarzan and the Forbidden City* occur. Tarzan fails to find his son and returns to the plantation, meeting Jane there.
Nov., 1913 to Jan. 12, a Monday, 1914	The events of *Tarzan and the Jewels of Opar.*
Feb. to May, 1914	Tarzan saves Meriem from rape and the rest of the events of *The Son of Tarzan* follow.

June to July, 1914	Tarzan and Jane in Kenya; Korak and Meriem in Europe with Meriem's parents; Barney and Victoria Custer visit the Greystokes (see *The Eternal Lover* by E. R. Burroughs).
Aug., 1914, to Oct., 1918	The events of *Tarzan the Untamed*. Also, a "lost adventure," during which Tarzan traced the route on the map of the dead giant Spanish soldier.
Nov., 1918, to March, 1919	The events of *Tarzan the Terrible*.
April, 1919, to Nov., 1921	The events of *Tarzan and the Golden Lion* begin.
May 7, a Tuesday, 1921	John Armand Drummond Clayton, Korak's and Meriem's son and Tarzan's grandson, born at Cadrenet Château, Normandy.
Nov., 1921	The end of *Tarzan and the Golden Lion*.
Dec., 1921, to Oct., 1922	Tarzan and Jane in Kenya except for one trip to London to see the newborn Jackie (John Paul).
Nov., 1922, to Dec., 1922	The events of *Tarzan and the Ant Men* (excluding the fictional part of this biography).
Jan., 1922, to May, 1926	Tarzan and Jane in Kenya and then on visits to England, Rome, Berlin, and other parts of Europe.
June, 1926, to March, 1927	The events of *Tarzan, Lord of the Jungle*. Professor Porter and Mr. Philander die in March in London within a few days of each other.
April to July, 1927	The events of *Tarzan and the Lost Empire*. *Tarzan at the Earth's Core* would have occurred between *Tarzan*

	and The Lost Empire and the next volume, but it is entirely fictional.
July 1, a Friday, 1927	Meriem's father, the retired General Jacot, dies at Cadrenet Château, Normandy.
Aug., 1927, to Dec., 1928	Tarzan divides his time between English and African estates.
Jan. to May, 1929	The events of *Tarzan the Invincible*. Ave atque vale to La of Opar.
June to Dec., 1929	Tarzan and Jane stay at the Kenyan plantation.
Jan. to April, 1930	The events of *Tarzan Triumphant*.
May to early Sept., 1930	The Greystokes in England, France, and Kenya. Tarzan takes a jungle vacation.
Middle of Sept. to middle of Nov., 1930	The events of *Tarzan and the City of Gold*.
Late Nov. to Jan., 1931	Tarzan is at the Kenyan plantation.
Jan. to April, 1931	Major part of *Tarzan and the Lion Man* (excluding the fictional parts).
June 1, a Monday, to June 11, a Thursday, 1931	The events of *Tarzan and the Leopard Men*.
June, 1931, to March, 1932	Tarzan and Jane are at Greystoke plantation or in England.
April to July, 1932	Tarzan visits the United States; final "Hollywood" part of *Tarzan and the Lion Man*, though the screen test for a Tarzan movie is fictional.
Aug., 1932, to April, 1933	Jane in England and France; Tarzan in Africa.
May 1, a Monday, to June 23, a Friday, 1933	The events of *Tarzan's Quest*.

Late June, 1933, to May, 1934	Tarzan and Jane in England and Kenya.
June 1, a Friday, to Sept. 7, a Friday, 1934	The events of *Tarzan the Magnificent*.
Sept., 1934, to early Sept., 1938	Tarzan, Jane, and grandson on a round-the-world trip in 1935; Tarzan goes up the Amazon in 1936, looking for the Maple White Land described in Doyle's *The Lost Land*, and he has another Lost Adventure. In 1937 and 1938, he is in Africa with several jungle vacations between his plantation duties.
Sept. 7, a Wednesday, to Sept. 29, a Thursday, 1938	The events of *Tarzan and the Jungle Murders*. (There is no chronology for *Tarzan and the Champion*, since this is entirely fictional.)
Oct., 1938, to May, 1939	Tarzan and Jane in East Africa.
June 1, a Thursday, to June 25, a Sunday, 1939	The events of *Tarzan and the Madman*.
July, 1939	Tarzan loses his memory in an accident while returning home from Abyssinia. He wanders around in the jungles of Mt. Elgon.
Aug. to Oct., 1939	The (non-Mayan) events of *Tarzan and the Castaways*.
Nov., 1939	Tarzan returns to Kenya, says good-bye to Jane (who follows him to England later), and joins the R.A.F. in London.
Dec., 1939, to Oct., 1942	Tarzan, as John Clayton, flies bombers. He submerges his ape-man persona deep within himself. Esmeralda is killed by a bomb in London. Tarzan is promoted to group captain. "Bunny," Lord Tennington, is killed in the North Sea.

Nov., 1942	Tarzan is transferred to the Far East theater.
Nov. 3, 1942	Tarzan's son, John Paul, marries.
Nov. 24, 1943	John Paul's son, John, born.
Jan. to Feb., 1944	Attached to the U.S.A.A.F. as an observer for the British.
March 13, a Monday, to Dec. 7, a Thursday, 1944	The events of *Tarzan and the Foreign Legion.*
May 1, 1945	John Armand, Korak's son, marries.
Dec., 1944, to Feb., 1946	Flies over Burma, China, and with the U.S.A.A.F. over Japan as an observer. Discharged in London.
March to April, 1946	Tarzan and Jane in Kenya.
May to Aug., 1946	He makes his final visit to Opar.
After Aug., 1946	?
Note:	Peter Ogden, editor of *ERB-ania*, believes that Tarzan was born in 1872 and that Burroughs purposely altered the date of his birth. This was to conceal Tarzan's true identity and to make the biography seem to be a work of fiction. This theory also explains the seeming Korak time discrepancy. However, this theory brings up more problems than it downs. Also, I have identified Tarzan, the real "Lord Greystoke," through research in Burke's *Peerage* and other works and have met him. I can definitely say that Tarzan was not born in 1872. And I can say definitely: *Tarzan lives!*

A SELECTED BIBLIOGRAPHY

Adamson, Joy, *Born Free*, Macfadden, N.Y., 1962

Adkins, Patrick H., "A Means of Authenticating ERB," *ERB-dom*, No. 29, Dec., 1969

Arbman, Holger, *The Vikings*, Frederick A. Praeger, N.Y., 1961

Ardrey, Robert, *African Genesis*, Atheneum, N.Y., 1963

———, *The Territorial Imperative*, ibid., 1966

Ashton, E. O., *Swahili Grammar*, Longmans, London, 1963

Austen, Jane, *Pride and Prejudice*, New American Library, N.Y., 1961

Baedeker, Karl, *Great Britain, Handbook for Travellers*, Baedeker, Leipzig, 1910

Barbour, Philip L., *The Three Worlds of Captain Smith*, Houghton Mifflin, Boston, 1964

Baring-Gould, W. S. (ed.), *The Annotated Sherlock Holmes*, 2 vols., Clarkson N. Potter, N.Y., 1967

——— (ed.), *Nero Wolfe of West Thirty-Fifth Street*, Viking, N.Y., 1969

——— (ed.), *Sherlock Holmes of Baker Street*, Clarkson N. Potter, N.Y., 1962

———, and Baring-Gould, Ceil (eds.), *The Annotated Mother Goose*, ibid., 1962.

Beyer, B. K. (ed.), *Africa South of the Sahara, A Resource and Curriculum Guide*, Thomas Y. Crowell, N.Y., 1969

Borgese, E. M., *The Language Barrier: Beasts and Men*, Holt, Rinehart, & Winston, N.Y., 1968

Boule, M., and Vallois, H. V., *Fossil Men*, Dryden Press, N.Y., 1957

Bourne, G. H., *The Ape People*, Putnam's N.Y., 1971

Brown, Leslie, *Africa, A Natural History*, Random House, N.Y., 1965

Brueckel, Frank J. "Physiological Aspects of Homo Minuniensis," ms. to be published in *The Burroughs Bulletin*

———, and Harwood, John, "Heritage of the Flaming God, an Essay on the History of Opar and Its Relationship to Other Ancient Cultures," *The Burroughs Bulletin*, Winter, 1971

Burke, J., *A Genealogical and Heraldic Dictionary of the Peerages of England, Ireland, and Scotland, Extinct, Dormant, and in Abeyance*, Henry Colburn, London, 1846. .

———, *Genealogical and Heraldic History of the Landed Gentry*, Burke's Peerage Ltd, England, 1914, 1939

———, *Genealogical and Heraldic History of the Peerage, Baronetage, and Knightage*, Shaw, London, 1930, 1947, 1949, 1956, 1967

Burroughs, Edgar Rice, *Tarzan of the Apes*, McClurg, Chicago, 1914; *The Return of Tarzan*, ibid., 1915; *The Beasts of Tarzan*, ibid., 1916; *The Son of Tarzan*, ibid., 1917; *Tarzan and the Jewels of Opar*, ibid., 1918; *Jungle Tales of Tarzan*, ibid., 1919; *Tarzan the Untamed*, ibid., 1920; *Tarzan the Terrible*, ibid., 1921; *Tarzan and the Golden Lion*, ibid., 1923; *Tarzan and the Ant Men*, ibid., 1924; *The Eternal Lover*, ibid., 1925; *The Mad King*, ibid., 1926; *The Outlaw of Torn*, ibid., 1927; *Tarzan, Lord of the Jungle*, ibid., 1928; *Tarzan and the Lost Empire*, Metropolitan, N.Y., 1929;

Tarzan at the Earth's Core, ibid., 1930; *Tarzan the Invincible*, Burroughs, Tarzana, 1931; *Tarzan Triumphant*, ibid., 1932; *Tarzan and the City of Gold*, ibid., 1933; *Tarzan and the Lion Man*, ibid., 1934; *Tarzan and the Leopard Men*, ibid., 1935; *Tarzan's Quest*, ibid., 1936; *Tarzan and the Forbidden City*, ibid., 1938; *Tarzan the Magnificent*, ibid., 1939; *Tarzan and the Foreign Legion*, ibid., 1947; *Tarzan and the Madman*, Canaveral, N.Y., 1964; *Tarzan and the Castaways*, ibid., 1965

All of the above are available in softcovers from Ballantine Books, N.Y., except for *The Eternal Lover* (*The Eternal Savage*), *The Mad King*, and *The Outlaw of Torn*. These three are available from Ace Books, N.Y.

Burton, Richard F., *The Lake Regions of Central Africa*, 2 vols., Longman, Green, Longman, and Roberts, London, 1860

———, *Two Trips to Gorilla Land and the Cataracts of the Congo*, S. Low, Marston, Low and Searle, London, 1876

———, and Cameron, V. L., *To the Gold Coast for Gold*, 2 vols., Chatto and Windus, London, 1883

Campbell, Joseph, *The Hero with a Thousand Faces*, Princeton University Press, Princeton, New Jersey, copyright © 1949 by Bollingen Foundation

Carr, John Dickson, *The Life of Sir Arthur Conan Doyle*, Harper & Brothers, N.Y., 1949

Cassirer, Ernest, *Language and Myth*, ibid., 1946

Cazedessus, C. E., Jr. (ed. and pub.), *ERB-dom & The Fantasy Collector*, a periodical devoted to Burroughs and advertisements for fantasy items. P. O. Box 550, Evergreen, Colo. 80439

Clark, J. D., *The Prehistory of Africa*, Praeger, N.Y., 1970

Clarkson, Steve (ed. and pub.), *The Man-Eater of Jahlreel*, American Press, Baltimore, 1970. A transcription from an original ms. found in a portmanteau supposed to be the property of the late Colonel Sebastian Moran. This may have been part of the ms. of Moran's *Three Months in the Jungle* but was, for some reason, not used.

Coon, C. S., *The Origin of Races*, Knopf, N.Y., 1962

Coriell, Vernell (ed. and pub.), *The Burroughs Bulletin*, the Baker Street Journal of periodicals devoted to the works of Burroughs. House of Greystoke, 6657 Locust, Kansas City, Mo. 64131

Costain, T. B., *The Three Edwards*, 1962; *The Conquering Family*, 1962; *The Magnificent Century*, 1951; *The Last Plantagenets*, 1962, Popular Library, N.Y.

Currie, Philip J. (ed. and pub.), *ERBivore*, an irregular periodical devoted to the works of Burroughs and others. 1224 Ingledene Drive, Oakville, Ontario, Canada

Darlington, C. F. and A. B., *African Betrayal*, David McKay, N.Y., 1968

Davidson, H. R. Ellis, *Gods and Myths of Northern Europe*, Penguin Books, Baltimore, 1964

Debrett, John, *The Peerage of the United Kingdom of Great Britain and Ireland*, 2 vols., G. Woodfall, London, 1816

DeCamp, L. S., *Lost Continents*, Gnome Press, N.Y., 1954

DeCudeville, Jean, le Conte, *Les Familles De Rougov et de Cudeville*, Patrouille, Paris, 1952

Defoe, Daniel, *The Life of Captain Singleton*, Classical Series, London, 1905

DeVore, Irven (ed.), *Primate Behavior*, Holt, Rinehart, & Winston, N.Y., 1965

Dod, *Dod's Peerage, Baronetage, and Knightage*, 2 vols., Sampson Low, Marston, and Co., London, 1898

Doyle, A. Conan, *The Complete Napoleonic Stories*, "Uncle Bernac," "Adventures of Gerard," "Exploits of Brigadier Gerard," "The Great Shadow," John Murrary, London, 1931

————, *The Complete Professor Challenger Stories*, "The Lost World," "The Poison Belt," "The Land of Mist," "The Disintegration Machine," "When the World Screamed," ibid., 1952

————, *The Conan Doyle Historical Romances*, "The White Company," "Sir Nigel," "Micah Clarke," "The Refugees," ibid., 1967

Doyle, J. W. E., *The Official Baronage of England*, Longmans, Green, London, 1886

Du Chaillu, Paul, *The Country of the Dwarfs*, Harper, N.Y., 1872

————, *Exploration and Adventures in Equatorial Africa*, ibid., 1861

Farb, Peter, and *Life* editors, *The Forest*, Life Nature Library, Time Inc., N.Y., 1961

Farwell, Byron, *Burton*, Avon Books, N.Y., 1965

Feldmann, S. (ed.), *African Myths and Tales*, Dell, N.Y., 1963

Fenton, R. W., *The Big Swingers*, Prentice-Hall, N.J., 1967

Firth, B. J., *Highways and Byways in Derbyshire*, Macmillan, London, 1905

Fraser, G. M. (ed.), *Flashman*, From the Flashman Papers, 1839–1842, World Pub. Co., N.Y., 1969

———— (ed.), *Royal Flash*, from the Flashman Papers, 1847–1848, Knopf, N.Y., 1970

Gaboriau, Emile, *Monsieur Lecoq*, Scribner's, N.Y., 1904

————, *The Widow Lerouge*, ibid., 1923

Glines, C. V., Jr., *The Compact History of the United States Air Force*, Hawthorn, N.Y., 1963

Goodrich, Norma L., *Myths of the Hero*, Orion Press, N.Y., 1962

Graves, Robert, *The Greek Myths*, 2 vols., Penguin, N.Y., 1955

Greenberg, J. H., *Studies in African Linguistic Classification*, Compass, New Haven, 1955

Grimal, P. (ed.), *Larousse World Mythology*, Prometheus Press, N.Y., 1965

Grimm, Jacob, *Teutonic Mythology*, vol. I, Dover, N.Y., 1966

Gronow, R. W., *The Reminiscences and Recollections of Captain Gronow . . . 1810–1860*, Viking, N.Y., 1964

Guirand, F. (ed.), *Larousse Encyclopedia of Mythology*, Prometheus Press, N.Y., 1959

Haggard, H. Rider, *She*, The Works of Haggard, Walter J. Black, N.Y., 1928

Hallet, Jean-Pierre, *Animal Kitabu*, Fawcett, Conn., 1969

————, *Congo Kitabu*, ibid., 1967

Harrison, Michael, *The Exploits of the Chevalier Dupin*, Mycroft and Moran, Sauk City, Wis., 1968

————, *In the Footsteps of Sherlock Holmes*, Cassell, London, 1958

————, "A Study in Surmise," *Ellery Queen's Mystery Magazine*, Feb., 1971, Davis, N.Y.

Harwood, John, "The Tarzan Theme in Real Life," ms. to be published in *The Burroughs Bulletin*

————, and Howard, Allan, "Tarzan Encyclopedia," ms. to be published in *The Burroughs Bulletin*

————, and Starr, H. W., "Korak—Son of Tarzan?" *The Burroughs Bulletin* ₩16, 1966

Heuvelmans, Bernard, *On the Track of Unknown Animals*, Hill & Wang, N.Y., 1959

Horn, A. A., and Lewis, E., *Trader Horn*, Simon & Schuster, N.Y., 1927

Hornaday, W. T., *Two Years in the Jungle*, Scribner's, N.Y., 1885

Hornung, E. W., *The Amateur Cracksman*, Scribner's, N.Y., 1908

————, *Raffles*, ibid., 1908

Howland, Wriothesley, *The Howlands of Streatham, Including the Narrative of John William C. Howland, Esq., Sole Survivor of the Wreck of the Antilla*, Balham Hill, Surrey, 1960

Huxtable, T., *Sidepaths of the Midlands, With Some Observations on the Dukeries*, Low, Marston, and Co., London, 1890

James, E. O., *The Ancient Gods*, Putnam's, N.Y., 1960

Johnson, Frederick (director), *A Standard Swahili-English Dictionary*, Oxford University Press, 1963

Jones, T. W., "The Man Who Really Was Tarzan," *Man's Adventure*, Stanley, N.Y., March, 1959

Joyce, James, *Ulysses*, Modern Library, N.Y., 1934

Kelly, Amy, *Eleanor of Aquitaine*, Vintage, N.Y., 1950

Keltie, J. S. (ed.), *Statesman's Year-Book, 1888*, Macmillan, London, 1888

Kent, William (ed.), *An Encyclopaedia of London*, E. P. Dutton, N.Y., 1937

Kenyatta, Jomo, *Facing Mt. Kenya*, Vintage, N.Y., n.d.

Kimble, G. T., *Tropical Africa*, 2 vols., Anchor, N.Y., 1960

Leach, M., and Fried, J. (eds.), *Standard Dictionary of Folklore, Mythology, and Legend*, 2 vols., Funk & Wagnalls, N.Y., 1949

Leakey, L. S. B., *Adam's Ancestors*, Harper Torchbooks, N.Y., 1960

Leblanc, Maurice, *The Confessions of Arsène Lupin*, Walker, N.Y., 1967

————, *Herlock Sholmes Versus Arsène Lupin*, J. S. Ogilvie, N.Y., 1910

Lee, Dal, *Dictionary of Astrology*, Paperback Library, N.Y., 1968

Ley, Willy, *Another Look at Atlantis*, Doubleday, N.Y., 1969

Lloyd, A. B., *In Dwarf Land and Cannibal Country*, Scribner's, N.Y., 1899

London, Jack, *The Sea Wolf*, Macmillan, N.Y., 1959

————, "When the World Was Young," *The Night Born*, Grosset & Dunlap, N.Y., 1913

Longfellow, H. W., *Hiawatha*, H. M. Caldwell, N.Y., n.d.

Lorenz, K., *On Aggression*, Bantam, N.Y, 1967

Lupoff, R. A., *Edgar Rice Burroughs: Master of Adventure*, Ace Books, N.Y., 1968

Magnusson, M., and Palsson, H. (translators), *King Harald's Saga*, Penguin Books, Baltimore, 1966

Marbot, J. B., *Adventures of General Marbot, By Himself* (ed., J. W. Thomason, Jr.), Scribner's, N.Y., 1935

Mark, Alexandra, *Astrology for the Aquarian Age*, Simon & Schuster, N.Y., 1970

Matthews, C. M., *English Surnames*, Scribner's, N.Y., 1967

Maxon, Arthur, and Finnegan, Paul J., "The Real Life Bases of Some Fictional Characters," ms. to be published in *The Burroughs Bulletin*

McKinstry, L., and Weinberg, R., *The Hero-Pulp Index*, 1970. Contains all the titles, publication dates, publishers, and the authors of the original issues of *Doc Savage*, *G-8 and His Battle Aces*, *The Shadow*, and *The Spider* magazines. Robert Weinberg, 127 Clark Street, Hillside, N.J. 07205

McNeile, H. C. (Sapper), *Bulldog Drummond*, 1920; *The Black Gang*, 1922; *The Third Round*, 1924; *The Final Count*, 1926; *The Female of the Species*, 1928; *Temple Tower*, 1929; *Bulldog Drummond Returns*, 1932; *Bulldog Drummond Strikes Back*, 1933; *Bulldog Drummond at Bay*, 1935; *Challenge*, 1937, Hodder & Stoughton, London. Most of the above are partly fictional. Gerard Fairlie's Drummond books are not listed because his are all fictional.

Mewhinney, H., *A Manual for Neanderthals*, University of Texas Press, Austin, 1957

Montagu, Ashley, *The Human Revolution*, Bantam, N.Y., 1967

Moorehead, Alan, *The Blue Nile*, Dell, N.Y., 1962

————, *The White Nile*, ibid., 1960

Morris, C. W., *Signs, Language, and Behavior*, Prentice-Hall, N.J., 1946

Morris, Desmond, *The Human Zoo*, McGraw-Hill, N.Y., 1969

————, *The Mammals*, Harper & Row, N.Y., 1965

————, *The Naked Ape*, McGraw-Hill, N.Y., 1967

Morris, Ramona and Desmond, *Men and Apes*, Bantam, N.Y., 1968

Moskowitz, Sam, *Under the Moons of Mars*, Holt, Rinehart, & Winston, N.Y., 1970

Mosley, Leonard, *Duel for Kilimanjaro*, Ballantine Books, N.Y., 1964

Mountjoy, A. B., and Embleton, C., *Africa, A New Geographical Survey*, Frederick A. Praeger, N.Y., 1967

Nicolas, N. H., *A Synopsis of the Peerage of England*, 2 vols., J. Nichols and Son, London, 1825

Northrop, H. D., *Wonders of the Tropics, or Explorations and Adventures of Henry M. Stanley*, Franklin, Richmond, 1889

Odgen, Peter (ed. and pub.), *ERBania*. A periodical devoted to the works of Edgar Rice Burroughs. 8001 Fernview Lane, Tampa, Fla., 33615

Orczy, Baroness, *The Scarlet Pimpernel*, Dodd, Mead, N.Y., 1905. The two sequels to the above are not listed as these are undoubtedly entirely fictional.

Osborne, Richard, *Clubland Heroes*, Constable, London, 1953

Papworth, J. W., *An Alphabetical Dictionary of Coats of Arms*, Genealogical Pub. Co., Baltimore, 1965

Parker, J., *A Glossary of Terms Used in Heraldry*, Charles E. Tuttle, Rutland, Vt., 1970

Parkinson, C. Northcote, *The Life and Times of Horatio Hornblower*, Little, Brown, Boston, 1970

Porter, Jane, *The Scottish Chiefs*, Scribner's, N.Y., 1956

Rachlis, E., *Early Automobiles*, Golden Press, N.Y., 1968

Radin, Paul, *The Trickster*, Philosophical Library, N.Y., 1956

Reynolds, Vernon, *The Apes*, Dutton, N.Y., 1967

Roberts, S., *History of French Colonial Policy*, 2 vols., P. S. King & Son, London, 1927

Roe, A., and Simpson, G. G. (eds.), *Behavior and Evolution*, Yale University Press, New Haven, 1958

Rolland, V. and H. V., *Illustrations to the Armorial Général By J.-B. Rietstap*, 3 vols., Heraldic Book Co., Baltimore, 1967

Roy, John F., "Red Star versus Forbidden City," *ERB-dom*, No. 23, April, 1968

——, "The Strange Quest of Tarzan," ibid., No. 14, Oct., 1965

Russell, Whitworth, "The Wreck of the Antilla," *Survivors*, Rackham, London, 1887

Rutherford, G. E., *History of the Rutherfords of England and Germany*, S. Baker and G. Leigh, London, 1768

Sanderson, Ivan, *Book of Great Jungles*, Julian Messner, N.Y., 1965

Sapiro, Leland (ed. and pub.), *Riverside Quarterly*, a periodical of high scholastic quality, emphasizing the science-fiction and fantasy literatures and occasionally containing articles on E. R. Burroughs. Box 40, University Station, Regina, Canada

Sayers, Dorothy L., For all Lord Peter Wimsey chronicles except *The Nine Tailors*, write to Harper & Row, Publishers, N.Y. For *The Nine Tailors*, write Harcourt, Brace & World, N.Y., or Lloyds Bank Limited, London.

Schaller, G. B., *The Deer and the Tiger*, University of Chicago Press, 1967

——, *The Mountain Gorilla: Ecology and Behavior*, ibid., 1963

——, *The Year of the Gorilla*, ibid., 1964

Scherer, Wendel, *From Freetown to the Congo: My Search for the Lost Peers*, Tylson and Edwards, London, 1891

Schweinfurth, G. A., *The Heart of Africa*, vol. I, Low, Marston, and Co., London, 1873

Schweitzer, Albert, *African Notebook*, Henry Holt, N.Y., 1939

Scott-Moncrieff, D., *Veteran and Edwardian Motor Cars*, B. T. Batsford, London, 1963

Shaw, G. B., *An Unsocial Socialist*, Modern Library, N. Y., n.d.

Smith, Edgar W. (ed.), *Profile by Gaslight*, Simon & Schuster, N.Y., 1944

Smith, Frank, *A Genealogical Gazetteer of England*, Genealogical Pub. Co., Baltimore, 1968

Smithson, H. A., Rev., *Was the Real Sir Percy Blakeney a Percy?*, A Study of British and French Government Documents, 1792–1796, privately printed for the Smithson and Percy families, 1932; reprinted in unauthorized edition, London, 1954

Spencer, Paul, "The Mystery of the Red Star of Tarzan," *The Burroughs Bulletin* #15, 1964

Starr, Frederick, *The Truth About the Congo*, Forbes, Chicago, 1907

Starr, H. W., "A Case of Identity or, The Adventure of the Seven Claytons," *Baker Street Journal*, New Series x, i, Jan., 1960

Sturluson, Snorri, *Heimskringla*, vol. II, Everyman's Library, Dutton, N.Y., 1964

————, *The Prose Edda*, University of California Press, 1964

Taylor, R. L., *W. C. Fields, His Follies and His Fortunes*, New American Library, N.Y., 1967

Tempels, P., *Bantu Philosophy*, Présence Africaine, Paris, 1959

Tompkins, A. J., "The Wondrous Words of E.R.B.," *The E.R.B. Digest*, Number One, March, 1967, Melbourne, Australia

Turnbull, C. M., *The Forest People*, Anchor, N.Y., 1962

Turner, E. S., *The Court of St. James*, Ballantine Books, N.Y., 1959

Van Lawick-Goodall, Jane, Baroness, *My Friends, the Wild Chimpanzees*, The National Geographic Society, 1967

Verne, Jules, *Around the World in Eighty Days*, Lancer, N.Y., 1968

————, *20,000 Leagues Under the Sea*, Scholastic, N.Y., 1965

Wagner, Leopold, *Names and Their Meaning*, Gale Research Co., Detroit, 1968

Watson, Lyall, *The Omnivorous Ape*, Coward, McCann & Geoghegan, N.Y., 1971

Wellard, J., *Lost Worlds of Africa*, E. P. Dutton, N.Y., 1967

Whitaker, J. (ed. and pub.), *An Almanack*, J. Whitaker, London, 1872, 1873, 1888–1946

Wilson, Colin, *The Outsider*, Victor Gollancz, London, 1956

The World Almanac and Book of Facts, New York World, N.Y., 1889–1946

Yerkes, R. M. and A. W., *The Great Apes*, Yale University Press, 1929

Yngman, Henry Stone, *Chronicles of the East Riding, Including a Narrative of the Falling Star of Wold Newton, 1500–1800*, Scarborough Issuance, Scarborough, 1803

MAPS

Africa (North and West) 153, 63 miles to one inch, Michelin Tyre, Stoke-on-Trent, printed in France, 1968

Africa in Maps, Martin, Geoffrey, A., Wm. C. Brown, Dubuque, 1962

Afrique (Centre et Sud) 155, (Nord-Est) 154, 1 cm pour 40 km, Pneu Michelin, Paris, 1969

A Map Book of Africa, Ferriday, A., Macmillan, N.Y., 1966

Buxton and Matlock, sheet 111, one inch to one mile, Ordnance Survey, Seventh Series, Chessington, 1961

316

318

319

320

322

323

frame works, duel with the count, gets first job as French secret agent, 91; investigates Lt. Gernois, foils Rokoff, almost joins the Arabs, meets Hazel Strong, thrown overboard, reaches land, 92-93; saves Busuli, 94; lives with Waziri, 94; defeats Arab slavers, becomes Waziri chief, 95-96; goes with Waziri to the city of gold, 97; sees the city, 98; enters, Waziri flee, 98-99; captured by Oparians, 99; taken to sacrificial altar, 100; sees La for the first time, 101; saves La, 101; hidden by La, escapes, 102-03; leaves Opar by secret exit, 103; takes gold out, buries it, saves Jane and Clayton, 103; hurt by Jane's seeming love for Clayton, stays in jungle, 105; thinks of La and Opar, 105-06; goes after Jane to Opar, 111; rescues Jane, hears Clayton's confession, exposes Thuran as Rokoff, marries Jane, leaves Africa, 111; in England learns how to be "civilized," and hears the family history, is unhappy; 113-19; returns to Gabon, 120; leads the great trek, 120; learns German in German East Africa, arrives at Greystoke plantation, 120-21; settles the mangani in Uganda, 121; gets "immortality" treatment, 121-22; returns to England, 122; returns to Kenya, saves again, helps deliver his son, John Paul, visits d'Arnot in Paris, 123; marooned by Rokoff, 124; gets off island with Mugambi and the "beasts," finds Svenssen, learns about Jane's and baby's escape from Rokoff, 124; rescues Jane, watches Sheeta eat Rokoff, saves Jane from a rapist, returns to England, 125; learns his son is safe, 125; denies Jane's theory that his son has inherited his primitive nature,' 127; forbids Jack to see trained ape, 127-28; finds his son, Korak, in Africa, and in England he returns Jacot's long-lost daughter to him, 129; adopts his cousin, John Drummond, 130; goes on a jungle vacation, 131; looks for Korak, has some unknown adventures, *Tarzan and the Forbidden City* is fictional, ghost-written, comments on humanity, 131-32; reads Burroughs' fictionalized version of his youth, 132; corresponds with and then meets Burroughs, sees Tarzan movies, 133; returns to Kenya, is financially ruined, goes to Opar again, 135; warned by witch doctor, followed by Werper into Opar, suffers amnesia, reverts to early ape-man state when

a tunnel collapses, has his diamonds stolen by Werper, 136-37; is captured by, and made love to by, La, regains his memory, rebuilds the plantation, saves Meriem, fails to recognize Malbihn, stops Tantor from killing Korak, is reunited with Akut, goes to London, reveals to Jacot that his lost daughter is Tarzan's daughter-in-law, 137-38; visited by the Custers in Kenya, 139; in Nairobi on business, 143; unaware that Jane is not dead, 144; hurries home from Nairobi on news of World War I, 144; thinks Jane is murdered, swears revenge, 145; arrives at Kilimanjaro battle, 145-46; looses a lion into German trenches, carries off Major Schneider, kills von Goss, 146; falls in with Bertha Kircher, takes Jane's locket from her, is knocked out by her, spares her at Wilhelmsthal, decides to return to Gabon, 147; almost dies of thirst, finds a giant skeleton in armor and an ancient map, terrorizes deserters from German forces, finds a mangani tribe, 147; uses ju-jitsu on Go-lat, saves Bertha Kircher, lassoes an airplane, 147-48; throws Usanga out, winds up in the lost city of Xuja, escapes, 148-49; is saved by British soldiers from hunting lions, is badly wounded, discovers that Kircher is an English agent, that Jane isn't dead, sets out to find her, 149; is looked for by a newspaper reporter, 150; turns to Nairobi, learns Korak is at the Argonne front, sets out again on quest for Jane, 155; spends two years in searching, crosses deserts and morasses into vast mountainous area, finds some animals long extinct elsewhere, 155-56; befriends Om-at and Ta-den, 156; has adventures in Pal-ul-Don, learns to control the *gryf*, 157; becomes known as Tarzan the Terrible, finds Jane, is saved by Korak, who shoots Obergatz, 157-58; hopes that civilization never comes to Pal-ul-Don, 158; tells interviewer the true story behind *Tarzan the Terrible*, speaks of Cathne and Athne and Nemone, 158-59; returning from Pal-ul-Don, finds a dead lioness, 161; raises her cub as a pet, 161-62; is ruined financially, sets out for Opar again, is accused by mangani of shooting them, 163; drugged by Flora Hawkes, 163; saved by La from Cadj, 165; escapes with La to the Palace of Diamonds, 165; leads a revolt, is saved by Jad-bal-ja, the Golden Lion, restores La to her throne, 165-66; robbed of diamonds

Tarzan *(continued)*

by Kraski, reunited with Jane, 166; solos and crashes in the Great Thorn Forest, 167-68; captured by Alalus female, teaches Alalus males to revolt, 169; captured by Khamis, breaks loose, convinces Obebe that he is indeed the River-Devil, 170-71; goes back to plantation, frustrates Miranda, 171; is in West Kenya and Europe for three-and-a-half years, then in Abyssinia, knocked out riding on Tantor, 173; captured by bandits, rescued by Tantor but left to die, his attitude towards death, 173-74; vine-swinging a movie invention, his tree-traveling limitations, 174-75; saved by the mangani, involved with greedy humans again, 175; saves a gorilla (or a baboon) from a python, is saved by gorilla from Stimbol, 175; question of Tarzan's title, fights with armored knights, 176-77; hurls a war lance through a knight, is helped by Jad-bal-ja in fight against the Arabs, 177; tells interviewer true story behind *Tarzan, Lord of the Jungle*, appears for first time with Nkima, 177-78; looks for Erich von Harben, comes to Castra Sanguinarius, 178-79; fights as a gladiator, saved by his mangani friends, 179; is saved by Nkima and the Waziri, rejects offer to be Caesar, finds Erich, 179-80; *Tarzan at the Earth's Core* is all fictional, 180; spends a year and a half at plantation or in England, then visits mangani, hears of strangers, 183; saves Colt's life, plays a trickster joke, goes to Opar, is imprisoned, escapes, 184; rejects La's love for final time, foils Zveri's plot, says hail and farewell to La, 184-85; grieving for La's hurt, goes to Midiam in Abyssinia, meets his cousin, Lady Barbara Collis, 185; attacked by bandits, kills many, 186; rescues a strange white man, goes to valley of warring cities of Athne and Cathne, outfights Phobeg, rejects Nemone, is chased by Belthar, the great god-lion, 186; is saved by Jad-bal-ja, buries Nemone after her suicide, is loafing with Jad-bal-ja when a rifle shot sounds, 186-87; saves a movie company, goes to Hollywood, is rejected when he tries out for lead role in a Tarzan movie, returns to Africa, 187-88; kills the duke of Buckingham, 188; most of *Tarzan and the Lion Man* is fiction, his encounters with the Leopard Society mostly true, loses memory, is regarded as a ghost by natives, 188; his amnesia testifies to his desire to

be an ape-man again, 188; shares Kavuru elixir pills with Nkima and others, gets pills synthesized by American surgeon cousin, 189; in Abyssinia again, investigates rebellion rumors, involved with the Lord Mountford mystery, the Kaji diamond, Athne and Cathne again, takes Gonfal diamond home, buries Zuli emerald, gives Wood and Gonfala good advice, 190; solves a jungle murder, becomes God in Alemtejo, finds the man who thought he was Tarzan, loses memory, caught by old enemies, 190-91; kills three men but is caged, shipped out, regains memory, escapes, has adventures on a South Pacific island, returns to Kenya, says goodbye to Jane, flies R.A.F. bombers over Europe, 191; transferred to Far East theater, 191-92; observer on U.S. B-24 bomber on Sumatran mission, 195-96; shot down, parachutes, exultant at being in jungle again, 196-97; leads American crew, teaches them jungle survival, confirms Rosetti's belief he's crazy, finds Sing Tai, rescues Corrie van der Meer, 197; kills a tiger, is revealed as Tarzan to the "Foreign Legion," his duality described, 197-98; tells of hatred of killing for revenge or pleasure, revenging Kala's death, 198; makes friends with a Sumatran Tantor, saves an orangutan from a python, battles Oju, an orang, 198-99; captured by white criminals, escapes, 199; identifies himself as Tarzan to Dutch guerrillas, behaves in an affable quite human manner now, 199-200; has shed his Trickster role, is all business in war, makes friends with a monkey, Keta, reveals how he got his prolonged youth, says he would like to live forever, 200; tells his attitude of Death, is captured by the Japanese, rescued through Keta, 200-01; is blown out of a boat, makes his last kill, is rescued by an English submarine, exits smiling, 201-02; pinch hitter for Mary, 202; is the lost heir of myth and fairy-tale, 203; is the changeling, the unpromising hero, the precociously strong and clever, 203-04; speaks to animals, has many animal helpers, is heir to magical gifts, 204-05; is a Trickster and battler against evil magicians, 205; is a revenger of father's death, a great inventor, rescuer of maidens and slayer of dragons, a wanderer, a plunger into the underworld, 205-06; is reborn, resists the Seductresses,

326

328